"Don'ː
Tieran
And I
you."

That sounds like a challenge.

A challenge I very much want to indulge in.

That foreign part of me wants him to earn the right to touch me, to *mate* me.

I suddenly feel possessed by the need to run, to make him prove his worth. To *challenge* him.

No. Not just him. *Them.*

A crash comes from the living room, the window shattering and eliciting a feral growl from Tieran. I inhale sharply, his rumble sending a tremor through my limbs.

Caius shouts something I don't quite catch, the incoming snarls reverberating all around me and eliciting shivers from deep within.

Run, my wolf demands as Tieran releases me to handle one of the shifters who has just entered the kitchen. *Run!*

I've always been able to tame her, to keep her down.

But not anymore.

Not since she took over during our initial shift.

I'm a slave to her needs now, and I do exactly what she says.

I sprint for the broken window, leap over the edge, and bolt full speed into the forest. My human legs are far more powerful and faster than my wolf's legs because I've spent two decades learning how to move on two feet instead of four paws.

This is why I won my trials. I'm fast. I'm strong. And I know when to pick my battles.

I choose this battle now.

I choose today to fight.

CARNAGE ISLAND

SAVAGE CLAWS & FORBIDDEN BITES

To: Becca

Welcome to Carnage Island...

LEXI C. FOSS

Carnage Island

Copyright © 2021 Lexi C. Foss

Editing by: Outthink Editing, LLC

Proofreading by: Jean Bachen, Katie Schmahl & Matt Foss

Cover Design: Paradise Cover Design

Cover Photographer: Wander Aguiar

Cover Models: Zack, Ive, Wayne, and Daniel

Published by: Ninja Newt Publishing, LLC

Print Edition

ISBN: 978-1-68530-065-4

❀ Created with Vellum

To Matt, this dream wouldn't be possible without you.
Thank you for being my fated mate.

CARNAGE ISLAND

A REJECT ISLAND NOVEL

CARNAGE ISLAND

A REJECT ISLAND NOVEL

Welcome to Carnage Island.
Home of brutal chaos.
Blood and tears.
And nefarious schemes.

A half-breed.
A reject.
A wolf without a mate.

My family doesn't want me.
My Alpha disowned me.
And my mate rejected me.

So I've just been given a new pack assignment.
Carnage Island.
Home to the worst of wolf kind.
Vicious claws. Cruel beasts. Wicked deeds.

I'm not one of them.
But I'm not a Nantahala Wolf either.
I'm something distinctly other: an Omega trapped in an
Alpha's skin.

One step toward my fate, and all the males turn their heads.
I'm fresh meat.
Property to be claimed.

Hide-and-seek is now a game of life and death.
With claws and teeth.
And malice and pain.

Only the strongest will survive.
Enter at your own peril.

Author's Note: This is a dark shifter story with Omegaverse undertones. Three Alpha males, one Omega female. There will be biting and violence because these Alphas will stop at nothing to protect their mate. And she'll claim them back just as fiercely.

A NOTE FROM LEXI

Oh, wolves. They make my heart happy. I love their brutality, fierceness, and that underlying animalistic passion that burns the pages.

Carnage Island has all of that.

There are also Omegaverse vibes in this novel, which means there may be some scenes of dubious consent that can make a reader uncomfortable. There's violence as well. However, these Alphas are heavy on the worship vibes. Once they sink their teeth into Clove, they don't let go. And honestly, she's not all that keen on letting them go either.

So while there are Omegaverse undertones, this book may come off as a little "sweet" to those who love brutal Alphas who bend their Omegas without remorse. There are hints of that here, but it's not nearly as dark as some of my other worlds. If you're craving a bit more bite, and stronger themes of dubious consent, I would check out *Andorra Sector*.

But if you're in the mood for something that blends the dark with the light, flip the page.

There will be knotting.

There will be nesting.

There will be chaos.

These Alphas are lethal, and they'll do anything to avenge and protect their little Omega.

And oh, dear moon, they absolutely love to bite…

INTRODUCTION

TIERAN

High Pack Notice: All rejects must report to Wolfe Island for immediate processing and island assignment.

Here's the thing they don't tell you about this "reject" assignment—not all rejects have to report to Wolfe Island for assignment.

Alphas, for example, are at the top of the hierarchy and therefore immune. They're allowed to choose if they want to mate or not. Just like they're allowed to choose if they go to their respective Reject Island or remain with their packs.

However, their rejects always go to Wolfe Island for pack reassignment.

While the Alphas typically choose to remain with their original packs.

It's not that way for all wolves, but it's certainly a standard for most of them.

It's fucked up. Cruel. And absolutely corrupt.

Of course, the Elders won't admit that. They sit on their pretty thrones on Wolfe Island making all the rules.

But I'll let you in on a secret: Carnage Island? Yeah, it's not under their control at all. They just think we obey because we're so far out in the ocean that we have no other choice. They also assume we're reliant on them for the minimal resources they provide, thus ensuring we behave out here.

And they believe they sent me here as some sort of punishment for my crimes.

As though I would let anyone ever tell me what to do.

Those Elder idiots don't realize that their flawed perception of our location allows us to prosper without their notice. Half of my wolves here aren't rejects at all, but soldiers preparing for the ultimate revenge.

Not with the Elders—I honestly don't give two fucks about their penchant for regulation and pack assignment.

No. What I care about is how I've been personally wronged. How my pack has been painted as the enemy in a battle we never actually wanted to join.

But we're all in now.

The Santeetlah Pack and Nantahala Pack will pay for their crimes.

In blood.

Because the Black Mountain Pack is coming for them.

And our enemies just gave me the perfect weapon to use in our fight.

A female of mixed origins.

My pretty, petite wolf.

My intended queen.

Our future.

Once I teach her how to heel…

Welcome to Carnage Island, little one.
Are you ready to play a game?
It's called hide-and-seek.
You hide.
We seek.
And then… we bite.

CLOVE

Energy hums through the air, causing the hairs along my arms to stand on end.

Deep breaths, Clove, I tell myself. *And don't look up.*

History is happening all around me as the wolves enter the clearing on both sides.

Nantahala and Santeetlah.

Two packs of similar origins who have fought for centuries over this land.

But today, we'll join as one.

Because of my agreement to mate the Santeetlah Pack Alpha's son.

The other females in my pack are jealous. Our matings are all arranged, and I definitely won this year's prime candidate—a future Alpha.

And not just any Alpha, but the Alpha who will lead the union between our packs, with me by his side.

I take another deep breath, attempting to calm my inner wolf. Kneeling agitates the animal lurking beneath my skin. I don't typically submit. But this ceremony requires it.

Just as it required me not to truly meet my inner

animal until today.

Hence her growing excitement.

I've never been allowed to shift.

It's part of the tradition among our two packs that the females don't shift until their chosen mate calls upon their wolf. The process allows us to grow our other strengths before our wolves, making us concentrate on perfecting our human form first and foremost.

Females create life.

Males protect it.

Thus, females focus on preparing their mortal bodies for procreation.

While males learn how to fight in their strongest form —as wolves.

My stomach flips at the notion of finally meeting my animal. We've bonded for so long, and after tonight, I can finally embrace her to the fullest.

She's softer than my mind but still fierce in her own way. I can sense her need to shift, her desire to run free in the woods on four paws instead of two feet.

But I've denied her for twenty very long years.

Tonight, I tell her. *Tonight, we will run with our mate by our side.*

It'll be his job to show me how to function on four legs. To embrace my animal half. To flourish in the trees beneath his protective gaze.

My wolf snorts at the notion of someone else protecting her. She has claws and teeth for a reason. But it's how the males in our packs thrive.

"Let them think they're in charge," my mother has always said. "Our animals know the truth."

Females bear the children. That gives us a certain amount of power that no male can take from us. Even if they try to control us in certain ways.

My mother ensured that I understood how the games are played in this world.

I know when to bow—such as now—and when to fight. All because my mother wanted me to know the truth about this world and how to survive it.

I can feel her eyes on me now, watching my every move. She's anxious. It's an irritation I sense against my skin, the nerves of my pack making it that much harder to remain still.

Because the Santeetlah Alpha and his son are approaching.

We've met a few times to establish the requisite chemistry. Tonight is the final test—a dance among our wolves.

His father, Alpha Crane, clears his throat.

I don't move. I just breathe, keeping my shoulders relaxed and my eyes on the ground.

My intended mate stops before me, his feet bare, just like my own. However, I can see the edge of his jeans flirting with his ankles.

Unlike him, I'm without clothes.

Because I'm ready for him to call upon my wolf, to set my animal free. Some packs are blessed with magic that allows them to shift while wearing clothing. My wolf type doesn't possess that kind of enchantment. And neither does his. Which means he intends to strip after he's forced my shift.

I don't mind.

All I really want is to feel my fur and stretch out my legs.

And run, I think wistfully.

"Today marks a momentous occasion," Alpha Crane says, his deep voice reverberating through the clearing like a rolling thunder.

Goose bumps pebble down my arms in response, his power evident in that vibrating tone alone. Alpha Bryson carries a similar presence, but not quite as overwhelming. Perhaps because I've grown up near him.

My father is his Beta, otherwise known as the second-in-command. Which is one of the reasons why I've been given the honor of mating Alpha Crane's son. The responsibility would have gone to Alpha Bryson's daughter, and did, when he tried to strike a truce with the Black Mountain Pack.

And, well, that did not go as planned.

The Black Mountain Alpha's son rejected her.

No.

He did worse than reject her.

He *slaughtered* her.

And the Black Mountain Alpha responded by *laughing*.

"The Santeetlah Pack and the Nantahala Pack will unite beneath a mating union," Alpha Crane continues. "One both Alpha Bryson and I have blessed—the mating between my son, Canton, and the Nantahala's highest-ranked eligible female, Beta Gafton's daughter, Aspen Clover Donough."

I don't react to him using my full name. Canton knows I prefer to go by Clove. That's what matters.

"Together, we will build a more powerful territory and provide a united front against those who intrude on our land." Alpha Crane releases a low growl, the sound making my stomach twist. "The Black Mountain savages think to attack our land and our people. No more. We will unite as the Santeetlah-Nantahala Pack and show them that our wolves are superior to their beastly ways!"

Howls take over the night, sending another shiver down my spine.

Our packs are uniting as one, the wolves joining

together in harmony as our ceremony officially begins.

I'm not allowed to join in on the howls; none of the females are. Not that there are many in attendance tonight. Most are home, protecting their offspring with a few enforcers remaining behind.

My mother is here because of me.

Just as Alpha Bryson's mate is here to show her support of this union.

The rest are males, their animalistic aggression a hot wave in the chilly winter air.

My wolf whines inside, begging to be released. I resist her, just as I've always done, the pain in my heart spiraling through my veins and sending electric shocks to my fingertips. It's never felt natural to suppress her. But I do what I have to for my pack.

I do what I *need* to do… to survive.

Canton places his hand on my head, his fingers running through my hair. He's pleased that I'm obeying and remaining still while everyone howls, including him. It's a display of my loyalty to him as my intended mate. It's a show of understanding my place in our packs.

I may possess the heart of an Alpha, but I will never be *the* Alpha. Men are stronger. I accept that. I accept my place. I accept *him*.

On most days, I think, recalling my mother's warnings about choosing my battles.

Swallowing, I wait for the men to calm and the next phase of this ceremony to begin.

Canton circles me, his eyes roaming over my exposed skin. I can feel his approval and interest. He knows he'll finally be allowed to taste me tonight. My own interest is slickening my thighs. He's an Alpha in his prime, a beautiful specimen of a male with a jawline I've wanted to lick from the moment I first met him.

Canton leans down to press a kiss to my temple, his breath warm as he whispers, "I can smell your arousal, Clove. You're already ready for me, aren't you, sweetheart?"

I don't answer. Not because I don't want to, but because I can't.

He chuckles, his lips meeting my temple again as he adds, "Good girl."

Another test—one I pass. Because I know better than to move or reply. I don't even clench my legs despite the desire pooling between them.

I focus on my wolf instead and my excitement to finally feel her outside of my heart.

The need to shift is all-consuming now, with the moon an added seduction against my skin.

But I have to wait. Canton will call on me when he's ready, when he's finally chosen me publicly.

"I approve," I hear him growl, a few of the wolves chuckling at the clear intent in his tone.

I've never attended a mating ceremony, but I've heard stories. Sometimes the males claim their females for the pack to see, not just via their bite, but per their bodies as well. I'm hoping Canton doesn't go that route. I want the freedom to run once he allows me to shift.

But I won't be able to fight him whenever he forces me back into human form.

So he could technically make me shift quickly between forms, claim me, and then let me run.

Or he may never let me run at all.

It's a fear I've harbored all my life. I've met females whose mates prefer them in human form. However, I think Canton will approve of my wolf and let me frolic. Our meetings have all been positive, and the fact that he calls me Clove says he respects my choices.

A low hum of growls ignites in the air, the wolves anticipating the final bond.

I've missed whatever Alpha Crane has said, my mind too focused on what comes next.

Canton's palm encircles the back of my neck as he steps into my space, placing my head near his upper thigh. He's tall and wider than me, as are most male shifters. I've always been petite for my status, my Alpha tendencies inside more than outside.

"Close your eyes," Canton says softly, his opposite hand going to my cheek in a tender caress. "This is going to hurt."

I do what he requests, my body alight with nervous energy. It buzzes through my veins, sending tingling sensations to my fingertips.

The final test.

Canton releases a low growl, one that causes my wolf to whine inside me. She doesn't want to be forced out; she wants to *choose*.

But that's not how this works.

She's not in charge here. Canton is, and she has to respect that, or we'll both pay the ultimate price—*rejection*.

He growls again, this time with a little more force, sending vibrations down my limbs. I compel myself to breathe, to remain calm, to let him control my change. But his third growl is harsher now, demanding that my animal comply and causing my bones to snap beneath his power.

By the fifth growl, tears are rolling from my closed eyes, my wolf fighting the call of our mate.

"It's natural to fight," my mother warned me before the ceremony. "Just let nature take its course. The Alphas want a strong mate. And you're the strongest of all of us."

Canton's grip on my nape tightens, his growl becoming even more aggressive.

I lose count of how many times he snarls.

I'm too lost to the sensation of my bones snapping and shifting, the movements foreign and painful.

How do the females submit to changing back for the claiming? I wonder, my insides turning to liquid fire as a whimper escapes my lips. *How do they enjoy the claiming?*

I've heard that the claiming is a beautiful ceremony filled with passion and pleasure.

But I can't imagine feeling that right now.

I bite my tongue to keep from screaming as my legs finally give out from under me. Canton keeps me in my position with his hand on my nape and my cheek.

It hurts.

It feels as though he's going to snap my neck.

It's unnatural.

I need him to release me, to let me finish my shift. Is he punishing me for taking too long? Is he holding me like this to prove he's in charge?

I whine, my body his to control entirely. What more does he want? I can't… I can't fight him. He's too powerful. Too masculine. Too *Alpha*.

He finally releases me and unleashes a growl that vibrates through every inch of my being, the wolf inside him demanding that my animal come to life.

She snarls in response, but neither of us can fight his call.

I curl into a ball as the shift takes over entirely, my body contorting in ways it's never done before.

This must be why they don't allow us to meet our inner animals until our mating. It *hurts*.

As much as I want to see my animal, I don't appreciate the pain it requires to meet her. I feel weak. I feel unworthy. I feel *soft*.

A mewl leaves my lips unbidden, my limbs shaking as

the final phases of my transition hit my core.

And then everything stops.

The agony. The fear. The anticipation. It just melts away as silence descends.

Peace.

My wolf yawns and stretches, pleased to finally be free.

Except the sudden intake of air around me has my wolf's ears flattening in concern. She doesn't like that sound, and neither do I.

I sniff, trying to draw out the cause of concern. It ruffles my fur, the stench of it growing by the second.

"What the fuck is this?" Alpha Crane demands. "Some sort of sick joke?"

I blink, confused.

Canton is no longer beside me, he's over ten feet away and glowering at me with a look of disgust that goes straight to my heart.

I lift my head, the sensation a bit strange as the muscles in my neck are new to this form.

I can't stand yet, my limbs still awkward beneath me.

I glance down to try to figure out where to put my paws and how to…

White fur.

I stare at it.

Why do I have white fur?

It should be black. All Nantahala Wolves have black fur. Santeetlah Wolves have brown fur.

The Black Mountain Pack is home to the Carnage Wolves.

And Carnage Wolves have white fur.

White fur, like snow.

White fur, like…

Like *my paws*.

Oh, moon… I'm in trouble.

9

CLOVE

"Explain yourself!" Alpha Bryson shouts.

I shiver, my focus instantly going to the male I've revered all my life. But he's not looking at me. He's looking at my father.

And my father… is glowering at my cowering mother.

"I… I…" she stutters, her skin as pale as my fur. "I didn't know… I…"

"You didn't know?" my father repeats, his tone holding an edge of fury that I've never heard from him before. "How could you *not* fucking know?" He points in my direction. "She's a goddamn mutt!"

"I thought she was yours," my mother whispers. "I… You have to believe me. It… He found me… I tried to fight… But I…"

Her statements are all garbled. Maybe because I can't hear beyond the pounding in my ears. Maybe because she can't seem to explain herself.

"I swear, I had no idea," my father says, his words for Alpha Bryson. "I'll take whatever punishment you require. This is not a reflection on our pack. It's a reflection on me and my whore of a wife."

"He raped me!" my mother shouts. "I tried to fight him! I… I thought… I prayed and hoped she was yours. I…"

"They are known for their savagery," Canton mutters. "It's possible."

Alpha Crane snorts. "You're naive and young and have a lot to learn."

"I'm thirty," Canton points out. "And I've faced those beasts in battle, Father."

"That doesn't explain her not reporting it." Alpha Crane utters the words with authority and a hint of disgust. "We wanted your best female, and this is what you give us? A mutt of unknown origin?" Alpha Crane spits on the ground near Alpha Bryson's feet. "I've never been more insulted than I am right now."

Alpha Bryson says nothing, his eyes wandering to me before settling on my trembling mother. "What will fix this?" he asks. "I can offer them as slaves."

My heart stutters. *What?*

"You can kill them," my father adds. "Do whatever you desire. I reject them both."

"Gafton—"

My father's hand resembles a whip on the wind, slamming across my mother's cheek and sending her to the ground. "You will *never* speak my name again, you fucking whore." He follows it up with a kick to her stomach, then another to her head, knocking her out cold on the field.

My wolf reacts with a snarl, furious at his treatment of his mate.

Mates are meant to be revered and cherished and protected.

His eyes find mine, the fury in those dark orbs unlike any I've ever seen. He takes a step toward me, but Alpha

Bryson holds him back with a palm to his chest. "This isn't your punishment to give, Gaf."

"No, it belongs to my son. He's the one most insulted here. He's the one you've duped with an unqualified mate. He will choose their fates." Alpha Crane looks at Canton. "The decision is yours."

I try to stand, but my legs are awkward and refuse to hold my weight.

This… this has to be a nightmare.

How can I have white fur?

My mother was raped?

By… by a Black Mountain Wolf?

My heart is pounding so hard in my chest that I don't hear Canton's approach. But I smell him, the scent of cedar and man calling to my wolf on a base level.

Mate, she whispers to me, purring in approval.

But the feeling is not reciprocated.

I can see the hatred in his eyes, the fury at having this whole arrangement ruined by my white coat.

Except, I'm still me.

I'm still the wolf my parents raised me to be.

I… I just have white fur.

Not black.

Maybe he'll demand I never shift again?

A laughable suggestion. Because our children will still be tainted by my mixed heritage.

He crouches before me, his striking blue eyes glittering beneath the moonlight. I try to bow my head, but my wolf refuses. She wants to challenge him, to challenge them all.

She refuses to accept whatever fate he chooses for her. She's too strong to bow.

Yet she can't even stand.

I scream at her to lower her eyes.

She doesn't.

And Canton starts to glare. "You dare challenge me, little wolf?"

No! I want to scream, but I can't. I can't speak. I can't move. My wolf is in control now. I've denied her for so many years that she's absolutely refusing to let me run the show now.

He growls.

And to my absolute horror, my wolf growls back.

"You're just proving to me and all my men that you can't be tamed," he tells me, his voice almost sad as he shakes his head. "A shame. I could have added you to my harem." He stands fully, his shoulders squaring in a way that makes my wolf snarl.

She wants to rip him apart.

Because she's *rejecting* him.

The realization hits me square in the chest, shocking me into silence.

And allowing my wolf to gain that much more control.

I'm on my paws now, my legs stretching as she takes in the field of aggressive males. They smell wrong. Feral. Unacceptable.

She wants to shred them all to pieces.

Especially the one I've called Father all my life.

She's furious at him for hurting our mother. Seeing her dark hair sprawled across the ground, her eyes closed, her lips bleeding from my father's slap, has my wolf taking a bold step forward.

Canton growls, this time menacingly. "Do not move," he tells my wolf, his voice holding a power similar to his father's.

My animal snarls in response, not bending to his will.

"*This*"—Alpha Crane points at me—"*this* is why we fight the Black Mountain Pack. They don't understand hierarchy because their wolves are feral creatures without rules. They fuck and kill and do not obey."

My wolf snorts as though she can understand his words.

She disagrees wholeheartedly, her disrespect having nothing to do with a lack of understanding and everything to do with her refusal to bow to him as her Alpha.

I don't understand the inclination or where it comes from, but I can't deny the sensation of rightness thrumming through my veins.

I don't belong here, I realize. *I never have.*

That's why my mother always lectured me on when to display my backbone. Other girls didn't need that lesson, but I did. Because I've always been stronger. I've always questioned our methods.

While all the other females merely accepted them as law.

I thought that was what made me an Alpha female.

But my wolf tells me now that it's never been about my inquisitive spirit. I've questioned everything all my life because I don't belong here.

The wolves start to chant, causing the fur along my back to stand on end.

They want Canton's decision.

They want vengeance.

They want *blood*.

Because they blame me for existing. And my father's expression tells me he blames me, too.

He's not my father, I think.

Yet he raised me. Loved me. Groomed me for this position today. And now he's disowning me before the pack.

I don't hear the words, my heart beating too fast in my

ears for whatever he's saying to register in my mind. But disapproval and hatred radiate from his stiff form.

He kicks my mother again.

She's not even awake or moving, the asshole taking advantage of her prone form.

He picks her up and tosses her at Alpha Crane's feet.

My wolf growls again, furious at the sight of a male treating his mate with such disrespect.

Alpha Crane nods at two of his men. They prowl forward with hungry eyes, picking up my mother's lifeless form and dragging her toward the trees.

My wolf steps forward, my fur standing on end.

But a growl from Alpha Crane holds me captive, confusing my senses.

Not my Alpha, my wolf thinks.

Yet my paws are frozen to the earth.

I don't understand this power. It doesn't feel right. My wolf wants to fight it, to claw her way out of his hold and destroy everyone in her path.

Alpha Bryson adds his own growl, forcing my legs to buckle beneath me, bringing me down to the earth. "She's going feral," I hear one of them say. "She's useless to us."

A conversation follows, something about my mother paying for her sins.

"Send her to Carnage Island," someone suggests, the words sending a blade of ice down my spine. "Let those animals rip her apart."

No, I want to say. *No, please don't.*

But my wolf won't let me shift back into human form.

Maybe because I don't actually know how to do it.

My *mate* is supposed to teach me that. Yet he's standing next to his father with his back to me, treating me like I'm nothing. Like I didn't just spend the last six months going through the mating trials with him.

None of this makes any sense.

I should be frolicking in the trees right now, basking in the scents of the earth, and—

An agonized scream reaches my ears, causing my wolf to perk up.

Mom…

Chuckles follow.

Hungry growls, too.

My *father* does nothing, his face expressionless, as my mother pleads for them to stop. I can't see them, but I can hear them. I can *smell* what they're doing.

They call her a whore.

They call her worthless.

They tell her she's going to die on her back.

My wolf growls low, the urge to move clawing at my instincts and shattering the hold around my paws.

In the next moment, I'm sprinting across the earth toward my mother's screams.

She's crying.

I'm coming.

She's in pain.

I'll save you.

She's terrified.

I'm almost—

A larger wolf tackles me to the ground, the fierce snarl one that I recognize. *Canton.* He has me pinned to the earth beneath his much larger body, his jaws on my throat.

My wolf doesn't accept his dominance, fighting beneath him with all the fury and terror inside me, trying to free herself from his weight.

It's useless.

I can barely breathe beneath him, his canines in my throat and piercing the skin.

He's going to rip my head off, I realize, panicking. *He's going to kill me!*

My spirit renews my fight, turning from anger to an outright need to survive.

But he won't move.

He's too big.

He's too strong.

And I've only just met my wolf. I can't control her at all.

A whimper escapes me, my eyes locking on those vibrant blue ones, so familiar in his wolfish features.

My mother's screams begin to fade.

The world is darkening.

My life… is over.

I try one last time to swipe my paw at Canton, but it's too late. My limbs no longer work, my body fully subdued beneath his growling form.

This is my end.

A nightmarish reality.

A cruel fate.

The last sound I hear is my mother calling my name. "*Aspen…*"

And the world goes black.

VOLT

I fucking hate wearing suits. They're claustrophobic and suffocate my wolf. And the damn ties make me want to choke something.

Not my own neck.

Someone else's neck.

Like the human sitting across from me.

Fortunately, he's useful.

Unfortunately, he's the reason I'm in the suit.

I wait patiently as he counts the cash in front of me, showing me the bonus he's giving me for a job well done.

He gave me a mark. I carried out the assignment without any inquiries or assistance required. And now I'm being paid for it.

"You military types are unnervingly silent," he says.

I don't reply. He assumes I'm military because I'm good at what I do. I don't bother correcting him because I don't need to explain myself. I'm a freelance assassin. The suit is just my version of a mask.

If he saw the claws beneath, there would be questions.

And I really fucking hate questions.

This guy has several on his mind. I can see them in his

dark eyes. But he's smart enough to keep his mouth shut, instead thanking me with cash.

He slides the final payment across the oak desk. "Send my best to your brother."

I nearly snort as I slip the thick envelope into my jacket pocket. Tieran isn't my brother. He's blond with blue eyes and about two inches shorter than my six-foot-five frame. But sure, we look exactly alike, what with my dark hair, matching eyes, and inked arms.

Standing, I dismiss myself without a word.

If this jackass needs another hit, he knows who to call.

My brother.

This time I do snort.

Tieran will fucking love that.

Caius looks more like me than fucking Tieran does.

Not that the human knows Caius. His specialty in this world is making deals and putting people in debt. Specifically, *our* debt.

I'm the assassin.

Tieran's the boss.

Fucking brother, I repeat, shaking my head as I make my way out of the rich dick's house. His private security steers clear of me, fully aware of my reputation for death.

Or maybe they can just smell the stench of it on my skin.

Whatever.

There are worse reputations in life than being seen as the literal Grim Reaper.

I push outside and take in a deep breath of fresh air. It calms my soul, allowing me to exist in the serenity of the moment. Two more guards immediately jump out of my way, their eyes averted.

They have no idea what I really am, and they're still submitting.

Pathetic mortals.

I take my keys from the waiting valet and slide into my favorite toy. It's one of the perks of off-island life.

The Elders think they're so smart, sending all the rejected wolves to their "Reject Islands."

It's their way of controlling the chaos associated with breaking fated bonds.

Some wolves can handle the rejection. Others can't. It's the ones who can't that created this new order that mandates all rejects to report to Wolfe Island. That's where they make assignments, sending the wolves to their new packs.

The Elders police some of the islands more heavily than the others.

But not Carnage Island.

No, they let us police ourselves.

Because they're too chickenshit to deal with our level of savagery.

I carefully navigate my way around the giant fountain in the middle of Rich Dick's driveway. It's a pompous centerpiece that I doubt anyone actually likes. But it successfully keeps me from gunning the engine—I save that for once I'm through the gate and speeding out of the neighborhood.

The tie is the first to go, the damn silk resembling a rope that I want to set on fire.

I unfasten the top button of my shirt next.

Then I hit the Dial icon on my screen.

Tieran answers on the first ring. "You on your way back?"

"Yeah," I tell him. "Cash in pocket."

"He count it again?"

"Yep."

"Saves me the trouble," Tieran drawls, and I can

picture him leaning back in his office chair and kicking up his feet on his desk. He's probably wearing jeans and no shirt. Lucky bastard. "One of these days, we're going to have to kill him."

"Yep," I repeat, fully aware of that future task. "He thinks we're brothers."

Tieran grunts. "He's an old fool blinded by his cash."

"As long as he keeps paying us, he's useful."

"Until he starts asking questions," Tieran returns. "Of which I'm hearing a few rumbling through the circle already."

"Hmm," I hum, fully prepared to turn around to handle the issue.

"Not now," Tieran says, reading me easily even through the phone. "We'll see how it plays out. And in the interim, we'll indulge in the incoming shipment."

"Incoming shipment?" I repeat.

"From the Elders," he clarifies. "Fresh meat."

"Female?" I ask hopefully.

Tieran wouldn't waste my time on this unless the fresh meat is female or someone from our past.

"Female," he confirms. "That's what I've been told, anyway. A feral little thing, too. She apparently killed her own mother."

I whistle, intrigued. "Sounds like my kind of woman."

I learned long ago that family isn't about blood. It's about loyalty. If I could kill my mother, I absolutely would. But my father already did it for me. Right before taking his own life.

Worthless fucking wolves.

"She's a half-breed," Tieran goes on, ignoring my interjection. "I guess her mother dabbled with a Carnage Wolf, created a mutt, and so her mate rejected her upon turning."

I frown. "What? How old is she? Five?" That's how old most pups are when they first shift.

"No," he scoffs. "Twenty."

"And she just found out about her lineage?" I ask, confused as hell. "Wouldn't that have been obvious with her first shift?"

"She's from the Nantahala Pack," he replies, those words alone explaining everything.

"Fuck."

"Yeah," he agrees. "Rather than send her to their island, she's coming to ours because of her violent outburst and mixed heritage."

"I see." I turn onto a main road that will take me to the highway, the wheels squealing in protest at my rising speed. "Are we throwing a welcome party?"

"Caius is working on it."

"Taking bets on who fucks her first?" I guess, grinning.

Carnage Wolves love sex. It's a carnal part of us ingrained into our animal spirit. Not just for men, but for women, too. And Carnage Island is severely lacking in the female department, giving the new wolf her pick of bedmates.

"Among other things," Tieran replies.

"Alpha or Beta?" I ask. The answer will influence my bet. And I don't bother guessing Omega since that's too unlikely to be true. It would also cause a riot on the island.

"Reese claims she was rejected by an Alpha's son, so I'm guessing she's an Alpha," he says. "Alpha Crane's son, to be precise."

I nearly freeze in my seat. "Shit."

"Yeah. Word is the two packs are trying to merge and this little wolf put a kink in those plans when she turned out to be a half-breed."

"Fuck," I breathe, impressed and a bit enthralled. "Have you confirmed that with your father?"

"Not yet," he replies. "I've left him a message, though. And Reese is trying to find out more for us."

I nod. Reese is one of our informants on the Elder council. If anyone can find out the truth, it's him. But it would be good to know what Tieran's father has to say about it.

He's the Black Mountain Alpha, after all.

"Sounds like we're in for an intriguing evening," I murmur.

"Quite," Tieran agrees, his English accent coming through—a trait he picked up from his Omega mother. And maybe from her English mate as well. Being a rare Omega allows her to have multiple mates, the Alpha of her circle being Tieran's father. But the other two males in her nest are both Alphas in their own right; they merely choose to bow to Tieran's dad.

Similar to how Caius and I allow Tieran to lead.

The three of us are all Carnage Wolf Alphas.

But Tieran is the strategist.

I'm the brawn.

And Caius is the brains.

"I'll be there in about fifteen minutes," I tell Tieran.

"I'll have the yacht prepped and waiting," he replies, ending the call.

Well, this day just improved drastically. Once I rid myself of this stuffy suit, I'll be all wolf.

And maybe I'll have an Alpha toy to play with tonight.

It's been a long time since I entertained a female capable of taking my strength. The two Betas and the single Alpha on the island claimed their males before I even had a chance to offer myself. So I've been forced to indulge my needs with humans instead. Which is pretty much like fucking glass.

Not fun for me.

Not fun for her.

Not fun all around.

But a pretty new wolf? Mmm, yes, please.

Maybe I'll engage in Caius's game.

Depends on how the welcome party goes.

Welcome to Carnage Island, little wolf, I think with a grin. *I hope you like to bite.*

CLOVE

I can't shift.

I've tried for four days, and my wolf won't allow me to return to human form.

The guards think I'm being defiant. The intake judge called me *feral*. And the social worker in charge of my case stated she couldn't help me because I didn't want to be helped.

If only that were true.

My wolf refuses to let me defend myself in human form. Everyone thinks I killed my mother because Alpha Bryson told them I did.

He claimed that I turned feral when I found out my true lineage.

He acted like he felt bad for me.

He called it a "sad, helpless case." And then went into a speech about how he couldn't put me down, that it wasn't my fault for being born this way.

Yet he didn't have a single problem with Alpha Crane's wolves killing my mom.

And he didn't care at all about laying the blame for her murder at my feet.

My wolf is furious. *I* am furious.

But I'm also terrified.

They're taking me to Carnage Island, home of the cruelest wolves in existence.

Because they think I killed my mom.

I want to cry. I want to scream. I want to *bite*.

They put a muzzle on me, my snarling only adding to the rumors of my feral state. My wolf is pissed and wants to kill the guard who clamped her mouth shut.

He keeps looking at my wolf with a hungry gaze, his nose twitching as he scents me.

I growl in response, my animal allowing the sound through.

He smiles, clearly amused by my show of defiance.

I am such a dead wolf, I think, sighing.

The boat zips along the water, leaving the land behind as we head toward my new home. For however long I survive, anyway.

Something I know my former Alpha is counting on.

"She won't make it long enough to talk," Alpha Bryson said to my father before the officials arrived the other night.

I was barely lucid at the time, my head pounding from Canton knocking me out.

Part of me thought it was all a dream.

But one glance at my paws told me it was very real.

I lost consciousness again soon after that. Then I woke up in a cell, where my social worker read the charges to me.

My mom's dead.

My pack disowned me.

And the Elders think I killed my mother in a fit of rage.

Panic and fury suffocated me in the next moment, causing my wolf to react aggressively.

Which was when the guards knocked me out with a tranquilizer.

That happened to me three times in the last few days.

I very much do not want to go through it again while on our way to the most dangerous island on earth. So I'm focusing on my breathing and trying not to freak out.

But my mother's screams continue to reverberate through my mind.

She begged them to stop.

They laughed.

My own father allowed it to happen.

Not my father, I remind myself.

But he was still her mate.

How could he be so cruel?

Why didn't she tell him the truth? a small part of me whispers. She should have told him about the Carnage Wolf and what he did to her.

But then she would have lost me.

My father would have made her abort the child.

I wouldn't exist.

That's why she didn't tell him.

Because of her love for me.

And now she paid the ultimate price with her life.

A tear longs to sneak from my eye, but my wolf refuses it. She's still very much in charge and presenting a confident air that has me cringing inside.

It's a bravado I don't feel.

She's in survival mode, not allowing me to run the show. If I'd been able to speak during my trial, I might have been able to negotiate where the Elders sent me.

But no.

My wolf cemented our fate by snarling at the intake judge instead.

I try to close my eyes, to just relax in the open ocean

air. Alas, the guard moves to the right, keeping my wolf on high alert.

At least I can't feel the wintry air. My fur keeps me warm as we zip along the water to the islands off the coast of Canada.

Only Wolfe Island can be reached by a bridge to the mainland. All the Reject Islands beyond it are accessible by ferry or helicopter only.

Or, in my case, via speedboat.

Probably because these guards want to drop me at the water's edge and escape before the Carnage Wolves can sense their presence.

I've never actually seen one up close, the Black Mountain Pack having never crossed into our village back home. The pack enforcers guaranteed our safety there.

But no one is guaranteeing mine here.

I'm in a damn cage.

One I suspect these assholes are not going to let me out of.

I shiver at the thought. If my wolf allows me to shift, then I can use my fingers to free us.

Assuming I can even shift with a muzzle attached to my head.

I frown inside, uncertain. These are the types of things I've never been taught.

The boat begins to slow, the guard up ahead yelling, "Get her ready!"

Mister Muzzle stands, his lips curling in a way that makes my skin crawl. "My fucking pleasure."

My wolf sits down in the crate, staring at him. The complete opposite of what I want to be doing right now. She's acting like a damn obedient dog, her ears perked, tail slightly wagging.

"I knew you would come around," he says, crouching down. "Why don't you shift so I can see you better?"

My wolf cocks her head like she can't understand him.

It's disorienting to feel so detached from her and out of control. I imagine it's how she's felt all these years while I suppressed her—something I'm realizing now isn't natural.

Because I saw a few pups running around on Wolfe Island.

Female pups.

"I'm not letting you out until you shift," he says.

Well, that's not happening, I want to tell him.

Instead, my wolf lies down with a sad little huff.

I have no idea what she's doing, and I've given up trying to understand. So I just roll with it. If she wants to mope, then we'll mope.

The guard frowns. "I can't let you out in wolf form, little one."

Which means he plans to dump my crate on the island. Awesome.

The boat slows to a stop, the guard's lips twisting.

"Yo! Push her off and let's go!" the guard from the front calls back to us.

Mister Muzzle sighs and shakes his head. "All right." He reaches forward, his fingers on the latch. "Try to attack me, and I'm going to toss you in the water to drown in this cage. Be a good wolf, and I'll let you swim to shore."

Wow, those are amazing options, I think, rolling my eyes.

But my wolf doesn't move, just continues to watch him.

He opens the door and she sits up, tail wagging happily.

"Well, go on, then," he says, pointing to the shore that I can now see is about a hundred feet away. He wasn't kidding about swimming.

My wolf whines a little and paws at her muzzle.

He narrows his eyes. "I'm not falling for that."

She sighs, lying down again.

"What the hell, Jack? Push her overboard already!" the impatient guard demands.

Jack doesn't move, his eyes on me. "All right. Come here and I'll remove it. But if you bite me, you'll regret it."

My wolf sits up again, wagging her tail like an obedient pet.

I wonder if he realizes that I'm not in control at all, that she's running the show entirely.

His smile suggests he thinks it's all me.

And it should be since *I* am the human here.

But I feel locked away, similar to how I used to push her to the back of my mind.

I can feel and hear and see everything. I could even taste the rotten food they gave me in my cell. However, I couldn't stop myself from eating it.

Just like I can't stop this ridiculous wagging now.

"Come out here like a good girl, and I'll take it off before you jump," Jack says.

My wolf stands and stretches, obviously understanding him. Although, I don't think it's his words she processes so much as his tone and movements. There's an animality in her that doesn't assess phrases the way a human would.

Which is why I should be able to control her.

He reaches for my face and I try to recoil back, but my wolf stays absolutely still, allowing him to undo the muzzle. He's cautious, carefully pulling it off my head.

And my wolf lunges for his throat.

He curses, throwing me overboard with his robust strength and sending me into the water by the boat. "Fucking bitch!" he shouts.

"And you're a fucking idiot," the other guard snaps back.

The boat begins to sputter as they take off, the blades on the back nearly catching my tail as they go.

My wolf sinks under the waves, uncertain of how to swim.

And the water is *cold*.

Like ice.

I'm frantic, trying to take over, to tell her how to doggy-paddle, to give her a way *up*. But she won't let me free. She won't listen to me!

We're sinking.

Water is swirling around us as we claw at the murky depths, trying to figure out how to float or reach the surface.

My wolf is whining.

I'm screaming.

Then brawny arms are suddenly around my torso and dragging me up. "What the fuck are you doing?" a male demands, his voice making me shiver inside and out.

Well, not out.

My wolf is snarling at him, furious at his touch.

"Oh, quiet," he snaps back, his Alpha energy shimmering across my fur in a manner far more potent than Alpha Bryson's ever did.

This male is power personified.

And it instantly calms my wolf.

She submits with ease, allowing him to drag us to shore.

I wonder, just for a moment, if she's faking it like she did on the boat.

But no. I can sense the lack of tension in my body now, the true will to submit to someone she believes is a stronger being.

He doesn't immediately release me, instead rolling me

to my side and staring down into my wolf eyes with a clinical look.

I stare back at him, mesmerized by his ebony irises. So dark and alluring. At least until they narrow in confusion. "You're not an Alpha," he tells me.

My wolf grumbles in response, clearly not approving of his tone.

Or maybe she really does understand him.

Hell if I know anymore.

"Shift," he says.

I don't because I don't know how. Because my wolf won't let me. Because apparently, I've gone mad and allowed my animal to take over.

"She can't," another voice says, this one slightly accented and radiating even more power than the Alpha beside me.

How is that even possible?

Wait… I glance sharply at the newcomer, my wolf finally allowing me to take over for just a second. *How do you know I can't shift?* He's the first to sense it. The first to realize I can't control my wolf.

But any elation I feel dies as he steps forward, his aura humming with electric superiority.

This is an Alpha.

Well, so is the guy beside me.

Both of them are Alphas.

Carnage Wolf Alphas.

Oh, moon…

I swallow, my insides turning to ice as I suddenly remember where I am.

"Shh," the male beside me hushes, lying down as though to appear less aggressive.

It doesn't work.

He's too big, too *Alpha*, to appear any less intimidating.

"You're all right," he murmurs, his voice deceptively calm.

I am definitely not *all right,* I want to tell him. I'm the complete opposite of all right. I'm fucking terrible. I'm trapped in my wolf form, accused of a murder I didn't commit, and currently being cornered by two *Carnage Wolf Alphas.*

"Well, she's a bit wetter than I expected," a third voice says, shooting ice through my veins. "Not that I'm complaining. A wet woman is always welcome in my presence."

Make that three *Carnage Wolf Alphas.*

I clearly pissed off a moon deity in my past life.

Because my world has been officially turned upside down in the last few days. And now I'm going to die at the hands of these savage beasts.

Except the one beside me is stroking my fur with a reverence I don't understand. And he's… he's humming?

Why is he humming?

My wolf is completely relaxed, lying beside him like a wet log of fur. She has no concerns about being surrounded by these Alphas. Actually, she's… *content.*

What is happening?

"Why can't she shift?" the male beside me asks.

I perk up at that. *Yes, why can't I shift?*

"I have a few guesses," the one with the slight accent replies. He's crouching beside us now, his intense blue gaze taking in every inch of my form. When he leans in to sniff me, I stiffen. At least inside. However, my wolf merely stretches like she wants to show off her legs for him.

Then, to my absolute horror, she starts to roll onto her back and show him her belly.

What the fuck is wrong with you? I demand, livid. *You were all fierce and angry, and now you want to submit to these three Alpha males?*

"Hmm, I see you've taken control," the blue-eyed Alpha murmurs, reaching down to stroke his palm along my exposed abdomen. "Are you protecting your human, little one? Hiding her from some sort of trauma?"

I consider that for a moment. *Is that what you're doing?* I ask my errant animal. *Are you allowing me to heal before you give me back control?*

"Or maybe your Alpha mate didn't give you permission to shift back?" he continues, his brow furrowing with the suggestion.

My mind reels with the possibility.

Canton inspired my wolf to come out. But he never forced me to change back.

Is that why I can't shift? I wonder, my heart skipping a beat. *What does that mean? Will I be stuck like this until he brings me back?*

Oh, moon… Canton will never help me. Not after everything that's happened.

I'm going to be trapped forever…

"She can't attend your party in this state, Caius." The strong Alpha speaks in a soft tone, but his words are underlined with authority.

"No shit," the third Alpha drawls, moving closer. "She'll be mounted by all the wolves in this state."

My wolf reacts to that, a low whine leaving her throat as she starts to hide her belly again. The blue-eyed Alpha allows it, giving her space to curl into a protective ball. But he continues to run his fingers along my fur, just like the one behind me now. He's still humming, the sound oddly soothing.

"She's not an Alpha," he says again, this time talking about me rather than to me. "A Beta?"

The blue-eyed one traces his fingers along my neck and then up to my snout to draw a line to my nose. "She's small," he says. "And submitting like an Omega." He leans down to sniff me again, then shakes his head. "Her half-breed genetics are confusing my wolf."

Caius joins him in squatting before me, his soulful eyes finding mine. He studies me for a moment, his grayish irises seeming to swirl with knowledge. "She's not feral."

"No, not at all," the blue-eyed one agrees. "Just very scared."

Caius nods like he's responding to some sort of unspoken question. "I'll cancel the welcome party."

"Tell them she's exhausted and needs a few nights before she meets the pack," the blue-eyed Alpha says, his gaze still on me.

"Where will she stay until then?" Caius asks.

"In our den," the one behind me says. "Where we can keep her safe."

"And determine if she's a Beta or..." The blue-eyed one trails off, but the others seem to understand the rest of his statement, because they grunt.

Or what? I want to ask. *An Omega?*

That's impossible.

My mother always called me an Alpha female. All my tests suggested the same. It was what made me suitable for Canton.

But these men keep saying I'm not an Alpha.

And after feeling their strong auras, I very much understand why. Because compared to them? Yeah, I'm definitely *not* an Alpha.

But an Omega?

I almost snort.

I'm definitely not *that* either.

The blue-eyed male sits back on his heels for a

moment, combing his fingers through his thick blond hair. "I'll come with you, Caius," he says. "Her scent is already in the air. They'll have questions."

The two of them stand at the same time.

Caius grins, but it's not a friendly sort of smile, more of a challenging one as he looks at the male behind me. "I suggest you move quickly, V."

"I always do, C," the Alpha drawls, his chest vibrating my back and making my wolf sigh in response. She really likes his rumbling hum. It's almost like a purr. "Do you want to run with me, sweetling?" he asks softly. "Or would you prefer I carry you?"

What is happening right now? I wonder, a bit dazed by this unexpected treatment.

All three males are staring at my wolf expectantly— which I anticipated when hearing I would be sent to Carnage Island, except it isn't the kind of expectant glimmer I worried about seeing in their wild eyes.

Instead, they appear intelligent.

Not carnal.

Caring.

Not savage.

Patient.

Not demanding.

I swallow, uncertain of what I want to do. It's up to my wolf, but she's not moving. She just seems to want to curl into the Alpha behind me and bathe in that rumbling purr emanating from his chest.

"Carrying it is," he says then, moving to stand.

My wolf perks up, irritated by the loss of his warmth.

But that rumbling sound from his chest lulls her into a placative state as she shuffles over to lean against his legs.

He's wearing suit pants and nothing else.

I follow my nose and find his shirt, jacket, and shoes

piled haphazardly on the beach only a few feet away. He wasn't wearing those when he pulled me from the water, which means he stripped them off before diving in.

"You got this, V?" the blue-eyed one asks, his attire of jeans and a bare chest similar to what I grew up seeing in the village.

"Yeah, I got this, T." That addictive purr underlines his words, making me shiver again.

The one called T nods, causing his blond hair to fall into his face. He pushes the errant strands back with his hand before looking at Caius. "Let's go break some hearts."

"And maybe some jaws," Caius says.

V glances at me, his expression suddenly tired. "Yeah, I think that's a given."

TIERAN

T he female's scent slithers around me, perfuming the air and filling my lungs with each breath.

There's something intoxicatingly sweet about it.

Something I want to *taste*.

"She tried to kill Jack," Caius says conversationally as we walk in the general direction of the main docks. It's the location where the guards should have taken the girl. But instead, they went to the opposite side of the island, where they couldn't anchor their boat.

Cowards, I think. "They were going to throw her cage in the water and let her drown. I think her assassination attempt is warranted."

"He was technically helping her by letting her out of the cage and removing the muzzle."

"Because he wanted to fuck her," I return.

Caius's silvery eyes gleam knowingly as he looks at me. "And you don't?"

I grunt. "Entirely not the point. I didn't try to drown her."

"Fair," he replies. "Well, it's a good thing you

anticipated their usual fuckery. She would have drowned if Volt hadn't pulled her out."

I grunt again, this time in agreement. Volt and I were disembarking the yacht when we saw the speedboat heading in the wrong direction around the island. The idiot guards didn't even see us, too caught up in their own fuckery to notice.

Or maybe they just didn't care.

Carnage Island is seen from the outside as an overgrown dystopian nightmare.

It's the front we provide to scare them off.

And it works.

But in this case, it almost cost an innocent wolf her life.

"I fucking hate the archaic methods some of these packs follow," I mutter. "She couldn't swim because no one has taught her how to be a goddamn wolf."

It infuriates me.

Black Mountain Pack is all about embracing our animal at a young age. Sure, we have our hierarchical nuances with Alpha, Beta, and Omega dynamics, but we never suppress our wolves. It's forbidden to even try.

"She would have died," I continue, my fists clenching with the urge to hit something.

"Do you think she can swim in human form?" he asks.

I shrug. "With the Nantahala Pack in charge of her upbringing? Who the fuck knows? I'll be surprised if she can even read."

Caius sighs, dragging his fingers through his thick brown hair. It's longer than usual, the ends touching his ears and falling into his face when he releases the strands. "I can't believe she's part Nantahala Wolf. She looks all Carnage to me."

He's not wrong. That white fur is flawless on her. "She doesn't smell like a Carnage Wolf."

Well, that's not fully true.

She does smell like a Carnage Wolf to an extent. But there's something underlying her fragrance that's distinctly *other*, and it's throwing off my wolf's ability to understand her.

"Hmm," Caius hums as we reach the crest of the hill that leads down to the main docks. "They're not going to be pleased by this development."

"They'll live," I reply, leading the way.

It's become a tradition to play a game with the female newcomers. But as there are only three on the island, I think the males will give us a little flexibility for this round.

Particularly as she's in no condition to indulge us right now.

Her wolf is in control, not the human inside. Consent is a touchy subject among our kind. Alphas tend to take what they want to an extent. We're stronger and faster. But our women are always willing.

And while her animal may want to play, the human inside is clearly hurting. I could see it in her eyes, the struggle deep within.

"We'll have to help her shift later," I tell Caius as we near the docks. "I suspect her mate never released her from his hold."

"An odd thing to do since he clearly rejected her."

"It's a power trip. He's not relinquished his control, because he wants her to suffer." Which means her former intended is an absolute ass. Not surprising, given his ties to the Santeetlah Pack. "Or it's a result of her not knowing how to manage her wolf."

Equally as likely, considering her upbringing.

"Or the wolf is protecting her," Caius says, echoing my earlier comment.

I nod. "We won't know until we spend more time with her."

"Something that will obviously be a hardship for all of us," my best friend drawls. "That scent alone is going to drive me wild in the best way."

He's not wrong. That delicious aroma clings to my skin even now, causing my wolf to want to run back to the den to greet her. To welcome her home.

An insane urge.

But my animal has always guided my actions.

I won't fault him for declaring his desire without even knowing the female's name. He has the ability not to overthink things. If he wants something, he states it flatly.

And right now, he wants her.

Not long-term. Just a taste.

Something I may indulge him in, assuming I can pull the female back into human form.

However, there are more pressing issues to address first, such as the cluster of male wolves waiting on the docks. They're all standing around, grinning in anticipation, their eyes gleaming with intrigue.

Most of them are Alphas.

Some are Betas.

No Omegas. Because we don't allow Omegas on this island. Not that they would ever be sent here. Omegas are prized among my kind. They would never be rejected. They would be revered and worshipped instead.

And most of the wolves here weren't rejected at all.

Just artificially rejected for the purpose of falsifying records and allowing more Carnage Wolves to come here.

Although, there are a few here who are absolutely insane as a result of their very real rejection. They're not Carnage Wolves, just rogue beasts that created the need for these Reject Islands.

Those males are not allowed to play our games. They stay occupied with other menial tasks that keep the island alive. And they provide a decent front for us to hide behind.

"Gentlemen," I greet as I step onto the dock. "You may have noticed the lack of a shipment arriving."

A few of them chuckle, while the others nod.

"Guards dropped her in the water on the opposite side of the island," Caius explains, infusing a hint of annoyance into his tone. "She's... displeased."

I nod. "More than displeased. She's a bit broken, to say the least."

Several of them frown now, glancing at each other before looking at me. "She's not a present from your father?"

The other three females were presents—otherwise known as *volunteers*—for the males on the island. They were bored and wanted to play. So my father falsified their rejections to send them here to satisfy their own urges, as well as our men.

This female definitely didn't qualify for that.

But I asked Caius to set up the games as an introduction to our life, thinking she might appreciate some playtime.

Clearly, I was wrong.

"She's from another pack," I say vaguely, not ready to reveal her origin yet. Otherwise, the men will hate her on sight. And until I decide what to do with her, I really don't want to cause more problems. "We'll need to postpone the games."

"Who is she?" Alpha Kin demands, his muscles bulging as he folds his arms over his chest. "Where's she from?"

"That's her story to tell, not mine," I deflect. "Which is

hard for her to do since she's currently in wolf form and refusing to shift."

Alpha Dirk grunts. "Then make her shift."

"I will," I promise. "But I came here with Caius to deliver the news first. Once she's ready, we'll reschedule the introductions."

Alpha Dirk and Alpha Kin share a look, their brows furrowing. "We want to see her," Alpha Kin says then, looking back at me. "We want to assess her for ourselves."

Because you can smell her, I translate, sighing to myself.

These two have always been a problem. Which is precisely why my father sent them here—he wants me to master them to prove my worth as Pack Alpha.

Which, unfortunately, means I have to use my fists more than I'd like.

But leadership has its requirements—both good and bad.

"I've assessed her," I tell them. "And she needs time before she meets the rest of us."

"So you're keeping her for yourself," Alpha Dirk hedges.

"I didn't say that," I reply, already bored with the posturing. "However, I'm deciding as Carnage Island Alpha to give her time to shift before we play our usual games."

"I think this needs to be discussed," Alpha Kin says, glancing around at the other Alphas and Betas in the crowd. "She's not from your father. She's from the Elders. That makes her open for debate."

"I agree," Alpha Dirk declares. "She smells different, too. Sweet. Like an Omega."

This causes several growls of agreement to go through the crowd.

It doesn't matter that she was wet and dropped off over

two miles away from here; we're wolves with enhanced senses.

They can also likely smell her on me and Caius, despite the fact that I barely touched her.

"Are you hiding her because she's an Omega?" Alpha Duncan asks, his hazel eyes flashing with irritation. "Is this all a ruse?"

"I want to see her for myself," Alpha Pan adds. "Prove to us she's incapable of shifting, and we'll discuss it more."

I raise my brows. "We'll discuss it more?" I repeat the words with a humorless laugh.

This is exactly why I accompanied Caius. Not because he couldn't handle himself, but because I suspected this female's scent would addle some brain cells.

"Let's say she is an Omega," I say, infusing a healthy dose of sarcasm into my tone. "What would stop me from claiming her? No, hold on, let me rephrase that. *Who* would stop me from claiming her?"

My question is met with a handful of growls, mostly from Alpha Kin and Alpha Dirk.

"Do you require a lesson on why I'm the most suitable Alpha for her to choose?" I ask, my English accent thickening my dark tone. "Because I'll happily oblige."

It's been a few weeks since my last challenge. I'm certainly due another one now. It's how I maintain my status and prepare for the future.

Alpha Dirk mutters something about my cock under his breath. Or maybe he calls me cocky.

He's not wrong.

I'm not up here by mistake.

I'm up here as a result of my heritage and hard work.

Alpha Kin and Alpha Dirk may be wider and taller, but I'm faster and sleeker. I'm also more intelligent.

"Is she an Omega?" Alpha Duncan asks, his tone holding a touch of awe to it.

"If she was, do you think I'd be down here placating you all?" It's a carefully worded question meant to disguise the answer.

Because I don't know.

She doesn't smell right.

But her wolf certainly acted like an Omega, showing me her belly and calming from Volt's purr. She seemed perfectly content to let us protect her, something only an Omega wolf could ever do.

However, until I meet the woman beneath the fur, I won't know for sure.

"That's not an answer," Alpha Pan intelligently points out. "I want to meet her, Tieran."

"And you will, when I decide it's time," I tell him, displeased by the lack of respect in his address and in his tone.

These men may respect me on the battlefield, but it's been hard to win their favor as a leader.

Another reason why my father sent me here.

Well, that and the Elders mandated it.

But that's another story entirely.

"I'm protecting her as I would one of our pack," I continue. "If you can't respect that, then we have other issues to discuss."

"How do we know that you're not just keeping her for yourself?" Alpha Dirk demands.

"Because I'm standing here talking to you instead of fucking her," I retort, mimicking his position by folding my arms. "If I want her, I'll take her. Regardless of your input or involvement in the situation. So it's a moot point, and you're merely wasting my time with this bullshit."

He growls.

I snarl back.

And some of the Alphas take a few steps away from us.

Scents can make wolves do stupid shit.

Like attacking the superior Alpha on the island.

Which Alpha Dirk does now by throwing the first punch.

The only reason I don't outright kill him is because I understand he's being driven by lust more than intelligent thought.

If he wanted to truly challenge me, he wouldn't do it here or now.

I duck his punch and counter him by slamming my fist into his groin. He's too big and slow to see me coming, my reflexes far outpacing his as I whirl around behind him and follow up my hit with a kick to the back of his knees, sending him to the ground.

Then I jump and land my heel on the back of his neck, forcing him to complete the fall and face-plant against the rusty old dock. It's the one we maintain for Elder purposes —to help add to the overall beat-up flair of the island.

The nicer dock is hidden on the other side in an alcove protected by tree cover.

That's where I keep the yacht and other boats for my men.

Alpha Dirk grunts into the decaying wood, moaning as I take a knee on his back.

"I could kill you," I tell him, my voice bored as I lean down to continue speaking against his ear. "I could take the silver blade from my pocket and slit your pathetic throat. But I'm not going to do that. And do you want to know why?"

His response is unintelligible because his mouth is currently kissing the dock.

"You're one hell of a warrior when not thinking with

your dick," I go on, answering my question without bothering to wait for his clear interest in the response. "So take a breath. Walk it off. And you'll realize what I'm doing is the right thing for our pack."

I shove off of him and meet Alpha Kin's stare directly.

He holds it for a beat before looking away.

Alpha Pan and Alpha Duncan are next.

They don't hold my gaze, their eyes averting in respectful submission.

"Good." I brush my palms off on my jeans, taking a step backward toward Caius. He's the only one behind me because he's the only one I trust at my back. "Give me a few days to sort this out with our newcomer. A proper introduction will occur when she's ready."

They don't respond verbally, just nod in agreement.

There are about twenty of them.

If they wanted to really push this and challenge me, they could as a group.

But too many of them already respect my role as Pack Alpha.

It's these troublemakers that give me grief. Mainly the idiot on the ground and his buddy Kin. They'll heel eventually. They always do.

VOLT

The little wolf follows close behind me as I lead her up the hill to our den. When I reached down to carry her earlier, she stood up and shook out her fur, then gave me a lopsided grin. It seemed to be a dare from her animal, or maybe an invitation.

Shrugging, I kicked off my pants and shifted.

Then she happily trotted along beside me up the path.

Tieran was right—her animal is definitely in control.

I can see the conflict in her eyes every time I glance at her, the general confusion as to why her wolf is so easily trusting mine.

It's dangerous.

I'm dangerous.

But the little wolf seems quite taken with my purr, so I continue to emanate the sound to soothe her.

It's a natural reaction after observing her terror in the waves. My animal is hell-bent now on protecting hers.

The word *Omega* whispers through my mind. She doesn't smell right, but something about her is calling to all my instincts.

Some wolves have fated mates.

Carnage Wolves have a different form of fate—Alphas are inherently drawn to Omegas because they can take our knot. They're also excellent with children and feisty as fuck.

We can technically choose to mate Betas or other Alphas, but most of us crave Omegas.

It's only natural. We're driven by the need to procreate, something Omegas are built to do with an Alpha.

It's all about the knot.

And the alluring heat cycle Omegas go through every few months.

I've never experienced that wondrous bliss myself. But I've heard about it from other Alphas, and I've witnessed the rut it inspires in unmated Alphas as well.

If this female turns out to be an Omega, we're going to have an island full of problems.

I reach the top of a hill, one that overlooks several of the others, and lead the little wolf toward our den.

We settled in this location because of its protective properties. No one can sneak up on us here. And we can see for miles in every direction, giving us the opportunity to scout for potential incoming aircraft or boats.

We also have state-of-the-art tech that provides alerts as well.

I shift back into human form to check the exterior monitor near the cabin door when we arrive, wanting to ensure there are no existing threats nearby. The only residual alarm on the screen is from the guards' earlier shipment—which is currently sitting beside me and staring at a nearby tree with interest.

Another confirmation that the female inside isn't in control. Otherwise, she would be eyeing the surveillance equipment.

Or *my* equipment, since it's currently eye level with her wolf.

But her animal is more taken with the trees.

"Are you hungry?" I wonder out loud.

She cants her head at me in that curious manner she did on the beach. It's not the same way she tricked the guard. This is genuine. Relaxed. *Happy.*

Definitely her wolf, I think, fighting a grin. Because the female inside would not be nearly as pleased with her current predicament.

Which is why Tieran wanted to postpone the welcome party.

We need to coax the human out first.

Which will require a bit of finesse and potentially some Alpha growls.

I purr for her instead, wanting to keep her happy as I open the door and step inside. She follows like an obedient little wolf, her nose taking in the scents of our living room and dining area.

I expect her to head toward the kitchen, but she plops down to roll around on a rug in the living room instead.

Leaning against the wood-paneled wall, I watch as she scents off the rug, her belly fully exposed.

The human inside must be cringing.

Or maybe she's too broken to even realize what's happening.

With a yip, the wolf jumps to her feet again, her agility impressive, considering she nearly drowned thirty minutes ago, and she takes off down the hallway.

I follow with a shake of my head, amused.

It's like having a puppy.

Except this female is definitely full grown.

She heads into the guest room first because it's the

closest to the living area. "This is where you'll sleep, if you're good," I tell her.

She snorts like she can understand me and scoffs at the bed before turning around to march back into the hallway toward the back stairs.

"It's rude to take yourself on your own tour," I say conversationally as she bolts down the wood stairs to the level underground. "Tieran wouldn't appreciate this."

Not that I care.

He'll live.

She walks right by the two offices at the bottom of the stairs and toward the rooms near the back. Mine is first, the door partially ajar.

She slips inside, her nose leading the way.

I take advantage of her self-possessed tour to grab a pair of flannels and tug them on.

She doesn't even notice, too busy sniffing every inch of my room. When she spies my bed, I narrow my eyes. "Do not—"

She jumps right into it and starts to roll around, scenting off my sheets and blankets.

Sighing, I just shake my head.

This little thing is going to cause all sorts of trouble.

She hits Caius's room next, noting his penchant for blue silk and rolling around happily in his formerly made bed. I don't bother fixing it. He'll know she was in here by her scent alone. May as well ensure he knows just what she was up to.

The final door is closed.

She paws at it and grunts.

"You don't want to mess up Tieran's bed, sweetling," I tell her. "He won't be pleased about it."

She sits down in defiance, staring straight at the door.

"How about we go upstairs for some food instead?" I offer, suggesting a meal again.

The daring little wolf just huffs and lies down, clearly wanting to go inside Tieran's room.

"You're a bit of a brat, aren't you?" I say it endearingly because I'm amused by her antics. "All right. If you want to piss off the Carnage Island Alpha, I'll allow it. But don't say I didn't warn you."

She perks up as I open his door.

Then she darts inside to start her sniffing tour all over again.

Tieran's room is the darkest in terms of tones and general aura. But his bed is made with the same precision as Caius's—which the little wolf promptly destroys.

She shoves her snout between his pillows, the black silk at odds against her white coat. A loud snort follows, her tail wagging happily.

I lean against his door frame, grinning as she uses her little claws to dig at the blankets.

Tieran's going to lose his fucking mind when he comes back.

I'll do my best to stand in his way, but the little wolf really needs to learn some manners. So I'll have to hand her over to him at some point.

She sighs happily as the comforter and top sheet move out of her way, allowing her to properly scent off his bed. Except she doesn't roll as much here. Instead, she curls into a ball in the center.

Claiming her spot.

I arch a brow. "You sure you want to do that, sweetling?"

She closes her eyes in response.

"All right," I say, chuckling as I push away from the

door frame. "I hope you enjoy spankings, sweetheart. You've more than earned one."

Of course, I'm partially to blame since I opened the door—something I'll own up to when Tieran returns.

Until then, I busy myself in the kitchen, making dinner for four instead of three.

The moon is rising when Tieran and Caius finally return, their arms full of shit from the yacht. We left it all there earlier when we spotted the guards going the wrong way around the island.

Tieran sets my folded clothes on the table, the suit in relatively good condition, considering how I left it on the beach.

Caius has the envelope of cash in his pile, along with a laptop bag and several other items from our trip to the mainland.

"Where's the girl?" he asks, frowning at finding me alone in the kitchen.

"Taking a nap." She hasn't made a single sound since I left her downstairs.

"In the guest room?" Tieran's tone and expression tell me he knows she's not there because her scent is too subtle on this floor.

"No." I smile, already anticipating his reaction. "She found a more comfortable place to sleep downstairs."

His brow draws downward. "Where?"

I shrug. "Follow your nose. You'll find her."

But the way his eyes narrow tells me he already knows. "Fuck. Tell me you didn't let that mutt into my room."

I frown at him, but it's forced and mocking. "You're asking me to lie? I thought our brotherhood was built on truth."

"You fucking dick."

My lips curl back upward. "Sorry. She's cute when she begs."

He growls. "I would throw your suit back down to the beach, but I know you wouldn't care."

"Not at all," I agree. "But feel free to do it anyway."

Caius distracts the grumbling Alpha with a beer. "She's scared and chose your bed because it made her feel safe. Take it as a compliment."

"Yeah, because I love fresh salty fur in my bed," he mutters at him, taking the beer and nearly breaking the neck of it.

I return to the stove, flipping the salmon steak once more to sear the opposite side. "If it makes you feel better, she rolled in all our sheets."

"That doesn't make me feel better," he bites back.

I shrug. "At least her salty fur comes with a sweet perfume."

"Great. So I'll feel grimy and want to jerk off." He slams his beer down on the counter. "I'm going to go see if I can't coax the human out of her furry shell so we can have an adult conversation about boundaries."

"Try not to go too hard on her," I call to him. "She's cute."

He grunts, disappearing from view as he enters the living area.

"Someone's in a mood," I say, glancing at Caius. "The beach party not go well?"

"Dirk challenged him." Caius picks up Tieran's beer to take a swig. "T put him in his place right quick, but he's concerned."

"About the girl?" I guess.

Caius nods. "Her scent is like a drug."

"Like an Omega, you mean." I've scented a few before,

and they were all sickly sweet, just like the little darling downstairs.

"Yeah. It's going to rip this island apart."

I turn off the burner before sliding the salmon onto a tray for the oven. I only sear the outside before baking it to help with texture and seasoning.

"It also may be exactly what we need," I say, thinking out loud. "An Alpha isn't complete without his circle."

Caius takes another sip of the beer, his eyes more silver today than gray. They often change with his mood. When they shift to green, it means he's angry. Silver and gray tend to imply he's feeling more relaxed or content.

Green is a rare look on him.

Silver is the most common.

"Maybe fate brought her here," he suggests after a beat. "He needs an Omega. Maybe she's ours."

A snarl echoes up from downstairs, making us both freeze.

"Well," Caius drawls, clearing his throat. "Assuming he doesn't kill her first."

CLOVE

My wolf has a death wish.

She's a fucking psycho.

And she's going to get us killed.

Because she decided to take a nap in the Carnage Island Alpha's *bed*.

His low growl from the doorway is a warning I feel to my very core. But all it does is draw a little whine of irritation from my suicidal wolf.

She picks up her head, yawns at him, and proceeds to flop over to her other side.

And closes her eyes.

I scream at her to move. To bow. To *run*. Anything but just relax in the Alpha's bed as though she belongs there.

"I see," he says, his tone holding a lethal note that makes me wince inside.

This is not going to end well.

"I think we need to have a conversation about etiquette and common decency, little one." He sounds calm. Too calm. And because my wolf's eyes are closed, I can't see his face. But I hear him prowling toward me, his presence a darkness threatening to suffocate me from the inside out.

Tieran, V called him.

A name I know very well.

A name I've feared for years.

Tieran isn't just the Carnage Island Alpha.

He's the Black Mountain Alpha's son.

The same one who slaughtered Alpha Bryson's daughter. That's why he's here—not for being rejected, but for slaughtering his mate.

And my wolf decided to nap in his bed.

Now she's ignoring him, content to relax in his presence, utterly unaware of the growing tension in the room.

I really am broken. It's the only explanation for her relaxed state and my inability to wake her the fuck up.

His palm comes down on my rump, making my wolf yelp in surprise. "Off," he demands.

She snarls in response.

And he snarls right back, the angry sound loud and reverberating through my ears.

My heart actually stops. I feel it stutter. Just as I sense my wolf's inability to breathe.

She's terrified.

Fucking finally.

But rather than fight or run, she freezes, like she's forgotten how to move.

"Off," he repeats, his tone one that would bring me to my knees if I were in human form. His Alpha energy is intoxicating and overwhelming and so damn thick that I can't see straight.

Or maybe that's my wolf losing her sight. She hasn't taken a breath in too long a time. Our lungs are aching. Yet she remains frozen, his snarl having rendered her incapable of functioning.

He reaches for us and I beg her to run, beg her to do

anything other than sit here like a disobedient pet on his bed. But she refuses me.

She merely shivers as his hands take hold of her scruff to guide us off the bed.

He's not rough, but he's not gentle either.

And he curses at whatever he sees in his sheets.

"All right, little brat," he says, lifting me effortlessly into his arms. "I think I know what you need."

My vision is starting to blur with black spots.

My wolf is feeling unbalanced.

My lungs are *burning*.

She's lost all control of her motor functions and has obviously forgotten our will to survive. Because my wolf is still frozen, just in his arms now.

At least inhale, I beg her, my heart splintering at this helpless sensation. I feel so shattered. So utterly useless. So... so... *lost.*

I'm not this girl.

I'm not meek or unintelligent.

I should have control of this situation.

But I... I just don't. And I have no idea what to do.

The room is so dark now that it's black.

And my damn wolf refuses to—

Water hits my head unexpectedly, drawing a sharp intake of air from my wolf that she releases on a low whine of disapproval.

"If you want to sleep in my bed, then you're at least going to be clean," Tieran says as he sets me down in a space bigger than my bedroom back home.

A shower, I realize, noting the marble and various heads. *Who needs a shower this big?*

"Sit," he demands, talking to me like a dog.

Which I would normally be pissed about, but my wolf

is behaving like an untamed canine, so his treatment is probably deserved.

My wolf huffs, ignoring his command.

And tries to leave the shower instead.

He grabs me by the scruff to pull me back. "Oh, no, you don't. You're filthy from that cage and the ocean. And since you refuse to let your human take over, I'm bathing you." He uses his grip to force my eyes to his. "And if you're a good girl, I may even brush you."

I shiver inside.

Something about that promise feels so… *intimate.*

He releases my scruff to stroke a hand down my neck to my throat. "I see you in there, little one," he whispers, his intense blue eyes holding mine. "I know your wolf has taken over. We'll help you regain control."

His soft voice soothes some ache deep inside me.

Until I remember his name.

Tieran Black.

The monster who slaughtered his mate.

His eyes narrow as though he can read my mind.

Or maybe he can smell my fear.

Rather than comment on it, he guides my wolf beneath the water again and proceeds to bathe her. She yelps and growls a few times, but he doesn't snarl back like before. He just runs his fingers through my fur, massaging a woodsy scent into my coat.

It reminds me of pine trees.

I want to inhale it, to bathe in it, but my wolf is too busy sputtering as the water touches her snout. She is not a fan of this experience at all, not understanding the intimacy of having an Alpha take care of her, or respecting his patience as he rinses away the suds.

She just keeps yipping at him.

Which earns her a rap on the nose. "Quiet, errant one."

I almost snort. Because I've called her that once or twice already.

"I will never understand why the Nantahala Wolves choose to suppress their females for so long," he mutters, making me freeze inside.

You know what I am?

"If you'd been raised in my pack, you would have started shifting around age five. We consider our animal forms sacred, and we embrace them at a young age to avoid the possibility of disassociation." He turns off the water to grab a towel. "But I suspect your males do this as a way to control you. To make sure you have to rely on them to be one with your beast."

My wolf growls a little as he starts patting her down, clearly not appreciating the manhandling.

He sighs and spreads the towel out on the floor. "Want to dry yourself, then?" he asks, standing.

She stares at the offering, allowing me to see the splash of white cotton against the obsidian marble floor. Then she dives into it as though she expects it to be a big fluffy cloud and starts rolling around, happily scenting herself off his towel.

The Alpha chuckles, clearly amused. "Well, as sad as it makes me to see a shifter be so far separated from her animal, I'll admit you're kinda cute."

My wolf huffs.

"*Very* cute," he corrects, squatting to rub my now exposed belly. "Are you going to let me brush you, pet?"

My heart skips a beat.

Or it feels like it does, anyway.

Because the way he said that shoots warmth through

every inch of my being. If I were in control, my body would be on fire right now.

My wolf sits up and cocks her head, clearly interested in his tone.

He sits on the floor, his jeans still sopping wet, and leans back against the sink cabinet behind him. Then he meets my gaze again as he lifts a hand toward my neck.

I can't see what he's doing because my wolf is staring him down, but I feel the comb gliding through my fur. I almost purr with delight, the sensation making me want to lie down and let him do whatever he wants with me.

His reputation haunted my teenage years, following me into adulthood.

Yet I can't help but give in to the sensation he's evoking now.

I've never experienced anything like it, and it's... it's *heavenly*.

I sigh, as does my wolf, leaning into his touch as he chuckles again. "You just need a little love," he says. "Maybe that'll help calm you down enough for your human to take charge for a bit, hmm?"

My animal doesn't seem to hear him or care what he's saying. She's too lost to his touch.

But I hear him.

And I understand just fine.

He wants to encourage my wolf to retreat, to allow me to shift. Because he knows she's in charge.

Why? I wonder. *Why are you helping me? And how do you know?*

Is this normal?

Do females often find themselves disassociated from their wolves?

I've never heard about it in my pack, but it would

explain why so many females weren't allowed to shift, even after their mating.

Or maybe… maybe they didn't *want* to shift for this very reason.

Why would my pack design this failure? I understand the point of focusing on procreation and ensuring the health of the children, but this feels debilitating.

Controlling, I think, recalling what Tieran said about how males probably do this to *control* their mates.

My insides burn for an entirely different reason now.

My mother always said it was about letting the males think they're in charge.

But they suppress our wolves on purpose.

They tell us it's natural, that all packs do this.

Tieran said his pack starts shifting at age five, something I wouldn't be inclined to believe, given his reputation. Except I *saw* pups running around on Wolfe Island.

Female pups.

Which means that even if Tieran is lying to me, so was Alpha Bryson. So were my mother and father and my entire damn pack.

And while I know Tieran's reputation, I'm almost inclined to believe he's not lying, because he has no reason to. He's helping me. He's the only one who has been able to sense my disassociation and give me potential causes for it.

"That fire in your gaze is beautiful," he murmurs, drawing my attention to him. "I can almost feel your anger, little wolf. Do you want me to help you shift back? Because I can. But it'll hurt. Forcing a shift always does, which is why Alphas tend to shy away from it."

I blink at him.

Or my wolf does, anyway.

Or maybe it's me.

It's hard to say. I feel so disconnected and lost that I'm not sure what is up or down.

But his words… his statement… his comment about Alphas shying away from commanding others to shift.

That's… that's not true. Alphas in my pack do it all the time to their females. It's part of the mating ritual. It's supposed to be sacred and special, something the male does for his chosen mate.

Or is that just another way to control the females?

My jaw clenches.

Really clenches.

Momentarily confusing me because *I* made my wolf gnash her teeth.

And Tieran's knowing gaze suggests he saw it, too.

"You're a fighter," he says, approval underlining those words. "Do you want to try to take control yourself, or would you like my help?"

He's already helping, his words alone seeming to give me the power to override my wolf. At least subtly.

Or maybe that's my anger.

Anger he's awakened with his truths and his outside perspective.

Have I been suppressed my whole life? Living in a world meant to keep women down, to control them, all to, what, impregnate them?

What was the point of all the tests? The trials? Me proving my worth as a mating candidate?

They tested my speed, my agility, and my strength. To do what, ensure I was able to produce a worthwhile pup?

I… I don't understand.

It feels too wrong. Too outlandish. Too *insane* to be true.

Yet I can't deny the resounding veracity in my soul that Tieran is telling me the truth.

He continues to brush my fur, waiting for me to give him my decision. Or perhaps waiting for a sign.

I can't exactly speak.

But I can blink.

And my jaws appear to be clenched as a result of my own frustration.

What else can I control? I wonder, attempting to move my head to look at Tieran again.

My wolf obeys.

His eyes lock with mine once more. "Good," he murmurs, his eyes grinning. "Try lying down."

I do.

And my wolf allows it.

"Sit back up," he says.

I lift up and meet his gaze again.

He nods. "That's it. You've broken down some sort of wall between you, helping to blend your wants and needs. To turn human, you'll need to take full control and tell her to heel. Which, given what I've observed of your animal, won't be easy."

"We could try feeding her," a deep voice suggests from behind me, causing me to spin on my rump to inspect the newcomer. *Caius.* I recognize his scent. *Peppermint and spice.* I'm not sure when I cataloged that information in my mind, but it's there, giving me his identity along with his familiar voice.

He has thick brown hair, an athletic physique, pretty silver eyes, and a kind smile with dimples engraved in his cheeks.

"Well, hello, gorgeous," he says, crouching in the doorway. "Don't you look all nice and clean?"

Tieran grunts behind me. "She's not a dog."

"Says the male who was down here giving her orders to sit and lie down and *off*," Caius returns without missing a beat, his gaze still holding mine. "How about some salmon, hmm? Maybe that'll help placate your wolf enough to submit to your wants and desires."

The sensuality in his voice stirs heat inside me, just like Tieran's brushing request.

Something about these males, perhaps their power and Alpha auras, is calling to a foreign part of my being. I can feel it simmering beneath their knowing gazes, threatening to take control and leave me a writhing mess on the ground.

That part of me doesn't care that my wolf is still in charge. It wants to wake up and steal the reins.

The competing sentiments cause a low whimper to escape my lips. Except it sounds oddly needy, like I'm begging for something I don't understand.

"Well, that wasn't on the menu, but we can absolutely arrange it once you're back in human form," Caius says, his dimples flashing again as he straightens in a ripple of muscle that makes me drool.

Literally.

My wolf is drooling.

Wow, I think, irritated all over again. *Put your jaws together.*

She does.

Which gives me pause again and I narrow my eyes. *Stand up*, I think.

She obliges.

Walk.

Again she listens but pauses to rub against the male in the doorway, earning her a quick scratch behind the ear. "I like her," he murmurs. "Let's keep her."

"Again, she's not a dog," Tieran tells him.

"Oh, I'm very aware of what she is, T," he drawls. "Volt is, too."

Volt? I think, pausing just outside the bathroom door in the bedroom. *V must be Volt.*

And he happens to be standing in the entryway that leads to the hall, his arms folded as he braces himself against the door frame. "How was your bath, sweetling?" he asks.

I shake out my coat in response, pleased that my wolf listens to me again. *Is it my anger that caught your attention?* I wonder. Because I'm still mad. I can feel the burn of it in my gut, itching for an outlet.

My pack raised me to be weak, to disassociate from my wolf.

They rejected me for being white.

Then raped and murdered my mother in front of me.

And pinned the blame on me.

Yeah, I have a lot to be furious about. I'll just keep channeling it until my wolf lets me convert back into a human.

At that point, I'll evaluate my next move.

Which will probably be to run.

Maybe.

Depending on how these Alphas react.

"I'll admit it's a rather bland punishment," Volt adds as Tieran follows me out into the bedroom. "I expected something a little more intense."

"Yeah? And who let her in my room, again?" Tieran pauses beside me to draw his fingers through my nape.

"It was that or leave her begging by your door. I chose to indulge the pretty beast instead." Volt sounds completely unapologetic.

"Hmm." Tieran's touch leaves my fur as he saunters over to begin stripping his bed. "Since you let her in here knowing she was a filthy mess, I think you should have to clean it up." He starts pulling the bedding together to create a giant ball.

My wolf wags her tail, excited about this new game.

I tell her to stop.

This time, she doesn't listen.

The second the bedding is in the air, I jump to catch it in my mouth, then I take it to the corner to lay it on the ground and start spreading it out with my paws. I have no idea why I'm doing this, but it's oddly soothing, so I let it happen.

It's similar to how my wolf wanted to roll in their beds, to scent off their sheets.

But different because I'm creating this myself. Sort of, anyway. It's like we're working together toward a goal only my wolf understands.

I lose myself to the task, stretching out the sheets, pawing off the salty grim, then smoothing it in a way that feels right. The comforter is next, the soft, dark fabric heavenly to my teeth and nails. I fluff it up a little, then nuzzle it with my nose until it's in the right position, creating a bed on the floor.

Pleased with the design, I plop down in the center of it and turn to face the three Alphas.

They're all gaping at me.

"Did she…?" Caius trails off, swallowing.

"Just start making a nest?" Tieran finishes for him, his voice sounding hoarse. "Yeah. Yeah, that's exactly what she just did."

I blink. *A nest?* I glance down at the bed I made and cock my head. I've never heard someone call a bed a nest before. But I guess it sort of resembles a nest.

Standing, I shake off the need to retreat to my *nest* and focus on Caius.

He mentioned food.

That sounds very nice right now. Maybe after, I can try

the whole *taking command* thing that Tieran mentioned and see if my wolf will let me walk on two legs again.

The males say nothing, their gazes still locked on me.

I give a little yip, trying to say *food*, then wander up to nudge Caius's hand.

It's bold, but I'm starving now. Something about making that bed has awakened my hunger.

I can't even remember the last time I ate.

And the scents coming from upstairs are practically screaming for me to run up and taste them.

Caius runs his fingers through my fur, his touch reverent. "I think she wants to eat," he whispers.

"She's going to want to do a lot more than that," Volt says, taking a step backward into the hallway. "But yeah. We should... we should eat."

"Yeah," Tieran agrees. "We really should."

Caius chuckles, his fingers still drawing through my fur in a way that makes my wolf want to purr. "Come on, beautiful. Let's feed you and see if you can't shift back after."

CAIUS

An Omega.
She has to be one.

She's small, smells divine, and just started making a fucking nest in Tieran's room out of his soiled sheets.

It would also explain her wolf's inherent trust in us to protect her.

Omegas are drawn to Alphas, just as we're drawn to them.

And I am absolutely fucking drawn to this little beast with her pretty white fur and intelligent brown eyes.

Her scent is a goddamn beacon as well, practically radiating *fuck me* vibes all over our den.

I lead her to the dining room to find the table set for four.

Which is obviously not going to work since she's still in wolf form.

I frown, searching for a better place to set her food down.

Volt has already sliced up the meal into bite-size pieces, likely anticipating her wolfish state. That also explains why he chose these lipped plates. They're almost like bowls, but flat on the bottom with edges.

Picking up her dish, I glance at the ground beside the table and decide that's not going to work. She can't eat at our feet.

Volt and Tieran seem to feel the same way, as they both are searching for a better place to eat while the little wolf leans against my legs and gazes up at me wistfully.

I doubt she's eaten much, if anything, since being shipped off to Wolfe Island.

"Let's eat in the living area," Tieran suggests, picking up his plate and fork. He swapped his wet jeans for a pair of sweats before coming up and seems to be quite comfortable with our little visitor now, as evidenced by the small grin he gives her. "We can gather around the coffee table."

Volt nods, grabbing his plate as well and taking it to the room before coming back for mine.

Tieran returns to grab our drinks, which leads me to ask, "Do we have a big mug?" Because our little wolf is going to need some water with this meal.

"On it," Tieran says, already on his way back from the living area.

The female is still pressed up against my leg, probably because I promised to feed her.

I lead her into the living area where Tieran is setting down pillows to function as chairs. Then he takes the seat on the floor that gives him the best view of the room and the door and gestures for me to sit beside him. Volt settles across from me, and the female sits next to me.

I set her bowl on the table. Then add her mug to the edge. It's still a little tall for her, so I end up setting it on the ground.

She huffs a little but lies down to eat.

Or she tries to, anyway.

She keeps snorting, her nose hitting the lip of the plate as she attempts to daintily take a bite.

"No need to be polite or elegant here," I tell her. "Just dig in and use your tongue."

"Or let your wolf guide you," Tieran suggests. "It's all about finding balance between you and your wolf. Once you start truly working together, you'll feel better."

She glances up at him, then dips her snout into the water mug and sneezes.

"Tongue, beautiful," I say again. "Use your tongue."

"And your wolf," Tieran echoes, taking a bite of his salmon steak.

She continues to try to eat, her agitation palpable. These are the sorts of skills that should come naturally to a wolf, but she's never been taught any of them—a realization that irritates me to no end.

But she doesn't give up. She tries various ways to eat, including lapping up some of the salmon with her tongue.

And after ten minutes or so, she finally finds a groove that allows her to enjoy her meal.

We could have scattered it on the ground or fed her from our hands, but these are life skills she needs to survive.

This time she laps up the water rather than sticking her snout in the cup.

Volt goes to refill it when she finishes.

And she drinks a whole second cup.

When he starts to stand again, she snorts and shakes her head.

Tieran smiles. "Well done, little one. Do you think you can try shifting now?"

She stares at him for a moment, her gaze hardening. After several minutes, she huffs and plops down.

Tieran studies her, humming thoughtfully. Then after a moment, he nods. "We'll try again tomorrow."

She sighs in response to that, her dejection hurting my heart. Shifting should come naturally to all wolves. But her pack purposely stunted her growth.

It's one of the many reasons I hate the Nantahala Pack.

And the Santeetlah Pack isn't much better.

They thrive on masculine superiority.

Yes, Alpha males are superior to others of our species. However, that doesn't mean we should belittle those born weaker than us. We're meant to protect them, not harm them. Which requires hierarchy within a pack and devout obedience.

But it also means knowing when to nurture, something we are all trying to do with her now.

"What's your name?" I ask, deciding a distraction is needed to help pull her away from her failure. As Tieran mentioned earlier, it's very likely that her former mate is the reason she can't shift.

Which means one of us is going to have to force her back into human form.

But that would be too much for tonight.

Something Tieran clearly already realized when he said she could try again tomorrow.

The little wolf peeks up at me, her dark brown eyes blinking.

While Tieran received a report of her incoming arrival, he was never given her name. Just all the details about her pack origin, the Alpha's son who rejected her, and how she supposedly killed her mom.

I'm struggling with that last bit.

She doesn't strike me as a killer.

Although, she did try to maul Jack.

So maybe she is a little beast after all.

She stands, her eyes on me, and pokes me in the chest with her snout. "Yes, I would like to know your name," I confirm, not clear on why that earned me a nudge.

The little wolf shakes her head.

"You won't tell us?" I'm not sure I like that response.

"Maybe she wants us to confirm our names first?" Volt suggests.

A fair request. We missed our introductions on the beach, what with being concerned for her life and all.

But she huffs before I can properly introduce myself.

"Well, this would be easier if you shifted back into human form," I say conversationally.

She nudges me again, this time with a bit more strength.

Then lies down before I can react and curls her body like a crescent moon.

"Oh, I see." My irritation with her perceived defiance melts away in an instance. "Your name is either Caius or begins with *C*. I'm guessing the latter."

She stands up again and wags her tail.

"It begins with *C*," I confirm.

She gives me her version of a wolf smile. Then lies down again on her belly with her legs stretched out behind her and in front of her.

"An *I*?" I guess.

She doesn't move.

"An *L*?" Volt says.

She stands up again with another tail wag.

"*C-L*. What's next?" I ask.

She blinks at me, her rump hitting the ground. After a beat, she starts howling. She immediately stops when we all wince. Then she tries again, only softer this time.

Volt and I share a look.

But it's Tieran who smirks and says, "Clever little thing."

"What letter is it?" I ask, completely at a loss.

"Well, as *W* sounds weird after *C-L*, I'm guessing she's trying to say *O*," he drawls as he stretches his arms over his head. Eating on a pillow on the floor isn't exactly comfortable.

The female stops her howling and pants happily once more.

"*C-L-O*." I'm not sure if that's a full name or not.

She confirms it's not complete when she stands again, this time bumping Volt with her snout. "Clovolt?" he teases, his fingers brushing the fur near her ear. "A strange name, sweetling."

She grumbles, making me laugh. "*C-L-O-V*."

"Clov," Tieran murmurs. "Clover, maybe?"

She moves away from Volt to sit by Tieran, her head cocked.

Which must mean he's either close or said something right. "Is it Clov or Clover?" I ask her.

Tieran holds up his hands. "Left is Clov. Right is Clover."

She puts her head between his hands.

"Clov… with an *e*?" I guess.

The little wolf perks up, panting.

"Clove," I repeat. "With an *e*."

"Short for Clover?" Tieran asks.

She licks his cheek excitedly. Then freezes at realizing she essentially just kissed him.

My lips curl, curious to see what he'll do.

This sort of easy candor isn't exactly normal for our trio. But this is definitely a unique situation. It's not every day an Omega ends up in our lair. They're exceptionally rare, a diamond among our kind, and they deserve our worship and devotion.

Which is why I'm not surprised at all when Tieran merely runs his fingers through her fur while saying, "Clove is a beautiful name." He adds a little purr to the statement, causing her to practically melt at his side. "I'm Alpha Tieran, as I imagine you've already figured out. That's Caius and Volt." His voice holds a note of wonder, my best friend clearly smitten with the girl.

Yeah, she's definitely an Omega.

Volt saving her wasn't exactly surprising. He would have been smitten with her the moment he heard she killed her own mother. That dance with Jack on the boat would only have cemented his desire.

However, the innate softness we all seem to be displaying for her is absolutely unusual for us.

Sitting on the floor and trying to teach her how to eat as a wolf? Yeah, that's not something we would normally do.

Tieran would be more likely to lock her in a cage with her bowl and tell her to figure it out.

Volt would have suggested letting her go to fend for herself—something Tieran would have vetoed on principle because it's his responsibility to protect all members of the pack.

And I would have taken my plate down to my room to ignore them all.

Yet here we sit around this table, captivated by this pretty little wolf when we don't even know what she looks like yet in human form.

Her scent is a big part of the allure.

But it's also the innate sweetness to her aura and the fighter we can all see lurking in her eyes.

This female is going to be fun once she shifts back into her human self.

"Are you tired, little one?" Tieran asks when Clove yawns.

She leans into him a little more, seeking the comfort of his Alpha touch—another thing only an Omega would ever truly do.

It's possible this is the result of whatever trauma led up to her killing her mother, or perhaps the trauma of that specific event.

But I suspect it's so much more.

Because her aroma is intoxicating and a drug to our senses.

Unless she's been sent here as some sort of glorified trap. Pheromones can be altered, after all.

And if that's the case, she'll die. Painfully.

"Hmm, I'm translating that as a yes," Tieran muses as she yawns again. "I don't suppose you want to sleep in the guest room?"

She seems to consider it, but the shiver in her fur tells us everything we need to know—she won't feel safe there.

"Just let her have her nest," I say, taking the decisions away from her. I'm not trying to be cruel or pushy. I just want to make it easier on her. Somehow, I just know she'll opt for the guest room and then not sleep a wink.

Tieran's expression says he suspects the same.

It's the fighter beneath her skin, and now that she has control of her wolf, she'll try to be independent. But her wolf knows what she needs—Alphas capable of protecting her from the predators outside.

Besides, it'll be easier having her sequestered at the back of the den. That scent of hers is a beacon, and someone may just be stupid enough to try to follow it in here.

I would prefer to be the one to properly welcome whatever idiot is suicidal enough to enter, and not leave Clove upstairs to defend herself. While that leap at Jack's throat was impressive, it would not be enough to take down a determined Carnage Wolf.

And especially not a Carnage Wolf Alpha.

Clove doesn't protest, instead choosing to follow Tieran as he leads her to the stairs. "I believe you know the rest of the way," he tells her. "I'll take the guest room for tonight so you can have your space."

She seems to pause at that, the female inside thinking.

But a little nudge to her rump with his palm has her scurrying down the stairs.

He waits a beat, likely listening for her to do as she was told, then returns to the living area to start picking up dishes.

"She has to be an Omega," I say conversationally as I help carry several empty plates to the sink.

"No shit," Volt agrees, helping as well. "T just gave up his room to her. Only an Omega could accomplish that."

Tieran snorts. "She's fragile, and I don't want to risk her wolf taking complete control again."

"You really think that's why she can't shift?" I wonder aloud. "Or is it the Alpha dick who did this to her?"

"We'll know in the morning." He starts scrubbing plates, telling me he's even more distracted than he cares to admit. Because Tieran only cleans when he's thinking seriously about something.

Volt and I share a look, then clear the rest of the living room while Tieran takes on the domestic chores in the kitchen.

By the time he's done, I know he has a plan because there's a strategic glint in his blue eyes. "We'll test her in the morning, see if she's ready to take back complete control. If she's not, we'll give her another day or two under our protection to see if that helps."

"And if it doesn't?" I prompt.

"Then I'll do what needs to be done." He doesn't sound happy about it. I don't blame him. Commanding a shift hurts the other wolf, and that's the very last thing any of us would want to do to an Omega.

But part of being an Alpha is knowing when to take charge and force situations for the betterment of the other party.

And, in this case, it'll be to Clove's benefit to learn how to shift back.

She'll hate him for it at first.

However, she'll eventually forgive him.

Probably around the time he knots her.

No Omega can resist an Alpha's cock.

Perhaps that'll be her final test to see if those pheromones are real or not. If she dies, she lied. If she survives, she's ours.

Tieran's wrist begins to vibrate, his watch warning him of an incoming call. "It's my father," he says, turning off the water. "I'll let you know what he says about the girl."

He disappears from view, heading down to his office.

Volt and I share yet another look—something we seem to be doing frequently tonight.

"Want to take bets on which idiot tries to find her first?" I ask him, referring to the Carnage Wolves.

"A bet against you?" He snorts. "They had better be good stakes."

"Winner knots the Omega first?" I suggest. It doesn't have to apply to Clove, just whoever our future Omega may be. It just happens to be her presence here today that gives me the idea for the bet.

"I think she'll be choosing T for that," Volt replies,

confirming that he agrees Clove isn't just an Omega, but *our* intended Omega. "Her wolf picked his bed, after all."

"A given. I meant the winner between us knots her first —*after* T." Because we're an Alpha circle. If T mates her, we all mate her. And given how comfortable she seemed with us tonight, I doubt that'll be much of an issue for her. However, again, this bet applies to whoever the Omega of our future is—which I very much hope is sweet little Clove.

Volt considers it. "All right." He makes his pick.

I make mine.

And the bet is on.

CLOVE

Roughly two days in a den with three Carnage Wolf Alphas has turned everything I know about their kind upside down.

Tieran has a reputation for cruelty because of how he killed his mate.

Yet he's treated me respectfully, allowing me to sleep in his room on my pile of sheets in the corner and ensuring I not only eat but know how to eat. He keeps dropping little hints about how to connect to my wolf, too.

It's... confusing.

I can sense his feral aura and his need to dominate. His Alpha energy is a thick presence against my skin that demands I submit.

But he's been almost gentle with me since I arrived.

Even the bath punishment was rather kind.

However, there's an air about him this morning that has me wondering if everything is about to change. I can feel it coming from upstairs, his dominance a suffocating wave that surrounds my very spirit.

He's coming for me.

I don't know how I know that, but I do. It's a warning

in the air. A caution my wolf picks up on just as well as I do.

Am I overreacting? I wonder.

All three males have been *kind*, a claim I really can't make about any of the Alphas from the Nantahala Pack.

Volt, Caius, and Tieran are different. They're Alphas, yet caring. Dominant, yet tender.

I slept well my first night in their den, then Tieran and I spent yesterday talking about how shifters control their wolves. He attempted to show me how to shift by demonstrating himself, but I was too enthralled by the majestic display to truly follow his advice.

The moment his pants came off, I was captivated.

Something that confused me because I grew up around naked men who frequently shifted into wolves.

But Tieran is a whole new breed of male. He's tall, lean, and sleek. Yet with white fur instead of black—a trait that only makes him more beautiful.

Volt tried to help as well by changing into his wolf. He also maintained that magnetic air of dominance, edged with a hint of lethality that had my animal sitting up and taking notice.

Caius didn't participate.

Instead, he focused on making food for us all. Mine came cut up in pieces, making it easier to eat—something that endeared these Alphas to me even more.

I can't understand why my pack fears them so much.

But the energy wafting off of Tieran now gives me somewhat of an idea. I can't tell if he's angry or tired or perhaps annoyed that I spent another night in his room while he took the guest bed.

I shouldn't have agreed to these sleeping arrangements.

I only did that because my wolf felt more comfortable in the "nest" she made. And Tieran keeps saying how important it is for me to be one with my wolf, not separate ourselves. So I thought it was the right decision.

However, as he prowls into the room this morning, I can't help but feel that it was a very bad choice.

He goes straight to the shower without looking at me.

I stand up and tiptoe from the room, trying to avoid his mood.

Caius meets me in the hallway, his expression giving nothing away. "How'd you sleep, gorgeous?"

I can't actually answer him, so I just rub against his leg in response because he seems to like that style of greeting. It's a sign of affection between wolves, something I really have no right to give, but these males welcomed me into their home. I have no idea why they're being so nice to me. However, I'm thankful for it.

They've turned my nightmare into something akin to a dream.

My anger hasn't abated.

My sadness is still there, too.

But they've somehow introduced a lightness to my heart that I long to embrace. It may all be a trick or some cruel way to lull me into a state of comfort. Nevertheless, my wolf seems to trust them, which makes me want to trust them, too.

Caius runs his fingers through my fur, telling me how soft and pretty I am. It's the same thing he said yesterday.

And just like yesterday, he squats before me and asks if I'm hungry.

I pant in response—my equivalent of a "yes" that he seems to translate with ease.

He winks one silver eye at me and stands again. "Follow me."

I don't really have a choice since his direction is the only way to go. But I would probably follow him regardless. He possesses an air of happiness about him that I find alluring.

Caius is definitely the playful one of the trio. Volt is the protector, his lethal aura one that makes my wolf want to roll over on her back in immediate submission. And Tieran is the leader.

Which is why I can't shake this sensation of unease against my fur. Tieran's displeasure can't be good. The fact that he didn't even acknowledge me says I'm the cause of that displeasure, or something about me has him on edge.

Maybe I'll take the guest room tonight.

Assuming they let me continue staying here.

It's not escaped my notice that this experience is a gift, not a natural occurrence.

Volt meets us in the kitchen, a bowl in his hand. "Morning, sweetling," he coos, setting the bowl on the ground. "Better eat. Tieran has plans for you today."

My stomach flips over at his words. *Plans? What kind of plans?*

I'm not sure I want to spend time with him in his current mood. I can still feel his dominance wrapping around my neck like a noose.

He's either been holding it back, to help make me feel at ease, or it's particularly strong today.

Given the last two days of treatment, I suspect it's the former. And for whatever reason, he's done hiding his Alpha persona from me today.

Is he going to make me leave? It's something I should want —freedom. But these Alphas haven't given me cause to want to run. If anything, they've given me very good reasons to stay.

I've never been one to rely on others for my survival. My mother trained me well for a reason. However, this island is nothing like the home I grew up in. I've not been given a proper tour of the lands, but I can sense the dangers lurking here.

The dangerous wolves.

Their Alpha spirits.

The violent undertones of their need to survive.

I shiver, and Caius strokes his fingers through my mane again. "You're safe, Clove," he whispers. "We won't let anyone hurt you."

Words I long to believe, but how can I trust three men I've just met? *Because they've literally proved through actions that they won't hurt you,* some part of me says. Maybe the words are driven by my wolf. Or perhaps it's my intelligent side trying to slap some sense into me.

I focus on the bowl and the fresh fruit mingled with oats. It's not something I would have anticipated eating on Carnage Island, but so far, nothing about this place is what I could ever have anticipated.

In addition to me actually being here.

As a Carnage Wolf.

I lap up the meal while Caius and Volt sit on the floor with me. They've not eaten at the table for any of our meals, and I find the gesture heartwarming.

Another direct conflict to everything I thought I knew about Carnage Wolves.

Tieran joins us several minutes later, his hair still damp from his shower and a pair of jeans slung low on his hips.

He doesn't look at me, instead focusing on breakfast and taking a chair at the table rather than sitting on the ground.

I consider trying to slip from the kitchen unnoticed, but the way he's seated puts me in the center of his vision.

"Do you want to try shifting again, Clove?" Volt asks as he takes my empty bowl and places it in the sink.

I almost grumble.

I've been trying to shift since being carted off to Wolfe Island. It's not like I want to be in this form. I would love to be able to walk on two legs and use my voice.

But even with me being able to control my movements now, I can't seem to shift at all. I've tried searching for the pain I felt when Canton made me change during the ceremony. I've tried telling my wolf to heel. I've tried fantasizing about being human again. I've tried calling on my mortal half. I've done everything Tieran and Volt suggested, and nothing.

"She can't," Tieran replies, that hint of anger touching his tone. "That fucking Alpha has a hold on her spirit. I'm going to have to break it."

I shiver at the dark promise in those words.

Caius and Volt both glance at each other and then at Tieran. "Where?" Volt asks.

"I'm still debating," Tieran mutters. "Her cries are going to call the wolves to her regardless of where I do it. But we need a place where we can properly protect her."

My cries? I repeat. *He expects me to cry?*

Does he think I'm weak because I can't shift? Because Canton has a hold on my spirit?

How is that even my fault?

My pack never taught me how to fight, and the whole ceremony is about letting his wolf bond with mine. How was I supposed to know this would happen?

I went through with the ceremony because I was the strongest eligible female of my pack. It hurt like hell, but I didn't scream, did I?

I honestly can't remember much beyond the pain.

And the agony of losing my mother right after.

My heart aches just thinking about it.

Her screams will haunt me for the rest of my days.

"She's strong," Volt says, interrupting my thoughts. "She'll take it."

"I'm more concerned about how she'll react afterward and what she might do to any of the wolves that come to investigate." Tieran sets down his fork, his tone flat.

Caius stands to join Volt at the sink, his gaze on Tieran. "It's their own hide if they come up uninvited, T. Let them pay the price for disobeying your directive."

"I mean, watching her attack them would be fun," Volt puts in. "A total fucking turn-on, actually."

"I'm not worried about her attacking or killing anyone," Tieran bites back. "Her mother was easy prey. I'm more concerned about the others scaring her or doing something worse."

My mother… I trail off, blinking at him. *My mother was easy prey?*

Did he really just say that?

Their conversation continues, but I can't hear it over the thumping in my ears.

What does he know about my mother?

Why does he consider her easy prey?

Does he know who raped her? Who… who *sired* me?

Or is this about how she died?

A palm lands on my scruff, the fingers digging in as Tieran suddenly squats before me. "Do not growl at us, little one. You will not like the consequences."

I blink. *Growl?* When did I growl?

"Better," he says, his gaze hard. "I don't have a choice. Either I force your change, or you remain a wolf. And the latter isn't acceptable."

He thinks I'm growling because he wants to help me back into my human state?

I snort.

Which causes his eyes to narrow, the irises suddenly resembling ice.

Oh, moon, that is not the response he wanted to hear… But it wasn't in response to his statement. Well, it was, but not for the reasons he probably thinks.

If I were human, I would explain.

But as a wolf, all I can do is grumble—which I do—and that just worsens the situation entirely.

"All right." He releases me and stands abruptly. "I guess we're doing this here."

"Uh, T, maybe—"

"No, Caius. I'm done with the disobedient act. I want a person to scold, not a wolf."

What the hell? I want to snap. *I'm not being disobedient!*

Which, of course, comes out as another grumble.

And earns me an icy glower from the Alpha.

Okay, yeah, and I'm a dead wolf again. Awesome.

CLOVE

Tieran growls, the menacing sound wrapping around me in a thunderous vibration that pierces my heart and shoots lava through my veins.

It *burns*.

I immediately cower, trying to hide from the venom in his aura. It flows around me, ensnaring me in his Alpha web and demanding my full focus.

Moon…

I was right about him dampening his Alpha energy these last few days. Because this feels like a whiplash to my senses, his power an avalanche threatening to suffocate my entire being.

He growls again, this one even more intimidating than the last.

I can feel my wolf whimpering and my soul screaming for mercy.

But he merely squats again, blocking any escape attempt I may make.

This is the monster I've been warned about. The savage beast who slaughtered his mate.

He probably did this to her before ripping her apart

with his teeth.

I'm going to die here.

My animal growls, refusing to go down without a fight.

Which only makes the Alpha snarl, demanding obedience.

I can't breathe.

It's all too much.

My body is breaking beneath the power of his wrath, and he isn't even touching me.

My fur is melting, morphing, leaving me behind as a shell of nothing but skin and shattering bones.

He's only growled three times. Maybe four.

But my body is responding to his demand, shifting back into human form in the most excruciating display of submission.

I hate him.

I despise his growl.

I loathe his Alpha powers.

I want to kill them all. I want to shred them for making me feel so small and alone and helpless.

This is the worst punishment of all, the degradation of my spirit and taking all the control away from my mind. Forcing me to morph into a state without my permission.

Part of me knows it's what I need.

Part of me understands that he has to do this to break Canton's hold.

But that part of me is no match for the living wrath building inside me. The need to lash out. To make him kneel. To make him *bleed*.

I lunge at him, my hands resembling fingers and nails instead of paws and claws. But it doesn't matter.

I slam my palm against his face, my other going to his chest to scratch jagged grooves down that flawless skin.

He doesn't fight me.

He doesn't even retaliate.

He lets me slap him again.

Lets me drag my nails down his pec a second time.

And doesn't budge when I try to shove him.

His eyes are no longer icy. They're full of heat, the blue orbs resembling a deep ocean of need that makes my knees weak.

I suddenly want to attack him for a whole new reason.

He's almost a foot taller than me and solid muscle. All pure Alpha male. It calls to a foreign part of me that has only awakened in the last few days. A part of me that inherently trusts this male and considers him hers.

I don't understand it.

Fated mates don't exist for my kind. It's why we have arranged matings.

Yet I feel an undeniable pull toward him. One I'm helpless to ignore.

He growls, this time the sound more sensual than aggressive. It causes my stomach to clench, my thighs slickening with *need*.

This is so much more intense than the arousal I felt in the field with Canton.

This is visceral. All-consuming. *Carnal*.

His palm wraps around the back of my neck, pulling me to him. There are no words. Just savage heat.

He's bleeding because of me.

And I like it.

I want to lick the marks, to stake my claim.

So I do.

It's natural. It's necessary. It's *glorious*.

He growls again as I lap at the wound on his pec, his grip tightening around my nape. I have no idea what I'm doing or why I'm doing it, but I'm following the urges of my inner animal, allowing us to function as one.

She wants him.

Therefore, I want him.

No, it's more than that. I *need* him. There's an ache inside me that only he can soothe. I feel it now, throbbing between my legs and demanding I take this Alpha and make him mine.

He's a perfect specimen. The *right* kind of male. The one I should have met all along.

My spirit guides me in this discovery, forcing me not to think about anything other than this beautiful male and the power emanating around him.

Except we're not alone.

I can feel their eyes on us, their hunger a palpable wave that brands my skin and makes me that much hotter.

They're not marked.

They're not bleeding.

I want to claw at them, too. Sink my nails into their flesh and tear, then drink from their wounds.

What is wrong with me? I marvel, my mind clouding with foreign urges and intense feelings.

I feel reborn. Like a brand-new shifter. Like I'm finally the wolf I was always meant to be.

It's freeing and suffocating at the same time.

Lively and deafening.

Overwhelming and right.

A finger trails down my spine, the touch molten against my skin. Lips caress my shoulder, Caius's warm breath against my ear as he says, "You're stunning, Clove."

The praise goes right to my heart, causing it to skip another beat.

I can barely breathe.

And yet, when I inhale, it's a cloud of musk and male. Peppermint. Pine trees. And coppery ash.

My thighs clench. Those scents are undoing me,

making me want to kneel for reasons I can only begin to understand.

This is what my claiming should have felt like.

The day I embraced my mate.

Not all the pain and death.

But this beautiful heat filled with renewed life and meaning.

I lean forward to lick Tieran's chest again. He rumbles in response, the sound part growl, part purr. I sigh, utterly captivated by that vibration. I want to melt into him. Do whatever he needs so long as he quells this storm brewing inside me.

His hand remains on my nape, holding me close to him.

He's aroused.

I feel the brand of his heat against my lower belly through his jeans. It takes restraint not to remove them. Somehow, I know that's the wrong thing to do.

He's in charge now.

Hell, he's always been in charge.

And while part of me wants to defy that, to *challenge* him, another part of me longs to bathe in that superiority and allow him to be my guide.

It's a conundrum I don't understand.

A mixture of fates that don't blend well with each other.

How can I want to submit and challenge him in the same thought?

Volt's mouth meets my opposite shoulder, his identity easily known because of his scent. He's the source of copper and ash.

Death, I think. *He reminds me of death.*

But addictive and right.

Caius is the spicy one, the refreshing mint I crave to taste on my tongue.

And Tieran is the source of masculinity and grace, the one filling my lungs with a pine-like scent. He's the master of the forest. The pack Alpha. The leader who demands my submission yet craves my fire.

It's all incredibly intoxicating, this knowledge and power and intimate union.

I can't remember why I was angry before.

I can't even remember the events of yesterday.

All I want is to indulge in these males and bathe in their strength.

My insides clench painfully now, that storm reaching a violent point in my lower abdomen and raining passion down my thighs.

Tieran growls.

Caius hisses.

And Volt hums in approval. "Slick," he says.

"She's going into heat," Tieran replies, his voice gruff, his pupils blown wide.

"How much time do we have?" Caius asks.

"Not long," Tieran tells him. "We need to fortify the den. They're already on their way here. I can feel them pounding up the hill."

He releases my neck, drawing a whimper from my throat at the loss of contact. I feel as though we've been standing here for hours, glued together by this warmth pooling inside me.

But it's really only been minutes.

Maybe even seconds.

It's all so surreal and unfocused.

A pulsating spasm in my lower abdomen causes my knees to buckle. Tieran catches me instantly, his hands branding my bare hips.

I mewl, leaning into him, needing more.

"Hold her," Caius says. "We'll handle the perimeter."

Tieran growls, the sound making me whimper as another pang vibrates through my belly. It hurts. I *need*. But I don't understand what this is or why it's happening.

On some level, I... I sort of do.

He said I'm going into heat.

I've witnessed that among females in my pack, but I don't recall it being painful or all-consuming like this.

It's something that only happens to mated wolves.

Usually, their males take care of them throughout the cycle by keeping them pleasured and fed. It lasts only a few days.

And it typically ends in pregnancy.

That's why heat cycles are so spare and rare for my kind, happening every few years. I've never experienced mine. I shouldn't be falling into the cycle now.

I'm not properly mated.

But ohhh, it's... it's *intense*.

I swallow, my vision blinking in and out as I sway.

Tieran's palms are still on my hips, his chest a blanket of warmth before me.

I lean into him, my tongue tasting his skin and trailing down to the grooves I left in his chest. He'll heal soon. No, he's healing already. He's no longer bleeding, and something about that upsets my wolf.

I want to claw at him again, to re-mark him, to *claim* him.

"Tieran," I groan, his name a rasp of sound in my mouth.

"Shh," he hushes. "I've got you, little one."

There's so much I need to say. So much I want to do. But I can't seem to remember any of it now. My body is begging me to seek relief from this Alpha, to quiet the stirring of sensations deep inside.

I moan.

He hushes me again.

And howls pierce the air outside.

Angry howls that excite my inner animal.

A chase, she's thinking. *We're about to go on a chase.*

I'm not sure I like that idea. I don't quite understand where the inclination and knowledge are coming from either.

But she's anticipating it, her adrenaline flooding my veins and allowing me to stand once more.

"Don't even think about it," Tieran tells me. "You run; I'll chase. And I won't be happy when I catch you."

That sounds like a challenge.

A challenge I very much want to indulge in.

That foreign part of me wants him to earn the right to touch me, to *mate* me.

I suddenly feel possessed by the need to run, to make him prove his worth. To *challenge* him.

No. Not just him. *Them.*

A crash comes from the living room, the window shattering and eliciting a feral growl from Tieran. I inhale sharply, his rumble sending a tremor through my limbs.

But there's something more.

A scent lingering in the air.

Like rain on a murky night, I think, momentarily distracted by the familiar aroma. *I've smelled that on a wolf before.*

When?

Where?

Oh, but I hurt…

I tremble, another quake rocketing through my veins, derailing my focus once more.

Caius shouts something I don't quite catch, the

incoming snarls reverberating all around me and eliciting shivers from deep within.

Run, my wolf demands as Tieran releases me to handle one of the shifters who has just entered the kitchen. *Run!*

I've always been able to tame her, to keep her down.

But not anymore.

Not since she took over during our initial shift.

I'm a slave to her needs now, and I do exactly what she says.

I sprint for the broken window, leap over the edge, and bolt full speed into the forest. My human legs are far more powerful and faster than my wolf's legs because I've spent two decades learning how to move on two feet instead of four paws.

This is why I won my trials.

I'm fast.

I'm strong.

And I know when to pick my battles.

I choose this battle now.

I choose today to fight.

TIERAN

"**F**^{*uck!*}"

That little brat is going to hurt herself. Or worse.

I growl as I snap Alpha Kin's neck. He'll heal. It'll take a day, but he'll survive and that's what matters.

The Alphas are being driven by rutting lust.

On a deep level, I understand that.

It doesn't make me any less pissed.

It would be so damn easy to take the silver blade from my pocket and drive it through Alpha Kin's heart. *That* would kill him, an act that a dark part of me feels he deserves. But I ignore the darkness and join Caius in the living room.

Alpha Dirk is unconscious with a shard of glass embedded in his chest.

Volt is standing just outside the doorway handling two more lust-drunk Alphas.

Caius jumps through the window with me on his tail. The wind tells me what direction Clove went in.

"Go!" Caius demands. "We'll be right behind you."

I don't stay to debate the options or strategize our best

plan. There isn't time. Instead, I take off after the fleeing Omega.

She's just inspired chaos on the island.

Her pheromones—which are absolutely fucking real—are going to drive all the Alphas mad. Maybe even the Betas.

She's an unclaimed Omega going into heat.

And she's *running*.

This is a goddamn nightmare.

If someone wanted to derail our entire operation on the island, *this* is the way to do it.

A possibility I will analyze after I catch her.

I leap over a fallen log, landing on my bare feet in the grass. Then I pause to inhale, searching for the little Omega with my nose.

Snarls sound to my right as two wolves come barreling toward me.

Volt leaps between us, still in human form, and takes them down with a set of throwing blades.

"Try not to kill them!" I shout at him. Those knives are silver. I can feel the heat of them from here. Which means the wolves won't be able to heal unless the blades are removed.

He responds with a grunt, yanking out his knives as he passes the two knocked-out Alphas. Then he takes off toward the woods to tackle a third wolf with his bare hands.

He's going to be either furious or elated when this is done. The psychotic bastard loves the taste of blood. But the cause of all this insanity is troublesome.

And still running, I think, catching her scent on the wind.

I take off toward her, my heart pounding in my chest.

If another wolf finds her first…

I cut off that line of thought.

That is not going to happen.

I bound over the earth, my bare feet used to the rough terrain.

She's naked, alone, and has no idea where she's going.

But her scent seems to be… diminishing.

I frown, pausing again to sniff the air. *Where are you, little one?* I wonder, trying to seek her out above the other fragrances of the island.

It's early winter, and we've already experienced our first snow, but it recently melted, thickening the streams that lead to the ocean below.

They're made of fresh water until they meet the bottom, which doesn't carry a strong scent but can wash away the natural perfume of others.

Humming, I bend to touch a nearby stream, my focus on the mud beneath the surface, searching for footprints.

Clove is small because of her Omega heritage, making her light on her feet.

But she's clever.

Because she's running down the stream in an attempt to mask her scent.

It almost works.

Except I've spent the last two days inhaling that sweet perfume, and while the water may dilute it, it's still there, lingering in the wind like a beckoning kiss.

I prowl behind her, my senses on high alert for potential intruders. This is my chase. Not theirs. I will destroy anyone and everything in my path. Then I'm going to teach the little brat a lesson in possession that she won't soon forget.

The only reason I'll even consider going easy on her is because I know she's new to this. She has no idea what she truly is. Fuck, I don't really know what she is.

A Carnage Wolf Omega, definitely.

But she's also a Nantahala Wolf.

What will that do to her genetics? Will she be able to take an Alpha's knot the way an Omega should? Or will her heat cycle be pure agony with no benefit of release?

I'm starting to understand why she killed her mother. I'm furious on Clove's behalf. Her heritage should never have been kept from her.

Although, I strongly suspect her mother did it to protect her.

Which makes the entire situation utterly fucked up.

And her running isn't helping.

However, my wolf is rather pleased inside by the chase. He likes that this female is challenging him. It's making him hungry to capture her, mount her, *claim* her.

Fuck.

I move faster, my animal riding me hard.

My ability to maintain control is why I'm the Carnage Island Alpha. It's what makes me suitable to lead. Because I'm not giving in to the rutting lust—a consequence of an unclaimed Omega going into heat. All available Alphas will react to her need to mate, her yearning for the *knot.*

I can feel their desire on the wind, their animalistic aggression mounting with each passing second.

Volt and Caius are the only two I trust on this island not to lose themselves to the rutting madness. They're strong wolves, which is why we're a triad clan. It's not about intimacy. It's about power. We feed off each other and provide necessary balance.

Like now.

I can sense their power overshadowing the others, their infallible control allowing them to be my weapons while I hunt our prey.

Little wolf, little wolf, I echo, pursuing her down the

stream. We're almost to the ocean, a fact that has more than impressed my inner animal.

She's fast.

Smart.

Worthy.

How this little Omega ended up here is the only thing that may keep me back from outright claiming her the moment I find her.

Because I don't know how she'll actually react.

She's not a pureblood.

What will that do to our potential mating bond?

I reach the water's edge, my gaze narrowing.

"Playing hide-and-seek won't lessen your punishment, little one," I murmur, aware that she's close.

My beast is growling in excitement, loving that she not only gave us chase but also hid. He wants to sniff her out and drag her beneath him, then bite her throat. Not hard. Just enough to claim for the world to see.

But three Alphas join us in wolf form, none of them Caius or Volt. I can sense them up on the hill, battling the others.

The daring little Omega has sent the entire island into a lust-driven battle.

There will be hell to pay once this is resolved, and not just because I'll have to dole out punishment to my men, but because they're going to be furious that I kept her from them.

Our pack is built on trust.

I defied that trust when I didn't allow her to meet the men. It was in her best interest, not theirs. It's almost fortunate that she ran, because I can say they were all given an equal opportunity to claim her.

Assuming I survive this battle.

Because two more wolves have entered the beach, their focus on me as the prime predator on this island.

I'm their main competition when it comes to claiming this Omega.

Therefore, they want to rip me to shreds.

"You are all going to regret this when your senses come back," I say conversationally as I unfasten my pants.

I could beat them in human form.

But I'll be faster in wolf form.

Of course, shifting is going to give my animal the upper hand in this battle of wills between us. Clove may suffer the consequences.

However, it's better than letting these five wolves find her and take her. They won't give her a chance to choose.

And I don't have to make her choose.

Her wolf picked me when she selected my bed.

The rest has just been a testament of patience and me not wanting to hurt her by forcing her transition.

Had I known she would go into heat, I may have chosen a different place to coax her back into human form.

Or I may have done it exactly like this.

Because this is how I'll win her.

She's nearby.

She's watching.

I can feel her eyes on me, her wolf waiting to see her chosen mate in action.

She wanted to challenge me for a reason.

Not only do I accept that challenge, but I intend to win it, too.

"You can't say I didn't warn you," I say, the words not just for the five males circling me but also for the errant little Omega who ran when I told her not to. "Let's play."

CLOVE

I'm panting.

Wet.

Freezing.

And utterly captivated by Tieran casually removing his jeans.

He kicks them off from his ankles, his body already morphing into a giant white wolf. It takes him milliseconds, his shift akin to taking a breath.

The five wolves growl in response, lunging at him as one.

I hold my breath, my heart beating chaotically in my ribs.

But Tieran's snarl comes out above the rest, his body moving with a power that makes my knees weak.

He knows I'm here. Because those words were for me, not the other wolves.

You can't say I didn't warn you.

He did.

He told me not to run.

That he would not be happy when he caught me.

And for some sick and twisted reason, that sends a shiver of excitement down my spine.

I tried to throw him off my path by moving through the stream to distort my scent. I even rolled in some mud. But he found me far faster than I could ever have anticipated.

A fact that pleases my wolf to no end. She's practically doing flips inside me, telling me to fall from this tree and lie prone on the ground for him to take us. She's not worried about him at all, even with the furious sounds coming from the fight below.

Two of the wolves are already unconscious, their throats ripped out from Tieran's teeth.

It's a gory sight, one that should make me queasy.

Yet my legs clench with unhindered *need*.

I'm on fire despite my frozen skin. Every part of me burns for him.

No, not just him.

Them.

Because I can hear Volt and Caius, too, their howls piercing my senses and calling to my inner wolf. She *knows* them. I don't understand how, and I'm beyond questioning why.

My instincts are leading me now, just as they have from the moment I turned.

I'm embracing my animal and allowing her needs to become my own.

No more suppression. No more fighting the urge to shift or to run or to indulge in my more savage inclinations.

My pack took all this from me.

And I'm taking it all back now.

I cling to the branch as Tieran roars. One of the wolves has a hold of his scruff, his black eyes mad with a hint of unhinged savagery.

My heart stutters.

It's another Alpha.

No, they're *all* Alphas.

And they're fighting to claim me.

It's an inherent understanding of the process that I don't fully comprehend. My wolf is the one who grasps the scene more than I do. She's the one who wanted to test Tieran, Volt, and Caius. She's the one hoping they'll *win*.

Seeing the mad wolf on Tieran's back has me—the woman—hoping Tieran wins, too.

Because I don't want to be anywhere near that crazed animal.

Tieran flips him off and goes right for his neck, ripping it out in a show of violence that seems appropriate here on *Carnage Island*.

He doesn't celebrate the victory or lord over his kill.

Instead, he focuses on the remaining two Alphas, his growl underlined in furious power that has the other males taking a step back.

Tieran howls then, the sound making me nearly lose my grip on the branch.

I feel compelled to kneel. To submit. To do whatever he desires so long as I gain his favor.

It *hurts* to hold on.

But if I fall…

No. Fight it, I command myself. *Don't. Let. Go.*

My fingers strain to hold on, my limbs shaking with the effort as he unleashes another howl, this one even more powerful than before.

An Alpha taking hold of his pack.

An Alpha telling the others that enough is enough.

An Alpha reminding his wolves who is in charge here.

The fact that I want to bend says so much about my shifting allegiances. It says I consider myself a member of his world. And not just that, but a part of me is already his to command.

I whimper, my grip slipping.

A third howl bites into the air, and I can no longer hold myself steady. My fingers refuse to listen to reason, my hands releasing the branch and causing me to tip off my perch.

From over twenty feet up in the air.

Moons.

Wind rushes by my ears, my body tumbling from the sky to the earth below.

Only to be caught in a pair of waiting arms.

I yelp, the strong bands bruising my skin from the force of my fall. The air whooshes from my lungs, a moan echoing deep inside me that can't be heard because of the lack of oxygen.

A soft purr rumbles in my ear, my head immediately cradled against a muscular chest. "You're like a sweet little angel falling from the sky," a familiar voice murmurs.

Volt.

"Too bad I have to give you to the devil," he continues, gently setting me on the ground.

I inhale sharply, my lungs burning from the loss of air.

It's a mistake.

I'm immediately inundated with a mixture of alluring scents.

Pine trees.

Ash and copper.

Peppermint and spice.

All underlined by a mixture of feral masculine deliciousness.

A low moan escapes my throat, my insides clenching with a foreign need that feels so much more intense than before. It… it *hurts*.

I curl into a ball, only for a snout to press into my neck, the pressure freezing me in my prone form.

The huge wolf growls, causing my animal to perk up with immediate interest. *Tieran.* I recognize his presence, his Alpha energy the source of my fall.

I go limp beneath his touch, aware that he's very much the superior predator on this island.

It seems everyone else has conceded as well, his howl bringing all the others to their proverbial knees.

Or maybe he slaughtered them all.

I'm really not sure, and I'm too focused on his snout to ask.

He inhales deeply, the sound reverberating against my neck as he draws his snout along my throat. I swallow, making him growl again.

I can feel the man beneath the fur, controlling the desire radiating from his beast.

His restraint is addictive. It makes my wolf want to push him. I'm not sure why or what she's hoping to accomplish, so I ignore the urge and remain still as he draws his nose down to my breasts.

My nipples bead for him, begging for his mouth, his teeth, his *hands*.

But all he does is take in my scent, his low grumble telling me he doesn't appreciate the mud marring my skin.

He nudges me to my back, his lethal mouth trailing down to the apex between my thighs.

My legs part for him, my skin damp from the water and mud and the desire that seems to be pouring out of me. I've heard about the mating process, how it can make females react in wanton and animalistic ways. But no one warned me about this agonizing ache or the abundance of *fluids*.

A groan slips from my lips as my insides pulse, slickening me even more at my heated center.

What is happening to me? I wonder.

Tieran rumbles, making my muscles tense.

Then his tongue slides between my folds.

Not as a wolf, but as a *man*.

He shifted without me even noticing, too lost to the sensations his presence evoked from me. Too lost to whatever the hell this is. Too lost to—

Ohhhh…

His tongue is divinity incarnate.

I've completely lost my mind.

He's licking me, just a few feet away from the waves. He's licking me *there*. He's tasting me. He's taking me. He's—

His teeth skim my clit, eliciting a scream from my throat.

"Hmm," he hums, crawling up and over my body. "Do you need something, little one?" His blue eyes are blazing with liquid fire, his aura blistering with a convoluted mixture of fury and arousal. I can feel it lapping at my skin, threatening to burn me from the inside out. "I told you not to run," he whispers, his lips less than an inch away from mine.

My wolf tells me to arch into him, to feel the power of his body against mine.

I do.

Because I'm helpless to her instincts.

Helpless to whatever is happening to me.

"I think you need another bath. Maybe I'll make you take one alone, draw out this agony until you're ready to really beg." Such dark words, ones that make my wolf whine in protest.

I wrap my legs around his waist, the bold move purely instinctual, and grind myself against him.

Fuck, I've never felt this hot before. Like I'm seconds away from exploding. Except I can't find the match to finish lighting my fuse. "*Tieran*," I groan, grabbing his shoulders and digging my nails into his flesh.

He narrows his eyes. "Topping from the bottom, I see." His palm finds my throat, giving it a brutal squeeze. "That's not how I work, little one. I'm Alpha. I top. You're an Omega. You submit."

I start to shake my head, his words making no sense. *Not an Omega*, I want to say, but his grip is too tight on my throat to allow words.

"You ran," he continues. "You ran and made me chase you. I fought for you, Clove. I'm still wearing their blood, too. It's on my tongue. Just like your sweet cunt." His mouth seals over mine, making me taste his words, the decadent flavor of copper and musk sliding easily down my throat.

I groan in response, eager for more.

He chuckles as I suck on his tongue, my beast taking charge of my human form. She's starving and he's her lifeline.

I'm merely an observer now, aching inside as my body begs for a release I don't understand.

His arousal is hard between my legs, and *so hot*. I mewl, pressing into him again, then suck his tongue even deeper into my mouth.

I want everything. I want him. I want… to feel *full*.

"Please," I whisper. "Please, Tieran." I don't even know what I'm asking for. But on some base level, I do. I want him inside me. To fill me. To *please* me.

I dig my nails even more into his skin, drawing blood as I shift my body below, grinding against his massive length.

Oh, moon.

I saw it when he shifted the other day.

I saw it again when he shifted today.

And now… now I'm feeling it against my much smaller body.

It's enough to make me still, to realize how terrible an idea this is.

My wolf may want that monster inside me, but it is *never* going to fit.

And what is that bulge near the base?

I boldly reach between us to touch him, my mind splintering between reason and need. "Why…?" I manage to ask, my fingers grazing the bulbous mass near his groin. It's not his balls. It's at the top of his shaft. And it's *pulsating.*

"Why what?" He reaches between us to wrap my palm around his thick cock, allowing me to *really* feel that length.

And yeah, that's not going inside me.

He's way too big.

A thought that makes me whimper because my wolf is demanding I try.

"Are you asking why I won't fuck you yet, Clove?" His eyes glimmer with cruelty as he stares down at me. "Because I'm not sure I want to claim you. Maybe I should issue my own challenge, hmm?"

My wolf snarls in my head, furious with his words.

And to my horror, some of it comes out through my mouth.

Which makes him chuckle and draw his nose across my cheek as his lips meet my ear. "Don't worry, darling. My wolf is just as enamored with you as you are with him."

My animal immediately calms.

But I don't.

"I don't understand," I finally manage to breathe, my

grip tightening near his base again. "Help me understand." It's a plea that brings tears to my eyes. Because all of this is foreign. I'm trying to give in to my animal, to do what she's demanding I do.

However, feeling his erection in my palm has oddly grounded me in reality.

He's so much larger than Canton.

It should be impossible.

It *is* impossible.

He's not going to fit.

And something about that makes me want to cry.

Or maybe it's the fear of knowing he's going to force it that causes my eyes to water.

I feel so weak. So lost. So... so *hot*.

I groan inside and out. *I'm losing my mind.*

"You're going into estrus," Tieran says, his palm suddenly on my cheek, his thumb wiping away the tear from my skin. "It's the heat cycle for Omegas, likely caused by you finally meeting your wolf and allowing your Carnage traits to come out to play."

I shake my head. "Not an Omega." It comes out as a fragment, my brain incapable of full thought. I'm torn between understanding and demanding he fuck me.

It's a conundrum that has me whimpering all over again.

And I hate it.

I *hate* feeling weak.

"I'm not this wolf," I say out loud. "I'm not. I'm strong. I'm... I'm..." A spasm in my lower belly makes me scream, the agony ripping through my veins and sending me spiraling back into a fit of lust and need.

The world starts to move around me.

My thighs feel wet and cold.

My heart thuds loudly in my chest, echoing in my ears.

Another scream leaves my mouth, that pain inside splintering into pulses of torturous vibrations.

I'm dying, I think. *This is death.*

Because it's killing me.

Those vibrations make it impossible to breathe.

I can't even scream or beg for help.

It's a lost cause.

Because all I am now is pain.

Pain. Pain. Pain.

Until nothingness takes hold.

And then… I start to float.

I breathe.

I settle.

I drown.

Water. Light. Water. Light.

Where am I?

Who am I?

What is this new place?

I blink, the bright sun dim above my head.

Did they throw me into the ocean? My heart cracks at the thought. *Am I back where I started?*

Or was it all a dream? Did I actually drown? Were the Alphas a product of my own imagination?

Water splashes in my mouth, and I gasp awake.

Surrounded by marble.

In a tub filled with masculine scents.

CLOVE

"Shh," someone hushes, reminding me of my dream on the beach. "You're all right."

Those are the words Volt said, too. Exactly the same. But his voice is hoarse now, like he's straining himself for some reason.

"Open," another voice says, something touching my lips.

I don't think.

I obey.

And something salty touches my tongue, the taste of it making me groan. I swallow on instinct alone, my mouth immediately seeking more.

But the flavor is gone.

Instead, I open my eyes to find a pair of beautiful blue eyes staring down at me. "Better?" Tieran asks, his voice low.

"More," I say instead.

He smiles, his finger drawing a line across my lower lip and leaving more of that delectable substance behind. "You're going into heat, Clove," he says as someone draws fingers through my hair.

It's then that I realize I'm floating in water. Not in the ocean, but in a massive bathtub. And there's a man beneath me. Naked. His arousal is a brand against my rump as he holds me steady in the water.

Volt, I think, his heat strangely familiar now. His coppery scent is all around me, too.

I blink up at Tieran, inhaling his woodsy cologne and moaning as it stirs that pulsating agony in my stomach once more.

"You need a knot," he says, his finger disappearing. "*That* is what you were feeling earlier, little one. My knot."

I vaguely recall stroking his cock and caressing that throbbing bulb near the base.

His finger is at my mouth again, more of that salty substance meeting my tongue. I lick him greedily, that flavor an addiction I don't understand.

"That's precum," he tells me, reading the question from my eyes. "From my cock."

I want to be embarrassed. I want to shy away and hide. But that's not what I do at all. Instead, I just say, "More," again. It's like I need his essence to survive. I need his brand of whatever this is to *breathe.*

Volt hushes me again, his fingers combing through my hair, his lips caressing my neck.

Then Tieran feeds me more of his addictive flavor, stirring a wanton noise from my chest.

"You're showing all the signs of a Carnage Wolf Omega entering the initial stages of estrus," he says softly. "You need an Alpha to see you through it. That's why your animal tested us. She wanted to ensure we're worthy of this gift."

Gift? I repeat to myself, my lips too occupied by his finger to speak.

"We're going to help you through this. We're going to

protect you. And we're going to claim you." He says this all matter-of-factly. "You're ours now, Clove."

Volt kisses my shoulder. "Welcome to Carnage Wolf life, sweetling."

"And welcome to our underground den," Caius says as he enters the room with a towel. "First up on our tour is the bedroom, where we intend to intimately introduce you to the silk sheets." He holds out the towel.

Tieran slips more of that delicious substance into my mouth, then lifts me from the tub and allows Caius to swathe me in a towel.

It's then that I realize we're all naked.

And wet.

The bath was a group activity, something that causes me to glance back at the massive tub. It's definitely built for a party of five or six and not the shower Tieran used to bathe my wolf.

Caius must have exited while I was temporarily lost.

I still feel a bit hazy, like I may be pulled back into that fog at any second.

"Try to breathe," Tieran says as he carries me into the bedroom. "I want you lucid for our first time."

I blink at him. "Lucid?"

Is he expecting me to black out during this?

What will he do to me then?

Rape me like those wolves raped my mother?

"Clove," he says, his tone demanding my complete focus, the Alpha in him staring down at me. "Calm down." He adds a little purr to the words, causing my body to relax.

I didn't even realize I tensed until my muscles begin to loosen.

Only then do I notice my nails in his shoulder.

"S-sorry," I whisper. "I don't want…" I trail off.

"You don't want what?"

"What happened to my mom," I finish, my eyes falling.

He lays me on the bed, his fingers finding my chin as he pulls my gaze back up to his. "What happened to your mom, little one?" Something about his voice soothes me, almost like a drug lulling me into sleep.

Only it's more than that.

It's heavier.

It's that rumble in his chest, I think dreamily. *I really like that sound.*

"Clove," he says, his tone softer now. "What happened to your mom?"

I stare at him, temporarily grounded once more. "They raped her." My voice is barely audible. "They… they killed her." My eyelids fall, then flare open again as I grab his shoulders. I haven't been able to speak all week. Someone has to know! "I didn't kill her, Tieran. I swear I didn't kill her."

Tears cloud my vision. It feels so good to finally say that.

But it's quickly followed by anger.

Anger that so many people refused to give me a chance to speak.

"They called me feral," I continue, my vision blurring in a sea of red. "They never gave me a chance to defend myself. Because I couldn't shift. I—"

A sharp spasm in my belly cuts off my thoughts, dragging me under that hazy torment once more.

Tieran's finger finds my tongue, but the taste of his essence isn't enough anymore. It's no longer the antidote I require. It's… it's…

"*Fire*," I breathe, writhing on the bed and curling into a ball of exquisite need.

Tieran's palms land on my hips, his body bigger than

mine and forcing me to unfurl on the mattress beneath him.

I start to cry, terrified of what's about to happen, yet craving it at the same time. I'm not sure if I'm sad or elated.

I can't decide.

I can't fucking think.

Pressure meets my core, the sensation of it shooting spikes through my veins.

I scream.

Then I cry out as the pressure increases, swirling, *licking*, drawing out pure bliss from between my thighs.

My fingers find Tieran's hair as I urge him on, riding his face in a furious display of need underlined in a hint of insanity.

This isn't me.

It's my wolf.

No, it's *us*.

Oh, fuck it.

I don't care. I just want to *feel*.

And ohhh, he's helping me feel a thousand things at once.

His fingers enter my slick channel, curling up to find a spot deep within that shoots me to the stars as his tongue continues to drive me mad.

I'm a mess of sensation and moans. I'm demanding more. I'm begging for him to fuck me. I'm losing my damn mind, and I just do not care.

The first wave of pleasure hits me unexpectedly, sending me soaring to the moon and back in the blink of an eye.

It's immediately followed by a second and a third thunderous climax, the pleasure all foreign and new to my spirit.

I've dabbled a little on my own.

But never with another.

It's forbidden to play with a male who isn't my mate.

Which I suppose makes Tieran my mate now. *Does that mean he'll slaughter me when he's done?* I wonder idly, a hint of fear caressing my mind. But it's there and gone in a second as he sends me tumbling into oblivion for a fourth time.

Or maybe it's all the same orgasm.

I'm losing track of time and space.

All I know is that I crave his heat. I need him to calm my beating heart. I need his essence. "Tieran," I breathe.

"I know," he says, crawling over me again. "I know, Clove."

Does he, though? Does he realize how badly I burn? How much this hurts?

His cock slides through my dampness, drawing another of those foreign sounds from my throat. I sound like I'm dying. Fuck, I feel like I'm dying.

Tieran's thick head nudges my entrance, drawing me back just long enough to inspire a deep-seated worry inside.

Only to scream in the next instant as he thrusts inside.

The bastard just split me wide open.

Speared me with his cock!

Is this how his previous mate died? Is this how he destroyed her?

Tears flood my vision, but his lips are suddenly on mine, his purr a rumble in his chest that has my wolf sighing inside.

It's so confusing.

It's... it's...

I start to pant.

Because he's... he's moving.

And now...

Oh, moons.

It's a slow shift of his hips that should shoot agony through my limbs, but all I feel is heat. Blissful, amazing *heat.*

I arch into him, taking him impossibly deeper.

It's not enough.

I want more.

I want his power.

I want the Alpha to fuck me.

But he's kissing me, his tongue a benediction against mine, his body a brand searing my very being. I bite his tongue, demanding his focus. "*More,*" I growl.

He chuckles. "You'll get what I give you, little one."

That is not good enough.

And I tell him that with my nails, dragging them down his back as I pump my hips up to meet his.

He growls a little, but his gaze holds a note of amusement. "Still trying to top me, hmm?" He catches my lip between his teeth and bites down hard, drawing blood. "I'm Alpha, baby." He drives his hips forward to punctuate his point. "I'm the one with the knot you need." He licks the blood from my lip, a soft rumble following from his mouth. "You'll submit."

I buck into him instead, my nails digging into his back.

If he wants me to submit, he'll need to work for it.

His lips curl, his eyes flashing with his wolf.

"Keep fighting me," he says, his palm wrapping around my throat as he thrusts harshly into my aching heat.

I wrap my legs around him, squeezing out my demand since I can no longer speak.

He growls in approval, his wolf so close to the surface that I can almost taste his feral nature.

This is dangerous.

He is dangerous.

But I've lost the ability to worry about what he may do to me.

All I can do is hold on and dare him to fuck me harder, which I do by writhing beneath him.

He smiles, but it's not a kind look on him. It's dark. It's predatory. It's sexy as hell.

This male is the epitome of Alphas everywhere.

He's the one who makes other Alphas bow.

Except maybe Caius and Volt, who are both standing nearby, watching, their gazes searing my flesh.

I can feel their need, sense the rising inferno building in the room between the four of us.

It's overwhelming and intoxicating, and I'm absolutely done fighting this. What's the point? I'll die if this Alpha doesn't come inside me. I need his essence like I need air.

"Please, Tieran," I choke out, his palm loosening enough to allow me to breathe, but the dominance is there, the threat lingers, and his savagery is just beneath the surface, threatening my very existence.

But there's a glimmer in his gaze that I trust.

A hint of knowledge and coherency that tells me he hasn't lost himself in this cloud of need. He's still very much in control. It's me who has lost myself to this passionate oblivion.

He's my anchor.

The one who will forever ground me.

The Alpha that my wolf craves to mark as her own.

His feral smile turns kinder now, the glint in his blue eyes morphing into one of pleasure. "There you are," he whispers. "My sweet little wolf. My intended."

I'm utterly lost to him now.

This Alpha.

This powerful being.

My wolf's chosen one.

She wants them all. The whole circle. And there's nothing I can do to stop her now.

I'm finally starting to understand what he's been telling me about going into heat. It's a dangerous mindfuck that threatens my very sanity.

It turns me into a being of lust.

An animal lost to her instincts.

And while a part of me knows this should truly concern me, I can't help giving in to it.

I kiss Tieran.

I sink my teeth into his lip to make him bleed.

And I swallow the aftermath of our mingled essences.

He growls.

I growl back.

And our frenzy turns into animalistic insanity.

He's brutal.

I'm feral.

Our beasts are mating through our skin, the wolves driving us toward a rapture that will probably kill me.

I don't care.

I chase after it.

And he chases me.

He drives me forward.

He destroys me.

He *owns* me.

His palm squeezes my throat, cutting off my airway, demanding I look at him and beg him with my eyes to release me.

But he doesn't.

Instead, he fucks me harder.

Then he roars as he reaches the precipice of his climax, and exquisite agony shoots into my core.

I scream, the unexpected penetration sharp and

sending me spiraling into a darkness I can't navigate without light.

It's terrifying.

It's amazing.

It's melting me from the inside out.

Air fills my lungs, Tieran forcing me to breathe. Sensation hits me in my belly and ripples out to my limbs, leaving me a writhing, crying mess beneath him.

But it's a good feeling.

Like I've been ripped apart and put back together again.

As though I've finally become one with my wolf.

He's still shuddering on top of me, his lips whispering reverently over mine.

It goes on for hours.

Maybe actually only minutes.

That pulsating knot inside me hot and filling me to completion over and over again.

Until it finally starts to withdraw, leaving me empty and aching for so much more.

I meet his gaze, see the very real concern in his depths and the care deep within.

He doesn't really want to hurt me. He wants to test me. To mate me. To see how much my wolf can take to make me a worthy mate.

I understand because my animal feels the same.

Which is exactly why I claw at his back again.

Why I lift my hips into his.

Why I growl and snarl at him to do it again.

He smiles, his lips brushing mine. "Challenge accepted, Clove." It's softly worded and underlined in hedonistic need.

He takes me harder this time, pushing me to my very limits before we both explode in hot waves of ecstasy.

His teeth skim my shoulder and neck, the Alpha deciding where he wants to claim me.

But he doesn't bite me yet. It's a taunt. A promise. There are more tests to come. A trial he wants my wolf to pass.

Which is when he finally releases me and rolls me toward Volt and Caius, who are waiting on the bed with hungry expressions.

I almost weep, my body exhausted and used.

But that tightening sensation inside me tells me I need them.

And I need them now.

I don't even think; I just crawl, taking Volt inside me as I straddle his waist. He groans, his palms finding my breasts as I move.

Caius sits up beside me, his fingers weaving into my hair as he tugs me into a kiss that is all heat and passion and sex.

He doesn't hold back, his tongue dominating mine in a manner similar to Tieran's, but different, too.

Volt tweaks my nipples, a low growl coming from him as he demands my full focus.

I leave Caius's mouth and continue to writhe, only to find myself on my back in the next breath with Volt stealing my vision.

He wants me to see him, to know him, to be here *with* him.

I can sense that desire radiating through his Alpha energy, and I accept it by pressing my lips to his.

He purrs, pleased.

And I growl, demanding more.

I hear Tieran chuckle, but it's quickly lost to the sounds coming from Volt's chest.

He's thicker than Tieran, stretching me wider, but he's

not as long. His strength is different, too. He's all muscular prowess and confident thrusts.

A different pace.

A harsher style.

And his eyes hold an edge to them that tells me he's going easy on me right now. That one day he's going to be rougher. Perhaps even sadistic.

My wolf mewls in response, approving of his inner beast and the dark urges shining in his ebony irises.

"That's it, sweetling," he whispers. "Take me. Embrace me. *Mate* me."

I bite down on his lip just like I did with Tieran, the impulse one driven from deep within.

And he groans in response, almost immediately biting me back, and our kiss becomes a passionate exchange of blood and sensuous lunacy.

I lose track of time.

All I feel is him.

All I know is him.

All I sense is this moment and the need pounding inside me, begging for his knot.

I'm going to die in this bed, and it's going to be the most blissful death in the existence of wolf kind.

I welcome it with my legs wrapped around his waist and my fingers knotting in his thick, dark hair. He kisses me as though I'm his reason for being.

And together we lose ourselves to the blissful madness of the moment, his knot finally exploding inside me and taking me into that dark land of intensity.

This time, I don't stir.

Because I can't open my eyes.

I just drown there in the passionate oblivion.

And allow my soul to fly. Fly. Fly.

CAIUS

"She's beautiful," I whisper, stroking my palm up and down her thigh, offering her comfort as she begins her descent into true madness.

Estrus is a multiday affair, and we're only in the first few hours of her heat cycle. She was beautifully aware for the beginning, something I know Tieran is pleased about. He wanted her to be aware enough to consent and participate in the union.

But he didn't bite her. Not truly, anyway.

I understand why.

He wants to make sure she accepts all three of us first.

I have no doubt that she will. She responded to my kiss with a passion I felt all the way to my soul.

She wants us all.

And once she wakes up, it'll be my turn to knot her.

Our sweet, beautiful Omega.

A diamond we never anticipated finding on this island.

The Alphas are going to be furious when they wake, but we won her fair and square. And now she's sequestered away in our underground den. Not the one she's been in the last few days. That home is for the others to be able to easily reach us when needed.

No, this home is deep underground with a tunnel only we know how to traverse.

We built it on the off chance we needed to hide from the Elders or an attacking pack.

It's large enough to house all the wolves on the island, but the three of us are the ones who know how to reach it. We've never shared the details with the others because it wasn't necessary. One of us is always on the island, even when the others are conducting business on the mainland.

Such as the other day—Volt and Tieran left while I remained to guard the pack.

It's always been this way since we first arrived seven years ago.

"She's a fighter," Tieran says as he finishes wiping away the fluids from her sweet pussy. She was a virgin, something that didn't surprise any of us. But she didn't notice, too lost in the beginning stages of her heat cycle to feel anything other than pleasure.

Well, and maybe a little pain.

But she embraced it.

She took Tieran's knot gloriously, her body built for our brand of fucking. Then she allowed Volt a brief taste.

I kiss her inner thigh, humming against her pulse. "I'm next, gorgeous," I tell her softly.

She doesn't stir.

I don't expect her to for at least another hour.

And when she does, it'll become a sex marathon.

Volt is already preparing supplies in the kitchen, ensuring we have enough water and nonperishable food to keep her healthy.

I already gathered all the linens I could find down here and created a pile beside the bed.

This is our joint bedroom, the one we only intended to use if this underground bunker became full of other wolves.

We have our own quarters that we maintain, which would go to the pack as needed. But I stripped those beds to add their sheets to the pile. Omegas like the scents of their mates. They prefer it to clean linens.

Some of our dirty clothes are in the pile as well.

The Omega will choose what she wants.

And we'll help in whatever way she needs.

"We need to find out what happened to her mother." Tieran speaks softly, but I sense his underlying fury. It rivals my own, instantly sobering my otherwise heated thoughts.

I lift my gaze to his. "Yes." I don't need to say anything else. I didn't even need to confirm.

"And we need to kill that pansy-ass Alpha who suppressed her ability to shift and defend herself," Volt adds from the doorway. He has on a pair of gray sweats, his chest bare.

There are little indents in his shoulders from where Clove clung to him, just like Tieran's. Except Tieran also has healing scratch marks down his back.

Our little Omega is quite the violent vixen in bed.

Which just makes her that much more perfect for us.

She's also one hell of a fighter, not only in the way she challenged Tieran, but in her general survival as well.

After everything she's been through, she managed to embrace her wolf and Omega spirit. That alone is absolutely awe-inspiring. Everything else just makes her that much more extraordinary.

I run my palm along her leg again, petting her and offering my adoration via touch.

"My father confirmed her mating with Canton, son of

Alpha Crane." Tieran's dark tone implies how fond he is of the Santeetlah Alpha and his son.

It rivals my own level of fondness—which is around a negative one hundred on a scale of zero to ten.

"Killing him will be an act of war," Tieran continues. "A war we are not ready for yet, given that more than half the island just challenged us over Clove."

"They were lost to the rut," I say. "And the fact that we beat them without permanently killing them should win us some favor."

"And nearly half of the Alphas proved strong enough to control their urges," Volt adds. "They're worthy warriors, T."

"Worthy but not quite ready. I need their devotion and respect. It's the only way we'll win this fight." He draws his fingers through Clove's silky brown hair, the color reminding me of dark chocolate. It matches her eyes, which pop beautifully against her alabaster skin.

Gorgeous, I think, momentarily distracted by her beauty.

The three of us should be lost to the rut now, down here surrounded by her Omega perfume.

But we're oddly in control.

Perhaps because her heat hasn't truly started yet. That playtime before was just a prelude to the event to come.

Volt's and Tieran's knots temporarily sated her initial lust. But when she wakes, this room will become a beautiful display of carnality.

And I cannot fucking wait.

"Winning this Omega will give you their devotion," Volt says quietly, his gaze on our sweet Clove. "It's the final stage of your Alpha legacy."

It's what we've been working toward for a decade. Being sent here seven years ago was a minor setback that we quickly used to our advantage. That event is the source that carved the path of our joint future.

The day Tieran was framed for murder.

"Do you find it ironic that Clove was also framed for murder?" I wonder out loud, shifting the topic with my thoughts. "Or is it too coincidental?" She came from the pack that framed him, after all.

"Do you think she's here to fuck with us?" Tieran asks.

"Do you?" I counter. He didn't claim her. I know it's because he's not done testing her. But are the coincidences of her arrival holding him back as well?

His fingers are still in her hair, his eyes sliding down to take in her delicate features. She's fully exposed with just her calves twisted in the sheets. It's common for an Omega in heat to be too warm, so we didn't cover her.

But it's also for our benefit, as we can see her toned thighs, shapely hips designed to take an Alpha's knot, flat stomach, and pert tits.

She's stunning.

A feisty wolf wrapped up in a tiny Omega package.

I draw my palm up her thigh, loving the way goose bumps trail in the wake of my touch. She's still lost to sleep, but her body knows her intended mate.

Her nipples bead as though she can sense our eyes on her.

And the sweet aroma of fresh slick graces the air, making all three of us rumble in hungry approval.

"If she's been sent here to fuck with us, it's without her knowledge," Tieran says, the authority in his tone suggesting he's not willing to debate his decision.

As I agree with him, I don't bother trying.

And Volt merely smiles. "Setup or not, she's ours now. And I look forward to killing her former punk-ass betrothed."

I smirk. "Blades or bullets?"

"Blades," he replies without missing a beat. "He'll suffer." The promise isn't just in his words, but in his eyes, too. Volt likes to kill. He lives to spill the blood of others. It's why he's so good at what he does.

I nod. "Good." I'll be claiming a front-row seat for that event. Watching Volt kill never gets old.

"You can't take him out yet," Tieran reminds him, a note of authority in his voice.

Volt just looks at him.

"I mean it, Volt," Tieran says. "I know you want to deliver his head to her as a gift, but think about how much more powerful that gift will be if you can avenge her mother, too."

Volt considers him for a moment. "A box full of rapists' dicks topped with an Alpha's severed head."

He means that literally.

Something that makes me want to gag, but I can't help agreeing with the sentiment. "She'll love it," I tell him. Or it may terrify her. But she'll have to accept Volt's penchant for death and torture eventually.

He'll never hurt her.

He'll just kill *for* her.

Which is exactly what he does for me and Tieran.

It's also how he contributes financially to our growing empire.

He takes the term *enforcer* to a whole new level of meaning.

"Let's try not to scare her too soon," Tieran cautions.

Volt snorts. "She's a fighter, T. She even challenged you."

Tieran's lips quirk up. "Yeah. She did." And the heat in his gaze says how much he enjoyed that little show of disobedience.

"She needs to know who we are," Volt continues, pushing off the door to saunter toward the bed. "And I mean more than just about how we fuck."

"Well, I think she'll be learning those traits first," I drawl, grinning down at our sleeping beauty. She should have already been introduced to my knot, but Volt won our bet earlier, giving him access to her sweet heat before me.

Soon, gorgeous, I think at her, my hand trailing up close to her delicious mound. I don't actually touch her, just enjoy the warmth coming from her center before sliding my touch back to the middle of her thigh. *Soon.*

Tieran's studying her, his fingers having shifted from her hair to her face. He leans down to trace his nose along her cheek, his wolf rumbling in his chest. "Her scent isn't as strong now," he says, his brow furrowing. "It should be drugging us, but my beast feels calm."

"Maybe from knotting her already?" I guess. None of us have ever been with an Omega before. We've heard stories, witnessed the call back home, and smelled the effects of Omegas in heat. But Tieran's right—we should be almost out of our minds with lust right now. "Do you think something's wrong?"

"I think our Omega has mixed genetics and may not do what we expect," he replies, sitting up again, his gaze still on her. "We'll continue preparing, but I want to take advantage of this prolonged moment of lucidity to talk to my father."

Volt settles on the bed, stretching out beside our Omega. "Don't worry, T. We'll keep her company in the interim."

Tieran presses a kiss to her temple before slipping off the bed.

I take his place beside her, sandwiching the female

between me and Volt. "Yeah, we've got this covered, T," I echo.

He grins again. "Try not to break her, yeah?"

"Don't take too long," I counter, not making any promises.

Because they're not needed.

This little beauty is a treasure, and when she wakes up, she'll see just how much we intend to worship her.

CLOVE

I wake to a pang in my lower belly, my thighs trembling with an aftershock of pain that elicits a low whimper from my chest.

Ugh. It feels like a tree fell on my head.

Every part of me aches, but especially my insides.

I groan, trying to curl into a ball, only to come up against a hard wall of flesh. I freeze, my heart leaping into my throat.

Warmth washes over me, touching me all the way to my toes.

"Morning, gorgeous," a deep voice rumbles, fingers combing through my hair. "Well, evening, technically. You've slept all day."

I swallow. *Where am I?*

Everything feels so hazy.

So unclear.

So… so… *unreal.*

Because the fantasy unfolding in my mind can't be accurate.

Tieran forcing me to shift. Followed by a chase. Volt catching me. Both of them… I shiver, the vivid memory of having them inside me making my thighs clench, which stirs another whine from deep within.

Because *ow*.

"Shh," the masculine wall hums.

Caius, I recognize, his peppermint scent surrounding me. But there are hints of pine and coppery ash, too.

I force my eyes open and take in all the smooth skin in front of me.

Caius's chest is a work of art. All tapered lines and lean muscle. His shoulders are just as firm, as are his arms and his abdomen.

He's not as big as Volt. He's also missing the ink on his arms and chest.

Volt is all strength and intimidating muscle.

Caius is sleek, almost panther-like.

And Tieran is all power.

The three of them together are an intoxicatingly dangerous situation. They represent a dark drug I shouldn't crave. Yet I find my gaze slowly sliding up the strong cords of Caius's neck to take in the five o'clock shadow of dark hair dusting his chiseled jaw, all the way up to his grayish-green eyes.

"Hi, beautiful," he whispers, his full lips curling into a welcome grin. "How are you feeling?"

I swallow again, trying to dislodge the rocks that seem to have taken up residence in my throat. "Sore," I manage to choke out. "Confused."

The latter is an admission I hate to make, but a necessary one. Because I really am confused. I'm not sure what's real and what's not, or how I ended up here.

Or why I feel this sudden urge to rub all over his body and bite his neck like he's my male to claim.

But I *really* want to lick him.

No, my wolf wants to lick him.

Maybe we both do.

It's hard to distinguish her needs from mine, something that makes me frown. *I can't suppress her anymore,* I realize. That place I used to put her in my mind to block the temptation to shift is no longer there.

It's... gone.

Like it never existed at all.

What does that mean?

"What's happening to me?" I ask, shivering as a chill chases away my warmth.

Caius shifts to drag a blanket up over us both, then reaches around me for something. "Here," he says, returning to his position alongside me. "Drink." He presses a bottle of water to my lips, tipping the contents into my mouth.

I accept the refreshment gratefully, the cool liquid calming the ache in my throat. He helps me finish half the bottle before moving to set it on the nightstand behind him.

He lies down again, his gray-green irises searching my features as a lock of dark hair falls over his forehead. I reach up to brush it from his eyes, wanting to see his face, then freeze as he smiles. Because that was a decidedly intimate act on my part.

But we are lying in a bed.

Me, naked.

Him—I glance down—in a pair of gray sweats.

He follows my gaze, his lips quirking up even more. "Hmm, you want my knot, gorgeous? Or are you just admiring the view?"

"Your knot?" I repeat in a whisper.

"My cock," he rephrases, cupping my cheek to draw my gaze back up to his. "Omegas crave their Alpha's knots.

And as you're on the edge of some sort of unique heat cycle, I would understand your need."

"That's the bulb..." I trail off, recalling how Tieran practically split me wide open before giving me the most amazing pleasure of my life.

Volt soon followed.

And then...

I *flew*.

My thighs tingle with the memory now, my insides heating at the remembered sensation of falling into oblivion.

"It was real. Not a dream." The words come out soft, the statement meant for me more than Caius. But he clearly hears it.

"Depends on the dream," he replies, his thumb tracing my lower lip. "If you mean that spectacular display of sex and passion earlier between you, Tieran, and Volt, then yes, very real. But if you're talking about my knot, then that part's a dream. One I'll happily assist in making come true."

I meet his intense gaze, my heart beating a chaotic rhythm in my chest. "I don't understand what's happening to me." I already said that once, but it's worth repeating. "Nantahala Alphas don't..." I'm not sure how to say this. "They're not like this."

They don't share their women.

They don't have knots.

And from what I know of the mating experience, it's nothing like what I just went through.

Which makes me frown.

I press my hand to my neck and shoulder, noting the smooth skin.

"I... I wasn't claimed," I say, even more confused now.

"No," he confirms. "Tieran has to initiate it first by blessing the claiming."

"But wasn't that…? Didn't Tieran say…?" I'm not sure how to finish my sentence. I feel overwhelmed. Broken. *Incomplete.*

"Take a breath for me," Caius says, his palm slipping to my nape as he guides me from my side to my back on the bed. "Inhale, Clove."

The demand in his voice wraps around me, compelling me to obey. My wolf doesn't want to defy him. She wants to submit. And my mind is too cluttered with questions to fight the urge.

"Keep breathing for me, and I'll try to help you understand," he says. "I assume you don't know much about Carnage Wolves other than we're supposedly savage and cruel, yeah?"

I confirm with a slight nod. "Nantahala Wolves fear your kind," I admit softly.

"*Our* kind," he corrects with a hint of chastisement in his tone.

"Yes." It's just weird to consider, as some of this still doesn't feel real. And a week ago, I was a Nantahala Wolf who very much feared Carnage Wolves.

"We'll come back to that," he says. "I'll give you a little dynamics lesson first."

Dynamics? I repeat, my gaze slipping downward to where his hips rest against mine.

His lips quirk. "Oh, we'll get to that dynamic in a few minutes, gorgeous. I'll even provide a hands-on demonstration."

I shiver, liking the sound of that. "Nantahala Wolves don't have a, um, *that.*"

"Large cocks?" he asks.

"A knot," I whisper, my cheeks heating.

The sparkle in his gaze tells me he already knew what I meant and wanted to tease me. "It's only Carnage Alphas that have them. And only Carnage Omegas can accept them."

"Accept them?" I repeat.

"When we fuck normal wolves or humans, our knots stay at the base," he explains. "But when we take an Omega, the knot connects to her, creating a bliss unlike any other. Or that's what I've heard and now observed, anyway. I've not yet experienced it for myself."

His gaze heats with the words, his focus falling to my mouth before slowly returning his eyes to mine.

"You've never had sex with an Omega?" It comes out as a question, but I already know the answer because that's what he said. I just don't know what else to say, and I want him to keep talking, to explain all this to me.

"Omegas are exceptionally rare. Most Carnage Wolf packs only have five or six, compared to maybe fifty Alphas and a hundred Betas. It's why we develop clans within the packs."

My brow furrows. "Clans?"

"Compatible mate groupings based on power and strength," he defines. "Tieran and Volt are my clan. We share power and protect each other."

"Like a mate-circle," I translate, awed by this concept. "Nantahala males often have harems to satiate their hunger, but only one mate."

Which is the purpose of the trials in my pack. Only the most eligible females win a mate. And the ones entirely rejected from the harem and mate process go to the Reject Islands.

Caius snorts. "The Nantahala Alpha has created a society that favors men and enslaves women. The male wolves have harems because they like to fuck, not because of some animalistic need to sate themselves. They don't understand pack dynamics the way we do."

The contempt in his tone sends a chill down my spine. He very clearly dislikes my former pack. Given everything I've been through, I'm inclined to agree.

"They purposely suppressed my wolf," I tell him, my eyes narrowing. "I thought it was to keep myself pure, to be the perfect mate. But I feel the wrongness of it now. My wolf never wants to be caged again."

"Carnage Wolves don't suppress our animals," he replies. "We embrace them. And we embrace our needs, too. That's the purpose of our clans—Alphas need Omegas to procreate and to feel alive. But there are so few of them available. That's why we form a circle. It's not just about protection; it's to share our chosen mate as well."

My eyes widen. "Your clans only take one female mate?"

He nods.

"And also a harem?" I assume out loud since male wolves have needs, and to only be able to take one female mate per clan would mean they need more females on the side to sate their hunger.

"You're thinking like a Nantahala Wolf, not a Carnage Wolf, so I'm going to forgive that insult," he replies, making me frown. "Carnage Omegas are the center of our clans, Clove. They're the jewel we all crave and desire. No other being could ever compare. So no, we do not take other women. Once we have our Omega, she's all we desire. She's *everything*." His gaze turns intense again. "*You* will be our everything."

I gape at him. "M-me?"

"Yes, Clove. *You*." He presses his lips to mine, his kiss gentle yet maintaining an air of dominance at the same time. "You're our missing jewel, the Omega we've been waiting for. We never expected to find you here, but that just makes this mean more."

"You've been searching for an Omega?"

He nods. "Tieran has visited a few Carnage Wolf packs to meet eligible Omegas. There have really only been two that he's met, but they were both clearly taken with other Alpha clans, and while Tieran had the power to claim whomever he wanted, he didn't feel right about them."

I blink. "I… I thought he was betrothed to Alpha Bryson's daughter? Did he visit these packs before or after…?" I almost finish with the words *he slaughtered her*, but the dark gleam in Caius's gaze has me trailing off instead.

"He was never *betrothed* to the Nantahala Wolf. Our kind can't take other wolves as mates. A Carnage Alpha needs a Carnage Omega, something *Bryson* knows very well." He utters the name with fury, causing my wolf to shiver beneath my skin.

She doesn't like his anger.

Neither do I.

But I also know it's not directed at me.

"That's Tieran's story to tell," he continues. "So I'll let him do the honors. But you need to understand that Carnage Wolves and Nantahala Wolves are not the same."

I try to dip my chin to tell him I understand, but his hand on my cheek stops me, his gaze intently holding mine.

"We value our relationships, and that includes cherishing our mates." He nips at my mouth, the gesture more playful than cruel, his mood shifting from angry to relaxed as he pulls back to gaze down at me.

"Most packs have an Alpha and a Beta and a few other official roles, but that's not how we operate," he continues. "We have an Alpha clan at the top, meaning we typically have at least three Alphas in charge of a pack. There's always one that's stronger than the rest, but that Alpha chooses the strongest among us to support him."

"So, similar to the Alpha-Beta dynamic where the Beta takes over if the Alpha is away," I translate.

"Similar, except our Alpha clans are even more closely knit. We can actually develop the ability to speak between our minds once we've found our Omega mate. She's the heart and key to everything. That's why you're so important, Clove. You're our heart, or you will be once you go into a proper heat cycle."

I frown. "This wasn't, um, proper?"

He chuckles. "No, gorgeous. Estrus usually lasts at least five days, sometimes even up to eight or nine. You only touched the cusp of your potential. We think it was brought on by finally connecting to your wolf, but we're not sure why it stopped. Once you fell asleep, it sort of… dissipated."

"And that's not normal," I say, reading between the lines.

"No, it's not. But your situation isn't exactly normal, either."

"Because I'm a half-breed."

"A half-breed who suppressed her wolf for…" He trails off, his gaze sharpening. "How old are you, Clove?"

"Twenty."

His eyebrows lift. "You suppressed your wolf for *twenty* years?"

I swallow, my chin attempting to move in the affirmative again, but his palm is still holding my cheek.

"*Fuck*," he breathes. "I mean, technically, it's more like fifteen, I guess, but Jesus, Clove. That must have hurt a lot."

"It's what we're taught to do." I don't say it defensively.

It's more of a sad statement as it comes out because I've realized how wrong it is over the last few days. How it's used to control the Nantahala females, not help them prosper.

I suddenly feel thankful for my fate.

Which then elicits a guilty pang in my chest.

Because my fate is directly tied to my mother's death.

"That explains your brief introduction to estrus," Caius says, his thumb tracing the hollow beneath my eye. "You'll likely go into a true heat soon. Maybe within the next few days."

"Nantahala Wolves don't really go into multiday heat cycles," I say. "I mean, they have their fertility periods where they mate, but it's not… it's not for eight days. Maybe a full day or two, and once every few years." So that's probably why my estrus only lasted a few hours. That's more typical of my kind.

Which makes me wonder how compatible I really am with these Alphas.

"I'm not an Omega," I continue, voicing my thoughts out loud. "My pack considered me an Alpha candidate because of my trials."

"Trials?" he repeats.

"They're tests designed to determine the most eligible Nantahala females for mating," I explain. "Like agility and strength exercises, as well as etiquette and the ability to teach. They groom us for motherhood but also test our traits to find the ones they want to replicate via procreation." It all sounds very clinical, and it is to an extent. "The purpose is to guarantee the best of the lines are continued."

He grunts. "And I'm guessing beauty plays a part in it?"

"It does because they want the most alluring females for the mating process."

"To appease the males," he drawls.

I don't comment because there's not much I can say, so I just shrug. Attractiveness has always been key among my former pack. They praise it and embrace it. Part of what made me one of the most eligible females was my physical appeal. The Alphas liked that I was petite and curvy.

Canton especially so.

He praised my appearance frequently during the mating tests.

"Carnage Wolves favor power and prosperity over all else. We mate based on strength compatibility, which is why Tieran's wolf likes your animal—you challenged him." He grins. "It's why we all like you."

"I challenged him when I ran." I vaguely remember that, my wolf having been in charge of the notion to flee. "My animal wanted to be chased."

"That's the Carnage Omega in you," he says. "It's overriding your Nantahala instincts, taking over your psyche and helping you become the wolf you were always meant to be."

"Unless who I'm meant to be is a mixture of the two," I say, frowning. "What if I can't go into heat like an Omega?"

He considers me, a deep crease marring his brow. "You *are* an Omega, Clove. I can smell it on your skin, taste it on my tongue. You'll go into heat like one. Today was just an appetizer to the meal to come." He kisses me again, silencing whatever I would have said back to him.

But my mind is reeling.

While I want to believe him, I'm not sure I trust my own genetics to play out the way he says they will.

I'm a mixed breed.

And these Alphas want a proper Omega for their circle. They value them as jewels. However, how can I shine when I'm tainted with my Nantahala heritage?

"Do you want your hands-on demonstration now, angel?" he asks softly, his groin pressing into mine. "Or would you prefer to indulge in that intimate discussion after dinner?"

CAIUS

I can sense her hesitation. Her concern is a sour taste in the air, one that makes me want to distract her with my cock, to prove to her that she's a Carnage Omega.

I understand she has Nantahala genetics in her as well, but the only way she could have been created is if an Alpha knotted her mother.

Which means her mother either also had Carnage Wolf ancestry or was a very unique breed of wolf.

Regardless, the Carnage part of her is going to dominate the Nantahala side. The process started when she first shifted.

She's becoming one with her wolf.

And when that merger completes itself, she'll very likely go into a full estrus cycle.

Which is when we'll claim her.

Tieran already spoke to his father about it, asking if he knew of any other half-breeds that turned Omega in the past. There was only one case Alpha Umber knew about, and that female did become a full Omega once taken by her Alpha clan.

He told Tieran this is his final test—to claim the

Omega. Once our clan is done, we'll gain the required favor of the pack, and Tieran will be able to return as the incoming Black Mountain Alpha.

It's almost a circumstance of fate that we couldn't complete the mating process with Clove. Because it means we have to protect her on an island full of eligible Alpha clans now. And not only that, but we also need to ensure they respect our claim without the official links in place.

It'll be a trial of honor, one we desperately need to pass for our dreams of vengeance to come to fruition.

I'm not concerned.

Neither is Tieran or Volt.

But our little Omega needs to understand that she's ours, that we're going to claim her even if her mixed heritage proves to be an issue.

Which I strongly suspect it won't.

"Volt's in the kitchen making something spicy," I say when she doesn't respond to my question about dinner. "He started cooking when we sensed you waking up, and Tieran is off working on his plan for damage control. So I'm in charge of taking care of you. Now, do you want to play with my knot? Or would you prefer to eat first?"

She blinks at me, her cheeks blossoming with color. It's an adorably innocent expression, considering what happened earlier today.

But that blush tells me her preference.

"Knot it is," I murmur, smiling.

She doesn't just need a distraction; she needs an unspoken vow.

Sometimes it's not about words but about actions. She can question her lineage all she wants. Her wolf will prove her wrong.

I press my lips to hers, coaxing her to open up for me with a gentle stroke of my tongue.

She does.

Because she's an Omega craving her Alpha's touch.

Clove wants my strength and reassurance. The sweet little wolf has been fighting alone all week, and I'm telling her with my mouth that she's no longer on her own.

She has me. She has Tieran. She has Volt.

We won't let her down.

We won't give up on her.

We will protect her until the end.

You're ours now, I'm telling her with my mouth. *And we will wait for as long as it takes for you to understand what that means.*

A soft shudder rolls through her, making me purr. I love her reactions. They're so potent and addictive. I want to taste her, to lick every inch of her body and feel her come against my tongue.

But I also want her to be confident.

I want her to recognize that her place is here with us.

Time doesn't matter.

Our wolves know their mates, and her soul calls to mine. It calls to us all. I felt it during her initial heat, that demand to take her and make her ours. It wasn't just from my animal's desire to rut; it was a yearning that came from my wolf's spirit.

This female sets all my blood on fire.

And I would be a fool to ignore that reaction.

Her palms meet my shoulders, not to push me away, but to explore.

I grin again, allowing her to pet me to her heart's content while I continue to kiss her softly with just a little bit of tongue.

She's sore. She's still tired. She's confused.

So I won't push.

But I will let her use me to sate her curiosity, which she

does as her small hands trail down my arms. She's letting her wolf lead. I can feel the pretty animal pulsating beneath me, calling to my beast and urging him to play.

This is what Carnage Wolves are all about—we thrive on sensation and life. We follow our instincts. We don't block the animalistic cravings inside ourselves, and we absolutely do not let our human sides rule our decisions.

It's why Volt can kill without a questioning thought.

How Tieran leads without remorse.

And it's what I truly love about being a Carnage Wolf.

I'm not shy. I take what I want when I want it. Because I can.

I slip my palm to her nape, asserting my dominance while continuing to kiss her gently. Her hands are near my sides now, running up my rib cage and back to my shoulders.

I don't rush her.

I let her lead.

She can feel my arousal. It's throbbing against her slick heat, beating a pulse of desire that she can absolutely sense through the thin layer of pants between us.

I pull back a little to study her alluring brown eyes. Her wolf peeks up at me, darkening the irises to a near-black shade.

"You can touch my knot," I tell her. "I won't make you take it. I won't even ask you to stroke it. I want you to be comfortable, Clove. I want you to understand who we are and why you're one of us."

I slowly roll off of her to my back and place my hands beneath my head, propping myself on the pillows while assuming an unthreatening position.

I'm essentially showing her my belly, just in human form.

An unheard-of reaction from an Alpha, but I trust this Omega. And I want her to trust me.

This is all about intimacy and learning and understanding the bond between our souls.

It's also about fucking.

About mating.

About *claiming*.

My dick is so fucking hard that I feel like I may explode at any second. It's been a bit since my last lay. I don't even remember the female; the mediocre experience was nothing compared to this.

And Clove has barely touched me.

Her eyes run over my torso with interest, her nostrils flaring as she licks her kiss-swollen lips.

I wait.

Delayed gratification has always been one of my favorite games. It's why I didn't mind losing the bet to Volt. He knows it, too.

Clove rolls toward me and goes up on her elbow, her soft hair sliding over her slender shoulder to pool in waves of brown silk. My fingers itch to touch her, but I don't move.

She releases a soft breath, then places her palm on my abdomen. It's light and tentative, her eyes flicking between my gaze and my torso. Then she bends to lick my neck.

I purr in response, pleased that she's letting her animal guide her. Because that move was pure wolf.

"Please keep doing that." Her voice is whisper soft, suggesting that wasn't easy for her to say.

So I don't ask her what she means.

I already know.

I reply by purring louder for her. She shudders, her nose pressing into my neck as her palm slides up to rest over my heart.

Alphas typically only make this sound for their mates, or on rare occasions when a troubled pack member requires soothing.

However, there are different levels to the vibrations.

The one I'm using now is the intimate reverberation meant for my intended Omega. It's a natural hum that comes from my chest, one I embrace fully because it clearly pleases my beautiful Clove.

Her bare thigh slides over mine as she tries to crawl closer, to lose herself in my purr.

I almost move to wrap my arms around her. But I don't want to disturb the moment. I let her find peace in my strength and in my presence. That's what mates are for.

Her lips trace my throat to my collarbone, her nose pressing into my chest as she inhales.

"Peppermint," she breathes.

"Hmm, you smell like honey and sweet cream to me." The perfect dessert. "And your slick is pure ambrosia, so decadent and intoxicating that I've been hard for you for hours."

There may have been a few periods of relief while she slept, but they didn't last long. One look at the beauty on the bed had me saluting her all over again.

Her brown eyes meet mine, her pupils dilated with a mixture of desire and contentment. I increase my purr again and smile as she presses her face against my pec.

"Nantahala Alphas don't purr," she says, the words souring my mood. She needs to stop comparing us to her former pack.

But I can't fault her entirely for it.

This is all new and confusing.

So for her, I'll be patient.

And I'll continue purring, too.

"Your Alphas don't do a lot of things that we do," I say,

my voice resembling a low growl as a result of the vibrations in my chest. "They don't cherish their females. They don't focus on pack bonds. They use fear to keep order. And…" I trail off and wait for her to meet my gaze.

She does, her expression softly inquisitive.

"And they don't have a knot," I finish. "They also probably couldn't handle an Omega's estrus. It's a lot of work to keep one satisfied for a week or longer."

But it's a challenge I'm very much looking forward to.

"Given how misogynistic the Nantahala Wolves are, I'm guessing they wouldn't even try to please an Omega mate," Volt adds from the doorway. "They wouldn't want to risk their reputation by failing, and they wouldn't care enough to try."

I lift my head to meet his gaze over Clove. She's still plastered to my chest, with one ear against my skin and her face turned in Volt's direction.

"Food ready?" I ask.

"I put it under the burner to keep it warm. Figured Clove wanted you as an appetizer first." He pushes off the door frame to saunter toward us. "When an Alpha offers to let you play with his knot, you indulge him, sweetling. Especially when he's the only one who hasn't tasted you yet."

"Don't ruin my fun, V." The bastard wants to push her along to kill my game of delayed gratification.

"Your version of fun is going to take all night," he drawls, joining us on the bed.

I shrug. "Not my fault that some of us have better stamina than others."

He snorts. "There's nothing wrong with my stamina, asshole. I just don't want to wait until tomorrow to play with Clove again."

"She's sore," I warn him as he draws his finger down

her spine. She's moved slightly, her cheek still pressed to my chest, but her eyes are on me again as Volt settles behind her. It was the same space he lay in before she started to wake up.

"I know how to properly care for a female," he says, his dark gaze filled with devious secrets.

"Tell me you didn't bring a knife in here," I reply, tensing. I'm *very* aware of his sadistic penchants. And Clove is not ready for that side yet, as evidenced by the way she's now frozen against me.

Or maybe that's because I stopped purring.

Volt takes over the rumbling vibration, his finger still tracing her spine. "I left the knives in the kitchen."

I relax a bit. "Good."

"But I want to see her play with your knot. Maybe even test her gag reflex, too." He waggles his brows.

I almost roll my eyes. His kink pushes a myriad of boundaries, something Clove is going to have to learn to accommodate.

Because there will be no other women now.

Just her.

The mere notion of bedding anyone other than our intended is abhorrent. There is just no one else in this world who will compare now. Not even another Omega.

It's amazing how I went from considering Clove's potential to *knowing* she belongs to us. It happened the moment she shifted back into human form.

One inhale and I was done.

Her scent claimed me instantly.

My wolf recognized her. My soul demanded I take her. And my heart started beating a new rhythm that exists only for her.

"Go on, sweetling," Volt urges. "His sweats aren't even tied. Just reach in and have a feel."

CAIUS

"V…" I'm not even sure what I want to say. He won't listen anyway. So instead, I focus on Clove and start purring again as I give in to the urge to touch her. I cup her cheek, "You're doing just fine. Ignore him."

"Yes, ignore me," he agrees. "And focus on that throbbing shaft in his pants instead. I can smell his need, sweets. Just like I can scent your interest. Give in and play. We don't mind."

Clove swallows as I sigh. He won't stop. It's something I've learned to just endure. "We've known each other all our lives," I confide in Clove as I release her cheek. "Volt never lies. He never exaggerates. And he always follows through on his word."

"Threats," Volt corrects. "I always follow through on my *threats*."

"Those, too," I concede.

He smiles. "Caius is the wordy one of the clan. And apparently, he's a closet romantic, too."

"Fuck you," I retort.

"No, I'm trying to convince her to fuck *you*," he says. "With her mouth."

I just shake my head and tuck my hands behind my head again. Clove watches me with a heated expression, her wolf staring at me again through her eyes. I allow her to see mine in return, which causes her lips to part in surprise.

"He's hungry," I say, unapologetic. "He wants to taste his intended mate."

"Yes, and Caius is torturing the poor beast by forcing him to wait," Volt adds. "But that's his schtick. It's what makes him hard."

"My version of a blade." One I'll use on myself as well as Clove. Because I love a good game of orgasm denial. "Control and self-restraint are my weapons in bed."

Clove's eyes widen.

"Thinking you prefer the food now?" I tease, purring with the words. "We can save this game for dessert if you prefer. Or even breakfast tomorrow." I really won't mind. She's been through a lot. I can wait for her to be ready.

Her expression hardens a bit as she studies me, some sort of resolve snapping into place.

There's my survivor, I think, intrigued by the shift from meek and innocent to fierce and determined.

This must be related to the trials she told me about, how she proved herself to be strong enough for an Alpha in her pack.

The mating requirements there are different.

Nantahala Alphas mate other Alphas because that's how they produce the strongest offspring. Yet the males want to control the females, hence their warped pack dynamics.

Meanwhile, Carnage Alphas need an Omega to even be able to procreate, which drives the whole structure of our hierarchy.

However, that doesn't mean our Omegas are weak.

They're delicate in size but mighty in spirit.

And Clove is proving to be no different.

She holds my gaze with a boldness now that has my abdomen clenching with excitement.

I purr for her, demonstrating my approval.

And then I groan as she places her palm directly on my groin.

No hesitation.

No holding back.

Just a knowing squeeze that has my muscles straining with the need to take her. To rip off my pants and *fuck* her.

I swallow instead, my hands still trapped behind my head.

She leans down to kiss my chest, my skin vibrating beneath her mouth as I strive to continue releasing those vibrations for her.

But it's hard.

So. Damn. *Hard.*

Especially with her squeezing my shaft like that through my sweats.

She travels down to the base, her body stilling above mine as she finds my throbbing knot.

I hold my breath, unsure of what she'll do.

And nearly growl as she begins kissing a path down my abdomen.

"You're a fucking natural at this, sweetling," Volt murmurs, his fingers still trailing up and down her spine.

He releases her as she nears the waistband of my sweats, his gaze fixated on the back of her head.

I follow suit, my chest stuttering as I force myself to inhale, to maintain that rumbling purr.

This is so much more intense than I anticipated. I'm going to fucking come before she even really touches me.

Her tongue tentatively tastes the skin beneath my pants, her mouth fixated on the muscle near my hip bone.

Then she slowly starts to tug my pants down.

It's fucking torture.

I'm going to explode.

I'm going to throw her on her back and thrust into her.

No.

I'm going to lie here and let her play.

Fuck. I don't even know what I want anymore. This game has escalated to a whole new level, and I'm absolutely fucking here for it.

My pants tangle around my knees as Clove seems to forget they exist. Her focus is on my groin, her eyes wide as she studies my aching cock.

"Lick him," Volt suggests. "See what he does."

I'm going to fucking kill you, I tell him with my eyes.

He grins in response, the mad bastard getting off on this sadistic twist of fate.

Clove runs her fingertips along the underside of my shaft to the knot at the base. It's a featherlight touch that causes my balls to tighten in anticipation.

I'm mesmerized by her.

Captivated by her every move.

She dampens her lips, her nostrils flaring as she takes in my scent.

"That's it," Volt murmurs. "Give in to the urge. You know you want to taste him."

I swallow, no longer capable of glaring at him for his unwanted commentary.

Because his urging appears to be working.

Clove's cheeks are tinted pink, her pupils blown with lust.

She glances up at me, seeking approval.

I nod, not even sure what she's asking to do. I really

don't care. My body belongs to her now. To torment. To lick. To touch. To fuck. Whatever she wants.

She bends, her silky hair tickling my abdomen.

A sharp exhale leaves my lungs as her lips taste my hip again. But then she starts to move, her mouth trailing wet kisses along my pelvic bone to my pulsating knot. She traces it with her tongue, the action so damn erotic that I nearly come undone.

My hands are fisted behind my head, the desire to grab her and thrust into her riding my spirit.

I want to claim her. Mark her. Declare my vows in blood.

The urge worsens as she slides her tongue up my shaft to the tip.

"Mmm, very good, sweetheart," Volt praises. "Taste him properly now."

She licks my head, a soft moan coming from her chest.

"Beautiful. Now lick him again. That precum is all for you, Clove. Don't waste it." Volt's words are fucking killing me.

Because she does exactly what he says.

And then she takes my cock into her mouth.

Not gently.

But completely.

Sucking me all the way down, as far as she can possibly go before lifting up.

"You can do better than that, sweetling," Volt says, his hand going to the back of her neck. "Relax your throat."

My abdomen tightens as he starts pushing her back onto my cock, her lips brushing my knot before she starts to gag.

He lets her pull away but again tells her to relax as he starts the process again.

Fire licks through my veins, making it hard not to

explode. But I want her to enjoy this, to understand it, to *embrace* it.

Her wolf is in her eyes again, her determination palpable as Volt tells her how good she is at this, how perfect she is for us, how he can't wait to feel her mouth on him, and how she needs to finish this task to earn her prize.

My cum.

It's what Omegas crave from their mates. It's how Tieran kept her grounded earlier—by feeding her drops of his essence.

I groan as Clove finds her rhythm, her wolf driving her as Volt continues to push her further, testing her limits.

She's so small.

Yet she sucks me down like a goddamn champ.

"Fuck, Clove," I breathe, panting with *need*. I can't keep my hands to myself anymore. I have to touch her. To stroke her. To show my appreciation for this intense experience.

Volt releases her head, allowing me to thread my fingers through her hair and help guide her pace.

Not that she needs my assistance.

She's turned into a cock-sucking professional.

Because she's given in to her wolf.

She's finally embracing her animal, coming to terms with who she is, learning to thrive as one—both beast and human.

It's glorious. Breathtaking. Fucking alluring.

"He's close," Volt tells her, his palms moving along her back, offering her comfort and his purr while she devours me with her mouth.

It's a hedonistic display, seeing him kneeling behind her while she sucks me off. I can almost picture him driving into her sweet cunt, knotting her as she gets me off.

Fuck yes.

Volt and I have never shared a female before.

None of us have, always choosing to play on our own.

But that's all changing now.

"Deeper," Volt tells her. "Wrap your hand around his knot and squeeze."

"*Clove,*" I grind out, reacting to her following Volt's command.

I could tell her what to do.

But I'm too damn lost to the sensations to focus.

Her fingers are massaging my knot, demanding I come.

I'm a slave to my Omega's needs.

"Swallow for me, gorgeous," I hiss, my limbs shaking from the impending insanity. "Take as much as you can."

I thrust deep into her mouth on a growl that vibrates through the room as I unleash my pleasure down her hot throat.

She sputters, the poor Omega unused to this act.

But she tries to swallow, her eyes watering from the intensity of it.

Her fingers continue milking my knot, her throat working around my shaft, her tongue laving my head to coax out every drop.

I pull out enough to let her breathe before going deep again, my orgasm rolling over us in monstrous waves.

It's unending.

It's excruciating.

It's the most amazing pleasure of my life.

And I've not even knotted her yet.

That sensuous part of me remains locked inside, but it reacts to her touch, shooting another spurt of cum into her mouth.

She swallows.

But the full force of my climax was too much for her to take.

It's all over her face, dribbling down her chin.

She's never looked more gorgeous.

I pull her up to me even as I continue to release a few aftershocks of pleasure, my need to kiss her far more pressing than the rapture spilling from my cock.

Her lips part on a gasp, my tongue snaking inside to duel with hers as I roll her beneath me.

She's so fucking perfect. I want her to know it. To feel it. To understand what our future together really means.

I kiss her soundly, then lick away the cum from her face, not bothered at all by my own flavor.

Espccially when she grabs me and pulls me back to suck the essence off my tongue.

I grin, loving this feral display.

I find some of the residual fluid near my groin and bring it to her lips. She sucks my fingers clean.

"Such a good little wolf," Volt says, reminding us that he's still here. He's taken his place alongside us, sans pants, hand on his cock, leisurely stroking. "Do you want more, sweetling?"

"Not yet," I tell him. "I want my appetizer first."

And I intend to enjoy it.

Right now.

Right between her slick thighs.

"Bon appétit," Volt murmurs.

Yes. Bon appétit indeed.

I start my path downward, my eyes holding Clove's gaze. "Deep breaths, gorgeous. I'm about to make you scream."

TIERAN

C love's moans reach my ears, causing my lips to curl. I told Caius and Volt to take care of her, and it appears they're doing just that.

Good.

I wrap up my email to one of my clients—he wants a discount for his project request, which isn't happening—and hit Send. Volt's skills are too impressive to ever earn a discount price, something my client will now understand. He can either pay in full, plus a percentage for the perceived insult, or go elsewhere with his bullshit.

We primarily do this to help finance projects on the island. Which makes it unnecessary in the grand scheme of our pack dynamics. But as Volt enjoys playing with knives and guns, it serves as a worthwhile effort on our part.

Caius's part of the business is where we make most of our money. He's a master blackmailer, always finding the right rich people to exploit and using it to our benefit. And it helps that Volt kills for some of them—adds fodder to the files.

Caius is also an expert at laundering funds through legitimate corporations and ensuring others are always in our debt. It's a skill he picked up from his dad, who happens to be one of my father's best friends and also the financial manager for the Black Mountain Pack.

Volt's upbringing was a little different. He came to Black Mountain as a pup, his father having gone insane and killed his mother before taking his own life. His Alpha father refused to join a clan and took a Beta for a mate yet impregnated an Omega to have a child—Volt.

It didn't end well.

And Volt's been dealing with the results ever since.

My father didn't approve of him for my clan, but it wasn't his choice. My wolf drives my needs, and he chose Caius and Volt.

And now my wolf wants Clove.

However, her falling out of her estrus is… problematic.

I can't mate an Omega incapable of providing an heir. That's my duty as Pack Alpha. And I refuse to mate an Omega only to fuck another to fulfill a requirement. That would destroy my clan.

Which leaves me with the very difficult decision of having to wait.

I need to know Clove can give us what we need before I mate her.

Until then, Caius and Volt can play. They can't truly claim her—not without my blessing first.

My wolf is pissed, but this is one situation where my human mind overrules his animalistic instincts. It's my responsibility as a leader to make the right choices in life— not just for me, but for my entire pack.

Unfortunately, this is one of them.

Sighing, I close down my computer and stand to stretch my arms over my head. I sent out a message to Alpha Duncan—one of the few who didn't attempt to challenge me earlier today over Clove—to call for a midnight meeting on the beach.

I'm going to address the pack and tell them what's happening with Clove.

Then I'll address the challengers, most of whom should be awake by now and healing.

I'll forgive them for their actions because I felt the rutting pull threatening to overtake my wolf and understand why they gave in to it. But I'll expect a show of respect from them.

Which will begin with them attending tonight's meeting.

Anyone who doesn't will be sternly spoken with and, depending on their response, permanently removed from the island.

I won't kill them.

But I will exile them, something I've only ever done once.

Since most of the wolves here are not true rejects, they're not relegated to the island. Most of the paperwork is all falsified as well, giving me jurisdiction to do as I please.

I don't particularly enjoy the authority. However, it is a natural skill.

Clove screams Caius's name, pulling me from my thoughts and making my lips curl. I wander toward them, wanting to grab some fresh jeans and a pair of boots from the closet in the den bedroom.

The erotic display on the bed momentarily arrests me, making me regret having a meeting to attend in ten minutes.

Clove's luscious brown hair is spilled across the silky pillows, her plump lips swollen and parted on a moan that goes straight to my groin.

Volt is lounging beside her, naked, and lazily stroking his shaft as Caius devours the sweetness between her legs. I swallow, her decadent perfume an allure that makes my wolf stir with need. I knotted her twice this morning, yet it feels like I could go a dozen more times and still not be satisfied.

She's beautiful.

And the way she's following her animalistic instincts right now is a divine sight that makes my wolf rumble in approval.

Her midnight gaze meets mine, her cheeks a stunning reddish shade. I walk toward her as though drawn to her by an invisible string and lean down to kiss her like I already own her.

Mine, my wolf says.

But I don't let him bite her.

Not yet.

Not until we know for sure that she's the Omega we should claim.

However, I purr for her, the sound one that comes from my wolf, demanding to be heard. He's already chosen her. He wants to worship her. He wants to give her comfort and prove himself worthy.

Alas, I pull away, the purr in my chest intensifying as I fight my inner beast.

Volt meets my gaze, his expression knowing.

I shake my head, telling him not to comment.

Thankfully, he doesn't.

I exchange my jeans and pull on a pair of socks with my boots just as Clove comes undone again on the bed.

Her scream is hoarser now, her body tensing in a way that suggests this orgasm was a bit more painful in nature. Caius notices and slowly stops his sensual torture, kissing a path up her abdomen to her breasts before reaching her lips.

She's still shaking from her orgasm, her body painted in goose bumps and shades of pink. "Give her a bath," I suggest from the doorway. "Help her relax."

Volt has already stopped stroking himself, clearly putting her needs above his—an action I've never seen him do for anyone other than his clan.

That gesture tells me so much about how sure he is that Clove belongs to us. He controls his wolf almost as well as I do, but on this, he's giving in to that urge to claim.

I envy him for that.

But it further proves that I need to be the one with the level head here, the one thinking about our future and what taking Clove may mean for our clan and our pack.

With one final wistful look at the bed, I leave and make the long jog through our underground cave to the surface. There is a series of traps here, all of which I know by heart, making it an easy ascent. But anyone trying to follow us down here would be in for a world of hurt.

Fortunately, no one attempted it earlier.

I reach the surface and continue my jog toward the beach, the moon illuminating my path through the trees. Most of the branches have lost their leaves, leaving only the fir trees to provide sufficient ground cover.

The scent of my pack welcomes me as I enter the beach a few minutes later, the shifters all standing around in human form. I do a brief count, surprised and pleased to find everyone here. Even the three females are present, their partners standing nearby.

Alpha Ebony is a rare female Alpha. She joined Alpha Duncan's clan shortly after her arrival on the island. Most Alpha clans are not intimate with each other, waiting instead for their Omega to join them, similar to what my own clan has done. I've seen Caius and Volt in action several times, but we've never shared. Not until today.

However, Alpha Ebony is intimate with both Alpha Duncan and Alpha Pan, creating a unique dynamic in their clan. One I suspect an Omega will very much enjoy in the future.

Just not Omega Clove.

She's mine.

Assuming she can fall into a true estrus, I remind myself.

Clearing my throat, I focus on the task at hand. "Thank you for joining me tonight," I say, addressing my pack. "I'm sure it comes as a bit of a surprise, considering this morning's events. However, my Omega is no longer in heat."

Omega Clove, not my *Omega*, I correct with a thought. But I can't bring myself to say it out loud, so instead, I continue by saying, "Clove is of mixed heritage. She comes to us from the Nantahala Pack, her mother having been a Nantahala Wolf, likely of mixed origin." As there is no other way to explain Clove's existence.

A few of the wolves bristle at the mention of the Nantahala Pack, but I ignore them. If I can forgive Clove for her origin, so can they.

It's not her fault she was born into a misogynistic pack with a penchant for framing innocents for their own murders.

I clear my throat again, calling order among the wolves who are still reacting to my statement. "She has a Carnage Wolf father whose identity remains a mystery to us at the moment. Her mother was raped, or that's what she said when Clove finally met her wolf the other night."

A few growls meet that statement.

They don't appreciate the insinuation that a Carnage Wolf would rape someone.

My father didn't like hearing that part either but promised he would look into it. He'll need to properly meet Clove to do a scent test. I don't recognize any pack aromas on her, suggesting the culprit may not be someone I know.

However, my father feels it's likely a Black Mountain Alpha, considering the close proximity to the Nantahala Pack. Clove's mother would never have been permitted to wander far, so on that basis, I agree.

That said, it still could have been a rogue.

Regardless, it's primarily my challenge. My father may help a little, but he made it clear that this is my Alpha task. "It may even be the one that will finally bring you home," he said earlier tonight. "Good luck, son."

This is the Carnage Wolf way—to earn our positions, even when born into them by blood.

And I fully intend to earn my Pack Alpha status.

Which includes winning over the wolves before me.

I continue by telling them what I know about Clove, how she was promised to Alpha Crane's son. How he rejected her. And how her sorry excuse for an Alpha claimed her to be feral, blamed her for killing her mother, and sent her to Carnage Island.

My wolves are growling now, furious at her treatment.

Omegas are precious, even half-breeds. However, I suspect they would have welcomed her even if she were a Beta or an Alpha. My pack values tolerance and respect, something they're proving now by giving me their undivided attention.

Even the Alphas I beat earlier are doing their best to show their support.

"I want to host a welcome party for our newest addition," I tell them all. "I know originally we designed a traditional game to play, but Clove is new to our customs and the ways of our pack. As such, I think this would be the best way to introduce her to our pack, unless one of you has a better suggestion."

I pause, waiting to see if anyone has any better ideas.

"I think a welcome party would be adequate," Alpha Duncan says.

"Me, too," Beta Clive adds, his voice soft yet holding a note of confidence in it. He's one of the few Betas on the island, a warrior I've come to respect these last few years.

"Have you claimed her?" Alpha Dirk asks, driving straight to the point. She's an Omega, and he wants to know if she's eligible.

"Not yet," I admit, allowing his interruption and providing a truthful answer. This pack is all about trust. I won't start lying to them now. "Her estrus cycle wasn't complete. I will wait until her next heat to properly claim her."

A statement meant to say, *She's mine, hands off.*

But there's an undercurrent to my words that many of them understand. I'm waiting until I know if she can properly procreate, something I have to do as Pack Alpha.

Which means they may have a chance with her if her heat cycle doesn't live up to expectations.

My wolf huffs in annoyance, disagreeing entirely with my decision. It's not often that we're at odds with one another, so it makes me decidedly uncomfortable. But I ignore the irritation under my skin and focus on my pack.

"I want her," I tell them honestly. "My clan does as well. We will claim her during her estrus." I allow them to hear my confidence in that coming to fruition, because I do believe she's meant to be ours. I just need that final fertility piece to make it a reality.

Which makes me feel like a right arse.

However, I've devoted my life to leadership.

I can't turn my back on it now.

"If anyone wishes to voice a challenge, I'll entertain it," I add, aware of how pack hierarchy works when claiming an Omega. "But I do believe I proved myself worthy this morning."

I look pointedly at Alpha Dirk before meeting the gaze of all those who challenged my clan earlier today. Most of them are fully healed, their wolf genetics having allowed them to regenerate quickly. But a few are in worse shape than others, such as Alpha Kin, who is decorated in a myriad of bruises.

Given that I broke his neck just over twelve hours ago, I'm honestly surprised he's awake. It'll take him another twelve hours or so to fully heal, something his eyes tell me he's not pleased about.

But he brought it on himself.

And I won't be apologizing for it.

I will, however, allow him to rest.

Not all Alphas rule through brawn and dominance alone. Some prefer compassion, a trait my father has taught me goes a long way in terms of leadership. However, there are also times when a demonstration of power is required to remind the pack who is in charge.

Which is something I do now.

Every single Alpha averts his eyes as I stare them down, deferring to me as their leader.

After several minutes of this show of authority, I nod. "Good. If that changes, you know how to reach me. Until then, take the next few days to rest and recuperate. I'll schedule the welcome event for three days from now."

Several shifters nod in agreement, pleased.

I stay to mingle and answer questions for the next thirty minutes. No one challenges me, but they do have a lot of questions about Clove and Alpha Bryson.

They want to know what I plan to do.

"Right now, nothing," I tell them. "But vengeance will be ours."

And soon.

Because tonight has shown me that the pack is almost ready and Clove might be key to finalizing our preparedness.

These wolves need a strong clan to fight behind.

And there's nothing stronger than a clan who has finally found their Omega. It completes our circle, giving the pack a heart to protect.

Clove may be that heart.

She may become *my* heart.

Time will tell.

I bid my wolves a good night after thanking them once more for attending, then make my way back to the den and the female waiting inside.

She's asleep, passed out between Volt and Caius. But they're both awake, their expressions expectant as I enter the room.

I quietly recap the meeting for them, telling them how the wolves agreed to a welcome party—something I mentioned to them earlier today when I realized Clove was no longer in heat.

They were already aware of everything my father had said as well, having vowed to help me with this challenge of discovering Clove's true identity and deciding how to proceed as a clan.

It's still very coincidental that she arrived here as a result of the Nantahala Pack. Alpha Bryson is a conniving dick, one who very well could have set all this up.

But one thing is clear to us all—Clove is innocent.

She has no idea who she is or how this has become her life, but she's embracing it through her wolf.

Our darling little fighter.

I lean over Caius to push some hair away from Clove's head, then bend to kiss her temple. She doesn't stir, Volt and Caius clearly having worn her out. She's clean, though, suggesting they gave her a bath like I requested. And her cheeks have a healthy pink tint to them, confirming she was thoroughly adored as well.

"Did you feed her anything other than cum?" I ask softly, my lips curling at the thought of her pleasing my clan.

"She ate some pasta," Volt confirms from behind her. He has his chest pressed into her back, his purr a soft rumble that seems to be keeping her asleep. Or maybe he's just too content to turn it off. Looking at her, I can understand the desire, as my wolf wants to rumble again, too.

Caius starts to move toward the edge, his arm brushing my chest, as I'm still leaning over him to touch Clove. He's trying to make a spot for me to join them, but I shake my head and straighten back up into a standing position.

"Keep her warm. I have a few more items to clear up in my office. I'll come to bed after." I just wanted to give them an update.

And also check in on Clove.

"You'll have to sleep at the foot of the bed, then," Caius says, cuddling back into her.

I grin. "I'll sleep between her legs and use her thigh as a pillow."

Volt perks up at that idea. "I'll do that. You sleep behind her."

"No, I already called my place," I tell him. "Stay there and keep purring. I'll join you all soon."

It's a promise I keep.

After about an hour of work, I crawl into bed to sleep against Clove's legs.

Except I don't do it in my human form; I instead shift into my wolf and allow my fur to brush against her warm skin.

She doesn't wake.

And I sleep better than I have in years.

CLOVE

I stare at the woman in the mirror, not recognizing her.

The last few days have been a mind-blowing experience, and not just in bed, but outside of it, too. Caius and Volt have seen to my every need—feeding me, bathing me, talking to me about life, and pleasuring me with their mouths.

They've not pushed me to take their knots again.

Just allowed me to explore and familiarize myself with them while teaching me about their pack and how they thrive on this island.

The Elders have no idea what they're really up to here or how many of the wolves on this island are not actually regulated rejectees. They're here training and thriving and using the land as their own.

I'm stunned by the information, but even more shocked that they provided it to me without a single hesitation. Like they already trust me despite barely knowing me.

Perhaps because they've been inside me.

Or because our wolves seem to harbor this age-old connection that surpasses the meaning of time.

Regardless of the reason, I'm thankful. Because I feel accepted here. Like it's where I've always belonged. I'm free to shift at will, free to wander the den as though it's my own, and allowed to use whatever resource I desire.

Yesterday, Caius showed me his laptop and let me browse the internet. Of course, staring in the mirror now, I realize he had a motive.

Because he told me to shop for clothes.

Clothes that I'm currently wearing.

"How did you have them delivered so quickly?" I wonder out loud as he finishes sliding on my socks. He showed me the outfit with one catch—that I allow him to dress me.

Which I did.

He tugs on the hem of my skinny jeans near my ankles, ensuring they're comfortable before pulling on one of my new knee-high boots. They don't have a heel, making them ideal for shifter life.

"I picked them up from the mainland earlier this morning while Volt was giving you breakfast." He glances up at the mirror, meeting my gaze with a knowing look.

My cheeks heat at the reminder of my *breakfast* this morning—which was Volt's cock down my throat. He's girthier than Caius, making him harder to swallow. But he patiently instructed me through it, just like he did the other day with Caius.

Then he returned the favor three times before showering and giving me some real food.

I assumed Caius was with Tieran, but he returned alone with a bunch of bags. *Because he went to the mainland,* I think, frowning as I recall what he just said. "How did you get to the mainland?"

The Reject Islands are supposed to be remote without mainland access. While he explained that life here wasn't at all what the Elders thought, he never mentioned anything about leaving the island.

"We have several speedboats and a yacht," he says. "As well as a residence on the coast, which is where I had your clothes delivered to this morning. It only takes about three hours to do a round trip, something Tieran does regularly. As do I."

I blink at him. "You go onto the mainland regularly?"

"For work," he explains. "We have to fund all this somehow. And the Elders just give us scraps. It's why the docks look like shit—we maintain the facade of being a dystopian world in order to make them think that's how we're living life here."

I glance around the elegant bathroom and peek through the door into the massive bedroom beyond. The mattress is fit for five or six big wolves, the furniture around is all crafted wood, and the technology of this place screams money. "They don't know this exists." It's not a question but a statement.

"Not at all," he says. "Nor do they know about our frequent trips inland." He finishes with my final boot and stands, his fingers running through my hair.

I start to turn, but he grasps my hips to keep me facing the mirror, then grabs a brush.

"We've explained a lot of the jobs on the island, which are all traditional pack roles for the most part. But there's a whole other level to what we do. And that's where the boats come in." He starts running the brush through my hair, the brown strands at odds against my cream-colored sweater.

"Which is why you go to the mainland regularly," I hedge.

"Yes. Tieran's father, Alpha Umber, owns a global finance organization that manages estates for some of the most elite humans in the world. But he does more than just that. Many of our clients are outwardly innocent, but inwardly nefarious. Which is where my role comes in. And Volt's, too."

I ponder that for a moment as he meets my gaze in the mirror. "What do you do?"

"I blackmail them," he tells me without remorse. "Or I make deals they can't refuse. It's all about reading the room and understanding motives. But I've always been skilled with money, something I've learned from my father, who happens to be Alpha Umber's chief financial officer."

"And the Elders have no idea?"

"Oh, they're aware of Alpha Umber's organization and the roles Black Mountain Pack plays in that company. But they're unaware of our involvement from here."

"Because they assume you can't leave the island," I say.

"Yes, and Tieran has been tasked with handling the more unsavory parts of the business, and those items are purposely kept quiet." He gathers my hair over one shoulder, kissing me on the neck. "His father wants our clan to work our way up the ladder, which has proved challenging since being sent here. But we've developed a good system over the last seven years."

"So coming here wasn't part of the plan."

He snorts, setting the brush back on the counter. "Not at all. However, our pack is all about challenges and proving our worth. So we've worked with what we have, aided minimally by Alpha Umber, and have grown from there. For example, the blackmail side of the business is new. As is Volt's role in the organization."

"What's Volt's role?" I wonder aloud as he finally lets me face him.

"Death, sweetheart," Volt replies as he enters the bedroom. His wolf ears must have let him hear our conversation, as he's still about twenty feet away but sauntering toward us in a pair of low-slung jeans and nothing else. "I kill for money."

I gape at him. "What?"

He shrugs. "I like pain. It's my skill." His eyes heat with the words, and I swallow. "Maybe you can come with me on my next assignment."

"I don't think that's a good idea, V," Tieran says, entering the room next.

Definitely wolf hearing, I decide. I couldn't hear them approaching because they seem to make no sound when they walk, the three of them skilled predators who move on silent feet.

"Why not?" Volt asks, pausing to glance at the approaching male. He's dressed similarly in jeans but also has on a pair of boots. "I researched the Senator yesterday. He's a prick who rapes women. I even found a video of him taking one of his barely legal interns last week. Not only will he be an easy kill, but he actually deserves it."

"A-a video?" I repeat, somehow stuck on that more than the rest of his statements. *I kill for money* should probably have been my first concern, but that news doesn't shock me as much. Volt possesses a lethal aura, one that definitely screams *murderous intent*.

"Yeah, I was using the camera in his computer to study his office layout and instead ended up watching his naked ass drill into a crying intern." He shudders. "I didn't actually need the extra detail to want to kill him, as I tend not to ask questions, but I think I'll enjoy making him suffer a little more."

"Hence the reason I don't think Clove should watch," Tieran interjects.

"I'm not shy about who I am, T," Volt tells him. "She

needs to know who she's getting into bed with, so why not show her?"

Tieran studies him for a long beat while I swallow, uncertain of how to feel.

Volt has a point—I want to know more about these men and their clan. My wolf already accepts them and considers them hers, but it would be nice to understand them better.

"Do you kill for fun?" I ask, interrupting the heated silence.

"Yes," Volt says without remorse. "I enjoy it."

"But you always have a reason for it, like the Senator raping women?" I press.

"I enjoy those kills more, but that's not always the case," he replies. "I take jobs to fulfill the lethal urges of my wolf, and I never ask questions. But I almost always learn something about the mark that warrants their death, which is why I usually end up enjoying the kill. On the off chance I don't, I make it quick."

All three men study me, waiting to see how I'll react.

I'm not quite sure how to feel.

Death is a part of life, and mortals tend to experience it far earlier than my kind. Shifters stop aging around thirty years old, and many breeds can live forever, unless taken down by silver.

But he's not talking about killing shifters. He's talking about assassinating humans.

Because he's paid to do it.

That makes whoever hired him the true culprit; Volt's just carrying out the task. Wolves take down prey every day, and while we may be part human, we are more animal than anything else. He's using his skills to make money to support the pack and also slaying whatever violent urges he seems to possess in the process.

I can't exactly fault him for that.

And... "I'm guessing this is where some of your blackmail comes from?" The thought leaves me on a question, one I direct at Caius.

He grins. "Yes, among many other things. Typically, when someone deals in death, they're playing with other darker schemes as well."

"Which you use to extort money from them," I translate.

"Not exactly. We mostly use it to maintain our favor for other business dealings." Caius must read the confusion in my features because he continues speaking. "Say there's a company we want to purchase and it's going to the highest bidder. We may find ourselves as that highest bidder, except it's the blackmail inflating the cost."

"Or we don't pay at all," Volt says. "And it's given to us as a gift for our continued silence."

"That, too," Caius murmurs.

"Why do you inherit companies?" I ask. "What do you do with them?"

"We repurpose them into legal organizations that we funnel money through," Tieran explains. "And we employ people who need it."

"Or keep the employees who were going to lose their jobs," Caius adds. "It's all a numbers game, but we make sure those who need our assistance receive it, all while funding our pack and keeping everyone comfortable."

"But they all have jobs on the island, too," Tieran points out. "And some of them help us run a few of the smaller corporations we've acquired. Nothing major, just business oversight and general management."

"That's in addition to the roles we talked about?" I ask Caius.

He shakes his head. "No, those roles are handled by

select wolves on the island. But there are more who help with external affairs. For example, Alpha Dirk's clan handles telecommunications both with our companies and on the island."

"We have a whole security division as well that reports up through Alpha Duncan's clan here," Tieran adds.

"Duncan's office is wicked." Volt grins. "It's where I go when I want to do recon because he has all the fun toys."

Tieran shakes his head, but his lips are curled in amusement. "You'll meet them all this afternoon, Clove. I'm sure they'll tell you all about what they do."

Volt nods. "And then I'll show you what I do later this week or early next week. The timeline is still being evaluated."

"Her going with us is still up for discussion," Tieran tells him.

"She needs to see who we are, T."

"Yes, but there are safer options than taking her to Virginia for an assassination," Tieran returns.

Volt grunts. "The Senator's house has three guards. He's cocky and an idiot. It's a cakewalk. And I'll have the whole thing under surveillance anyway, so she can watch from the car."

Tieran's jaw ticks. "Which means she could watch safely from here."

He sighs. "Not the same and you know it."

Tieran runs his fingers through his thick blond hair and sighs. "I'll think about it."

Volt doesn't push, just smiles and focuses on me again. "If he says no, I'll show you how I play with knives another way."

Caius and Tieran both glare at him, saying, "No," at the same time.

But I find myself smiling instead of shivering. My wolf

innately trusts Volt, and he's been rather sweet to me since I arrived. Sure, he may be a killer with some psychotic undertones, but I'm not sure I mind.

Actually, I find myself intrigued.

Which is why I say, "I look forward to learning more." Because I do. I want to understand him, to *know* him. Even if it's dangerous. Because my animal says that while he may be deadly to others, he isn't to us.

He isn't to *me*.

Something his eyes seem to display now as his dark irises meet mine with a smile. "I think she's ready to meet the pack," he says, his smile reaching his mouth now. "She's going to slay them."

"No," Tieran replies, causing all of us to look at him. "She's going to *rule* them."

He utters it with confidence.

Something I didn't realize I needed to hear until he said it, because we're not mated yet. He hasn't even touched me since he knotted me during my heat. A part of me had begun to question his interest. Yet he slept in the bed each night in wolf form, and his gestures suggested otherwise.

But all of this is just so new and foreign to me.

So it's easy to let a sliver of doubt creep inside.

However, his words now help wash that way.

As does the kiss he places against my mouth. "They all know I intend to claim you," he says against my ear. "Own it, Clove. They're going to love you."

I shiver, melting into his strength and thanking him for his confidence by brushing my lips against his chin.

"We should go." He pulls away, his smile still in his sapphire eyes. "It's time for the pack to greet you and show you what sets Carnage Wolves apart from the wolves of your past."

CLOVE

The Carnage Wolves are nothing like the savage beasts depicted by Alpha Bryson.

They're intimidating, yes.

But there's an intelligence to them that I admire. They're also polite and respectful. Even the Alphas treat me kindly, gazing upon me with an interest very unlike the wolves back in Nantahala Pack.

These Alphas are curious about me, the person. Not me, the woman. Well, there may be some of that intrigue, but several have remarked on how they're looking forward to me mating Tieran's clan.

It's formal yet laid-back.

And I feel safe with Caius and Volt on either side of me with Tieran at my back. There have been a few times he's possessively placed his hand on my hip or kissed my neck.

Which just makes my wolf preen.

Because Tieran is very clearly the Pack Alpha on this island. His dominance is a blistering heat against my senses that makes me want to kneel at his feet. But he keeps me upright with his soft touches and subtle commentary.

"Alpha Duncan is the security master I told you

about," he says, his mouth against my ear. "These are his clan mates, Alpha Ebony and Alpha Pan."

I nod to them all, a bit surprised to meet an Alpha female among all these Alpha males. I don't need Tieran to tell me that it's rare for a female to be a Carnage Wolf Alpha.

It's still a unique concept for me to grasp that Carnage Wolves have multiple Alphas, not just one single Alpha in charge.

In the Nantahala Pack, we only called Bryson the Alpha. There were other wolves with alpha-like tendencies, but they were never given the designation.

Whereas here on Carnage Island, approximately seventy percent of the wolves are Alphas. The rest are all Betas, and then a handful of rogue wolves.

The rogue wolves don't attend the ceremony, something Tieran mentioned as we wandered to the beach.

While he keeps them in line, they are free to roam the island at will so long as they don't interfere with pack business.

Those rogues are part of the reason the Elders created the Reject Islands—the rogues were the ones who went crazy upon being rejected. And several were sent here to Carnage Island because the Elders felt the Carnage Wolves were among the few who could keep them under control.

Seeing all these Alpha males together, I can understand why.

They're much larger than the Nantahala Wolves. Even Bryson would appear somewhat short compared to Alpha Duncan's clan. Ebony is over six feet tall with long, dark hair braided down her back. Her muscles are lean, but I can sense the power in her brown eyes. She's polite, just like the others, smiling at me in welcome.

"Don't let all the testosterone overwhelm you," she says quietly. "They'll tone it down once you're properly mated."

I shiver. *Properly mated.*

I want that. I want Tieran to claim me. It's an instinctual need driven by my wolf, her desire to be mated by the strongest Alpha a palpable presence in my mind.

But I can feel him holding back for now.

Because of my insufficient heat cycle.

He needs to know that I can properly mate him.

And part of me isn't so sure I can.

However, I push that away for now and continue the introductory tour. I meet several Betas, all of whom are not in a clan. Tieran explains that Betas can join an Alpha's clan when compatible. I'm not sure what drives that connection; however, I suspect it's related to power signatures.

Tieran, Caius, and Volt all exude a similar authority that feels overwhelmingly dominant when together. It's what makes them the strongest clan on the island, the wolves no one truly wants to challenge.

Although, a few do seem to hold Tieran's gaze a beat longer than appropriate.

Including the clan he introduces me to next.

"This is Alpha Dirk," Tieran says, his voice holding a note to it that sends a chill down my spine. "Alpha Dirk, introduce your clan." It's a demand that draws the Alpha's gaze away from my breasts and up to the male behind me.

I swallow as they stand off, the energy between them causing my knees to shake.

Caius takes my hand, giving it a gentle squeeze as Volt clears his throat. He's still shirtless beside me, his tattoos gleaming in the sunlight like battle scars. I've traced a few of them with my tongue, enjoying the unique patterns.

I asked him the other day what they represent, and he

merely replied, "They mean I like pain." Because apparently, he has to use a special ink tainted with silver to make them stay. Otherwise, his wolf heals them. There's another wolf on the island who does them—a Beta named Christian that I met shortly after arriving.

"This is Alpha Kin," Alpha Dirk says, his gravelly voice underlined with a hint of irritation as he gestures to the giant male beside him. He's taller and wider than Tieran, but his aura isn't nearly as dominant.

However, Alpha Dirk exudes power. Not quite as strong as the male behind me, but enough to certainly give him notice. He smells familiar, too. Like a mud puddle that's left behind after a storm. I can't quite place it.

Or maybe that fragrance is coming from the male beside him.

But I've definitely inhaled this fragrance before.

I just can't remember when.

And neither male is familiar at all, at least not in appearance.

Alpha Dirk clears his throat, his gaze landing on Tieran once more. "My clan is not yet complete."

Ah, so that's why Tieran made him do the introductions, I realize. It was a power play to show that Alpha Dirk's clan is inferior since he hasn't found all the compatible wolves for his circle.

Caius told me three is the minimum.

Hence *two* wolves being an incomplete clan.

Caius squeezes my hand again as Tieran kisses my neck, that touch of obvious possession warming me once more. "Alpha Dirk's clan oversees our telecommunications," he reminds me, repeating the detail Caius mentioned before we arrived. "They're our technical experts for phones, as there is no prominent cellular network out here."

"Yes, we use satellite tech," Alpha Dirk adds, some of the gravel in his tone disappearing as he speaks up about his work. "It's how we access the internet as well."

Tieran nods, his chin touching my shoulder. "Their work is impressive. It makes Alpha Dirk and Alpha Kin invaluable to our efforts here."

It's a compliment.

One I watch register in Alpha Dirk's features, his dark eyes lighting up. "Thank you. We take pride in our work."

Alpha Kin doesn't appear as impressed with the praise. He merely nods, his thick neck bulging with the motion.

That scent slithers around me again, making me wonder why I recognize it. Maybe I smelled them when I first arrived? Or were they among the wolves that attacked the other day when I started to go into heat?

I'll have to ask about it later. Tieran hasn't given any indication on who those wolves were, and it wasn't something I thought much about with them surrounding me.

But the way Alpha Kin is eyeing me has me somewhat concerned.

Alpha Dirk, too.

My wolf doesn't like them. She's huffing in annoyance and telling me to snuggle back into Tieran more, to demonstrate her mutual claim.

Fortunately, we don't remain long, the introduction complete, and we're moving again to another clan. This one has five Alphas in it, something Tieran says is rare but can happen. "The largest clan in Black Mountain Pack has seven Alphas and one Omega," he adds.

My eyes widen at that concept.

That's a lot of knots, I nearly say.

But I refrain and meet the final clan of two Alpha males and a Beta female. Their dynamic reminds me a bit of what I saw with Alpha Ebony. There was another Beta female as well, but she appeared to be with a lone Alpha— one Tieran didn't force to introduce his "incomplete" clan.

We're just wrapping up when a boat arrives at the docks off the beach. I wince, worried the rusted old wood won't function properly, but one of the large males exits the boat with ease. He looks at Volt and waggles his auburn brows. "Dinner's here."

Volt grins. "Excellent."

I frown, wondering if they caught a fresh batch of fish.

Then understanding dawns on me when the savory aroma of greasy cheese hits my senses. I nearly moan, the food one of my favorites—something I told Volt the other evening when he asked if I had any preferences for dinner.

I glance at him and find him grinning triumphantly. "She approves," he says, the words for Caius.

"I knew she would. That's why I didn't take the bet," Caius replies.

"What bet?" I ask, frowning again.

"Terms weren't discussed," Caius replies.

"This time," Volt murmurs.

That just makes me frown harder. "'This time,' meaning there's been another bet?"

"They're always making bets," Tieran puts in. "Caius usually wins, which makes Volt try that much harder."

"I won the last one," Volt points out.

"You did," Caius concedes. "I'll win the next dozen or so."

Volt snorts but doesn't disagree. "My prize last time was worth a million losses." He looks at me and winks. "Ready to eat, sweetling?"

I really want to ask what he won, but I'm almost afraid to find out. So I just nod instead, the alluring scent of pizza calling my name.

The boat is apparently full of boxes, all of them protected by warming bags.

Groans of approval rend the air, the wolves all appeased by this development.

It's a bit early for dinner, but the sun is already starting to set since it's winter here and we're much farther north than the Nantahala Pack region.

Tieran pulls me onto a blanket a little way down the beach, something I didn't realize was set up until my ass hits the fabric. Several other shifters have blankets as well, some of them choosing to sit closer to the water than others.

It's cold, yet most of the males are shirtless, their shifter heat keeping them warm despite the wintry temperatures. Tieran, Volt, and Caius are all just in jeans, but they added boots for this afternoon's event.

So I feel a bit overdressed in my sweater, jeans, and boots.

However, feeling Alpha Dirk's eyes on me again, I'm glad to have a fabric shield.

Being naked doesn't usually bother me. I grew up around nudity. But something about his clan unnerves me.

That scent is irritating my senses again.

Tieran joins me on the blanket, sitting behind me and bracketing me with his legs, momentarily distracting me from the other Alpha.

I shiver, the warmth of his touch calling my animal to the surface and causing her fur to brush beneath my skin.

He wraps his arms around me and guides my back to his chest, his lips caressing my ear. "What's wrong?" he asks in a whisper I'm certain no one else can hear, as it's extremely low.

"A familiar scent," I reply, turning so our lips are near

each other. "I'm wondering if it's from the other day…" I trail off, and understanding blossoms in his blue eyes.

"The Alphas who attacked the den," he says.

I nod. "Or maybe even before that?" A vague memory of recognizing a scent before stirs in my mind, but I can't quite place it. The events from that day are fuzzy and clouded by what happened in the den.

"Several of the Alphas from that day are here," Tieran admits. "But they were caught in the rut, something Omegas inspire in unmated Alphas. We all have an instinct to claim and to protect." He nuzzles my cheek. "Which is why I'm struggling to keep my hands off of you."

That makes me grin. "I don't mind."

"Good," he whispers, nipping my ear as I settle once more against his chest. "Because I'm going to hold you like this all night to ensure everyone knows we intend to claim you."

Assuming I go into heat again, I think, swallowing.

It's a constant thought in my head, swimming around and flirting with the doubt hiding in the corner of my mind.

I ignore it, allowing myself to enjoy the moment as Tieran holds me.

Caius and Volt join us with two boxes in their hands.

The pizza has my favorite toppings—pepperoni and sausage—proving Volt more than listened to me the other day. He may kill for a living, but there's a deep and thoughtful soul in there. One I'm going to enjoy exploring.

I want to know what makes him enjoy pain, why he possesses a lethal edge.

Just like I want to know more about Caius and his penchant for blackmail. What made him choose that profession? How is he so skilled at reading people? Is it a natural trait or a learned one?

With Tieran, I want to know more about his visions for leadership, what it means to be an Omega in his clan, and what really happened with Alpha Bryson's daughter. I've not possessed the confidence to ask.

Maybe I will tonight.

Definitely not here.

He picks up a slice and brings it to my lips, then takes his own bite out of the same piece. We share our meal like that, with him feeding me before himself, his purr a low hum against my back.

It's peaceful.

The Carnage Wolves are all relaxed as well, indulging in the pizza on the beach as the moon lifts into the sky. Several end up shifting soon after, frolicking in the waves and running through the frigid water.

The boat also disappears, going to some secret alcove in the island where they keep the proper dock—something Caius tells me about while we lounge in the sand.

This life is far different from the one I left behind.

It's definitely not what I ever considered possible.

More like a dream than a reality.

A dream I hope to never wake up from.

But I fear a nightmare lurks in my future.

One involving my Nantahala Wolf heritage.

A nightmare to consider later, I tell myself, drunk on life. *Just enjoy the dream. Live in the moment. And breathe.*

VOLT

"I want Alpha Dirk and Alpha Kin monitored," Tieran says softly from the foot of the bed.

This has become our nightly routine—Caius and I wear out our little wolf, then Tieran joins us for a chat after she falls asleep.

I know what he's doing.

He's avoiding fucking Clove because he doesn't trust himself not to claim her.

His wolf is riding him hard, something that was absolutely evident during tonight's welcome party. He couldn't keep his hands off Clove, his possessive instincts flaring to life in every conceivable way.

It was entertaining to observe.

Caius exuded a similar need to stake his claim, one driven by the fact that he hasn't knotted her yet. Although, he's not holding back out of fear of claiming her—we both know to wait for Tieran's blessing. No, Caius is just prolonging his gratification, as per usual. He's waiting until he can't deny himself for a moment longer. Then Clove will be in for the ride of her life.

And I fully intend to watch.

Maybe I'll even participate.

Help drive Caius over the edge and make him give up his steadfast control.

Mmm, that'll be fun.

"I don't like the way they watched Clove tonight," Tieran continues, talking about Alpha Dirk and Alpha Kin. "She also recognized their scents, likely from their attack the other day, which unsettled her. I don't want them near her."

Caius nods from beside Clove. He's lounging naked at her front, while I'm pressed up against her back. This seems to be the way we sleep now, which I don't mind at all.

"I'll take care of it," Caius says. "Alpha Duncan has some toys I can play with. But I'll keep it minimal and surface level."

Tieran dips his chin. "I don't want to invade their privacy. I just want to keep an eye on them when Clove's around."

I snort because they'll claim even that is an invasion of their privacy. But I agree heartily with his desire to keep them in line. They've disrespected Tieran one too many times, and Clove is the last straw.

"If they can't learn to heel when appropriate, they forfeit their right to privacy." That's my stance, anyway. I don't give two fucks about their self-decided importance. They've insulted Tieran with their constant disregard. "They broke into our den with the intent of taking our Omega. That alone is an offense that should have them exiled from the island.

"They were lost to the rut," Tieran replies.

I grunt. "As were many others, but they were the two who broke in first. And Dirk's strong enough to be a secondary clan for leadership. He should be able to fight the rut, just like we did." The fact that he couldn't says so much about his intentions. "He acted on the opportunity as a way to best you. His privacy is the least of my concerns."

"He's right," Caius agrees. "They forfeited their right to privacy when they challenged us for Clove. She's not yet claimed. Even if we didn't intend to keep her, it's still our duty to protect her as the lead clan."

I press my nose to the back of her head, loving the way her soft hair tickles my lips. "We are definitely keeping you, sweetling," I murmur.

Tieran says nothing for a long moment. Then finally he concedes with, "Just keep the monitoring light. If they complain, I'll handle it."

"They won't even know I'm there," Caius promises.

"I know." Tieran runs his fingers through his blond hair, then blows out a breath and meets my gaze. "And on a similar topic of surveillance, I agree with taking her with us on your next assignment."

My lips pull up into a grin. "I knew you would eventually come around to my side of things."

"But she'll remain with me in a safe place over a mile away, and we'll watch you through the cameras," he continues, ignoring my commentary. "It gives us an opportunity to show her a bit more about our lives while keeping her safe as well."

"Because I can't do that here without you?" Caius asks, arching a brown brow.

"Of course you can," Tieran replies, sighing. "But my wolf is feeling…"

"Needy?" I offer. "Possessive? *Hungry?*"

Tieran narrows his eyes at me. "All of the above." The confession leaves him on a rumble, his purr momentarily taking over before he can clear his throat.

Caius smiles. "You should just bite her, T." It's a taunt, one I fully approve of.

"Yeah, T. Just bite her."

He glowers at us. "Yeah, fuck both of you."

"If that's what it takes," I offer, shrugging.

He just grunts in response.

I know what's holding him back—his need to extend the Alpha line.

If she can't go into a proper heat, then she can't procreate.

Which means he has two choices: claim her and fuck another Omega to obtain an heir, or search for another eligible Omega.

The problem is that his wolf wants Clove. I can smell it. My wolf wants her, too. As does Caius's. Which makes her ours.

And that presents a conundrum.

One Tieran appears hell-bent on shouldering himself. Yet it's *me* he's worried about. A fact that pisses me the fuck off. He's also probably worried about what it will do to Clove if he has to fuck another Omega to create an heir.

His wolf may not even allow it.

Her wolf will despise him for it.

Our clan will suffer.

And it may all end in death.

Or that's been my experience, anyway. My father took an Omega to create an heir, yet he mated a Beta. Then he expected her—the Beta—to raise me as her own.

Mommy Dearest didn't approve.

She used me as a punching bag instead.

She loathed me.

The feeling was fucking mutual.

I dreamt of killing her so many times. But my father did the honors for me.

And my real mother, the Omega, was happily mated to a clan in another pack—the Black Mountain Pack.

Which is how I ended up on Alpha Umber's doorstep. His Omega wasn't my mother, but she lived in his pack. He took me in as his own and raised me with Tieran, and I maintained a very distant relationship with the female who birthed me.

A fucked-up history of injustice, one that's tainting my clan circle now.

"I'll be fine, T," I tell him, holding his gaze. It's a slight change in the subject of conversation, but it's one he immediately understands. "Clove isn't the bitch who raised me. She's strong. And she's ours."

He swallows, his gaze going to the sleeping Omega on the bed. She hasn't stirred once during our conversation, probably because Caius and I have kept up a steady stream of purring for her. Mine faltered a bit in the last few minutes, but his didn't.

It's enough to keep her comfortable.

To ensure she knows she's protected.

In a den that facilitates sleep.

The only thing missing is a nest—something she hasn't started creating despite the ample sheets and clothes strewn around the room. We even brought her the sheets her wolf slept on in Tieran's room. Nothing.

I brush my fingers through her hair and kiss the back of her head again. "Maybe you should try talking to her about it," I suggest softly, my purr starting up again. "Tell her the concern and see how she reacts."

"No Omega is going to be okay with her Alpha taking another female," Tieran replies, a hint of pain in his voice. "And I would never want to hurt her in that way. Once I make her ours, she'll be it for us."

Which brings about the real issue at hand. "Your wolf won't let you take another Omega."

"No, he won't," he admits. "So I need to make sure she's the right one."

"She is," Caius says, his voice certain. "She just needs a little more time to embrace her Omega wolf."

Tieran studies her, silent once more. Then he stands and shucks off his pants. "We should sleep. I'll make the preparations for her to join us on the mainland later this week. Until then, keep helping her accept her wolf."

My lips quirk up. "Such a hard task."

"So fucking difficult," Caius echoes.

"You have no idea," Tieran mutters, shifting in the next second to curl up against her legs.

"Try having her blow you," I tell him, aware that he can't reply now that he's in wolf form. "It helps take the edge off."

He grunts.

Caius grins. "It's pretty fucking amazing. She's a natural at it."

"Because she's ours," I say.

"Yep," Caius agrees, settling into the pillow and staring at the female between us. "Good night, beautiful."

"Night," I say, smirking since the words were for Clove and not for me. But we're a clan for a reason. We have our shared interests, and while we may not be physical with each other, we're still intimately connected.

And soon, we'll be mentally linked as well.

Via the bond to our Omega.

Our Clove.

Tieran may have reservations about her, but I don't. She's our future. And I'll do everything I can to prove it.

CLOVE

My wolf is agitated.

    I can feel her stirring beneath my skin, her fur rubbing against my nerves and demanding an outlet.

I just can't figure out if the outlet she craves is a shift or a good knotting. Maybe both.

I've dreamt about Caius, Volt, and Tieran every night since going into heat. Each dream is progressively sexier, driving me mad with need.

A need that Caius and Volt have both seen to several mornings this week.

Just without their knots.

Which seems to only make my dreams that much more sensual.

I want them inside me, and not just in my mouth.

My wolf hums in agreement before irritating my skin once more.

"You're in need of a shift," Volt says as he enters the room with a towel wrapped around his hips. We just finished playing in the shower.

Without the knot, I think irritably.

None of them have properly fucked me since my estrus, and that was several days ago. No, wait, a week ago.

My sense of time here is slipping.

It's been a while. That's what matters. And I want more than just a tongue between my legs.

Which makes me sound like a horny brat.

So I keep my mouth shut and just nod at Volt, agreeing with him regarding the shift. "I can feel her pressing against my skin."

"I can taste that need in the air," he says, and I wonder if he means my arousal or my wolf's desire to be released.

Perhaps both.

Volt is all about word play, something I'm very much enjoying about him.

"How about we go for a run outside?" he suggests. "It'll be a good way to burn off some energy before we leave."

Right. Today's the day we venture off the island, I remind myself. Volt told me the other morning that Tieran agreed to let me go with them, something that surprised me. I was both nervous and excited about it, a joint sentiment that hasn't changed.

"Come on, I'll show you how to navigate the corridor," he says, leading the way with that towel still wrapped around his waist. I have one as well that I keep on, padding barefoot behind him.

"Um, what if I can't?" I ask, voicing a concern I've had since initially shifting back into human form. "Or what if she won't let me shift back again?"

"Then I'll growl," he answers, adding a slight rumble to his words. "Tieran's not the only one who can tame your animal, sweetheart."

I swallow, because yeah, that sounded like a threat and a promise all wrapped up in a pretty Volt-sized bow.

Making him a present I want to unwrap.

With my teeth.

Just to see if he fulfills the vow in those words.

Yes, I have definitely lost my mind to this need to be knotted, I decide, trying to keep pace with him. But it's really not my fault; it's theirs. They're the ones who introduced me to the pleasure of their knots.

My thighs clench at the memory of it.

The way they dominated me.

The sensation of fullness.

The spiral of delirious sensation.

"Do you want to shift or fuck?" Volt asks, pulling me from my thoughts as he grabs me and pushes me up against the wall. I've been mindlessly following him down the corridor. We're outside the door now in the nature tunnel that leads us up from this underground cavern.

I blink at him, noting his palm around my throat. His opposite hand has a death grip on my hip as he slides his thigh between my legs. "Both," I tell him.

"I didn't lick you thoroughly enough in the shower?"

My lower belly spasms with a reminder of the two orgasms he gifted me in the last hour. "I enjoyed that."

He smiles. "I know you did. But you're saying you want more, hmm?"

I nod, swallowing. "Yes."

"How about a deal?" he suggests, his voice lowering as he more fully aligns his body with mine. His thick, muscular thigh presses into my core, eliciting a low whine from my throat. Because I'm already wet for him. I'm *always* wet around these males. It's something I don't know how to control and a consequence of my Omega genetics. Well, according to Caius, it's a *benefit*, not a consequence. But it makes me uncomfortable, especially when they growl.

Like Volt is doing now.

It's a hungry sound coming from his wolf, one my animal responds to with a whimper of need.

He brushes his lips against mine, the promise in that touch one that makes me melt. But he pulls back to meet my gaze. "Go on a run with me in wolf form for thirty minutes, then shift back, and I'll make you come until it's time to leave."

I shiver, his obsidian gaze glittering with dark intent. "And if I can't shift back?" I breathe.

"Then I'll tame your wolf with my growl," he says. "And afterward, I'll show you why Caius and Tieran don't want me to play with knives around you."

My stomach clenches at the dangerous undertones of that statement.

It's a part of him I shouldn't want to meet.

Yet my wolf is eager to take him up on the offer. She wants to indulge in our mate's darker inclinations, drive him over the edge, and demand he knot us into oblivion.

Over and over again.

With teeth and claws and savage bites.

"Okay," I whisper, liking this challenge.

He presses his lips to mine again, sealing our deal with a kiss that's underlined in hazardous need. I moan, seeking his tongue, but he releases me in the next moment and takes my towel with him. "Shift," he demands.

It's not a growled command, which means my animal is waiting for me to pull her out rather than being forced out by his Alpha authority.

I swallow and focus on my wolf, inviting her out to play.

She responds almost immediately, taking me to the ground on a sharp gasp, the pain of the transformation stealing the air from my lungs.

But it's not nearly as bad as when Canton initially drove my shift.

This is me being in charge, me letting my animal free, me choosing to embrace my wolf rather than being coerced into accepting her.

Fur sprouts along my arms and legs, my bones morphing with the magic of my soul. I sigh, letting it take over, and in what feels like seconds, I'm a wolf. I shake out my coat, feeling miraculously in charge.

My animalistic instincts are still there, her pull on my psyche strong and demanding, but I'm one with my animal.

I'm *free*.

Volt grins down at me, his gaze full of approval. "Beautifully done, sweetheart." He tosses his towel to the ground beside mine, giving me an unhindered view of his arousal. It's pulsating with need, his knot a beacon I long to stroke with my tongue.

But I maintain the urge, not wanting to indulge in that while in wolf form.

He seems almost disappointed, like he expected me to try it, but the expression is gone in the next second as he begins to shift into his massive wolf form.

I'm bewitched by his presence, the Alpha in him dwarfing my Omega wolf by at least a hundred pounds.

He's *huge*.

And he's magnificent.

All white fur and ebony irises, with perked ears and a snout that could easily take down prey twice his size.

He nips at my nose, the gesture playful. Then he bounds off down the tunnel, his sharp yip a command to follow.

My wolf takes off after him, elated by the chase and longing to show off her speed.

I'm surprised by how agile I feel on four feet now, my first shift having been awkward and clumsy. But I feel powerful now. *Right*.

I chase him without stumbling, avoiding the traps lying in wait for those who don't belong here. He points to them with his nose, warning me before leaping in a new direction to avoid another one.

Caius explained that these are here to protect the den, ensuring only the clan knows how to descend into the heart of the cave.

It's their most cherished home on this island, but it's also stocked with items and enough beds to house the pack should an emergency situation arise.

It's unique and beautiful and rather fun.

I dance along in Volt's wake, following his tail like a moving stick.

My wolf is panting in excitement, her spirit right alongside mine as we run together as one.

The outside air is a welcome chill as we burst free of the cave. Then Volt takes off up the hill on a jog that has me itching to keep up. There are no traps out here, just solid earth and a terrain dusted in a fresh sheet of snow.

I roll in it, thrilled by the frigid texture, then chase him down with a happy pant parting my jaws.

This is what being a shifter is all about, the freedom and excitement of nature. Embracing our wolfish souls and flourishing.

My heart is soaring, my spirit feeling full of vivacious energy and life.

I want to run forever.

Volt must suspect that because he takes me on a full tour of the island, darting past other shifters and showing me their homes. Most of them live in log homes similar to the one I stayed in on the first two nights. Others have dug out caves, creating their own dens.

He shows me the real docks and all the speedboats tucked into the hidden cove—it's really just disguised by leaves and a curling stream that heads inland. It's barely big enough for the yacht, which I suspect they built with specific sizing in mind to be able to push it up this stream.

After exploring the docks, he takes me to another area of the island where a few more buildings stand. One is a library. Another is an internet cafe of sorts. And the third appears to be a little coffee shop. All items I did not expect on this island, but they're hidden by lush pine trees, making them not visible off the island.

So I'm guessing the Elders don't know this exists at all.

Just like the abundance of power, which is sourced from the middle of the island—something else Volt shows me—and other advanced features.

It's a whirlwind tour that leaves me breathless.

A howl pierces the air, causing Volt to pause for a moment. He howls back, then leads me back to the docks rather than to the den.

I don't understand until I find Caius and Tieran waiting for us with bags and a basket of what smells like fresh food.

Oh.

We ran all day.

It went by so quickly that I didn't even notice the sun beginning to set in the sky.

Volt shifts back into his human form, his expression filled with mischief as he looks at Tieran. "Clove's wolf needed a run."

"I see that," Tieran says, his blue eyes meeting mine with a warm smile before focusing once more on Volt.

"But we should go. I don't particularly enjoy navigating the water at night."

My heart stutters a little. We spent all day running, which means Volt can't live up to his part of the deal.

I'm mildly disappointed.

But also elated that we ran all day.

So I'm conflicted on how I feel about that.

Volt's dark eyes find mine as he runs his fingers through his dark hair, making his tattooed arms bulge alluringly. "We'll play on the yacht instead," he tells me. "Assuming you can shift back."

Oh, my wolf approves of this challenge. As do I.

He folds his arms, giving me his full attention.

Caius and Tieran both stare at me intently, too.

I swallow, suddenly nervous. *Do they think I'll fail?* I don't scent any concern on them, just their usual scents of peppermint, pine, and coppery ash.

A delicious blend that makes me sigh.

I want to roll in their scents and bathe in their Alpha essence.

"Shift, Clove," Volt dares, his gaze glittering with wicked promise.

I take a deep breath, intimidated by the process of shifting.

Because the last several times I tried, my wolf refused to let me go.

However, this time she urges me on.

No, she does more than that. She *guides* me through it, helping me return to my human form. It doesn't hurt. It… it feels natural. And completely different from before when I felt blocked beneath another being's power.

Because Tieran only encouraged my shift the other day. He didn't maintain his hold. He literally set me free.

The way an Alpha should.

The way a mate should.

He didn't lord his power over me. He let me be the shifter I'm supposed to be.

Tears prickle my eyes as I complete my transformation and stand on my own. *I did it. I shifted.*

But the males around me appear expectant, not proud. They're still watching me with that subtle hint of intrigue.

When nothing happens, Tieran merely nods and says, "Well done, Clove."

Somehow that feels lacking in comparison to the triumph vibrating through my soul. Even Volt appears to be less than impressed as he says, "That was perfect, sweetling."

"A beautiful display," Caius echoes.

Their words are what I want to hear.

But something is missing.

Joy, I think. *Joy and… and…* I can't put my finger on it.

All I feel is a hint of disappointment, but I'm not sure if it's coming from them or from me.

Until I realize the source of it. The last time I shifted, I went into heat.

Were they waiting for that to happen now? Hoping that I would fall into a full estrus? To make me truly eligible as their mate?

I heard them talking the other night, their words chasing me into my dreams. Tieran needs an heir. Which means he needs an Omega who can procreate.

That's why he hasn't claimed me yet. It's also probably why he won't touch me. I'm not worthy enough in my current state, something that makes me bitter and annoyed.

I want to be good enough for them. I want these males to claim me, to knot me, to make me theirs.

Because my wolf has already decided that they belong to her.

But what if I never go into a proper heat cycle? Will they reject me? Find a new Omega for their clan?

Just the thought of it almost destroys me.

I've already been rejected once.

I'm not sure I'll survive it a second time, not when my spirit tells me these males are meant to be mine.

"Clove?" Tieran prompts, a frown creasing his forehead. "Are you all right?"

Am I all right? I almost laugh. But instead, I hear myself saying, "I'm fine." It's a lie that tastes wrong on my tongue. "I enjoyed my tour," I add, trying to focus on the positives.

Live in the moment, I tell myself. *Don't dwell on things you can't control.*

The latter is a phrase my mom used to say. She always told me to indulge in the pleasant part of life because I may never know when I'll need those memories to help make it through a potentially negative experience.

Looking back on it now, I can't help but wonder if she was preparing me for life as Canton's mate. She taught me to pick my battles, to hold on to my happy moments, and to know when to fight.

It seems she knew a lot more about my future than she ever let on.

Which makes sense, given my Carnage Wolf heritage.

"Hmm," Tieran hums, a hint of something in his tone.

He glances at Volt, who responds with an arched brow. Something passes between them that ends in a nod from Tieran.

"Let's get moving," he says. "Clove, say goodbye to Caius." He doesn't look at me while he says it, instead already turning toward the dock with several bags clutched in his hands.

Caius whistles low, looking at Volt. "Well, this'll be a fun trip."

"Indeed," Volt replies, taking the basket and bag from him. "Help her get on board, will you? I need to have a word with the captain."

I frown after him, confused by the sudden dismissal.

"Tieran isn't a fan of lies," Caius tells me conversationally. "None of us are."

I blink. "What?"

"My suggestion is to tell them the truth," he continues as though I didn't speak. "It'll lessen the punishment." He wraps his palm around the back of my neck and pulls me to him in the next breath, his lips sealing over mine before I can speak. "Try to be a good girl, Clove. They won't go too hard on you. Volt may even make sure you enjoy it."

I'm so confused. They're mad that I lied? About what? Being fine? They would prefer I complain about something they already know?

I shifted.

And I didn't go into heat.

End of story.

What more can I say? What can I change? Absolutely nothing. So I am *fine*. I'm here. I'm safe. I'm alive. And they are welcoming me to the pack as though I'm one of their own.

When I'm very clearly not.

I'm a half-breed.

But I'm not dwelling on that, right?

Right.

Or do they think I lied about something else?

"Caius," I start, hoping he'll give me more information.

But he merely kisses me and starts walking me

backward down the dock. By the time we reach the onboarding ramp, I'm panting.

"Mmm, yes, your slick will help," he whispers. "Just kneel and take it. And be *honest*." He nips my lower lip with the word and proceeds to guide me up the gangway to the main deck of the yacht.

Where he presses me up against a wall, cutting off my view of the luxury vessel.

His tongue steals my reply again, his skilled mouth kissing me senseless until I'm a panting mess on the ship.

"I'll miss you, gorgeous," he says softly. "But I mean it, Clove. Be a good girl. Kneel and beg. You'll be *fine*." He winks and escapes down the ramp while I gape after him.

"It's not nice to lie, C," Volt calls after him.

"But that's the moral of the punishment, isn't it?" he returns. "Try not to make her bleed."

"No promises," Volt replies as he pulls up the ramp.

He's put on a pair of jeans.

I have nothing. Just my skin.

And I suddenly find myself *very* naked.

"Follow me, Clove," he demands, leading the way as the engines start to rumble all around us. "The captain would like a word."

TIERAN

Something is bothering Clove. It started shortly after her shift, or perhaps was deepened by her shift, and led to her telling me she was fine when that clearly wasn't the case.

I don't appreciate lies.

I appreciate truths.

Details are not required. I won't push her to talk to me. But I do need her to tell me when something is wrong, even if she doesn't elaborate.

Honesty is imperative in a clan.

As Alphas, we'll push her boundaries and reach limits she may not be comfortable exploring, and if she doesn't voice her concerns, we may not know we've gone too far until it's too late.

And that's unacceptable.

Tonight's offense is obviously mild, and her punishment won't be harsh. However, I intend to use her little lie as a teaching moment.

Because we can't afford larger lies in the future.

"Are you all right to helm the yacht on your own?" I ask Beta Lock and Alpha Mackin. They are two of the wolves we typically take with us when sailing to the mainland.

Beta Lock is an expert yachtsman with a nautical engineering background, and Alpha Mackin is an enforcer in training. He's a lone wolf without a clan because he prefers his solitude. Which is likely why he didn't attack us during Clove's heat last week.

"Yep," Beta Lock says, taking control of the steering.

I often use the time at sea to relax and take a break from work, which means I usually captain the yacht for fun. But tonight I have an Omega who requires my guidance.

So I nod my thanks and exit the bridge to head down to the cabin below.

There are five rooms built to sleep up to ten passengers. It's not a large yacht, but it's sizable enough to help transport several wolves at once.

It's not what we would use for an island evacuation—we have speedboats for that purpose. Just in case.

The yacht is more about comfort and style.

It also adds to our overall grandeur, which is important for our public image—something our clients appreciate. After all, I am the expected heir to my father's global enterprise.

And humans love stalking the rich and famous.

However, my current status with the Elders forces me to maintain a low profile. Hence, we use gimmicks—such as the yacht—to maintain a presence without being seen.

Volt and Clove are waiting for me in the largest cabin, which happens to be the one I typically sleep in when we do an overnight trip somewhere.

"I brought the cargo to the room, just like you requested, Captain," Volt announces, making me roll my eyes.

Yes, I'm technically the yacht captain, but I don't use the title. It's pompous and ridiculous, something Volt definitely knows. Hence the reason he loves using it.

"Can I at least have a shirt?" Clove demands, taking in my boots, jeans, and navy sweater before looking pointedly at Volt's pants.

I consider her for a moment before glancing at Volt. "Do liars deserve clothes, V?"

"No, T. I don't think they do," he drawls, smiling as he takes in her hardening nipples.

She blushes, the color going all the way to her breasts. But it's not a flush of embarrassment. It's one founded in a fiery energy that has my wolf standing up and taking notice.

"I didn't lie. I'm fine and I meant it," she snaps.

"You don't sound *fine*," I point out, irritated by her continued lie. "Something's bothering you. I can smell it, Clove. Your distress disturbs my wolf. And lying about it pisses me off."

"Maybe I'm distressed because I'm now trapped on a yacht with two angry Alphas who apparently want to punish me for truthfully saying I'm fine," she bites back.

"I'm talking about your distress after you shifted, not the furious energy coming off you right now," I clarify as I shut the door and lock it. "I'm talking about you clearly lying to me when I asked if you were all right. And now I'm going to talk about why this is a problem and what we're going to do abo—"

"It wasn't a lie," she interrupts, speaking through gritted teeth. "I am fine. I just had a few unwanted thoughts. But they don't matter. I'm safe. I'm protected. *I'm fine.*"

I narrow my gaze.

"And I want clothes," she adds. "I didn't do anything

wrong. I even won Volt's challenges. But now I'm not in the mood for my reward because you both are being Alpha assholes."

I arch a brow at Volt. "Reward?"

"I said I would pleasure her until it was time to go, but only if she shifted without my help and went on a run with me."

"And then we ran all day," she mutters.

"Because you needed the run, sweetheart."

"Yes," she agrees. "Since I clearly won't be getting the other thing I need."

I frown, glancing at Volt and then at her.

"What other thing?" I ask.

She huffs and starts pulling the blanket off the bed. "Since I can't have clothes, I'll—"

Clove shrieks as Volt lifts her up off her feet and tosses her into the center of the bed. He's on her in the next second, capturing her hands over her head and pinning her to the mattress with his thighs.

"What other thing?" I repeat.

But she mutinously snaps her jaw closed, her teeth clenching so hard I can hear it.

"I see," I murmur. "Well, while you're being silent, I'll explain why lying isn't acceptable in our clan. You're an Omega. That makes you inherently weaker than us."

Her cheeks darken with fury, her brown eyes glowing with the need to rebuke my statement.

"It's a fact, Clove. We are bigger and stronger. And while you may harbor some alpha-like traits, they are not of the physical variety."

"She was pretty quick on her paws today," Volt offers, causing some of her ire to bleed out of her expression. "Definitely nimble and agile."

"Fantastic traits," I admit, "but they don't detract from

the reality that she's an Omega." I walk up to the bed to stare down at her, but she's too busy avoiding my gaze and biting her tongue to look at me. "Can you move, Clove? Can you push Volt off of you?"

He wiggles in response to my words, daring her to try.

She doesn't.

"You can't, can you? Because we are much stronger than you physically." I infuse a hint of dominance into my tone, making her shiver. "You're helpless to us. If we want to fuck you, we will. If we want to kill you, we can. And if we want to hurt you, there's nothing you can do to stop us." I grab her chin and force her gaze to meet mine. "Except for one thing."

She swallows, her eyes filling with furious tears. She hates being put in this position. But that's the point. *This* is what I need her to understand.

"You have the power here, Clove," I tell her. "You may be physically weaker, but we are slaves to your desires. A single command will release you. A *truth*. That's all you need, and Volt will do exactly what you tell him to do."

Volt may be a little unhinged and crave violence, but he's so smitten with Clove that all he needs is to hear the words and he'll do whatever she asks.

"That's why your words matter." I tighten my grip on her chin, demanding that she hear me. "Your *truth* is vital to the success of our clan. You don't have to tell us exactly what you're feeling, but admitting that you're not okay is imperative to how we function as a unit. Otherwise, we risk crossing a boundary that may cause irreparable damage."

Volt gathers her hands in one of his, pulling out a blade with another to set it against her throat. "Trust is crucial, sweetling. Without it, you could die."

A far more crass approach, one that is particularly dangerous, considering the yacht is gaining speed.

But I choose to trust Volt's steady hand.

And the startled glimmer in her gaze tells me the point is finally registering. "Tell him to put the knife away, Clove." I don't phrase it as a demand, instead offering it as a suggestion as I release her chin.

She slowly looks at Volt, her throat working beneath the metal edge.

He stares down at her, waiting.

"I asked for clothes and you denied me," she says. "Yet you're telling me my words matter. Well, so do your actions."

"Actions," I repeat. "Such as allowing you to roam our den as an unknown wolf. Feeding you without requesting anything in return. Giving you a safe place to rest. Ensuring none of the other Alphas attacked you when you went into heat. You mean actions like those?"

She doesn't reply.

"True words, Clove," I press. "Requests that actually mean something. Those are what matter. And we both know your request for clothes wasn't because you actually desired them."

"So I should just trust you to know my desires, then," she says bitterly. "To know whether I really mean something or not."

"That's the heart of our clan," I reiterate. "It's being open and honest with each other so we can trust our instincts. We could so easily hurt you, Clove. That's what we want to avoid. And to do that, we need you to be honest with us."

"Saying you're fine when you're clearly not isn't acceptable," Volt adds, his tone holding a darkness to it that makes Clove's eyes widen a little.

I nod. "You just shifted for the first time on your own,

and you were openly distressed. Telling us you were fine was a blatant lie."

"Think about the consequences of that," Volt tells her. "We just watched you shift, which was hot as fuck and one hell of a turn-on. What if I fucked you after that? You said you were fine. But maybe you were actually hurt. I could have made that so much worse."

"Except you haven't fucked me since I was in heat, so that scenario is a moot point because none of you want to knot me again," she grumbles. "At least not until I go into a proper estrus."

Silence falls on the heels of that pronouncement, followed by Clove's eyes rounding at what she just said.

"So that's the other thing you need," Volt muses after a beat, glancing at me before focusing on the blade at her throat. "Is that why you're all bent out of shape? Because you're craving our knots?"

I can see the denial forming on her lips.

Volt sees it, too.

So he presses the blade a little harder against her throat. "Think about what we've been trying to tell you before you answer that, sweetheart." He's not cutting her, just reinforcing his position.

It's not my favorite method.

But we're a clan.

A team.

And therefore, I'll let him play his role while I engage in my own.

I carefully join them on the bed, lying alongside Clove and tracing her jaw with my fingertip. "Are you upset with me, little one?" I give her an easier question to answer as I gently coax her gaze to mine.

Volt lets up on the knife a little, making sure the movement of her chin doesn't cause a superficial wound.

"Yes," she whispers. "I don't like this at all."

"Which part?"

"Being held down with a knife at my throat. Being chastised like I'm a child," she says, swallowing. "I said I was fine because I am fine. I'm… I'm disappointed that I'm not the Omega you need. But I'm healthy and safe, which makes me fine."

I frown. "Healthy and safe, yes. But emotions matter, Clove. If something is upsetting you, it's okay to admit that you're not all right."

"To what point?" she asks. "So I can complain about something none of us can change? It seems like a waste of time."

"It's not a waste of time at all. It's important to know how you're feeling so we don't make something worse." I slide my palm to her cheek, cupping it. "You're upset that we haven't knotted you, and now you're trapped beneath Volt with his knife at your throat. I think we can all agree that makes this much worse."

"Depends on if she enjoys knife play," Volt says.

I ignore him, my focus on Clove. "I can only imagine why you were taught to suppress your emotions, but that's not how Carnage Wolves work. We're shifters. We're passionate. We discuss our emotions freely. And most importantly, we trust each other to help us heal."

Which is exactly what I'll do for her now.

If she'll allow it.

"I want to knot you, Clove," I tell her. "Fuck, it's all I can think about. I've refrained because of my wolf. He's…" I trail off, searching for the right term. "He's *voracious*. I'm not sure what he'll do when I'm inside you again."

"And I've refrained because I'm enjoying your mouth." Volt lifts the blade to trace her bottom lip. "I've also been giving you time to understand our preferences and to learn your limits, something I can't do when you lie."

He removes the knife, sliding it back into the sheath built into his jeans before releasing her hands. Volt rolls to her side, trapping her between us and allowing me to take the lead.

I glide my fingers down to her throat, tracing the pink line left by Volt's dagger. He didn't break the skin, just marked it enough to leave a subtle claim behind.

"It's okay to be distressed," I tell her softly. "I think we are all a little on edge right now. But it's how we come together that matters."

"I just don't want to dwell on it," she whispers. "I want to enjoy the moment for however long it lasts."

My lips curl down, not liking the way she said that. "This isn't temporary, Clove."

"It will be if I can't give you an heir," she replies, making me wince.

That's not something I've admitted directly to her, which means she overheard one of us discussing it.

Perhaps she isn't as deep a sleeper as we thought.

"See?" She gives me a sad smile. "It ruins the moment, which is exactly what I wanted to avoid."

All my frustration with her little lie disappears in the face of the truth. She hid her distress from us because she didn't want to taint the experience. It's an honorable notion, but still a flawed one.

Because this is something we all need to discuss, not hide from.

"It's true that I need an heir," I say, clearing my throat. "And it's something we should discuss more."

Volt's midnight gaze meets mine, approval radiating in his depths. "Let's discuss it while we eat," he suggests.

"Caius packed a meal for us in the baskets since Clove and I went all day without food."

Her stomach rumbles in response, making my lips twitch. "A sound idea," I reply, reaching out to tuck a strand of her hair behind her ear.

There's a glimmer of disappointment still lurking in her features, confirming she's still sour with me.

But I'll make it better.

After we eat.

CLOVE

Volt gave me a shirt.

Then he fisted my hair and tilted my head back to examine my neck, his gaze intent as he bent to kiss the mark he'd left on my throat.

My skin still tingles now with the memory of the pleasure chasing away the pain.

A logical part of me is aware that I should be pissed at him for pulling a knife on me, but my wolf is too intrigued to allow that logical part to gain purchase.

Not once did I feel threatened beneath him. The tension in his body told me he was very much in control.

And the hardness pressed up against my core told me he was also very aroused by the position.

The whole display of power somehow kept me grounded. It made me feel safe despite the lethal blade against my skin.

He didn't use silver on me, just steel.

Maybe I would have felt more fear had it been the latter.

Regardless, I'm fascinated by the way my body responded to his. There was no fear, only mild interest.

And a hell of a lot of anger over the punishment they gave me for "lying."

However, I understand the reason behind their reaction —they value honesty. And saying I was fine qualified as a lie because, emotionally, I'm not fine. I'm scared that I won't go into heat the way they need me to.

They've introduced me to a world I never knew existed.

It would be just my luck for my Nantahala heritage to prevent me from truly embracing this new existence.

Volt brings a fork to my lips, telling me to open.

I comply, allowing him to feed me.

I'm not sure if he's apologizing for his knife or demonstrating the benefits of healing pain with pleasure. Likely the latter.

There's a heat to his gaze that's been there since I shifted back into human form. It intensified when he placed his weapon at my throat. And it's simmering now, like he can't wait for whatever he has planned for dessert.

Tieran is thoughtful and quiet beside him, his focus on our meal. He hasn't spoken much since agreeing with Volt that we should eat.

We're all sitting on the bed, but there are only two plates.

Tieran isn't eating.

Neither is Volt since he's too busy feeding me. Although, he sneaks in a few bites here and there.

These males confuse me. They were angry before, doing their best to punish me for being dishonest. But the moment I explained my view, Tieran softened with understanding.

It seems we all have a lot to learn about each other.

Which isn't surprising, considering the short time we've spent together. However, my wolf feels as though she's known them for years.

Tieran gently strokes my ankle, drawing my attention to him as Volt brings another piece of fruit to my mouth. The whole plate is littered with grapes, berries, and cheese. There's a smattering of some sort of seafood dip beside it that Volt uses to decorate crackers before bringing them to my lips.

It's delicious.

But my stomach churns with the residual effects of Volt's touch, the way his body pinned me to the bed while Tieran moved my chin.

Anger hums in my veins, emboldened by *need*.

It's an intoxicating combination of sensations, one that leaves me a little breathless as Volt gives me a piece of cheese.

They showed me a dominant side of them tonight that left me craving *more*.

I want their brand of punishment.

I want to play with Volt's knife.

It makes me question my sanity. These are the types of things I should fight, not accept. But knowing their reasoning for being upset somehow dampens my ability to feel fury.

Because deep down, I know they'll never hurt me.

They'll be harsh when they need to be, but never to the point of true damage. Just a teasing ache that they'll quickly soothe with their touch.

I swallow again, blindly accepting whatever Volt puts in my mouth.

I trust him.

That's the key lesson I learned today—I don't fear him at all.

And I want them to trust me, which means being open and discussing my feelings. I'm not sure I can always do that. But for them, I'll try.

"You need an heir," I prompt, looking at Tieran. "And if I can't go into a proper Omega heat, then I can't provide that for you."

There. I said it. The real issue threatening my future—the potential for me to be an incompatible host for his future child.

He swallows and nods. "Yes." He takes a cracker this time, covers it in more of that seafood spread, and brings it to my mouth before Volt can feed me another berry.

Volt doesn't seem to mind. He just pops the strawberry into his own mouth and chews, the cords along his muscular neck flexing with him. He has a few tattoos decorating his throat, and the pattern bleeds into his chest. However, his torso is mostly bare below his pecs, leaving the skin along his abdomen untouched. I idly wonder if he intends to fill that space with more designs someday.

"Alphas can only procreate with an Omega while she's in heat. It's why Alphas fall into the rut—they feel an intense desire to spread their seed and sate the Omega's lust. Only the strongest of our kind can fight the impulse," Tieran says, repeating some of what I've already learned from Caius.

"However," he continues, "that pull dissipates when an Omega is mated. It's a subtle change in scent that allows us to ignore the desire. Unless the Alphas are part of her clan, in which case, they're slaves to the rut."

"So we can't properly mate if I'm unable to experience a full estrus," I say, reiterating what I already know.

"No," he replies, surprising me. "My wolf is drawn to yours. If I bite you, we'll be mated. We just may never be able to procreate."

"Which is a problem because Tieran is the future Pack Alpha and he needs his line to continue," Volt says, placing another piece of cheese on my tongue. "But it's a moot point because you're going to go into heat again."

He speaks with a confidence I don't feel.

And the glimmer in Tieran's gaze tells me he doesn't feel that confidence, either.

I chew and finish swallowing before saying, "What happens if we mate and can't procreate?"

"I either abdicate or seek another Omega for the task," he says, his voice gruff as he glances at Volt. "And the latter isn't going to happen."

Volt narrows his gaze back at him, the two of them engaged in some sort of secret discussion between their eyes.

I clear my throat. "Is the reason it won't happen because you worry about how it'll impact the clan?" I hedge, wanting them to let me in on their silent disagreement.

"It'll destroy our clan," he says, making Volt grunt.

"You're not my father, T."

"Which is precisely why I won't take another Omega when our clan already has one," Tieran bites back.

My brow furrows. "If this is about me, then you have to know I would be okay with you fulfilling your duty elsewhere. I mean, most Nantahala males have a harem. My own father, well, not my real father…" I trail off and shake my head. "My point is, it's a concept I'm not entirely opposed to."

Both males gape at me.

"You would be okay sharing us with another female?" Tieran asks.

"I would accept that it's a required part of your nature," I reply, even as my wolf growls in opposition in my head. She doesn't understand male needs the way I do.

I grew up around men who needed a harem to satisfy their animal lust. "I told Caius this the other day, too."

"That you would accept us fucking other Omegas when you're *our* female?" Tieran presses, his jaw ticking with the words. Some of his anger from earlier is beginning to return to both his expression and his tone.

I clear my throat. "It's pretty common in the Nantahala Pack. The male urges are stronger. They require more… *satisfaction.*" It comes out a little less confident than before because both males are glaring at me now, their expressions suggesting they want to punish me again.

Which, of course, has my wolf doing flips of excitement inside me.

"How many orgasms have I given you today?' Volt demands, his change in subject making me blink.

"Uh…" I'm not able to respond, his fierce glower stealing the breath from my lungs.

"Two," he says. "And yesterday, I gave you three while Caius gave you two. So five total. And the day before that was six between the two of us." He sets the plates on the nightstand while he speaks, then pins me with a look. "How unsatisfied are you right now, Clove? How many orgasms could I give you before you would finally feel sated?"

I'm entirely bewildered by this abrupt subject change. I don't understand it. And I don't know how to answer him.

Which makes him growl.

Only it's not an angry growl. It's a different kind of vibration, one I feel stroking me right between the legs. "Show me your pussy," he demands.

I gape at him. "What?"

"You heard him," Tieran says, and his tone is just as

lethal as Volt's. "Spread your fucking legs so we can see you."

Volt growls again, causing my stomach to twist with an intensity I feel all the way down to my toes. "*Now*, Clove."

These males are going to kill me with their whiplash. "I don't understand what's happening."

"I'm about to make a fucking point," Volt says, his palm curling around my foot. I have my legs stretched out and crossed at the ankles. But in the next moment, I'm being spread open by Volt tugging one ankle toward him and Tieran grabbing the other.

I yelp, the cool air an unwelcome caress against my slick inner thighs.

But I'm too enthralled by this change in behavior and conversation to issue a complaint.

Especially not with the hungry way Volt studies my throbbing core. He growls again, stirring a moan from inside me as my interior muscles clench.

He's making me so wet.

So *hot*.

So damn aroused.

"Volt," I whisper as he unleashes another vibration, the sensations blistering inside to elicit a fresh coating of dampness between my thighs. I don't understand what he's doing or how he's doing it, but I suddenly *need* him to fuck me. To fill me. To *knot* me.

"Two orgasms today and look how slick she is," Volt says conversationally to Tieran. "I don't know about you, but that's all I need in my life."

"I'm pretty satisfied by it," Tieran replies, his tone a little less conversational and slightly more guttural. "You said it was six orgasms the other day and five yesterday, right?"

Volt unleashes yet another growl that makes me whimper. "Yep."

"And she's still this needy, hmm?" Tieran hums. "Seems to me she needs three of us to sate her needs. How could we possibly entertain another?"

"Why would we want to?" Volt asks.

"Why indeed," Tieran says, bending to kiss my calf as he stretches my leg out wider, further exposing me to them both. "Real wolves know how to properly satisfy themselves and their female, Clove. Real wolves don't take a fucking harem when they have a mate. Real wolves are faithful. *That* is why I can't just take another Omega on the side. Because I'm a real fucking wolf." He says all this as he starts prowling up my leg, his final statement a whisper against my inner thigh.

I shiver, finally understanding the shift in topic.

Caius told me he would forgive my insult regarding their need for a harem.

It seems he really wasn't kidding.

Because Tieran and Volt appear to be very insulted by the insinuation that they'll need more than me in their bed.

Except that's not how I grew up. This concept of mates being faithful isn't something I understand. Hell, even Canton said he considered adding me to his harem, and that was after rejecting me as his mate.

The comment didn't even faze me.

Because that's the Nantahala way, and the same applies to the Santeetlah Wolves, too.

But not to the Carnage Wolves, something Tieran, Volt, and Caius have all made very clear.

"When I make this pussy mine, it's the only one I'm ever going to desire," Tieran says, his blue eyes meeting mine as his tongue traces the damp seam between my legs.

I moan, the sensation igniting a fire in my gut.

Only it's not enough.

Volt's growls have worked my wolf into a frenzy, turning her into a keening mess inside me. "I need more," I whisper, pleading with them. "Please, I… I need *more*."

"Mmm, that truth tastes so fucking sweet, little one," Tieran murmurs before closing his mouth around my clit.

I bow off the bed, only to be pushed back down by Volt's palm. His dark irises overtake my vision as he leans over me, pinning me with ease to the bed. "Tell us exactly what you want, and we'll give it to you."

"Yes, darling," Tieran says, his breath hot against my sensitive skin. "Be honest and we'll reward you."

A tremble tickles my spine, making me squirm beneath them.

But I'm trapped.

Tieran has my legs and Volt has my torso.

Both of them are staring at me with intimate intent in their gazes.

All I have to do is say what I want.

So I do.

"I want you to knot me." The words leave me without remorse, my wolf rumbling in approval. "I *need* you to knot me."

TIERAN

I meet Volt's gaze.

There's only one way this is going to work, and the subtle nod he gives me says he understands that.

I don't trust my wolf not to claim her, which means I can't fully knot her. But Volt can. If he bites her, the bond won't snap into place. It needs my blessing as the clan leader.

And as much as I want to claim Clove, I can't.

Not yet.

We've only just begun discussing this situation, and her willingness to share me says we're not ready. Because she doesn't yet understand what it means to be our Omega. My anger isn't directed at her. It's meant for her pack and the sorry excuse for an Alpha who raises the Nantahala females to accept such disrespectful practices.

A harem is fine.

But not when you have a mate.

A mate is meant to be cherished and worshipped, not degraded to a life of constant servitude. To take other women while in her presence is just so fucking wrong. To force the women to just accept it is even worse.

I've known about Alpha Bryson's penchants for years.

Ever since he tried to give me his daughter as a gift. Not as a mate, but as a fuck doll.

Because he knows how Carnage Wolves operate.

Which makes Clove's existence all the more suspicious. Her mother was a mixed breed, something he very likely knew.

But Clove clearly didn't.

I know what she smells like when she lies now. Everything she's told us until her little statement today has been the truth.

Including the words she just said about needing our knots.

I circle her clit with my tongue, praising her for giving us the truth, then lick downward to lap up her decadent slick.

Definitely Omega, I think, purring in approval.

Only Omegas can produce this moisture, and the scent is fucking divine. I have no doubt that it's driving Alpha Mackin mad right now. But he won't dare come down here. He also has a deck full of fresh sea air to breathe.

Beta Lock won't be a problem. While they react to an Omega's need, they don't possess the same urge to take and claim.

Volt removes his jeans and shoes, then kneels on the bed to lift Clove's shirt. She's panting, ready for more, but we're going to take our time, savor her, and make every minute count.

She needs to understand that she will be it for us.

We will crave no one else.

"Omegas are so incredibly sexual," I say against her damp flesh. "It'll be a full-time job for us to ensure your needs are always met, Clove. We'll be too exhausted to take anyone else."

"Nor will we want to," Volt adds as he reveals her breasts. "You're all we'll ever want for the rest of our lives." He bends to take her stiff nipple into his mouth, causing her to cry out in pleasure.

At least until he bites her, which elicits a low hiss from her mouth.

"Don't ever insult us with the mention of taking other women again, Clove," I say, watching as Volt's tongue soothes the indent in her breast. He didn't break the skin, but he certainly left an impression. "We don't want a harem. And I will not take another Omega. Only you."

I nibble her sweet little nub, watching as passion blends with pain in her features. It's a beautiful sight, seeing her come undone, making her realize what it means to have us in her life.

"You're ours," I whisper.

"And we are yours," Volt says on a low growl.

She squirms in response, that sound a mating call from an Alpha to his chosen mate. Her reaction earlier told me that Caius hasn't explained that to her yet. Only the purr and other parts of our lives.

After tonight, she'll understand that an Alpha can bring his Omega to her knees with a subtle rumble.

Just like he can soothe her with a purr.

Or make her scream with his knot.

Omegas drive Alphas mad, but we know how to return the favor in kind.

I trace my tongue down to her entrance, prodding her and loving the way her muscles clench around me. "She's very ready for a knot," I say, humming in approval. "The question is…"

I palm her thighs, pushing her wider, then draw my tongue lower toward her back hole.

"Mmm, the question is, can she take us at the same

time?" I use my finger to demonstrate, sliding one in her ass before returning my mouth to her pussy.

She's so fucking wet.

So beautifully aroused.

And so damn *perfect*.

Because she moans as I breach her backside, our little vixen eager to take us in any way she can.

That's the Omega in her, the being driven to take whatever her Alphas want to give her and begging us to dominate her in every conceivable way.

Because that's what makes her feel safe.

That's what proves to an Omega that her Alphas will protect her.

She may not realize the animalistic drive behind this need, but Volt and I do. We were born to take care of an Omega just like this, to see to her every desire and protect her from the world.

We'll do just that.

And we'll avenge her, too.

If Alpha Bryson is somehow behind her existence and appearance on Carnage Island, he'll regret the day he played that card.

Because I'm going to fucking destroy him for what he's done to me and to Clove.

I add a second finger to her ass, my movement a little sharper than intended as my anger gets the better of me, but all Clove does is moan.

Her hand is fisted in Volt's thick hair, holding him against her tit and begging him to bite her again. He obliges, taking a rosy little tip between his teeth and biting down until she screams.

She rakes her nails down his back in response, drawing an approving rumble from his chest.

He enjoys giving pain almost as much as he enjoys receiving it.

I use her distraction to add a third finger. She contracts around me, groaning in response to the sensation of fullness in her backside.

There's no question as to what I'm doing—I'm preparing her—and she seems to be fully on board with what that means.

I reward her eagerness to play by sucking on her clit. Her ass clenches around my fingers, her slick pouring out of her in blatant need. She's soaking the bed, her Omega genetics preparing her to take our cocks.

We're big.

She's small.

But she's already proven more than capable of accommodating us between her legs.

It's her backside I'm worried about, which is why I start flexing my fingers, scissoring them inside her and ensuring I won't tear her apart.

Goose bumps pebble across her skin, her body vibrating with intensity as little whines leave her throat.

Volt finishes removing her shirt, then kisses her to swallow those sounds with his tongue while palming her breast.

She clenches around me again, her little nub throbbing against my tongue. She's close to coming. I consider letting it happen, but I want to be inside her, to feel that climax around my shaft while I'm fucking her.

It'll make me want to elicit more pleasure from her, to keep her coming the whole time we take her.

Volt and I have never shared a female before.

This is going to be violent and explosive and outright savage.

I need her to enjoy it, to fall into a wave of unending rapture while we pound into her.

So I don't let her come.

Instead, I nip her clit and smile when she screams.

It's a taunt. She wants my bite. And my wolf almost makes me break the skin.

But I'm just enough in control to tell him to heel as I pull away from Clove and strip off my pants and shoes.

Volt is soothing her pain with his mouth, kissing her and massaging her breast in an almost gentle manner. At least for him.

But his cock is fucking weeping at the sound of her agony.

The sadist in him enjoyed that, and I'm betting he wants me to do it again.

I don't. Because it's not what Clove wants.

And I want to prove to her that honesty is key between us, that we will do what she desires whenever she asks. I press my palm to her sweet heat, saturating my hand with her slick, then palm my shaft.

Yesss, I think, indulging in the heavenly sensation against my skin. It's fucking amazing and makes me want to slide inside her.

But that's not the plan.

"On your back, V," I demand, my voice gruff. "Clove, I want you to straddle him and put him in that sweet cunt. Then ride him a little for me."

"Normally, I would fight another Alpha commanding me," Volt says, his mouth against Clove's as he grabs her hips. "But in this case"—he rolls to his back, taking her with him—"I'll very happily oblige. Now wrap that palm around my shaft and put me inside you, sweetling."

She presses her hand to his chest to sit up, her legs automatically straddling him. Then she reaches between them, her fingers wrapping around his knot at the base of his dick and giving it a taunting squeeze.

Volt growls in response, making her shudder so violently she almost collapses against him.

I chuckle. "You have so much to learn, little one," I whisper, kneeling on the bed behind her and bending to kiss her shoulder. "Alphas have mating calls. It's one of the reasons I know we'll never desire another—you'll always respond to our call. Just as you're doing now."

"She's weeping all over my cock," Volt says, clear contentment in his voice. "Her body is more than ready."

"It is," I agree. "Take him inside you, little one. No teasing this time or he'll growl again."

She visibly shudders, her hesitation suggesting she's debating if she wants to test my statement. An Alpha's growl is an aphrodisiac to an Omega's senses, making it something she'll crave almost as much as our purr.

But never as much as our knots.

Which she seems to realize because she grabs him again, this time angling him upward and slowly sliding herself down.

Volt is patient and doesn't push her, aware that while her body may be built for us, we're still large. He may enjoy pain, but it's clear that he's decided she's endured enough for one night.

Or perhaps he recognizes that I'm about to deliver the edge to our fucking, the one that will make her scream in a brilliant condition of agonized rapture.

Because I won't be going easy on her.

My wolf has ridden me hard all damn week.

I *need* to take her, and it's going to be an intense battle of wills between me and my beast.

He may win.

Something that should concern me a hell of a lot more than it does right now.

Because seeing her take Volt does things to me.

It makes me wild. Unpredictable. A little unhinged.

She starts to move, her hips flexing as she dictates a slow speed that allows her to feel every thick inch of his cock. He palms her breasts in response, squeezing and kneading the alluring curves.

It's an erotic display of passion, one that makes my dick pulse in response.

I can't knot her ass. That's the point of this.

But I can milk my knot into her ass.

Which is exactly what I'm going to do while Volt holds her in a state of ecstasy.

I allow them a few more minutes of that sweet pace, my palm moving along my shaft in a similar motion while I remain kneeling behind her.

Once she appears to be lost to the bliss of fullness, I press my palm to her shoulder blades and guide her down for Volt to distract her mouth.

His hands leave her tits, one of his palms wrapping around her nape while his opposite arm encircles her back. He's ensuring she can't escape or jerk in a way that may do more damage than good.

Because this is going to hurt.

But once I'm inside, I'm going to make her see the stars in the best way.

I lean over her to kiss her shoulder again, my fingers taking more of her slick to press it in her back hole. Then I coat myself in her arousal, ensuring there's enough lubrication for what I'm about to do.

Volt's arm flexes beneath my torso as I right myself behind her again. Then I reach around her to slide my hand between them, my thumb unerringly finding her little bundle of nerves.

She practically mewls in response, her hips jumping forward to take Volt to the hilt.

He thrusts up at the same time, distracting her with his size as I line myself up at her back entrance.

As she jolts back from him, she senses me behind her, entering her, and freezes.

I thrum her clit once more, causing her to jerk again, this time backward before she thrusts forward.

A deep moan echoes from her throat, but Volt is too busy kissing her to allow the sound to fully escape.

His arm has tightened around her, trying to keep her in place as I continue pushing forward.

She tries to squirm, to thrust away from my entry, but that only makes her take Volt deeper, stirring a guttural noise from her.

I focus on her pleasure, trying to evoke as much of it as I can with my thumb while allowing her to acclimate to my entry.

I'm only a quarter of the way in, but the hard part is always the initial penetration. The rest is just her accepting my size and learning to enjoy the sensation of being full.

The boat rocks around us, telling me we're close to shore.

But I don't care.

We'll finish this on the yacht, then do it again in the house.

All fucking night, if I have my way.

Clove whines a little, her hips flexing again as I push myself deeper. "You're doing so good," I praise her, placing a palm on her back to steady myself. "So fucking good."

She whimpers in response, so I purr a little for her,

wanting her to know how proud I am of her for taking two of her Alphas into her tight little body.

"You're a natural, sweetling," Volt says against her mouth. "And fuck, this feels amazing. I've never shared a woman like this."

"Neither of us has," I echo, sliding in a little more. "Only with you, Clove. Only ever with you."

It's a vow I shouldn't make.

But it's a promise I feel all the way to my soul.

She's mine, I think, my wolf grumbling in agreement.

I circle her swollen nub and gently lower myself to her back again, my lips finding her shoulder. It's instinctual. It's where I want to bite her. How I want to claim her. And I can't fight the impulse to press myself against her.

Volt's arm slips out from between us, his palm going to her hip as I slide my hand around her throat. He releases her nape, giving me full access to her neck. I nibble and kiss my way to her ear. "I'm going to thrust the rest of the way inside you now, Clove. Then we're going to fuck you until you can't walk."

She groans in response, her mouth still occupied by Volt's lips.

I nuzzle her pulse, kissing her tender skin, and do exactly what I said I was going to do.

She screams, the intensity of having us both inside her causing shock to ripple through her sweet body. I don't stop massaging her sensually, coaxing her back to that nearly orgasmic state as Volt and I begin to move.

Not harshly.

Not yet.

Just enough to show her what we can do, to prepare her for the insanity we're about to unleash upon her.

She whimpers again, the sound adorably alluring.

She knows she can take us. She wants it. She just has to accept it.

"You're squeezing my cock so damn hard, sweetheart," Volt says, groaning. "You're so fucking hungry for my knot."

"You're strangling my shaft even more," I tell her, my lips against her ear once more. "Your tight little ass is begging me to unleash my power, to show you what I can do."

"Just say the words, Clove," Volt murmurs. "Tell us to let go, and we'll give you what you need."

She writhes between us, our wanton Omega giving in to the sensuality of the moment, learning how to accept both of us in her tight little holes.

I give her that moment, allowing her to adjust to our assault, waiting for her to tell us to fuck her.

"You're going to feel so good when you come," I whisper. "It's going to make us want to knot you for hours."

"Days," Volt corrects, thrusting up into her. "*Weeks.*"

I hum in agreement, nibbling her throbbing pulse.

She's falling apart.

Her mental walls are crumbling.

Her body is becoming ours.

The animal inside her is taking control, thriving in this moment of possession.

"Tell us to fuck you, Clove," I say against her ear. "Beg us and we'll do whatever you want."

She starts to shake between us, her climax mounting from the subtle shifts of our hips and my thumb against her sweet spot.

"More," she breathes.

"Be specific, little one." I want to hear her say it. I want to hear her unleash her desires on a demanding scream, to force our wolves to dance with hers. "Tell us to fuck you."

"Beg for our knots," Volt says, arching up into her on a thrust that draws a gasp from her pretty throat. "Give us your truths, sweetling. Command us and we'll obey."

I nip at her neck, not hard enough to bleed, just enough to ground her before she erupts. Because I can feel her pulse between her legs, the indication that she's about to explode. "Tell us now, Clove, or we'll stop." I demonstrate by pressing down on her nub rather than stroking it.

"*Fuck me,*" she cries out. "*Please fuck me.*"

Volt growls in approval, and I smile against her neck. "You're perfect, baby," I whisper. "So fucking perfect."

I slam into her, eliciting a scream from her that goes straight to my balls.

Volt does the same, the two of us pounding into her with a force that would break a human. But Clove takes us. Fuck, she does more than that. She *embraces* us. Her hips are moving just as fiercely as ours, her needy little clit throbbing against my thumb as I push her over the edge into oblivion.

Only, she doesn't lose her mind to the sensuous bliss. She demands more with her mouth and with her supple form.

She's a little sex beast, mewling and bucking and riding us more than we're riding her.

It's a sight to behold, one that has my groin tightening with the need to empty myself inside her. To sink my teeth into her flesh and bite. To knot her to completion and make her ours.

I just barely hold on to the lust captivating my mind, that subtle hint of duty lurking inside my thoughts and keeping me just this side of sane.

It fucking hurts.

I want to bellow, to growl, to fucking snarl at fate.

Instead, I take it out on her ass, let her feel my pent-up need, ravage her to completion, and claim her in the only way I can.

Volt curses, his own climax taking him by the balls and forcing him to unleash inside her.

I feel his knot enter her, hear the effect it has on Clove as she shrieks in rapturous delight. She's shaking, her body taking his pleasure and making it her own.

It tips me over the edge, forcing me to join them as I come in her ass. I just barely grab my base in time, holding my knot steady, not wanting to destroy her too completely.

Because if I shoot my knot up her ass, it will hurt.

She'll bleed.

And that's not the kind of blood I want to draw.

Instead, I milk myself, her presence enough to allow me to fully unload in her in a way impossible for anyone else.

Only an Omega can draw this sort of pleasure from an Alpha.

It's fucking ecstasy.

But it hurts, too.

Because my knot wants to be inside her, to experience her sweet heat to completion.

If I were in her cunt, I'd allow it. I fucking *own* her.

This is why I took her from behind. I knew it would be just enough to ground me, to make me harness my control, even if by a thread, to keep from truly hurting her.

Which allows me to refrain from biting her, too.

Volt is utterly lost to her, his mouth ravaging hers as he continues to unload inside her. She's oblivious, lost to the carnality of the moment.

I maintain control here, guarding them both as they lose themselves to the sensations.

She's full of our cum.

Full of our claim.

Marked by our intentions.

Possessed from the inside out.

It's glorious perfection.

I kiss her throat, whispering in her ear about how proud I am of her for taking us. How good she feels coated in our arousal. How I want to live inside her ass. And I promise to take her again and again.

She quivers in response, her body clenching around us in a manner that says she approves.

I grin and lick her neck. "You were absolutely made for us, Clove," I tell her softly. "And we were made for you."

I feel her relax between us, her body well sated.

She's going to fall asleep now.

That's fine.

I'll let her rest.

When she wakes, we'll fuck her again.

Prove to her that she's all we'll ever need.

Show her what it means to be a Carnage Wolf.

And demonstrate just how we intend to care for her —*our Omega*.

Our sweet, darling little Clove.

VOLT

"You look well knotted, sweetling," I murmur as I lift Clove out of the massive tub in the en-suite bathroom of Tieran's room. Caius and I have similar amenities in our rooms at this beachfront estate, but Tieran led me and Clove to his quarters upon arrival.

Where we promptly fucked Clove on his bed.

She slept.

We fucked again.

And then I carried her to the bath.

She dozed a little in my arms with her head pressed against my chest, reveling in my purr.

I washed her hair while Tieran climbed in to take care of her lower half. She's definitely sore there, as she flinched a few times while grumbling something about her wolf's unhealthy obsession with knots.

Her protest made my lips twitch. Then I purred louder for her, and she immediately calmed again.

She snuggles into my neck now, yawning as Tieran haphazardly wraps a towel around her. She's still in my arms, curled into my chest, and now she's cloaked with awkwardly placed cotton.

It can't be a more perfect moment.

Well, that's not true.

Tieran could have claimed her.

And Caius could be here, too.

So it's a near-perfect moment.

I study her sleepy features, smiling as she yawns again.

"Yes, definitely well knotted," I repeat.

I carry her to the bed, not caring at all that I'm still wet, and sit with her in my arms. Tieran follows with a comb, handing it to me to brush out her hair. "I'm going to put together a midnight snack and check on our morning arrangements."

I almost point out that it's after three in the morning, making it more like an early breakfast, but I let it go with a nod. Clove needs some sustenance after everything we just put her through, and I'm hungry as well.

Tieran doesn't bother with pants, just wanders out of the room in his towel. There are a few human staff members that reside at the estate to keep everything up and running, but they should all be asleep.

Besides, they're used to a little nudity where we're concerned.

They don't know about our true heritage. They just think we're eccentric and embrace it. We pay them well and keep them happy. That's all they really care about.

I comb through Clove's hair while she snuggles into me, my purr keeping her sated in an entirely different way from my knot.

She's so precious and small, so perfect and *ours*. I want to hold her like this for the rest of our very long existence.

I kiss the top of her head. "You did well tonight," I tell her. "Very, very well."

Her eyelashes flutter as she peers up at me. "Thank you," she whispers.

I frown. "For the compliment?" Because I should be the one expressing my gratitude to her, not the other way around.

She shakes her head. "For knotting me."

My eyes widen. "You're thanking me for fucking you?"

I nearly laugh, but she nods serenely, her lips curling. "Yes."

"Oh, sweetheart, no," I say, pulling her up to straddle my hips. "You're the one deserving of praise and gratitude, not me. It's my absolute pleasure to knot you. Always. In fact, I'll do it again right now if you want." I yank her forward, her barely there towel slipping and allowing my cock to press against her slick heat.

But she winces, a little whine coming from her.

Because she's sore.

So I kiss her instead, gently, telling her with my tongue how grateful I am for her, how much I adore her, how I intend to worship her for the rest of our lives. Then I slowly guide her down to the bed and continue the demonstration of how I promise to always take care of her.

But as I start to kiss a path downward, she flinches again. "Too sore for my tongue?"

"Yes," she admits, her voice low.

I return to her mouth, telling her with my tongue how proud I am of her for voicing the truth. "I never want to push you to the point of true discomfort," I tell her. "That doesn't mean I won't test your boundaries, but I'll never hurt you, Clove. Not truly."

I just may make her bleed a little with my knife.

Or bite her until she screams.

But nothing that would ever do real damage.

She sighs beneath me, completely relaxed again, trusting me to keep her safe. My chest warms from her regard, my wolf extremely appeased by her faith in us. Not only did she voice the truth, but she also accepted my truth in kind.

Which is why I feel the need to share another truth with her.

To help her better understand our situation.

"It's not you holding Tieran back," I confide softly. "It's me."

She tenses a bit, her thick, near-black eyelashes parting to reveal her gorgeous brown irises. "What?"

"It's my past," I explain, slowly rolling off of her to lounge beside her. She rotates with me, her long hair flowing over the pillow beneath her head as she settles into a similar position, facing me.

I tuck my arm under my head and rest my opposite palm on her hip, needing to touch her.

"What about your past?" she asks, fully alert now.

"My father mated a Beta." My hand wanders naturally along her curves, tracing her side before returning to her hip. I just want to stroke her, to make sure she understands that she will always be mine despite our current predicament.

She mimics my position by tucking her own arm under her head, then rests her palm against my chest. I purr in response, enraptured by her touch, then lean forward to kiss her. Nothing too sensual, just a peck of affection that brings a smile to her eyes.

"You're so beautiful, Clove."

Her cheeks turn a lovely shade of pink. But she doesn't thank me for the compliment this time, something that pleases me greatly.

So I continue speaking.

"Alphas and Betas can't procreate, but he went into the mating knowing that. He didn't join a clan, either. He simply picked her with no regard for the consequences." I shrug. "They were young. Only eighteen or so. It wasn't until he was my current age that he realized he needed an heir." Well, *needed* may be a strong word. More like *wanted*, but I don't clarify that out loud, as it doesn't really matter.

"How old are you?" Clove asks.

"Twenty-nine," I say. "Tieran and Caius are both thirty."

"And you went to Carnage Island seven years ago, right?"

I nod, confirming the history Caius gave her. "We were all twenty-two at the time. I'm only a few months younger than Tieran and Caius." They have summer birthdays, while I have a fall one. But that's not important.

Except she asks me for our birthdays next.

So I give them to her before asking for her own.

"I turned twenty in September," she admits before stating the day.

"Are you intimidated by us being older?" I ask, teasing.

She snorts. "Females are usually mated younger than the males in Nantahala Pack. I had a friend who mated a male twice her age last year. Of course, he didn't look older than thirty since we stop aging then."

"Carnage Wolves don't have a designated mating age. We form our clans first, then search for our Omegas. Some clans don't find one for decades because they're so rare," I explain. "We're fortunate to have found you when we did. Which brings me back to the claiming issue."

The smile in her eyes dims at that. "So your father realized he wanted an heir…" She trails off, prompting me to continue.

"And he found an Omega willing to give him one." I say *willing* with a bit of a sardonic twist because I'm not sure she was that willing. I think he found her at the right moment during a heat and didn't claim her but took her child away—*me*.

Which is why she's always struggled to embrace me. We never experienced that mother-son connection the way an Omega should with a child.

I clear my throat. "He took her during estrus. Impregnated her without claiming her. And when I arrived, he took me home to meet his Beta and demanded she raise me as her own."

Or that's the way the story goes, from what I've been told.

"It didn't go according to plan," I continue. "My *mother*, the term one I use because I called her that as a child, hated me. Every time she looked at me, she was reminded of what she couldn't provide for my father. And I became her outlet for that hatred."

I take Clove's hand to trace a scar along my chest, the ugly white line hidden by my blue ink.

"The tats help hide some of her handiwork, but the texture is still there." I shift a little closer and guide her hand up to my shoulder. "If you continue back, you'll feel the scars of the silver belt she used on me. They're light, as she wasn't strong enough to do a lot of damage, but it was certainly enough. And she bathed me in silver-infused water to keep me from healing."

Clove's features are ashen, her eyes rounding in horror. "And your father allowed this?"

"He said I had the spirit of an Alpha and could take the punishment for needing to exist." The words sound flat to my ears.

It's a past I haven't considered for years yet live with every day.

"That's horrible," she breathes.

I shrug. Because what can I say to that? I know it's horrible. But that doesn't make it any less true.

"He killed her when I was seven, shortly after my wolf started to mature. Carnage Wolves don't know their true designation—Alpha, Beta, or Omega—until their inner animal starts to grow, which is inspired by our first shift. Once my Alpha status was confirmed, he decided his work in this world was done."

Truly, it was the result of insanity. He didn't have a clan to ground him or an Omega to touch his heart. He went insane with misdirected power, unable to ground himself appropriately, and lost his fucking mind.

I explain some of that to Clove, using the experiment to explain why Alpha clans and Omegas are so vital to pack structure. "It's all about balance," I conclude. "A balance my father couldn't achieve. So he killed his mate and then himself, leaving me without a home. Which is how I ended up with the Black Mountain Pack. Because my Omega mother was part of an Alpha clan there."

I tell her about Alpha Umber and how he took me in, raised me alongside Tieran as though we were brothers. And I give her some insight into the fractured relationship between me and my birth mother, Gemma.

As Clove is new to the Carnage Wolf ways, I also provide a little history about the bond between Omegas and their children.

Then explain how that very much doesn't exist between me and Gemma.

Her eyes glisten with tears, her sadness over my situation prickling my insides.

I'm not used to having anyone care about me other than Tieran and Caius.

It feels nice to have Clove's warmth.

Even if it's under disappointing circumstances.

But maybe this helps her understand my desire for pain —it reminds me that I'm alive. Reminds me why we exist. Reminds me to enjoy every second as though it may be my last.

All things I tell her now.

Unleashing my every thought onto her and holding nothing back before finishing with, "So Tieran and Caius grew up witnessing my pain and anger. They were already best friends when I arrived, but they took me in, and the three of us grew up together. It didn't surprise anyone when our clan formed. Although, Alpha Umber isn't crazy about me being part of it."

Her lips curl down. "He's not?"

"No, he's not. Because he knows I'm broken. Probably irrevocably. But Tieran's wolf takes what he wants, and our beasts are well matched."

"I don't think you're broken," she whispers, making me smile a little.

"I am, but I embrace it rather than shy away from it," I say, drawing her touch back to my chest and pressing my palm to the back of her hand to hold her against my heart. "But Tieran doesn't want to risk making it worse. That's what I'm trying to explain—my history is why he won't claim you yet. He doesn't want to finalize our clan, then need to procreate with another just to fulfill his pack obligations."

We're all slaves to our inner beasts.

So while his wolf may not allow him to take another Omega right now, that doesn't mean the animal won't change his mind in the future.

Just like my father's did.

And although Tieran can control his wolf better than most, there are certain desires in life that we can't deny. No matter how hard we may try.

"Tieran's afraid his inevitable need to procreate will destroy me, and thereby destroy us." I know better. I've told him I'll be fine. But it's the clan leader's responsibility to do what's best for his circle. And Tieran will always put our needs above his own.

Which is why he's stuck in this conundrum.

"He has a duty to the pack to create an heir," I say. "But he has a duty to his clan to keep us sane, too. He's trying to figure out how to do both."

"And me being unable to go into a true heat is the crux of it all," she murmurs.

"We don't know that yet," I remind her. "You only just met your wolf for the first time. It may take years for you to fall into a proper estrus, or it could be a matter of days. All I know for sure is, you're ours."

I kiss her again, allowing her to feel the promise from my lips.

But I can sense some of her hesitation, the concern that she won't be enough. "I would never hurt a child," she says against my mouth, her tone adamant.

My brow furrows as I pull back to stare down into her fiery gaze. "Of course you wouldn't. Omegas are naturals with children. It doesn't matter who the mother is; an Omega is instinctually prone to care for the young. It's another trait that makes them so unique and cherished among our kind."

She narrows her eyes at me. "Then how could Tieran think I would threaten the sanity of our clan by harming another Omega's child. It would still be *his* child. I would never do that."

Ah, I think. "You've misunderstood what I meant. He's worried about how *I* will react to him taking another Omega when he has a mate. He's concerned it'll trigger me. Not to mention what it'll do to you. Omegas are possessive of their Alphas. You may not feel it yet, but you will when we claim you."

"Not possessive enough to hurt an innocent child," she repeats.

"No, you would never do that," I agree, softening my voice and adding a little purr. "As I said, Omegas love children. Even Gemma is affectionate toward me, despite our fractured bond and whatever my father did to her during his rut. She's still soft, never cruel. She's just distant."

"I wouldn't be distant. Not if it's Tieran's child." She sounds adamant, almost angry by the concept of disrespecting an innocent. "Nantahala males take harems, Volt." She presses her finger to my lips, silencing my rebuke to that. "I understand that's not how things work among your kind—*our* kind—but I wasn't raised with Carnage Wolves. I was raised to accept the wills of men."

My teeth grind together, not liking the way that sounds at all.

"It may not be right," she continues. "And I may hate it. No, I do hate it. The very thought of sharing any of you has my wolf wanting to commit murder. But under the right circumstances, I think I could accept it. That's what I'm saying."

"You won't have to," I promise her. "And I don't think Tieran will ever allow you to accept it, either."

"From what you've both said, he doesn't have a choice," she points out.

"Ah, but he does," I say. "He could abdicate." It's a potential scenario none of us have discussed, but it's one I know Tieran is thinking about. "He doesn't have to be the Black Mountain Pack Alpha."

It's what he's been groomed for, what we've all been striving for.

But he could choose his clan over duty.

It may not be the best choice. It may not even be a *good* choice. But it's still an option.

"I will never let him do that," Clove vows, making me smile.

"Which is why you're our mate," I tell her. "It's only a matter of time, Clove. You'll…" I trail off as my inner wolf perks up, going on alert.

I look at the door, finding it empty. But a hint of peppermint touches my nose.

Fresh peppermint.

"Caius is here." Which can't be good. If he's here, then something has happened. I scent the air, noting the influx of new scents—scents that are not typical around this estate. "And he's not alone."

I push off the bed, searching for my jeans.

"We need to go downstairs," I tell Clove. "Right now."

CAIUS

"We have a problem," I say as I enter the kitchen. There's no greeting required. Tieran would have smelled me coming, just as I followed my nose to him here.

He's wearing a towel, his damp hair suggesting he recently showered. As he usually stays up late, this doesn't surprise me. But the three plates of food before him suggest he's not the only one still awake.

That's a good thing.

Because I have a lot to say.

Tieran picks up a glass of water and faces me, his gaze taking in the four wolves at my back before arching a brow at me. He doesn't ask for an explanation with that look; he demands one.

Because I've very clearly broken protocol, something we both know I would never do without justification.

"Alpha Kin is working with the Nantahala Wolves," I say, driving straight to the point.

Alpha Pan growls at my back, still furious by what we overheard. "He's been taking advantage of his communications role on the island."

I nod, pulling my laptop from my bag to set it up on the

counter. "After seeing you off, I did some rounds, checking in on everyone, and saved Alpha Dirk's clan for last. But they weren't in their usual den. So I checked the island surveillance and couldn't locate them. However, I noticed a weird little ripple in the frame. Which led me to Alpha Pan."

I wake up my screen to pull up one of the feeds.

"And we discovered the feed was on a loop," Alpha Pan says.

"No *we* about it. Alpha Pan did all the work," I correct him, then show Tieran the loop in question. "He was able to override the glitch, which is what led us to find this."

The image changes to depict Alpha Kin on a satellite phone.

"That's not one of ours," Tieran says immediately.

"No, it's not," Alpha Pan agrees. "But we were able to hack into the frequency to listen in."

"I gave him permission," I add, meeting Tieran's gaze. He tasked me with keeping an eye on Alpha Dirk's clan but told me not to jeopardize their privacy.

It's a demand I clearly disregarded when I asked Alpha Pan to hack the satellite phone frequency.

But Alpha Kin's suspicious demeanor tipped me off.

Coupled with the strange loop in the feed, it was obvious he wanted to hide something. So, as acting Alpha on the island, I made the executive decision to fully monitor him.

I clear my throat. "Normally, I would have called to ask you first, but as Alpha Kin is in charge of telecommunications on the island…"

"You didn't want to risk him overhearing," Tieran finishes for me. "A wise decision, one I'm not disappointed about."

I nod. "Good."

"I'll always trust your judgment, C," he adds, his voice firm. "You know that."

He's right; I do. But it seemed important to explain my decision, as it went directly against his wishes. He values the privacy of his pack, preferring to maintain leadership in a more compassionate manner than a cruel one. It's what makes him a good Pack Alpha.

"What did I miss?" Volt asks, entering the room in a pair of jeans with Clove at his side.

Her sweet aroma swirls around me, momentarily captivating me and drawing me toward her on instinct. She's so beautiful with her pink cheeks and plump lips, her hair damp from a recent shower.

"Hi, gorgeous," I say, prowling toward her and wrapping her in my arms while Tieran summarizes what I've said so far about Alpha Kin.

Alpha Pan adds a few comments as he takes over my laptop. I don't stop him, preferring to hold Clove over pulling up the transcript. She settles against my side as I purr a little, ensuring she remains somewhat calm for what she's about to hear.

Alpha Kin's voice starts playing, his low tones slightly marred by static. But his words are clear. "Yeah, tomorrow," he's saying. "Richmond, Virginia." He gives the name of the Senator next, then the address. "I took it from their files. He'll definitely be there, as he just left with Tieran and Aspen."

Clove frowns at the use of her first name—something I recently learned about her. *Aspen Clover Donough.*

However, the voice that follows makes her freeze. "Good. We'll send a team in to dismantle the clan, then we'll proceed as expected. I'm sorry she's caused so much trouble. I didn't think she would be able to shift."

"You underestimated Tieran's growl," Alpha Kin replies.

"I'll clean it up," Alpha Bryson promises. "I should have killed the bitch the moment I realized she wouldn't be of proper use with the Santeetlah Pack. But I thought I could use her to cause a little chaos."

"Something that would have worked if Tieran didn't want her for himself," Alpha Kin says flatly. "Or if you had given me a heads-up to intervene. She could have been brought back to our den and properly silenced."

"I don't report to you," Alpha Bryson reminds him sternly. "If you think that's how this is going to go, then we're going to have a problem."

"Just fucking fix it. She's a distraction that's going to get us caught," he snaps, causing Tieran to arch a brow.

"I said I'd clean it up," Alpha Bryson bites back. "I'll take care of Volt, too. Consider it a gift."

"Do that and I'll forgive this bullshit," Alpha Kin replies, his tone as cold as ice. "Fuck it up more, and you're a dead man."

Alpha Bryson snorts. "Don't threaten me. The only reason you were upgraded to this position is because of your—"

The call goes dead after that, making Tieran's jaw tick.

"Alpha Kin hung up on him," Alpha Pan explains.

"Any guesses on what the rest of his sentence would have been?" Tieran asks.

"I have several," Volt drawls.

"*Helpful* guesses," Tieran clarifies.

"He could have meant clan leader," I offer. "Or perhaps a family member, like his father."

"Alpha Nick." Tieran scratches the light dusting of hair along his jaw, his eyes narrowing. "I'll pass it along to my father, see what he thinks. Until then, we clearly have a problem, just as you said."

"We do," I agree.

"Or an opportunity," Volt says. "He's about to send his enforcer team after us. If he's smart, that'll include seven, eight, maybe nine, wolves? So how many will he leave behind to protect himself?"

Tieran studies him for a moment. "Last I checked, he only had about eight qualified enforcers. Most of his wolves are too weak."

"Probably because they don't know how to properly mate," Alpha Pan adds, making me snort.

He's not wrong.

"He uses three for his personal guard," Clove says quietly. "And a team of twelve for the pack grounds."

"Those twelve are lower-level wolves that enforce boundaries around the women, making sure none of them run," Tieran informs her, his voice soft as he speaks to Clove. "His enforcer unit is who he takes to ceremonies."

She frowns. "I… I've only attended one, and I was on my knees for most of it."

My teeth clench at the thought of her being degraded in that way before the packs. Knowing Bryson, she was probably naked, too. "That fucker needs to die."

"No shit," Volt drawls. "That's what I'm getting at. We attack him when he thinks he's attacking us."

Tieran shakes his head. "He'll pull the enforcers back the moment he realizes we're not there."

"They won't get back in time to stop us," Volt points out. "Richmond is at least a three-hour drive to Nantahala territory, and that's if you're breaking all the speed laws in one of my toys."

"You could send a decoy," Alpha Pan suggests, his tone

contemplative. "You could send me." He and Volt exchange a look, the two of them sizing each other up.

They're a similar size and stature. Alpha Pan has the right color hair.

"I'll wear one of your long-sleeved shirts," he adds, noting Volt's tats. "It's winter. No one will think anything of it."

"I could go with him," Alpha Lance speaks up from the doorway. He's blond like Tieran, which is likely why he offered. A bit shorter, though, and a lot less intimidating in status. "Give me some of your clothes to mask my scent. They'll think I'm you."

"What about Clove?" Tieran asks, glancing at her. "I assume that's who he meant by 'Aspen'?"

"Aspen Clover Donough," I murmur, my arm still around her waist. "A beautiful name for a beautiful wolf."

"I prefer Clove," she admits softly.

"I know," I whisper, kissing her on the temple.

"What was the original plan?" Alpha Lance asks. "Are you joining Volt on the assignment or watching from nearby?"

"Watching from nearby," Tieran confirms. "Which Bryson would expect. She's a new Omega. He'll know that we intend to keep her close."

"So give me some of her clothes as well, or a piece of the nest, and I can lure the Nantahala Wolves to me by scent. It'll help us split their team, too," Alpha Lance says.

The mention of the nest has me frowning because Clove hasn't made a new nest yet. Not even with our clothes.

It's something that's been nagging at me all week.

She should be nesting.

Her wolf chose us.

So why isn't she building herself a proper den?

Because she doesn't feel fully at peace with us? She hasn't completely accepted us? Or is it because we haven't claimed her?

Something has left her uneasy.

It's something I hope to fix after we handle this mess.

"It'll also give us probable cause to retaliate," Tieran adds to Alpha Lance's points. "We'll capture the attack on surveillance, use it as proof that he attempted to take out my clan, and return the favor in kind."

"By killing the Alpha of Nantahala Pack," Volt translates, grinning. "I like it."

"It's a fair retaliation," I agree. "He's attempting to take out the future hierarchy of the Black Mountain Pack for the second time in a decade. We punish him accordingly, then send all the evidence to the Elders to back up our decision. They won't be able to hold us accountable."

"And they'll have to release us from Carnage Island," Volt adds.

"It's a brilliant endgame," I say. "Assuming you're ready to take the mantle."

Tieran looks from Volt to me and then to Clove. "It's my final challenge," he says, still staring at her. "All of this. If we do it right, then we'll be fit to lead."

"We're going to do it right." Volt's confidence is echoed in Alpha Pan's expression. Alpha Lance seems a little more reserved, but the glimmer of excitement lurks in his hazel eyes.

I study the other two Alphas I brought with me here— Alpha Ebony and Alpha Edwin. They're both grinning.

Which makes me grin.

"It's time," I say.

"It's time," Volt echoes.

Then we both look at Clove, waiting for her input. But

she's staring at us with an odd expression. Not confusion, necessarily. Just... uncertainty. "You're going to kill Alpha Bryson," she says.

"We are," Tieran confirms, stepping toward her and cupping her cheek. "Does that bother you?"

I hold my breath, curious as to what she'll say.

She grew up with Alpha Bryson as a leader. Oftentimes, packs look upon their Alphas as father figures. It wouldn't be surprising if she harbors an innate respect for the man, even if he's a colossal jackass.

Volt appears expectant as well, all signs of excitement fleeing his expression.

Her response matters.

As does her comfort.

If she's not—

"Alpha Bryson allowed the Santeetlah Pack to rape and murder my mother in front of me. Then he handed me over to the Elders, told them I killed my mother, and said I was feral, all the while knowing the truth—that I didn't kill my mother *and* Canton was the reason I couldn't shift." She sounds furious, and rightly so. Just hearing her repeat all that makes my blood boil.

It has Volt narrowing his gaze in response as well.

But Tieran is still stoically focused on her, his palm against her cheek, his gaze studying hers.

"Am I bothered by the fact that you want to kill Alpha Bryson?" she asks, repeating the question Tieran just voiced. "Absolutely not. But I don't understand what you mean by 'second time.' When was the first time?"

Ah, she wants to know about the betrothal. I never told her the full story. Because it's not my tale to tell. It's all on Tieran to rewrite the history in her mind, to distinguish truth from the lies.

"What did Bryson tell your pack about my supposed

betrothal to his daughter?" Tieran asks quietly. "Did he say I rejected her by slaughtering her?"

"He told us you rejected her, then you slaughtered her."

He nods. "Yes, that's the tale he spun for the Elders, too." He releases her cheek, his hand falling to her hip as he continues to hold her gaze.

"What's the truth?" she asks, a note of something in her voice that I don't quite understand. A knowing lilt. A hint of confidence.

And it results in a grin from both Volt and Tieran.

After a beat, I begin to understand—her lesson on the lie.

They told her why truth is important to a clan, and she's using it now to provoke Tieran into telling his story.

Not that he needs the coaxing.

He would tell her regardless.

But the word play is definitely a welcome breath of fresh air in the room. It means she's starting to understand our dynamic. And I fucking love that.

"Alpha Bryson offered me his daughter as a whore, not as a mate," he says, cutting straight to the heart of the story. "He knows that Carnage Wolf Alphas need Omegas for their clans. But he tried to seduce me into a deal between our packs by offering his daughter as a slave."

"Harem member," I correct him with a grin.

"To him, it's the same," Tieran replies. "And I refused, which he blamed on his daughter. He told her she wasn't good for anything and killed her in a fit of rage. Which doesn't exactly paint him in the best image, so he told the Elders I rejected her and killed her. And he convinced several of his wolves to back up the story."

"Was my father there?"

Tieran nods. "Yes. His Beta was present. Gafton, right?

He provided a full testimony to the Elders. And it's all a lie."

"Which you have proof of," Volt adds, making Clove's eyebrows hit her hairline.

"You have proof that he lied?" Her voice matches her shocked expression.

Tieran nods. "I do."

"Why didn't you use it?"

"Because it's not time yet," he replies, making her frown. "Carnage Island was the perfect location for me to become my own wolf. I took the opportunity as my first challenge."

"I don't understand," she says slowly. "You accepted the sentencing… because you wanted to be sent to Carnage Island?"

He considers her for a moment, his expression thoughtful. There's still so much Clove has to learn about our kind. It's a good thing we have an eternity to teach her.

"It's common for Carnage Wolves destined to be Pack Alphas to venture into the wild to find themselves, to prove themselves worthy through a series of challenges," Tieran explains slowly. "Accepting my fate from the Elders was the first challenge in my journey. Killing Bryson will allow me to close that chapter of my life, making it time for me to finally return to the Black Mountain Pack."

"Oh." She swallows. "So everyone will, uh, leave with you?"

"Not everyone," he says. "There are wolves who need to be kept on Carnage Island. And we'll ensure they survive and prosper. It'll be a secondary base for our kind, a shelter of protection."

"I see." She sounds breathless. "A-and me?"

He stares at her. "What do you think?"

"I…" She clears her throat, some of that confidence

seeming to seep back into her stature, the wolf inside her reminding her to tell the truth.

Good girl, I think, proud.

"The Elders think I killed my mother, that I'm feral," she says.

Tieran dips his chin. "Yes. Both of which are not true."

"But my mate rejected me."

"Not your true mate," he corrects her. "Just some pompous dick of a Santeetlah Wolf who thought he was your betrothed. But I think we all know that's not true now. Right?" He glances at Volt and then at me.

"Right," we echo.

"A Santeetlah Wolf can't be a true mate for a Carnage Wolf, darling," Tieran murmurs. "Once we explain that to the Elders, you'll be free. As will I, because I didn't reject or kill Bryson's daughter. And I can prove it." He shrugs. "I'll send them a lengthy letter when I'm done killing him. I'm sure they'll be riveted by the details and so tied up in red tape that they won't be able to see straight for months."

"Such a shame," I drawl.

Volt grins. "I still think I should bomb their headquarters."

Tieran shakes his head. "You can focus on Bryson's head for now." He looks at Alpha Pan and Alpha Lance. "You'll both go to Richmond, pretend to be us. I'll get you clothes." His focus goes to Alpha Ebony. "I need you to take Clove back to the island and keep her safe. And—"

"What?" Clove interjects. "No. I'm coming with you."

Volt and I share a look.

"No, you're not," Tieran says, the authority sharp in his tone. "We won't be able to focus with you there. You need to be somewhere safe, and right now, that's with Alpha Ebony and Alpha Duncan."

"He's my former Alpha," she says, her back straightening as she stares Tieran down. "I'm coming."

"No, Clove. My wolf will go absolutely insane if you're anywhere near the danger. I can't focus on you and my task at the same time. *I* need you to go back to the island. That's what you can do for my sanity and focus. Fuck, not even just mine. Volt's and Caius's, too."

I nod. "He's right, beauty. I won't be able to focus at all if you're there. I'll be too busy wanting to protect you, not myself."

Volt seems a little more conflicted, but he eventually agrees with a subtle tilt of his head. "This isn't about your abilities or your strength. It's not an insult, sweetling. It's about keeping our heads. You're still unclaimed. That does things to our wolves."

"Then cla…" she starts to snap back, only to trail off as she realizes what she was about to demand. Her jaw snaps closed, but her eyes breathe fire. She's pissed.

Because deep down, she knows we're right.

And she can't demand our claim. Not yet. Not like this.

"I'll bring his head back for you," Volt offers softly. "His balls, too, if you'd like."

She grimaces.

"I'll add your father to the pile," Volt continues. "Give me names. I'll find them and kill them. All of them. Just tell me who." His earnest promises seem to be thawing her a little.

"It's not about sexism or saying you can't hold your own," Alpha Ebony speaks up. "They're right. I can feel how agitated their wolves are even here. They can't fight in this condition. It'll get them killed."

Clove deflates. She knows she's defeated, but she clearly doesn't like it. And I hate it, too. If she were our mate, we could absolutely take her with us. We would be stronger as a full clan. Our mental hive mind would be in place. Our shared immunity. Everything.

But in this current state, she has to go back to the island.

"All right," she says, her tone indicating she's not happy about this but won't fight it. "I'll go back to Carnage Island with Alpha Ebony."

Tieran swallows, his expression uncharacteristically soft for him. "I'm sorry, Clove. But I promise we'll make this up to you."

"By bringing back Bryson's body for you to burn," Volt offers hopefully.

Tieran ignores him.

But Clove smiles a little. She knows Volt's trying. "Looks like we're having a barbecue, V," I tell him.

He grins. "Yeah?"

Tieran doesn't respond, his concentration still on Clove. It's like he wants to say something but doesn't know how. Which is again uncharacteristic of him.

"I would like to watch him burn," Clove says, her gaze on Tieran, not on Volt.

Which means she misses his ridiculous smile. Probably a good thing because he looks a bit psychotic. Even Alpha Lance takes a step away from him.

"We'll make it up to you," Tieran repeats, his palm finding her cheek again. "I promise, Clove."

"I believe you," she whispers back to him.

He presses his forehead to hers, a moment of intense emotion seeming to pass from him to her. It's enough to wipe that look off Volt's face and sober his expression. He steps forward, taking over her opposite side while I remain on the other.

Then the three of us hug her, our clan embracing our Omega.

It's a charged moment without words.

Just a passing of knowledge.

A vow of the future.

A destiny engraving itself in all our hearts.

Ours, I think, kissing her temple. Tieran takes her mouth, his own declaration passing to her with his tongue. And Volt nibbles her neck.

When this is done, we'll be taking her back to Black Mountain Pack as our Omega.

I can feel it in my soul.

She's the one who will push us through this final challenge.

The reason Tieran will finally ascend.

We're going home, I think. *We're finally going home.*

TIERAN

"Clove's safe with Alpha Duncan in his den," I say, reading the message from Alpha Ebony.

It's accompanied by a photo of Clove sitting on a couch, staring at security screens. Alpha Edwin is beside her, pointing at one of the monitors, probably explaining the technical jargon to her.

He's one of the other lone wolves on the island, similar to Alpha Mackin. They're brothers, actually. So it must be a family trait.

I run a palm over my face. My wolf isn't pleased. He didn't want to let Clove leave. Fuck, *I* didn't want to let her leave. But this is the right way to do this.

Except I hate it.

So it feels wrong.

Because we're not connected. If I bit her and completed the link, I would be able to talk to her right now. Find out what Alpha Edwin is really saying. Make sure she's okay. Happy. Healthy. *Safe*.

Instead, I have to rely on my pack to protect her. Something I normally wouldn't question, but Alpha Kin has proved that not everyone can be trusted.

We've been going through surveillance and details for the last few hours, Caius having brought the details on his laptop. We can't find any indication that Alpha Dirk is involved, which means it may be someone else on the island.

Or Alpha Kin's father, Alpha Nick.

I passed that tidbit onto my father, and he's handling the interrogation for me since we have other tasks on our agenda today.

"Do you think Clove recognized Alpha Kin's scent because he's been around the Nantahala Pack?" Caius asks after looking at the photo of her on my phone. "We thought it was just from the day of her initial heat, but maybe he's visited Bryson before."

"It's possible," I say, sharing the photo with Volt. He grins in response, then goes back to sharpening his knives.

This is why having a jet is useful. Not only can we work while we travel, but we can also carry weapons with us.

We'll be dropping Alpha Pan, Alpha Lance, and Alpha Mackin off in Richmond first. Then we'll be heading to North Carolina to pay the Nantahala Pack a little visit.

Beta Lock will be with us, as well as a handful of Carnage Wolves that Alpha Duncan quietly sent our way after Caius brought him up to speed via a secure line.

It took some doing, what with Alpha Dirk's clan overseeing telecommunications on the island.

But Alpha Duncan is the chief security expert for a reason.

Between Caius and Alpha Pan, they found a way to reach out.

And six more trusted wolves were able to join us before the jet took off.

They're all eager for blood.

We debriefed them about Alpha Kin and our plan to

take down Bryson. Their savage grins told me they're ready.

They're all helping Volt prepare the weapons, the hunger for blood a lethal kiss in the air.

My phone vibrates as Alpha Ebony sends me another text over the secure line we established.

D is working on setting up surveillance at the Senator's house. Your Omega is still fine.

The second message comes through while I'm reading the first, making my lips twitch.

She sends me another photo, this one of Clove yawning with a plate of food on her lap.

"Let me see," Caius says, noting the grin on my face.

I show him and he smiles, too.

Volt just smirks in response.

More updates and photos continue to arrive as we make the trip to Richmond. Each one helps me relax a little more, especially the last few of Clove sleeping in the corner of the couch. She's covered in my sheets, not from the den but from the bed we fucked in last night.

It's not a nest. Not quite. But it's close.

Volt and Caius both study the photo a little longer than the others, their eyes softening.

"You need to claim her," Volt says, his voice gruff. "She's ours, T. We'll figure out the heir later."

"I mentioned Clove to my dad earlier when I called him about Alpha Nick," I admit. "He reminded me that there's no timeline involved regarding my heir. And that Pack Alphas make the rules more than traditions do."

It wasn't necessarily his way of blessing the union, just him being wise. A good father. An even better Alpha.

I look at the photo again, and the sense of wrongness hits me once more. "She should be here," I admit. "And she would be if we'd bitten her." I meet Volt's dark gaze.

"It's my responsibility to make the best decision for our clan. But I'm struggling."

"So let us help you," he says. "That's why we're here."

"He's right." Caius's gray irises are highlighted by a rim of gleaming silver. "We understand your burden and need for an heir. But Clove isn't a normal Carnage Wolf Omega. She's been raised to process everything differently."

"Just because she may be able to live with it doesn't make it right to produce an heir with another Omega," I state flatly, irritated by the reminder of what she implied last night.

Caius snorts. "That's not what I meant, T. I'm saying her heat process is unique. She's only just met her wolf. It makes sense that there's a delay. However, in regard to what you just said, is your wolf giving you any reason to doubt her ability to give you an heir? Is he hesitating at all?"

"No. He's following his instincts and not considering potential repercussions for the future," I reply.

Caius stares at me. "Maybe because he doesn't sense any potential repercussions."

"Mine certainly doesn't," Volt says, stealing my phone to type something to Alpha Ebony. I don't even try to take it back. Not with that wicked blade beside him.

"Mine doesn't either," Caius says. "And while I may not need an heir, I certainly want one. Especially if it's with Clove."

"A pregnant Clove." Volt sounds like he's daydreaming. "Yes. Yes, I like that image."

So do I, I think.

"You need to consider it, T." Caius infuses a hint of steel into his tone, something that's not all that customary for him unless he really wants to make a point. Which he clearly does now. "Consider that your wolf isn't hesitating because he *knows* there's nothing to worry about."

My animal purrs in approval, making my chest ache at the need to release the sound. But I swallow it instead, much to his irritation.

"Hello, gorgeous," Volt murmurs, my phone at his ear now. "I just wanted to say that I miss you."

Caius and I share a glance, surprised by the softness in Volt's tone. He's usually amped up and ready to kill by now, but he appears to be completely relaxed.

"I miss you, too," Clove says, my shifter senses allowing me to hear her loud and clear. "Are you being safe?"

"Always, sweetling." Volt puts her on video chat so he can show her the plane and takes her on a tour.

"I've never seen him so smitten," Caius tells me. "He usually just wants to break women and leave them."

"He pulled a knife on her last night," I admit. "But she didn't even flinch."

Caius grins. "No, I doubt she would. She knows he'll never really hurt her, even at his craziest."

"Her wolf trusts us." That much has been evident since the start.

"And you keep telling her how important it is to listen to her wolf, yeah?" Caius gives me another knowing look. "Perhaps you should take that advice, T."

"I am listening to him. I'm just making sure he's right first."

"Except mating is meant to be animalistic. The drive to claim is stirred by our carnal needs, not our mental ones." He tilts his head. "You can't be strategic about everything, T. At some point, you have to let the wolf out."

"Stop trying to psychoanalyze me, C." It's a half-hearted statement. He's good at reading people, especially me.

"Just trying to help you find your way out of your ass," he replies conversationally. "You stuck your head so far up there that I'm surprised you can even see right now."

I snort. "Fuck you."

He grins. "Only if Clove is between us."

I consider that for a moment, my lips curling of their own accord. "V and I tried that last night. Three times. Definitely recommend it."

Caius's gaze glitters. "I'm knotting her first during her next heat." It's a bold statement, one I can absolutely counter as lead Alpha.

But I nod instead.

He's been denying himself that sweet pussy all week, taking her mouth instead.

I know it's part of his kink, his game of delayed gratification. However, it only seems fair to agree since he wasn't given the opportunity during her short estrus period.

"Oh, it seems we're missing a fun conversation, sweetling," Volt says, returning to us. "Caius wants to knot you. I think he's jealous about last night."

Her cheeks are pink on the phone screen as Volt turns her toward us. Alpha Ebony is right beside her, studiously ignoring us. But I see the tic in her jaw that says she wants to grin.

"Hi, little one," I say to Clove. "We're all thinking about you."

"We are," Caius agrees. "I hope you're being good, gorgeous."

"I was sleeping," she says, the sheets still wrapped around her in a nesting-like manner. "So I can't guarantee I was being good in my head."

Caius grins. "Oh? A naughty dream, then? Tell us more."

"I will when you get back," she replies, baiting us.

"Hmm, no," I tell her. "I don't want to hear about it. I want you to demonstrate the naughty dream instead."

"Yes," Caius murmurs. "Yes, I like that plan more."

Her face is bright red now.

And Ebony's lips are no longer flat, but tilted.

"We'll see you soon, little one," I say to Clove, loving that look on her face.

Caius takes the phone rather than hanging up, asking if Clove can give the phone to Duncan for a minute. She does, and the two of them start talking about the surveillance update in Richmond.

I listen idly as Volt settles in across from me. "She's ours, T," he says again. "Your wolf knows it. Listen to him."

I don't reply.

Because I don't need to.

We both know he's right.

Claiming her is a risk.

But it's a risk I need to accept.

Caius wraps up his conversation as the plane starts to descend.

The show is about to begin.

CLOVE

A lpha Ebony sets a plate down before me, her brown eyes smiling. "Eat."

My stomach churns, the notion of food making me ill. But I know she's right. I haven't eaten all day. My nerves are all tied up in knots, and my mind is fully focused on Tieran, Volt, and Caius.

They checked in again about an hour ago before turning off their comms.

We're all waiting now for the trap to play out.

Alpha Pan and Alpha Lance are in position.

Alpha Duncan has them up on the feeds.

And Alpha Ebony is busy trying to distract herself by feeding me.

I can sense her concern, the scent subtle but there. So I try to calm her by picking up the sub and taking a bite. She has her own plate as well, one she focuses on when she sees me eating.

Alpha Duncan wanders over to press a kiss to her head, his lips going to her ear. "He'll be fine," he says, the words low but easily heard via my enhanced senses.

I pretend I didn't overhear it, though, not wanting to intrude on their moment.

Their clan is different from Tieran's. Mainly because the Alphas are clearly intimate with each other. I saw Alpha Ebony kiss Alpha Pan goodbye, and it was a lot more than just a peck on the lips. It was hungry, reminding me of the way Volt likes to kiss me.

I like their dynamic.

But I also like that Tieran's clan is more brotherly than romantic. They don't seem shy about sharing me, but they don't appear to be sexually into each other either.

It just demonstrates that not all clans are the same. And I rather like that about the Carnage Wolves. Actually, I like a lot of things about the Carnage Wolves.

Including Alpha Ebony.

She's down-to-earth and tells it like it is. Which she does now as she says, "I know Pan will be fine. But I don't like leaving him to do this on his own." The words are for me since Alpha Duncan has already walked away.

"I know what you mean," I tell her. "I understand why I couldn't go with Tieran, Caius, and Volt, but I don't like it, either." The moment they explained it was about their wolves not being able to handle my nearness during a fight, I halted all my arguments to the contrary.

Because they were right.

But that doesn't mean I'm fond of the outcome.

They seemed to be trying to keep me as involved as possible today with their frequent calls, telling me where they are, showing me around the jet, allowing me to watch as they prepared their weapons.

Well, it was mostly Volt.

But Caius and Tieran both spoke to me as well.

And that helped calm my nerves a little.

However, they're firing to life again now as the monitor shows Alpha Pan scaling the fence of the property.

He does it with an ease that impresses me and makes Alpha Ebony grin. "He has such a fine ass," she says, sighing.

Alpha Duncan grunts. "No distractions, Ebs."

"Me?" She bats her long, black eyelashes at him. "Never."

He gives her an indulgent look, his hazel eyes glowing with a warmth that makes his intimidating form a little more acceptable. He's as wide as Volt but slightly shorter. However, he maintains a much more serious disposition, which he appears to soften just a bit for Alpha Ebony.

A growl comes from the screen, immediately grabbing the entirety of our focus. I've only eaten a few bites of my sub, but I push it away to concentrate on the screens.

Alpha Ebony tenses as a blur of motion crosses the field outside the Senator's home. "I count six," she says.

"Seven," Alpha Duncan corrects, pointing to another blur by the fence. "This one is watching."

"What about Alpha Lance?" she asks.

Alpha Duncan shifts monitors, the two of them studying the footage. "Only two so far."

"I'm insulted," Tieran's voice comes through the microphone. I didn't realize he was listening again. If they're on task, then they should be on the outskirts of Nantahala territory, waiting for the go-ahead. I want to ask, but my eyes are glued to the screen.

"I know. Seven to take me down?" Volt grunts. "Not fucking likely."

"He only sent two after me," Tieran points out.

"He's banking on Volt's attack weakening you emotionally. And he only wants to kill Clove, not you," Caius says.

Tieran and Volt both growl at that.

But a shout from the monitor silences them, everyone's focus on Alpha Pan as the Nantahala Wolves attack.

Gunshots fire. Snarls follow. But Alpha Pan anticipated the attack, and he's in a vest. He moves with impressive speed, opening fire in return as Alpha Mackin leaps into action. They're both dressed in Volt's clothes to help disguise the scents and mask Alpha Mackin's presence.

It works.

The Nantahala Wolves are shocked—I can see it on their faces, thanks to the night-vision tech on the surveillance feed.

I search the feeds, looking for my "father."

But he's not there, something I say out loud to Alpha Ebony.

"We'll find him," Volt promises via the comms, likely having heard me through the one Alpha Ebony is wearing. "If he's not there, he's with Bryson. Which would be my preference."

"Mine, too," Caius agrees.

"I would not want to be Beta Gafton in that situation," Alpha Edwin drawls from his position near the door. He's another intimidating warrior type, but with a thoughtful side I learned a little about today. He likes explaining things, such as the surveillance tools Alpha Duncan uses. He also told me about the secure line they created to fly under Alpha Kin's radar. I liked his teaching mannerisms. Something about them made me feel safer.

He's completely relaxed now, but his eyes dance shrewdly across the screens.

Alpha Duncan and Alpha Ebony are watching them, too. They seem to be holding their breaths, their focus solely on Alpha Pan.

It's not until he takes down the last wolf with Alpha Mackin's help that I hear them finally inhale.

Alpha Lance did his part as well, his voice bored as he says, "They shot the bundle of blankets through the glass. Idiots didn't even notice the missing head, too eager to do damage and run."

"And you chased them, yeah?" Tieran's tone has an intensity to it that cascades goose bumps down my arms.

Anything other than a positive response isn't going to be acceptable to him.

"I wrapped your clothes around two boxes and left them in the driver's side seat as a decoy before they even arrived. I snuck up behind them and shot them in the heads as they turned to run," Alpha Lance replies. "No chasing required."

"Good man," Volt replies.

"I had a good teacher," Lance says.

"Yeah, you did." Pride bleeds into Volt's tone. "The best."

"Is there enough surveillance footage for us to use as proof of intent?" Tieran asks, clearly done with that part of the conversation. Or maybe he's just eager to know if he can hunt Bryson now—a notion that has my nerves fraying all over again.

This was the easy part.

The assault on Nantahala territory is going to be a lot more intense.

"Yeah, Pan is taking close-ups of all the wolves now," Alpha Duncan says, watching a fourth screen that appears to be tied to whatever video equipment Alpha Pan is using. I think it's a camera secured by his vest. "I'm running the visuals through a database for a match. I'll have them any minute now."

"Good. Let me know when they're appropriately

identified." Tieran is in full Alpha mode now, his tone harder than I've ever heard it.

My wolf is pleased. She likes the demonstration of power.

But my stomach is still twisting with discomfort.

"Four positive IDs and counting," Alpha Duncan says, lips curling. "All Nantahala Wolves, Alpha T."

I try to look at the screen to see who they are, but the images are moving too fast. He's already scanning the next dead wolf, whom I briefly recognize as a male not much older than me. *No, that can't be right. He wasn't an enforcer.*

The image is gone before I can really see it.

"Make that five," Alpha Duncan adds.

"All I needed was one," Tieran drawls. "We're going in."

"Make it rain, gentlemen," Alpha Ebony says, excitement coloring her tone.

"I'll bring back souvenirs," Volt promises.

"Good," she replies. "Bloody ones."

"What other kinds are there?" he asks, sounding genuinely curious.

Tieran clears his throat. "Going radio silent in three, two…" He doesn't utter the word *one*, his comms already off.

My heart skips a beat.

What if something happens to them?

I didn't even get to say goodbye.

Was that intentional? A way to keep them focused on the task at hand? Because they don't need to say goodbye, as they'll be back soon?

My mind races, my skin going cold.

It's happening. It's really happening.

And I can't hear them.

I can't see them.

I can't feel *them.*

Alpha Ebony places a hand on my knee. "Hey. They need your faith, not your worry."

I don't bother pointing out the concern I caught on her face during Alpha Pan's part of the mission. She knows. She's just trying to offer support.

But it's not helping.

My wolf is frantic, pacing inside me, furious that she's not there. It feels wrong.

Something's wrong?

No, this is wrong.

I blink, trying to harness my panic.

But I can't seem to breathe.

Alpha Duncan crouches in front of me but keeps his hands to himself. A good thing because I'm ready to bite off Alpha Ebony's fingers. Her palm feels wrong against my jeans. I want that hand to belong to Volt or Tieran or Caius. No one else.

They're mine.

I should be there.

I should be *helping.*

Get it together, I tell myself. *This isn't helping at all. This is making it worse!*

But I can't seem to breathe right. My wolf is a frantic mess. She doesn't like being separated from them. She hates not knowing if they're okay.

There's a missing connection, a mental link that should be here that isn't.

"*Clove.*" Alpha Duncan's tone is stern, forcing me to look at him. His Alpha energy pours over me, demanding focus.

I avert my gaze, but my wolf is listening to him, craving that dominant air. It's not the right male or the right wolf, but she hears the authority in his tone. She knows he's safe. She trusts him.

She trusts Alpha Ebony, too.

It's an interesting sensation, having faith in wolves I've really only just met. But I'm doing what Tieran told me to do—I'm listening to my wolf.

"Alpha Tieran's our Pack Alpha for a reason," Alpha Duncan says, his voice softening a little but still holding that steel edge. "He's the best at what he does, and he has a team with him that's been training for this opportunity for seven years. I'm more worried about how much blood they're going to spill than—"

The ground vibrates beneath us as an explosion sounds in the distance.

Alpha Ebony is on her feet in a second with Alpha Duncan right beside her.

"What the fuck was that?" she demands.

Alpha Duncan starts pulling up island footage, searching for the cause.

Only for the screens to go black.

No.

Not the screens.

The whole damn room.

My wolf reacts, throwing me to the floor as another *Boom!* rocks the foundation.

Alpha Ebony snarls, causing my wolf to whine inside me.

I scurry backward into a corner, driven by my wolf's instincts rather than my own.

The door crashes open on the next breath, a bullet whizzing through the air and going straight into Alpha Duncan's head.

I'm frozen.

Shocked.

Not understanding how I can see until I realize my wolf is looking through my eyes.

I haven't shifted but she's entirely taken over my human form, protecting us both while my mind catches up with what's happening.

I try to meet her halfway, to share control, when all hell breaks loose in the room.

The assailants have silver.

Alpha Duncan is dead.

Alpha Ebony is shot next, her scream sending a shock wave down my spine.

Run. Run. Run.

My wolf is already moving, using our speed and small size to escape the room as Alpha Edwin tackles the intruder into the hallway wall. The gun goes flying.

But I don't stop.

I'm sprinting.

I know the way into the den.

It's safe there.

Safer than here.

I reach the end of the hall and take a left, barreling straight into a hard chest.

The familiar scent of home hits me square in the gut, my gaze darting upward to meet a pair of familiar dark hazel eyes.

Now I know why I couldn't find my "father" on those surveillance tapes.

Because he's here.

On Carnage Island.

And he has a silver knife pressed up against my throat.

VOLT

Tieran gestures for me to lead, aware that this is my sort of playground.

I take point, using my nose to lead the way. We've already doused our scent in mud, using decaying leaves and other woodsy items to make us smell more like the forest around us and less like Carnage Wolves.

But a strong shifter will be able to scent us coming.

Which is why we keep a good distance between us with me leading about twenty-five yards ahead.

It'll make it seem like I'm a one-off at first, potentially encouraging any enforcer types in the area to attack.

I have two guns loaded with silver bullets and over a dozen knives tucked into various places in my jeans.

One ballsy shifter won't be an issue.

Fuck, I could probably easily take down a dozen enforcer types in my current mood.

I move on silent feet, my boots barely touching the ground as I run through the trees. They're as familiar to me as the island.

Because drone technology is fucking amazing.

I've never actually been here, but I'm navigating the land as though I own it.

All those years of studying are finally paying off.

I palm a blade, aware I'm about to pass into monitored territory.

A rustle to my left is all I need. I throw the knife, lodging it into a black wolf's throat. His snarl turns into a breathy whimper that calls to the demons inside of me.

Death, I think, inhaling. *Sweet. Beautiful. Death.*

That silver will keep him from healing.

He'll be gone in five minutes, tops.

Too bad I can't stick around to watch.

I take down two more wolves in a similar sequence, then dart forward toward the first security hut. The Nantahala Pack only has about twelve wolves on rotating duty per shift—another fun fact learned by the drones.

Two wolves are waiting for me there.

Well, not waiting.

They're fucking chuckling at something on the television, oblivious to the lethal energy behind them.

"Seriously," I say. "Killing you is almost a favor to wolf kind."

I use my gun this time, taking them out before they even turn.

"Fucking idiots," I mutter, entirely unimpressed.

Until I realize there are four Nantahala Wolves trying to sneak up behind me.

No. Five.

I grin, turning to engage them.

But Caius and Tieran are already taking them down with a round of well-placed bullets.

I sigh.

Caius grins. "Can't let you have all the fun, V."

"What fun am I even having?" I ask, annoyed.

Then a bell starts to ring, announcing our attack, and my lips curl again.

"A lot of fun," I say, responding to myself. "Excellent."

I take off in the opposite direction of the bell, aware of the security tactic the Nantahala Pack uses when under attack.

We might have let a few drones explode for fun in the past.

Just to see how they reacted.

The technology was so well disguised and emitting such a low frequency that they never noticed them in the sky. And the ones that exploded were too destroyed for them to even begin to piece back together into something meaningful.

They knew where the explosions came from—Carnage Wolves.

But they didn't know what they meant.

They went on full alert for months after the first attack.

We were all very amused.

I leap over a log toward the bunker the Nantahala Pack favors. Three shifters are waiting for me, their statures much larger than the others'. They have guns, too. And don't immediately try to shift.

True enforcers.

Interesting.

I thought they would have all been deployed to kill me.

I'm actually pretty fucking insulted to learn that's not the case.

They pull out their guns, taking aim, but I use a tree as a shield, duck, and fire at a pair of knees. The owner goes down with a howl.

Music to my ears.

Two of our own enforcers join me, using the trees to

their advantage and coming up behind the Nantahala Wolves.

But the enforcers hear them, spinning and firing.

Only for Caius to send one to the ground with a bullet through the head.

Just as Tieran takes down the other with a knife to the throat.

"He didn't send all his enforcers," Tieran says, reading the scene like I did. "That's not a good sign."

"No, it's not." It's a sign that we should have reviewed the identities a little closer to find out how many enforcers remained behind.

But we have a decent team of nine, ten if I include Beta Lock. However, we left him in charge of guarding the jet a good ten miles away.

We used some four-by-fours to drive most of the distance.

Jogged the rest.

And now we're maybe half a mile from the heart of Nantahala Wolf territory.

"We need to find Bryson," Tieran says, heading toward the bunker.

It's where the pack goes to regroup and hide. Which makes it a very likely place to locate Bryson, as he'll be among the front line protecting those inside.

We encounter two more enforcers along the way, both of whom earn quick bullets to the head.

But as we reach the bunker, we quickly realize Bryson isn't here.

It's all women and children, with a few weaker males spread out among them.

They're shaking but taking defensive postures, which would be impressive if it weren't so sad.

Tieran frowns. "Where's your Alpha?" He infuses the

right amount of dominance into his tone to tell them what he is—a true Alpha.

A few of the females immediately fall to their knees. Others just avoid his gaze.

And the children cling to the adults, their confusion pungent in the air.

I share a glance with Caius. The rest of our pack has taken up a protective crescent around us, ensuring their top clan is protected from any unexpected attacks.

But none come.

Because Bryson isn't anywhere near here. "What kind of coward leaves his pack like this?" I demand. "Where's the honor?"

"He took their defensive line, too," Caius adds. "Because there's no way we've already cut through them all."

Tieran steps forward, his posture holding an air of dominance that he makes less threatening by putting away his weapons.

I still keep mine drawn, my hand at my side. I don't trust Bryson not to use this as a perfect opportunity to ambush us.

Caius must feel similarly because he keeps his gun out as well.

One of the females screams, drawing my attention and my gun to her, only to realize she's yelling about her child who has just escaped her grasp. He's maybe seven and running toward Tieran at full speed.

I take a step forward, ready to block the little tyrant.

But Tieran holds me off with his hand, then crouches to meet the little bugger's fist.

He slams it right into Tieran's shoulder.

The mother appears stricken, stumbling into a wall with her hand against her mouth.

However, all Tieran does is grin. "Nice hit, kid," he says, catching the boy's fist as he tries to punch him again. "You have fight; I'll give you that," he tells him, a little purr emanating from his chest in approval.

"Please," the mother whispers, tears pouring down her face. "Please don't. I'll… I'll do whatever you want. Just please don't hurt him."

"Will you tell me where your Alpha went?" Tieran asks as he catches the kid's other hand.

He's right—the kid has spirit.

Definitely Alpha caliber. He's growling and trying to tackle Tieran even while he has no hands. It's sort of adorable.

And really fucking sad.

"Your Alpha left a child behind to fight for you all," I say, shaking my head. "What a fucking craven."

"H-he t-took the Jeeps and headed down the b-back trails," the mother stammers, her hands on her chest as she tries to step forward. But a woman with long black hair holds her back, true fear in her features.

Because they think we're savage beasts.

What they don't realize is they've been living under the rule of a real monster for decades.

He feeds them lies about our kind to keep them scared. Because if they knew the truth, they would run toward us, not from us.

Tieran spins the kid around as he tries to kick him. "Stop," he tells him sternly, his purr intensifying. "I'm not going to hurt you or your mum." He wraps his arms around the boy, pulling him back to his chest in a backward hug. "You can relax, little Alpha. You did good trying to protect them."

The words are against his ear, his voice still stern but holding the nurturing touch of a Pack Alpha.

Tieran purrs a little more, the rumble distinctly different from the one he uses with Clove. This is a purr meant to soothe a pack member, which seems to be working wonders on the boy because he's sagging now in defeat.

In the next moment, the child is crying. But they're not tears of sadness. They're tears of fury.

"H-he left us. Papa left us."

My lips curl down. "Bryson?" Did he create another heir under our noses?

"His father is an enforcer," one of the others explains. This one is a male with shaggy hair who can't be older than fifteen. "They all left us."

"How long ago?" I ask.

"When the bells started," he replies.

Tieran looks up at the male. "Can you show me which direction they headed?"

The teen nods. "Yeah. And I can get you some keys, too."

"Jaxon," one of the females hisses.

"What?" the teen counters, a fresh anger painting a wave of red on his features. "Alpha Bryson just left us to face *that*"—he points at us—"alone. And so far, all they've done is let Jimmy hit their Alpha."

"That doesn't mean they won't do worse. They're Carnage Wolves," the female snaps.

"Yes, evil, savage beasts who pillage and plunder," I drawl. "Doing a hell of a lot of that right now, aren't we?"

"Your Alpha has lied to you," Tieran says, taking a different approach as he slowly rises from his crouched position with the boy still standing before him. "I have proof of those lies."

A few of them share looks.

Some of them don't appear to be all that surprised.

Others are more disbelieving.

The indoctrination of this pack is intense.

"But first, I need to find him," Tieran continues. "He's going to pay for what he's done to the Black Mountain Pack. After that, you'll all be questioned. Those found innocent of his crimes will be given safe haven in our territory. Because when I'm done with your Alpha and his enforcer line, there won't be much left of this pack."

He looks down at the child again, turning him to face him.

"I want you to go back to your mum and not leave her side. She's going to need your strength, little Alpha," he says, brushing his knuckles against his cheek in a gesture of favor from an Alpha to a pack member. "You did good, Jimmy. Now go protect your mum, yeah?"

The little boy stares up at him in wonder, then nods at the task he's been given and runs back to his mother. She's gaping at Tieran like he's grown three heads.

These fucking wolves, I think, already done with this scene. "Show us where they went," I tell the teen. *Jaxon*, I think, repeating his name.

Not that I need it.

But he immediately responds to my command, which earns him some points in my book.

A few of the wolves bristle, causing Tieran to tell two of our wolves to stay behind. "Keep them in line," he orders.

They both nod silently, using the Carnage Wolf intimidation tactic to do exactly what Tieran said.

I suppose that's one way to use our reputation to our advantage.

Are we deadly? Fuck yeah.

Savage? Maybe some of us.

But we're not cruel. Unless the other party deserves it. Which Bryson absolutely does.

Jaxon leads us to the Jeeps, telling us where to find a set of keys for the two left. I toss a pair to Caius, then take the other for myself.

"They went that way," Jaxon says, pointing in the direction of a dirt trail. "It ends at a cabin used for training."

"So he went to find more weapons," I translate.

Jaxon nods.

I glance at Caius, the ultimate expert on this terrain. "True?"

"True," he says. "I know the way."

"Then you get to lead," I tell him.

He grins. "Excellent."

"How many enforcers does he have with him?" Tieran asks, his hand on the passenger door to my new Jeep.

"Eight," Jaxon tells him.

Tieran and I share a look.

"He didn't send enforcers to Richmond," I say. "Not the main ones."

"No," he replies, concern tainting his features.

Shit. "He knew we were coming."

"Seems that way," he replies, his jaw clenching.

I'm about to slide into the driver's seat, but I pause, my chest suddenly twisting. "We have another mole." We already knew this because Alpha Kin said *us*. But who?

Tieran walks away from the Jeep, his finger near his ear as he starts to reactivate the comms.

All the hairs along my arms stand on end as I wait for him to make that connection. Which is why I notice Jaxon's flinch. His eyes start to widen, and I'm moving before I even hear the crack of the bullet.

I dive in front of Tieran, taking the hit to my shoulder and growling in the direction of the gun.

It didn't originate from Jaxon.

It came from the woods.

The little fucker led us into a trap.

Gunfire erupts around us, one of the bullets hitting him square in the head, killing him instantly.

Okay, so it may not have been an intentional trap.

"Looks like they found those weapons!" Caius shouts as he takes cover behind the four-by-four.

Tieran's at my side in the next instant, his knife digging into my arm to catch the bullet. "Don't waste your time on me," I snap.

"I need your fucking aim," he counters, cutting me deeper to yank out the metal.

It hurts like a son of a bitch, making me snarl in response.

He growls back, his animal in his eyes. "The comms are dead," he tells me as he finishes the quick medic job.

Our wolves are surrounding us, taking fire and returning it with the assholes in the woods.

From the growls, it sounds like we're winning. Not a surprise. We've trained under far worse conditions.

"Something's wrong," Tieran continues.

An explosion comes from the tree line, drawing my attention to Alpha Ion. He's grinning like a loon, having just unleashed a handful of grenades. Normally, I would be smiling right along with him.

But my heart is hammering in my chest. *Clove*.

I can hear her screaming.

I don't know how. I don't know why. But she's all around me, her pain echoing between the trees. It's like I'm losing my fucking mind.

Except Tieran is snarling with fury, searching for the source.

And Caius is howling.

It takes a beat for me to understand the source—a fucking speaker system.

"Smile for the camera, Aspen," a flat voice says.

"Yes, say, 'Free me,'" a second drawls, causing my jaw to pop in fury. *Alpha Kin.*

She shrieks instead, the sound unlike anything I've ever heard from her, and my blood is fucking on fire as a result.

"Make a choice," another voice says, this one deeper. *Bryson.* "Your lives or hers."

"Cease fire!" Tieran shouts at our men.

They immediately obey.

And Bryson chuckles, the sound victorious.

Only for Clove to scream again, the sound an agonized cry that goes right to my heart.

Three things occur to me at once.

We should never have left her alone.

If we were bonded, we would be able to talk to her.

And... *I'm going to fucking kill Bryson.*

CLOVE

Several Minutes Earlier

The silver burns against my neck, but I don't stop staring up at the man I once called Father. There's something different about him, a sense of indifference that feels wrong.

He's looking at me like he doesn't even recognize me.

Like he didn't spend two decades raising me as his own.

Most males leave the child-rearing to the females, but he often helped with my training as a child, ensuring I was the fastest female of my age. He pushed me, perhaps not kindly, but I am who I am today because of his influence.

Yet his expression registers absolutely nothing as he holds the knife to my throat. It's like he's frozen there, demanding I stay without even requesting it.

"Good job, Gafton," a new voice says, the source of it making my stomach churn.

Alpha Kin.

He steps into view, his intimidating size immediately making me want to shrink into a corner. It's also the look in his eyes that has me almost cringing. His fractured irises are blazing with fragments of colors that make him look half-mad. Like his wolf is trying to shift, and he's not allowing it.

Brown.

Green.

Brown.

Red.

I swallow as the array of colors shift, giving a whole new meaning to hazel eyes.

I'm guessing brown is the usual shade, as his hair is also a thick dark brown. But he appears a bit unhinged, like he's on the edge of going feral.

"Well, it seems Bryson has fucked everything up for me," the Alpha drawls, leaning against the wall and running his gaze over me. "And it all started with you." He shakes his head and sighs. "Why our father chose your mother, I'll never know."

I swallow against the knife at my throat. My former father isn't otherwise touching me, just frozen before me with that dead look on his face. He's barely even blinking.

What the hell is going on?

And what did Kin just say about my mother?

Our father?

"It was the beginning of their alliance, which proved fruitful for a while. But Bryson's lost his touch." Alpha Kin sounds disgusted by it, his expression darkening. "However, my father cherishes the relationship. So here we are."

He gestures to the hallway, to my former father holding a knife at my throat, and to himself. "A pretty awkward family reunion, I guess." He shrugs. "Well, Gafton's not really part of it. He didn't even realize his mate was part Carnage Wolf until recently."

My former father doesn't even blink at that, just continues to stare at me with the blade.

It's like he's under a trance of some kind.

Is Alpha Bryson doing this to you? I wonder. As Pack Alpha, he's capable of controlling anyone under his rule, even his Beta.

"Bryson knew, though," Alpha Kin continues. "That's why he brought her into the pack—her mixed heritage intrigued him. And he used it to his advantage by forcing her to play with our father. She was meant to be a glorified fuck doll—an Omega-like cunt capable of taking the knot, but a womb that rejects the sperm." He gives me a cruel grin. "What I imagine you'd become to Tieran and his clan eventually."

I'm listening to him, but not reacting. Because I know I'm more than a fuck toy to my clan.

And I'm too disturbed by the fact that my former father still hasn't moved. He's just… standing there… unblinking, holding me at knifepoint.

Can I jump backward? I wonder.

"Unfortunately," Alpha Kin continues, drawing out the word, his head tilting to the side. "Your mother didn't turn out to be the ideal fuck toy because she had you. So the playtime only lasted a night as a result, which almost ruined the alliance between him and our father. But Bryson negotiated to keep you while offering a few other perks to satisfy my father's darker inclinations."

His tone allows me to guess what those perks are, and the glitter in his gaze confirms they're crude.

"Breaking Nantahala Wolves by forcing them to take a knot is quite fun," he says, because apparently, I needed that detail in my mind.

I'm going to be sick.

Yet my former father still isn't moving.

Seriously, why aren't you moving? I think, locking eyes with my father while Alpha Kin continues speaking.

"I don't know why Bryson wanted to keep you. Maybe he thought you'd be an Alpha, someone he could mold into a weapon. Or perhaps he planned to fuck you when you came of age," he says. "Regardless, he found a use for you with that idiot Santeetlah Wolf. At least until you turned white." He steps forward. "So you ended up here, and we've now come full circle."

I swallow again, my gaze darting to Alpha Kin's crazed expression.

He's too close for comfort.

And he looks pissed.

"*You* have ruined everything. I tried to handle it, but Tieran was too fucking fast. And Dirk proved to be an incompetent ass." Alpha Kin shudders visibly, his eyes closing for a moment. His irises are fully brown again when he reopens them. "I told Bryson to fix it. He failed. And now I have to decide what the fuck to do with you."

The insanity in his expression disappears behind a mask of indifference similar to the one my former father is wearing.

It sends a chill down my spine.

"But we have a game to play first. I need you to scream." He reaches for me with lightning speed, slamming me back against the wall and taking the blade from my former father's grip. The sharp edge meets my shoulder, sliding beneath the fabric of my sweater to touch the skin. "It's too bad you're my half sister. Otherwise, we could have some fun first."

He drives the tip into my shoulder, shooting fiery pain through my body all the way to my toes.

"Can't have you dying yet, Aspen. You're my ticket off

this fucking island," he says. "And I have one more deal with Bryson to make—his life for mine."

I don't understand.

None of this makes any sense.

Alpha Bryson knew my mother was part Carnage Wolf. He knew a Carnage Wolf fathered me. Yet he still tried to mate me off to a Santeetlah Wolf by "using my sexuality."

When that failed, my so-called father disowned me and my mother—a female temporarily *traded* to a Carnage Wolf as a fuck toy by her own Alpha—-which led to my exile and her death.

And now my *half brother* wants to use me as some pawn?

He yanks the knife out, only to slash it across my cheek, drawing a hiss of pain from me that ends on a whimper.

A whimper I despise.

And my former father still doesn't fucking move.

It makes me want to hurt him. To kill him. To unleash all this anger on the man I trusted to protect me in this life.

I didn't choose to be the product of a rape.

Nor did my mother choose to be used by her own Alpha as a fucking sex pawn.

What else did he do to her? I wonder, recalling all the times Bryson visited our home.

How could you let this happen to her? I want to demand of the frozen male standing there, watching me endure Alpha Kin's insanity.

The knife touches my neck again as he spins me in his arms, pressing my back to his chest.

"Smile for the camera, Aspen," my father says flatly, holding up a phone.

"Yes, say, 'Free me,'" Alpha Kin coos in my ear as he presses the silver into my skin.

It doesn't slice this time. It just burns, causing me to shriek in both agony and fury.

Agony because silver fucking hurts.

And fury because I can't believe my former father is just standing there holding a phone, videotaping my torment.

Who even are you? I nearly shout. Instead, I scream as Alpha Kin licks my throat.

Everything about this is so damn wrong! Alphas are meant to protect. Mates are meant to cherish.

And this… this is the opposite of that. It's cruel. It's twisted. It's—

"Make a choice," a new voice says, drawing my attention to the phone. *Alpha Bryson*, I recognize, my blood going cold. "Your lives or hers."

No.

No. No. No.

"Cease fire!" Tieran bellows, his voice sending a chill down my spine.

Alpha Kin chuckles at my back, amused. He shifts the blade back to my shoulder, digging in again to reopen the wound he created there. It isn't deep but it *hurts*, drawing a scream from my lips that makes him laugh harder behind me.

Fucking sadist!

The silver leaves my skin, returning to my neck as he wraps his palm around my waist to hold me upright. He thinks I'm losing strength over this. Maybe I am.

Or maybe I can use that to my advantage.

He sees me as an Omega. A weakling.

But he has no idea who I really am, who I trained all my life to be.

I feign a shudder that earns me another lick to the

neck. I fight the urge to gag, my stomach churning in disgust.

"Well played, Bryson," he says as the male in question appears on the phone—which my former father is holding with blank eyes.

He's definitely under Bryson's hold, I decide.

Not that it makes anything different between us. He willingly handed my mother over to the Santeetlah Wolves. And he disavowed me in front of the pack. That was all him.

Not the Alpha studying me from the screen.

Bryson doesn't say anything for a long moment, his eyes assessing. I feel cold under his stare. *Dead.*

"What a disappointment you've proven to be, Aspen" are the words he finally chooses to voice.

And something about his statement makes me even angrier.

He's calling *me* a disappointment? After everything he's done to my mother? After everything he's done to me?

"Release her," I hear Tieran demand.

Alpha Kin snorts behind me.

"That's not how this is going to work," Bryson says conversationally, the phone's image angling down to the ground. "I make the calls here."

My jaw clenches. *Yeah. You always make the calls, don't you? With my life. With my mother's life. You're a fucking disgrace.*

Lava pumps through my veins, my wolf pacing angrily inside me, dying for a chance to *kill.*

Alphas protect.

Mates cherish.

Alphas protect.

Mates cherish.

She seems to be repeating those words over and over

again in my mind, her tail swishing in fury as the *Alpha* at my back continues to hold me at knifepoint.

The *Alpha* who is supposedly my *half brother*.

Maybe that's why his scent is familiar.

Or maybe I'm smelling my father on him.

It doesn't fucking matter.

I am not going to be a pawn, I decide. *I'm* done *being a pawn*.

My wolf roars in agreement, the snarl leaving my lips as I give her full control.

Alpha Kin isn't expecting it.

His arm was loose around me, not firm, the knife at my throat pressing but not cutting. So when I spin out of his hold, it's in a quick maneuver he's not ready to counter.

The silver cuts my skin.

But rather than scream, I embrace the burn and let it fuel my rage.

A roar escapes me, my wolf going absolutely feral.

I allow it.

I give her everything.

I let her *lead*.

My former father—*Beta Gafton*, I forcefully correct myself—lunges forward, finally fucking moving. But I'm ready for him, my wolf shredding my clothes as I shift in midair.

We collide and my paws take him down, the shift far easier than ever before. I didn't even feel my bones break. I'm too busy going for his throat.

I chomp down as I feel a bite of silver in my flank. I rip my jaws away from Beta Gafton's bleeding neck.

Alpha Kin growls behind me, the grating noise trying to force me back into my human form.

My wolf snarls as I fly around to face him. He's not

one of *my* Alphas. He will not control me. He will die instead.

But the silver blade in my rump is making it hard to focus on my movements.

It's actually making me a little uneven.

I stumble.

He smirks.

Then his wild eyes go to the snarling beast at my back.

All the fur along my spine stands on end as the knife is ripped out of my rump and Alpha Dirk darts forward to slam the blade into Alpha Kin's shoulder.

I blink, stunned.

Only to have a leg grabbed and twisted beneath me by Beta Gafton.

He's rabid.

Feral.

With wild eyes I don't recognize and an expression of pure animalistic fury.

"*You did this,*" he roars, leaping at me.

My wolf bounds out of the way, but the corridor is only so wide. I immediately hit a wall, which sends a jolt through my lower half.

I'm healing now that the silver is out of me, but I still feel awkward.

Except I'm on my four legs.

And Beta Gafton is on two.

I also have a fully functioning irate wolf running the show, while he's clearly lost his mind. Likely a side effect of Bryson controlling him, which is the only explanation for his blankness.

How did he even get here? I wonder as he attempts to attack me again.

My wolf reacts, going straight for his throat with the intention of finishing the job this time.

His arms come around me and squeeze so hard that bones start to crack, but my jaws are locked tight around his jugular.

He didn't expect me to leap.

And he thinks his strength is enough to intimidate me now.

But my wolf works through the pain, locking her teeth and ripping out his fucking throat. A harsh gurgling follows, his crazed eyes blinking in surprise as blood pours from the wound.

He's choking.

My wolf is licking her chops, appeased.

His knees buckle, his hands clawing at his throat.

When a bullet goes through his head.

A *silver* bullet—something I know because I feel the blaze of it in the air.

I spin toward the shooter to find Alpha Dirk lowering the muzzle to his side, his body covered in blood.

And a dead Alpha Kin at his feet.

I back up, my rump hitting the wall as I brace myself for whatever fight is about to occur. Because pure, unadulterated rage pours off of Alpha Dirk.

He's bigger than Alpha Kin.

Stronger.

Fiercer.

My wolf growls, challenging him because she doesn't know what else to do.

Alpha Dirk narrows his eyes in return.

Then a howl pierces the air, the source of it coming from the phone on the floor between us.

My legs buckle beneath me, my animal immediately submitting to the rage coming from that sound.

Tieran…

TIERAN

Several Minutes Earlier

Y*our lives or hers*, Bryson said.

I choose neither, I think as he enters the clearing with the phone near his side.

It's a mistake. He's still hooked up to the speakers, allowing me to hear Clove's response.

She's in pain and she's furious.

But he doesn't seem to realize that because he's grinning triumphantly.

The three enforcers at his back don't appear nearly as confident because they are all who remain of Bryson's team.

Meanwhile, all my wolves are still alive.

Because I have something he doesn't—*heart*.

He uses hive-mind manipulation and enslaved pussy to tame his wolves. That only allows for so much loyalty in a pack. And those wolves at his back don't appear too keen on dying for their insane leader right now.

Because they know that's what's about to happen.

A roar comes through the phone, the source of it all

Clove, and a loud crash follows. *Beta Gafton dropping the phone*, I translate.

Volt is moving before I can even lift my weapon.

He has two blades on Bryson's chest in the next breath, just as Caius sends a bullet into the enforcer closest to the Alpha. I take down the next two with my own gun, firing without thinking and giving them both a quick death.

Then I walk up to where Bryson is wheezing on the ground. "I choose your death," I tell him, aiming at his head.

And I pull the trigger.

There's one thing I've learned in my training—never prolong a death just to gloat. One never knows when the opposite party will gain the upper hand.

Just like we did now while Bryson paused to enjoy his victory.

"Cocky fucking wolf," I mutter, shooting him again.

"Well, that was anticlimactic," Volt says as he retrieves his knives.

"He needed to die," I say flatly.

I bend to pick up the phone, hoping to see the source of all the snarling coming through the loudspeaker.

But the screen is black. I try to unlock it, only to realize it's already live.

Which means either the camera is turned off or the phone is facing the gro—

My head snaps up as a fresh scent catches my nose. "Santeetlah Wolves," I hiss.

This isn't their fight.

They need to learn to back the fuck off.

And I'm about to show them why.

Because I'm fucking *done* with this war. Bryson caused it. I'm finishing it.

I don't wait; I *howl*.

All my furious energy and pent-up rage go into the echoing sound. It's a warning, one I hope those assholes heed. Because I will shred every single one of them.

I don't know if Clove is alive or dead. And I'm pissed that I didn't claim her. If I did, I would be able to feel her right now.

Instead, I'm staring at a black screen with a dead fucking Pack Alpha at my feet.

I'm fury incarnate.

A wolf mourning the loss of his potential mate.

An Alpha devastated by everything that's befallen his pack.

Alpha Crane responds with his own howl, attempting to regroup his likely startled wolves.

So I open my mouth once more, unleashing another wave of power. Only this one is amplified by the howls of Caius and Volt. The three of us sing in unison, capturing the night with our dark and deadly song.

Silence greets us when we're done.

I wait.

Alpha Crane appears several minutes later with only two wolves at his side.

Volt has his gun drawn. Caius, too.

But I just hold the phone, waiting for an image to appear.

"The Elders will hear about this, Tieran," Alpha Crane says, his disgust palpable as he takes in Alpha Bryson's dead body. "Using guns instead of teeth. It's despicable."

"I agree," I tell him honestly. "But Bryson is known for his silver tactics. I merely beat him at his own game."

A true wolf fights with claws and teeth.

But Bryson proved long ago that he wasn't a true wolf.

"Tell the Elders," I add. "I look forward to finally presenting my case."

Alpha Crane's brow furrows. "What case?"

I don't grace him with a response. He hasn't earned one. But I do offer him one final comment. "When I ascend, I'll be calling a meeting. I suggest you attend. We have a few items to discuss."

One being Clove's mother.

I continue checking the phone.

There are no sounds coming from it now.

Come on, Clove, I think. *Tell me you're okay*.

It's almost an appropriate punishment—me not knowing.

"You can go," Caius says calmly, his words for Alpha Crane. "We'll be in touch."

The Santeetlah Alpha bristles at being dismissed, so three of my wolves step forward *without* guns. They simply snarl.

And Alpha Crane stiffens.

He has a pack of weak wolves, similar to the one we just destroyed.

And he came without weapons.

I meant what I said about the guns. But that doesn't mean he trusts me to honor him in a fair fight.

He believes all the rumors, which are helping me in this situation.

Because he accepts our dismissal with a low grunt, making his displeasure at the insult known, and leaves with his tail tucked between his legs.

"*That's* Alpha Crane's heir?" Volt asks, sounding entirely unimpressed. "His son, right?"

"Yeah, the shaking one was his son," Caius confirms.

Volt snorts. "He looked ready to piss his pants."

"This phone doesn't appear to be working," I tell Caius, handing it to him.

He fiddles with the black screen, his brow furrowing.

I try my comms again and find them still busted. "Anyone else able to connect via comms?"

All my men shake their heads.

I hate this sensation of not knowing what's happening. Clove went quiet for too long again. The last sound I heard was her roar before Beta Gafton dropped the phone. Or I assume he was the one holding it since it was his voice that told her to smile.

Caius throws the phone on the ground. "It's broken."

"We need to go," I say, my heart in my throat. I fucking hate this. I hate that I can't feel her. I hate that I can't hear her. I hate that I have no idea what's happening to her right now.

"I'll reach out to Alpha Pan as soon as we get to the jet." Caius sounds as concerned as I feel.

I quickly put three of my men in charge of cleaning up here and tell them to head to Black Mountain Pack territory when they're done. I'll call my father on the way to let him know the plan.

"If anyone tries to hurt a Carnage Wolf while I'm gone, there will be hell to pay when I return," I say to those at the bunker on our way out.

Most of them are staring at me with reverence.

Some possess a hint of unease and distrust.

And only a handful glare at me. That handful is promptly taken by Alpha Ion. He'll start by questioning them first.

I start toward the path we came in on, when the little Alpha calls out to me. I turn toward Jimmy to see him chasing us down.

My heart is torn between embracing him and running

toward my intended mate. But the wolf in me makes me squat to his level as he reaches me on a pant.

"You kill Papa," he tells me, blinking innocently with the childlike words.

I swallow but nod. I won't lie to this tiny being. "Yeah, we did." All the enforcers here are dead. So unless his father ran, which is doubtful, then his dad is no longer with us.

His lips twist and he nods. "I take care of Mama." He sounds almost relieved by that, making me wonder how his father used to treat his mother. Because he isn't upset at all. Just accepting, almost to the point of thankfulness.

"Yes, Jimmy. Go take care of your mum."

He beams. "Thank you, Alpha."

My heart warms at the clear designation in his tone. His mom is waiting for him just beyond the trees, her eyes wide.

"He's a good kid," I tell her. "If you seek refuge with Black Mountain Pack, we'll turn him into an Alpha who can lead." Because he has the genetics. I can sense it in him.

She looks ready to cry. Not necessarily in sadness, but maybe with a hint of shock to it.

I clear my throat and stand, then ruffle the kid's hair. "Go be a good little Alpha and take care of your pack. I'll be back."

I turn away, just for the mother to say, "I hope Clove is okay."

All the hairs along my arms lift as I face her again. The entire pack probably heard that display with Bryson. We are nowhere near their cabins, so if the speakers are out this far, then they likely span the territory. Also, everything went down near the bunker.

So yeah.

They heard everything.

"She's a good wolf," the female adds.

"She is," I tell her, my lips almost curling. "And she's fine." I say it with a confidence I don't feel.

But I'm determined to believe it.

"He told us she was dead," the female adds. "Bryson. He said she went feral and killed her mom." She swallows. "Clove would never kill Serena."

"Another one of his lies," Volt says as he steps up to my side. "And we really need to go." He voices it gently but with a touch of urgency.

She nods. "Yes. G-Gafton isn't a bad wolf. He's… he's just under Bryson's control. But Kin…" She shudders, her shoulders turning in on herself as Volt and I share a look. "You're not like him."

"You've met Alpha Kin?" Caius asks, inching toward the female.

Her son is wrapped around her legs again, his face buried in her thigh as he tries to rumble for her in the same way I did for him.

It comes out as a grumble more than a purr.

Because he's not a Carnage Wolf.

"Alpha Bryson… he… he lets Kin…" Her violent tremble tells us all we need to know.

Jimmy clings to her tighter, and she clears her throat.

"There are two Carnage Wolves that he *introduced* to certain members of our pack. Always in secret. He didn't know that I…" She trails off, clearing her throat again. "He never knew that I saw it happen. I was only six the first time. But I saw what that Alpha did to Serena. His scent haunted me for years. It's how I knew when he returned. And then, one day, he brought *Kin.*"

"Do you know the name of the other man? The one you can scent?" I ask, gentling my voice.

She shakes her head. "I only knew Kin because he made Evelyn scream his name while… while he… he *killed* her."

I understand what she's saying. He forced his knot on her.

"What did he smell like?" Caius infuses a hint of his purr into his words.

"Like sour mud," she whispers.

My brow furrows. I'm not sure any of our wolves have that scent. "Thank you. We'll find him and make him pay for what he's done." It's a vow I intend to keep.

She nods again, her cheeks pink as she fights more tears. "I'm sorry. I know you need to go to Clove."

"We do," Caius confirms. "But we'll be back."

"And we'll bring her with us," Volt promises.

My throat constricts.

It's a promise I hope we can keep.

CLOVE

T_hey're here._
        It's an intrinsic reaction, one that causes the hairs along my nape to stand on end.

Alpha Dirk must sense it as well because he perks up in his chair.

"They're going to try to kill you," Alpha Ebony tells him conversationally.

"I know," he replies with a sigh. "I probably deserve it."

"You don't," she replies.

And I agree with her.

After Tieran's howl came through the phone, Alpha Dirk fell to his knees and bowed his head.

Not for Tieran.

But for _me_.

He remained that way as we listened to the aftermath of that howl, overheard Tieran's conversation with Alpha Crane, and his inevitable frustration over the phone not working on his end.

Not once did Alpha Dirk stir.

As the phone went quiet, my wolf started to move, sniffing the alpha male with interest.

He didn't move, allowing her to circle him while scenting the air for any signs of malevolence.

She found none.

I eventually stepped away from him with a grunt.

Only then did he start to sit up, his dark green eyes intense. "I won't hurt you, Clove. But I'll accept whatever punishment you wish to deliver. It's my responsibility to manage those in my clan, and I failed."

His words still swirl around me now, along with the acute disappointment in his tone and the sadness of his failure.

He blames himself for Alpha Kin's crimes.

I almost shifted back to tell him it wasn't his fault, but logic kept me in wolf form.

It *is* partially his fault. He should have suspected Alpha Kin's nefarious intent. I can't imagine Volt or Caius being able to do something so horrible beneath Tieran's nose.

So in that regard, I do blame him.

But I won't let him bear the punishment of another's sin.

I sit on my rump by the door, waiting for my intended mates to find me. I sense them prowling, *hunting*, their Alpha energies an aphrodisiac calling to my very soul.

They're coming, my animal is saying, her excitement palpable. *They're coming. They're coming.*

We've been sitting in the dark down here for hours. No phones. No way to communicate. Using our enhanced night vision to see.

Alpha Duncan is dead. And Alpha Ebony is healing, thanks to Alpha Dirk removing the bullets from her skin.

He did the same for Alpha Edwin, but he's still unconscious on the couch.

"Kin took out the telecommunication tower," Alpha Dirk said earlier. "And he cut the power to the island."

It's what tipped Alpha Dirk off that there was a problem—he could smell Alpha Kin's essence all over the sabotage. So he went looking for him.

And found him with me.

"I didn't think; I reacted," he told Alpha Ebony shortly after she woke up. "I ripped his throat out."

"Good," she replied. "He fucking deserved it."

They discussed a bit about what they thought happened, comparing notes between Alpha Dirk's observation of events and Alpha Ebony's pre-established knowledge of Alpha Kin's betrayal.

"He must have found the secure line that Alpha Caius and Alpha Pan set up," Alpha Dirk said at one point. "Or maybe he had his own surveillance set up to detect interference. Regardless, it's clear he warned Bryson since they were working together."

He uttered that last part through his teeth, his fury at the situation a palpable presence in the air. He clearly didn't know about that link until Alpha Ebony voiced it.

And now that he knows about it, he's still angry.

But he's remaining mostly calm at the desk, awaiting his fate.

Alpha Kin's and Beta Gafton's remains are sitting in the hallway as a pair of gifts—something Alpha Ebony suggested they do. "It'll give them enough pause to perhaps consider talking to you before ending you," she said after voicing the recommendation.

Alpha Dirk didn't necessarily agree but did what she told him to do after I grunted in agreement.

They fell into a brief conversation about my former father, wondering how he'd even managed to get here. Then Alpha Dirk confirmed something I already knew.

"He wasn't of sound mind," he said. "He was under his Alpha's control. I could see it in his crazed eyes when he attacked Clove."

Which explains why he stood as still as a statue after putting a knife to my throat.

But doesn't exactly tell us how he arrived on the island.

"Someone must have helped him," Alpha Ebony said, voicing my concern out loud.

The question is, *who?*

Alpha Kin's father?

I refuse to call the male *our* father because I don't know him, nor do I want to know him.

Just the thought makes me shiver.

"He could have just taken a speedboat from the mainland," Alpha Dirk told Alpha Ebony.

"Maybe," she replied, not sounding all that convinced.

I'm not convinced either.

It's a piece of the puzzle that's been swirling around in my mind on repeat for hours. *There's someone else involved*, I keep thinking, even now. *But who?*

From what Alpha Ebony said, Alpha Kin's father was taken into custody by Alpha Umber. So it can't be him.

A deep roar comes from the hallway, snapping my wolf's head in the direction of Volt's fury.

They're here. They're here. They're here.

My wolf wants to bound into the corridor to greet them, but I stay seated.

Because I'm protecting Alpha Dirk.

Alpha Ebony is right. They're furious, and they're going to try to kill him because my blood is in the hallway, as is his, from the fight.

Alpha Tieran is the first through the door, his gaze wild as he takes in the scene with a snarl.

Until he sees me sitting there, waiting.

He's in wolf form, his animal dwarfing mine.

His reaction is immediate, his wolf leaping forward to sniff my neck and nuzzle my throat.

Volt is next. Then Caius. The three of them are all in their beast forms, rubbing against me with purrs and growls and sniffing every inch of me to check for injury.

I let them, refraining from the instinct to do the same.

Because I need to keep my focus.

Volt is the first to react to Alpha Dirk's presence, his growl low and menacing. Tieran does the same, both males rumbling in disapproval and fury.

When Volt starts to stalk forward, I nip him on the flank.

He spins on me, growling at the unexpected bite. Then softens when he realizes it was me.

I stand then and move to sit between him and Alpha Dirk.

All three of my males watch me with interest, their confusion palpable.

"She's saying she's in charge of his punishment," Alpha Ebony translates for me, a hint of wonder in her tone. "*That's* why you've been sitting by the door."

I grunt in confirmation.

And now that my males are here, I can shift.

Because I feel safe again.

So I do, which turns out to be a mistake because Volt immediately tackles me to the ground in the next breath, his furry body covering all of mine.

"*Oomph*." The sound escapes me on a puff of air, leaving me a little light-headed.

"Get her a shirt," Tieran demands, apparently back in human form. "What the fuck happened down here?"

"Alpha Kin took out the communications tower and the power. Only his sat phone seems to work," Alpha

Ebony says. "But we couldn't figure out his password to make outgoing calls. And without access to electricity, which we need to power up the computers, we couldn't use anything to hack it."

A shirt appears in my peripheral vision as Caius kneels beside us. "Here you go, gorgeous," he says, his eyes more silver than gray as he scans my face.

Volt grumbles a little, shifting just enough to give Caius room to pull the shirt over my head.

"No one sees you naked except us," Caius explains, tugging the fabric down.

"I'm a shifter," I mutter at him. "I have to be naked to shift."

His eyes narrow. "*No one*," he repeats.

My mother's voice is in my head telling me to pick my battles. This is one I may fight him on later, but for now, I let him pull the shirt down while Alpha Ebony continues to report on what happened down here.

"Alpha Kin killed Alpha Duncan," she says, her voice void of the emotion I know she's feeling. "He tried to kill me and Alpha Edwin and would have succeeded if Alpha Dirk hadn't removed the silver."

"And you had no idea he was working with Bryson?" Tieran demands, his words for Alpha Dirk.

"No, but I should have known," he admits. "I failed as a clan leader. I failed as a Carnage Wolf. I failed as one of your Alphas. I'll accept whatever fate you assign to me."

"He saved me from Alpha Kin," I interject, still partially trapped beneath Volt's bulky form. Apparently, the shirt isn't enough for him. Or maybe he just likes lying on top of me. "This... this was after Alpha Kin told me he's my half brother. His father... his father raped my mother."

It hurts to voice out loud. But Tieran needs to

understand that Alpha Kin's loyalty was never to Alpha Dirk.

And while, yes, Alpha Dirk should have suspected the lack of allegiance, sometimes blood can be a powerful motivator in manipulation.

"But Alpha Dirk killed Alpha Kin, and he killed Beta Gafton," I say. "He acted in honor of the pack. In honor of *me*." It's something I instinctively understand, the way he bowed to me for nearly thirty minutes after Tieran's howl.

He was *submitting* to my wolf.

"Alpha Kin told you that about his father?" Tieran asks, stepping around Volt's wolfish head to meet my gaze.

I nod. "Bryson let him do it because he knew my mother was a half-breed. He thought she would make a nice... *fuck toy*... for his father." I cringe at the term, but it's the one he used. "Only, she ended up pregnant."

Tieran considers me for a long moment. "I'll have my father confirm his scent with one of the Nantahala Wolf witnesses."

I frown, not understanding what he means, but Volt distracts me by shifting back into his human form. His strong legs trap mine as he moves to lie more firmly on top of me with his elbows on either side of my head. He doesn't speak. He just kisses me. Hard.

Caius clears his throat.

Volt grunts in response, then buries his nose in my hair, inhaling deeply.

"Tell me everything," Tieran demands. "From beginning to end."

Alpha Ebony obliges, reiterating all the facts of what happened up until the attack. Then Alpha Dirk takes over to fill in the missing pieces, about how he went to the telecommunications tower to investigate the power outage and realized Alpha Kin had sabotaged it all and how he followed him here.

Where he found him attacking me.

I listen, partially numb to it all, and sigh as Volt begins to purr.

"We could hear you through the phone," Alpha Dirk concludes. "We chose to wait here for your return. It's deep underground, and not many wolves know how to breach Alpha Duncan's security."

"But you did," Tieran points out.

"Yes. I know how to breach a lot of security on the island, but that doesn't mean I use that knowledge."

"No, you just shared it with Alpha Kin," Tieran accuses.

"He was my clan mate." Alpha Dirk doesn't voice it as an excuse, just a fact. "I… I trusted him."

Silence falls.

The concept of judgment is heavy in the air as Tieran evaluates everything they know.

"Someone helped Beta Gafton reach the island," Tieran says. "I want to know who it was. Find out for me and I'll consider lessening your sentence."

Alpha Dirk nods, accepting the task.

Tieran is quiet for another moment.

Then he throws his head back on a howl that scatters goose bumps down my arms and legs. Volt and Caius immediately join in, answering his call and empowering it with their energy and strength.

My wolf purrs in response to their joint song.

Ours, she's saying. *These males are ours*.

Volt nuzzles my neck when the howling finishes, his tongue laving my pulse. Only for his head to snap back on a snarl in the next second.

I flinch.

Caius and Tieran are there in an instant, both of them burying their heads into my throat to sniff whatever inspired Volt's reaction.

Both men growl.

"Did Alpha Kin *lick* you?" The words are from Tieran, anger making them come out in a low rumble of furious sound.

I swallow, then nod.

All three of them snarl now, Volt jumping up off the floor and lifting me into his arms like I weigh nothing.

"Bring the bodies with you," Tieran snaps at Alpha Dirk. "You have ninety minutes."

I have no idea what he means.

That howl must have been a signal for something.

"Don't you dare help him," Tieran adds, looking at Alpha Ebony.

"He's not touching Duncan," she replies, her gaze intense as she challenges her superior. "He's *mine*."

Tieran considers her for a moment, then concedes with a nod. "Only Alpha Duncan."

She immediately relaxes, her gaze leaving his. "Thank you, Alpha."

He steps toward her, his palm wrapping around the back of her neck.

She tenses.

And he pulls her into a hug. "Thank you," I hear him whisper against her ear. "Thank you for taking care of our Clove."

She shudders, her shoulders losing their stiffness.

"Alpha Duncan was a good man," Tieran continues. "He will be honored."

She wraps her arms around him, returning the hug as another tremble works through her.

He embraces her, lending her his strength for a long

moment. Then he kisses the top of her head. "Alpha Pan will be here within the hour. He doesn't know yet."

"I'll tell him," she replies.

Tieran nods again, slowly releasing her. "Place Alpha Duncan near the water. I'll take care of the rest."

She visibly swallows and dips her chin in acknowledgment.

It's the first true sign of pain I've seen from her since she woke up. She's been holding herself together this whole time, her focus on protection.

Alpha Dirk's been the same, his expression stoic as he waited for Tieran, Volt, and Caius to return.

Volt carries me into the hallway, leaving Tieran to say a few final words to Alpha Ebony and Alpha Dirk. I don't know what they are because Volt and Caius start to purr so loudly that their rumbles are all I can hear.

It doesn't seem intentional, just them wanting to offer comfort as we move through the scene of carnage around us.

"I can walk," I tell Volt as he reaches another corridor.

He grunts in response. "I'm never letting you go again, Clove. Better just get used to being carried everywhere."

"Yep," Caius echoes.

Another battle I really don't want to fight.

Although, I could point out that they're both stalking through these halls naked when they just told me I'm not allowed to go without clothes in front of other people.

But I really don't want to argue about that either.

I just want to revel in their presence.

They're okay.

They're here.

They're alive.

I nuzzle Volt's chest, inhaling his coppery scent and sighing at the hint of ash in its wake.

He smells like death.

A death I would not mind experiencing.

Caius's peppermint essence tickles my nose next.

Followed by the strong fragrance of pine and male.

Tieran is suddenly there, taking me from Volt's hold and hugging me with a fierceness that makes it hard to breathe. "*Ours*," he growls, taking off in a run that has me wrapping my arms around his neck to hold on for the ride.

I almost repeat my ability to walk, but midnight air touches my neck, causing me to curl further into Tieran's heat.

I breathe him in, relishing his existence.

He takes me to the den, running through the cave with purpose and not stopping until he reaches the main bedroom.

Caius is already there, warming the shower. Apparently, the underground generators aren't impacted by the power outage on the island.

It's something I almost ask about, but I'm distracted by the onslaught of testosterone and strong male scents.

My shirt disappears to the floor, and Tieran's intense blue eyes meet mine.

"We're going to bathe you. Dress you. Then claim you before the pack." His palm cups my cheek. "You're *ours*, Clove. Never again will we be without you. Never again will you be alone. The ceremony is set. We're biting you at three beneath the moon."

TIERAN

T he shock in Clove's gaze tells me how badly I've fucked this up.

She's surprised we're going to claim her.

She shouldn't be surprised.

She should be *expectant*.

Instead, she's gaping at me.

I slowly lower her to her feet. Caius is immediately there behind her, grabbing her hips to provide balance. Not that she needs it. She's fully healed, just has a bit of dried blood on her.

And Alpha Kin's saliva.

My wolf growls inside at that.

He had no right to touch her, let alone *lick* her. If he wasn't already dead, I would kill him again.

I cradle Clove's face between my hands as Volt enters the shower last. I walk her backward into Caius, trapping her between us. "I should have bitten you the moment I knotted you," I tell her. "You've been ours from the moment that Volt pulled you out of the water."

"But... but we don't know if..." She trails off, swallowing. Then her brow furrows as her gaze drifts to the side. "Well, my mom did. So maybe…" She blinks back at me. "Is that what you're basing your claim on? That Alpha Kin's father was able to impregnate my mother?"

My eyes widen. "What? *No.*" Just the notion of it infuriates me. She thinks we only want to claim her now that we know how she was conceived?

That's… that's so beyond wrong it makes my wolf snarl in fury.

Not at her.

But at *me.*

He's pissed that I let it go this far, that she thinks the only reason I would actually claim her is to procreate.

"Do I need an heir?" I ask rhetorically. "Yes. But you know what I want more, Clove?" My palm slides from her cheek to the back of her neck. "*You.*" I press myself fully against her, aligning us from our knees all the way up. She's officially trapped between me and Caius without any escape. Because Volt is blocking the only exit.

Not that she appears all that interested in running.

"I… Okay. But we can't mate unless—"

I press my mouth to hers, silencing that statement. Because I'm so tired of hearing it. I'm so tired of thinking it, too. Fuck, I'm just so exhausted from this fight.

"You're ours," I say against her lips. "The rest will sort itself out."

She presses her palm to my chest, pushing me back a little. "But I may never be able to give you an heir, Tieran. Then you'll have to take—"

"Then I'll have to either rewrite the rules as Pack Alpha or abdicate," I say, refusing to let her finish that statement.

Because I won't take another Omega.

Only this one.

Only Clove.

"I'm listening to my wolf," I continue. "I'm taking my own advice… and letting him lead."

"About fucking time," Volt says, picking up the water sprayer and aiming it at Clove's neck. He does it in a way that doesn't splash her face, just washes away the presence of another male.

But her gaze is locked on mine, her expression giving nothing away.

"I'm sorry it's taken me so long to realize what matters most. It's not my heir or my duty to the pack. It's *you*, Clove. *You* define our clan. You're the heart we didn't realize we needed." I allow her to see my wolf in my eyes, to feel his desire in my touch.

Her gaze searches mine, her lips parting a little at whatever she sees inside me.

"I feel in my soul that you're meant to be mine, Clove." I tighten my grip around her nape. "You're meant to be *ours*."

She shivers, her pupils blowing wide. "I want to be yours," she admits in a whisper. "My wolf says you're already hers."

I smile. "And what did I say about listening to your animal?"

"To embrace her and let her thrive," she replies.

I nod. "And I've not been doing that with mine. I've been telling him to listen to reason, but our wolves don't care about rules or political discourse. They drive our passion. They drive our need. They tell us how to live." I push against her palm, closing the distance between us again. "And he's telling me to bite you, Clove."

"Then bite me," she dares.

Volt freezes beside us, a bar of soap in his hand.

It's not what I planned, nor what we announced with our howls.

But I owe this moment to our intended mate, not to our pack.

If she wants to be claimed here, in this shower, and not out on the beach before the wolves, then I'll oblige her.

And we'll present her as ours to the wolves.

I know in my gut they'll accept her because they already do. She's our Omega. The heart of our clan. Our future.

"Wash her neck," I tell Volt, needing her skin fully clean.

Her eyes glitter as she holds my gaze.

Caius hums in approval behind her, his arms slipping between us as he wraps his arms around her waist. "Ours," he whispers against her ear.

"Ours," Volt echoes as he uses the soap against her neck.

"Ours," I agree, releasing her nape to take the showerhead from Volt's other hand.

Her nipples are hard little points, her lips parted on a pant I can almost feel as I rinse the suds from her throat and down her breasts.

There's some dried blood on her shoulder that I clean off as well before focusing on her cheek. "Did he cut you anywhere else?" I ask, aware that there were wounds here that caused the dried blood to exist. Because it's her blood, not his.

She shakes her head.

"Did he lick you anywhere else?" Volt demands.

She shakes her head again.

"Did he touch you anywhere else?" Caius asks.

This time she nods, then gestures to the places he touched her. Which includes her back—presumably from holding her against him—and various places on her torso. "They both placed knives here," she points at her throat.

We proceed to clean every space with soap and water.

Then Caius takes over by washing her hair while Volt focuses on her thighs and the sweet space between her legs. No one touched her there, but he's being thorough.

All the while I watch, waiting for her to be ready for us.

It's a drawn-out game of delayed gratification.

I want to bite her.

And now I'm trying to decide where she'll bear my mark.

It needs to be somewhere everyone will see. I want there to be no question as to whom she belongs to.

Caius and Volt take turns kissing her as they worship her with their hands, their bodies primed to claim in more ways than one.

I'm hard, too.

Painfully so.

But my wolf is more eager to *bite*.

I take in her supple form, that flat belly, perky tits, curvy bottom. Fuck, she's perfect.

"We should never have waited," I say, repeating myself from earlier. "We should have claimed you from the very first day."

Which would have been impossible in wolf form.

However, it's the point that matters most.

"I'm sorry it took me this long to understand," I say, stepping into her space as Caius finishes washing her hair. I have her by the nape again, my opposite hand on her hip. "I'm going to spend however long it takes to earn your forgiveness."

"I'm not upset," she whispers.

"Then I'll wait however long it takes to earn my wolf's forgiveness," I clarify. "Because he's furious with me."

She smiles. "You ignored him. They don't like that."

"No, they don't," I agree, brushing my lips against hers. "They really, *really* don't."

I kiss her the way he tells me to now, all teeth and tongue and dominance. She practically vibrates against me, her body so fucking ready. I growl, the sound low and meant for a mate. She trembles in response, the alluring scent of slick touching my senses.

Volt rumbles in approval.

Caius, too.

All three of us are calling to her, demanding she prepare herself for our *need*.

I'm aware we're on a timeline.

But my wolf doesn't care.

And I meant what I said about allowing him to lead.

I release her neck to grab her hips, lifting her into the air and pinning her to the shower wall. I don't wait. I don't even play. I just thrust into her weeping heat and take her to the hilt.

She cries out in surprise more than pain, her body already acclimating to mine.

Because she was made for us.

Just as we were made for her.

"If I'm going to claim you here, then I'm going to do it properly," I tell her. "By making you come while I bite you."

She grabs my shoulders, her nails biting into my skin. "Then you'd better fuck me harder," she breathes. "Or I'm going to end up biting you first."

Volt chuckles. "Do it, sweetling. He deserves it for making us all wait this long."

I growl, slamming into her again and drawing a scream from her throat. "Hard enough?"

"No." She arches into me on a needy little moan, her

claws dragging down my arms. She hasn't shifted, not really. But her nails are sharp and potent.

And they're turning me the fuck on.

As is her mouth.

My palm circles her throat, my other hand staying at her hip as I drive the pace between the lower halves of our bodies.

But I let her dictate the embrace between our mouths.

Which turns out to be just this side of feral.

Her wolf has taken over entirely, driving our savagery and encouraging my beast to come out to play.

So I let him, giving in to the animalistic need to *fuck*. To *take*. To *claim*.

She's screaming.

I'm snarling.

And together we create a beautiful song of carnality.

The hot energy coming off of Volt and Caius only adds to our embrace. I can feel their eyes on me, waiting for that claiming moment.

It's intense.

It's right.

It's absolutely fucking *perfect.*

Her tight sheath squeezes my shaft, demanding my knot. I don't hold back. I don't delay. I just give in to her on a growl, not bothering to restrain my savage intent.

Clove falls apart, her body spasming as she accepts all of me inside her.

I erupt on a roar, my knot shooting out of my shaft to claim what's mine.

And I sink my teeth into her neck.

Right where that bastard licked *my* female.

Caius and Volt growl in approval, their collective triumph tipping me over the edge into the most intense climax of my life.

It's like I just started coming all over again.

Clove follows me right into that oblivion, her heart hammering against my chest as she fights my hold on her throat.

I finally release her from my mouth and my hand.

She darts forward, sinking her canines into my shoulder, her wolf needing to claim me back just as fiercely as I did her.

I hold her to me, embracing the bond as it settles into place.

But it's not fully complete.

She needs Caius and Volt, too.

I can't move without hurting her, my knot too deep inside to disengage. She's still pulsating around me, lost on a wave of orgasmic bliss created by my internal claim.

Volt and Caius are not deterred, their wolves driving them to join us on either side.

Caius's mouth goes to her breast.

And Volt falls to his knees.

Clove jolts as Caius sinks his teeth into her breast, right above her heart. Then she moans as Volt moves her leg away from my hip. I shift my grip to her ass, holding her up as he takes control of her knee, widening her to reach her inner thigh.

She moans as he finds the spot he wants, his teeth piercing her skin on a rumble of approval that goes straight to my groin.

We're a clan.

We're coming together as one.

And Clove is the center of it all.

Caius takes her mouth, her blood still on his lips. Then he guides her to his throat, where she doesn't hesitate to sink her teeth into his pulse.

It's an erotic sight, our little wolf showing her strength

and desire by claiming us with the same ferocity that we're claiming her.

Volt is last, his gaze heated as he stares down at her.

She doesn't go for his neck.

She goes for his chest, biting him in a place similar to where Caius bit her.

Volt purrs in approval—we *all* do.

And then she moans, her pussy throbbing around me with need.

Because apparently my knot isn't enough.

I'm about to grin, to say something to that effect, when I see her eyes, and everything stills.

Her pupils are so dilated that I can't see her irises.

She clenches around me again, her body trembling with an intensity I instantly recognize.

She's going into heat again.

Right now.

Right here.

With my knot already inside her.

CAIUS

C love's sweet aroma makes me so fucking hard I nearly come from the scent alone.

Tieran groans, his head falling to her shoulder. "*Fuck.*"

Yes. Yes, that's *exactly* what I want to do. *Fuck Clove.*

But Tieran is already inside her, his knot claiming the sweet heaven between her thighs.

Volt growls, as do I. Not in anger, but in hunger.

Our mate is going into heat.

Her gaze is liquid black, her pupils blown so wide I can barely see the whites of her eyes. That didn't happen last time.

Which tells me this is the real deal.

She's about to lose herself to estrus for days, maybe even a week or more.

And I cannot fucking wait.

"I have to address the pack," Tieran says, sounding agonized by the mere notion of having to leave her in this state.

But we just suffered a major loss with Alpha Duncan's death.

And experienced a huge win by taking down Alpha Bryson.

Tieran doesn't have a choice. This is where his duty as Pack Alpha will have to come first. "You can make it a quick speech," I tell him. "They'll understand."

"Alpha Duncan deserves better," he whispers, the pain in his voice driven by Clove running her lips along his throat.

She's not even listening, just tasting.

Because her wolf is leading her now.

Our feisty little hellion, I think, excited to play.

"It's Caius's due," Volt says. "He'll take care of her while you and I see to the pack."

"Yes, I'll take care of our Clove," I murmur, leaning in to kiss her neck. "I have more than enough saved-up tension to keep her occupied." Even if she makes me come with her scent right now, I'll still be hard again in seconds.

We've been engaged in sensual foreplay for what feels like forever.

I'm *very* ready to seek our mutual gratification, something I tell her with a kiss. She wraps her palm around the back of my neck, holding me to her as she devours my tongue.

Tieran curses as she arches into him.

"Not helping, C," he grits out.

I respond by palming Clove's breast, my thumb tracing my claiming mark. She mewls in response, her wolf needing her mates.

Now.

Tieran's head is still against her opposite shoulder, his body tense as he fights for control of his own cock. Knots don't obey reason; they obey passion.

And our little sex kitten is all about passion at the moment.

But he's clan leader for a reason.

Not just that, he's a fucking Pack Alpha.

Something he proves by mastering his own body now and pulling out of her slick channel. Slick and seed gush from her, drawing his focus to her pussy.

He falls to his knees, licking her from hole to clit, his wolf demanding his due. I press my forehead to hers, watching him devour her.

He's struggling, and it's a struggle I don't envy as the man in him tries to strive for dominance against his savage inner beast.

Volt's barely holding on beside us, his palm wrapped around his shaft as he pumps himself beneath the water. "We need to go now or we're not going at all," he says through clenched teeth.

Tieran grunts.

Then he forces himself up to his feet and takes Clove's mouth in a promising kiss. "Be. Good." He nips her lower lip. "We'll be back."

She growls as they step out of the shower, her wolf disapproving.

But the moment I take her mouth again, she sighs, her arms encircling my neck as she tries to climb me like a tree. I grab her hips, pinning her to the wall and taking charge.

She rumbles in protest.

Only to moan in the next moment as the head of my cock meets her clit.

"Yeah, we're doing this my way, gorgeous," I murmur, lifting her. She wraps her legs around me, her lower half moving to take me inside her slick heat.

But I palm her ass and grind her against my shaft instead.

Then I slowly walk backward out of the shower.

She mutters an incoherent complaint.

I ignore her, turning off the water as I move before grabbing a towel.

She's so small and light that I hold her to me with ease.

Of course, it helps that she's wrapped around my neck and panting passionately in my ear. She starts rubbing herself against my hardness, trying to entice me into slipping inside her.

But my palm on her ass holds her steady, keeping her from being able to slide in the direction she needs to accomplish her true goal.

I take her and the towel to the bed, tossing the fluffy cotton down onto the sheets before lowering her to the center. She doesn't even notice, too lost to the sensation of my skin on hers to care as I kneel over her.

Definitely in heat, I think, loving the way she's out of her mind with lust.

It was likely caused by our claiming. Her wolf just needed that final little nudge to embrace her Omega tendencies.

She wraps her legs around my hips again, grabs my shoulders, and yanks me down to bite my neck. *Hard*. Right over her mark.

I flinch. "*Clove*."

She clearly does not want to do this my way, the little beauty trying to top from the bottom.

I have half a mind to let her because, *fuck*, she smells good. She feels good. She's literal perfection in the bed.

And her pussy against my shaft is *killing* me.

I grab her throat, tugging her away from my neck, and push her back down on the bed. Then I bend to take her nipple into my mouth.

Her thighs tighten around my hips, her slick pouring over my dick in enchanting welcome.

Oh, fuck it, I think, slamming home inside her.

I can't take it anymore.

I can't keep waiting.

I need this. I need *her*.

I sink my teeth into her tit, drawing a scream from her that quickly melts into a moan as I lave the wound with my tongue.

Her nails find my shoulder, then rake dangerously down my back, her wolf punishing mine for the rough bite.

Or perhaps provoking me to do it again.

It doesn't matter, I'm too lost to her passion to focus anymore. I take her mouth, fucking her with my tongue as I pound into her tight heat like my life depends on it.

She moves with me, her body pure sex.

I roll to my back, taking her with me, then hold on for the ride as she sits up and takes me even deeper. Her breasts sway as she moves, her palms on my abdomen, her nails digging into my skin to create little crescent grooves.

I fucking love it.

I fucking love *her*.

"You're so beautiful," I say, thrusting up into her. She almost falls forward from the power of my hips, but her torso flexes, keeping her upright. "So good, gorgeous. You feel so fucking good."

She groans, frustration evident in her movements when I don't immediately knot her.

I sit up and pull her legs around me, ensuring our snug and tight fit. Then I wrap her in my arms, pressing my chest to hers.

Her ankles cross behind my back, her hips moving with a frenzy driven by her need to mate.

"You want my knot, beauty?" I ask against her mouth, my palm curling around her nape while my opposite arm forms a band around her lower back. "You're going to have to work harder for it."

She growls, her teeth sinking into my lower lip.

"Squeeze me," I say, pumping up into her. "Squeeze me with that sweet pussy of yours, Clove. *Demand* my knot."

Her thighs clench, the little deviant hearing me through her haze of lust.

She's in there, semi-aware of what I'm doing to her. But she's in this blissful state of sensation that overtakes all else.

I absolutely envy her.

It's similar to the rut, the need I feel to fuck her to oblivion over and over again, only I maintain my senses.

Because it's my job to take care of her.

To make sure she's not hurt.

To ensure she feels pleasure during this time of need, not pain.

To keep her fed, warm, *clean*.

It's a dynamic I've craved all my life.

And I finally have it.

With Clove.

"You're everything I've always desired," I say, kissing her as I force her movements to slow. "Everything I've always wanted."

Her hips flex against mine, her need a palpable presence that pulls at my groin.

And then she starts to *squeeze*, just like I said, those slick inner walls clamping down around my shaft and driving me wild.

"Yeah, gorgeous," I whisper. "Just like that." It's slow. It's intense. It's exactly what we both need.

I rock up into her, slower now, thoroughly claiming her as she massages me beautifully with her sensual muscles.

"You're so damn perfect," I tell her on a groan. "Don't stop, beauty. Don't fucking stop."

If anything, she clamps down on me *more*.

"*Fuck*, Clove," I breathe, my lips against hers. "You're killing me, love. And I fucking love it."

She thrusts her fingers through my hair, some of the brown of her irises bleeding back into the black.

I smile. "I knew you were in there." I just had to do a little bit of lovemaking to draw her out.

"*Knot me*," she demands.

"Mmm, I intend to," I promise, using my palm against her ass to help guide more of the motion and sinking impossibly deeper into her.

She seizes around me, her walls strangling my cock.

"Yes, Clove," I hiss, grinding against her and ensuring every part of her feels the movement, including her clit. "Fuck, you feel amazing. Make me knot you. *Command* me with your cunt."

Her entire body spasms as she cries out in frustration.

Then she grinds down onto my knot and squeezes me so hard that I explode up into her.

It's so goddamn intense that it fucking *hurts*.

I've never experienced anything like it, my knot never having left the base before.

She screams in response, her orgasm a cataclysmic wave of energy that wraps around us both and sends us spiraling into a sea of dark ecstasy.

I can't see.

And I don't even fucking care.

Not with the sensations exploding from below.

It's a new meaning of heaven.

It's rapture.

It's fucking *flawless*.

I kiss her, thanking her with my mouth as I guide us both back to the bed, panting as I pull her beneath me.

Then I begin to move again, my knot still inside her.

Because fuck, I need to come again.

And again.

And again.

She doesn't stop me. She *begs* me to do it.

And I do.

Taking her into rapturous oblivion with me on repeat as my knot just continues to pulse deep in her cunt.

It's amazing. It's life-changing. It's my new favorite existence.

Delaying our gratification was worth it.

But I doubt I'll ever be able to do it again.

Denying her is an impossibility. And denying *us* will never feel right.

My sweet little Omega just redefined my purpose in life. She gave me a heart. And she breathed renewed sensation into my soul.

"I love you," I whisper, aware that she's so lost to her heat that she won't remember me saying the words. However, I'll repeat them as many times as she needs me to.

For eternity.

VOLT

Tieran is a better wolf than I am.

He's somehow holding himself together for this speech and embracing the pack as though he has all the time in the world.

While all I want to do is return to the den and fuck our mate into oblivion.

However, it's Caius's turn. I'm just pissed I couldn't be there to watch him *finally* let himself fuck her.

"It's a new era for the Black Mountain Pack," Tieran is saying. "Because we're finally ready to go home."

Howls echo into the night, the wolves thrilled that we've handled the Nantahala Pack once and for all. The Santeetlah Pack is all that's left. But we'll save them for after Tieran ascends.

Alpha Bryson became our primary challenge seven years ago.

And now he's dead.

A bit anticlimactic for my taste, but that's Tieran's way. He's not the type to prolong torture or make someone suffer. When he has the upper hand, he uses it without remorse.

I'm just sad I didn't have a chance to take the bastard's head.

It would have made for a nice trophy in the den.

But I don't want it bad enough to go back there to take it. Not when Clove is in our bed right now, likely mewling and writhing in pleasure.

Fuck. I'm so damn hard.

I know Tieran is, too.

However, he's still speaking, voicing a tribute to the lives lost now.

It's really only Alpha Duncan, but he mentions the misguided enforcers from Nantahala Pack as well, saying they were not of sound mind with Alpha Bryson being their leader.

He mentions Alpha Kin, too.

Which is met with growls because he's already told the pack about his betrayal.

"He was still a Carnage Wolf," Tieran reminds them all. "But his actions against this pack will keep him from being properly buried." He looks at Alpha Dirk then and nods.

Alpha Dirk doesn't even hesitate. He picks up Alpha Kin's body and tosses him into the bonfire, drawing more howls from the crowd.

But Alpha Duncan is treated much differently.

His body is wrapped up for shipment back to Black Mountain Pack territory to be buried among the warriors of our kind.

Everyone is silent for the ceremony, which Alpha Ebony and Alpha Pan lead. They don't hide their emotions, their grief a palpable presence the pack embraces in kind.

Alpha Duncan was a good wolf.

A strong man.

An excellent clan leader.

He will be missed by us all.

All statements I don't say out loud but think as the final preparations are made for the transport of his body back to the pack headquarters.

Tieran helps Alpha Pan and Alpha Ebony carry him to the yacht. Beta Lock and Alpha Mackin are waiting to help guide the transport.

Alpha Pan and Alpha Ebony will go with Alpha Duncan.

Tieran hugs them all, saying a few private words to each of them.

Private words that I realize I can *hear*.

Not with my ears, but in my mind.

Because I can hear Tieran's thoughts.

My brow furrows. *Well, that's new.*

He glances at me, then returns his focus to the others.

Fully mated clans typically develop a telepathic link that allows mates to talk to each other, but I didn't realize ours would happen so quickly.

Actually, I wasn't sure if ours would happen at all, what with Clove being a half-breed and all.

However, I can *feel* her in my soul. *Hear* her in my mind.

And tapping into it is a *huge* mistake. Her need slams into my gut, causing my knees to buckle and sending me to the sand with a groan that I can't hold back.

"Right," Tieran says, clearing his throat. "Volt and I are needed back at the den. Our Omega has just gone into heat."

I don't see their reactions, my mind entirely focused on Clove's *need*.

"Yes, we're mated," I hear him explaining.

Which earns us a round of howls that only make me want to growl.

Mine, my wolf is saying. *Mine. Mine. Mine.*

Ours, Tieran replies flatly, directly into my mind.

It's loud enough and stern enough that it snaps through my drunken haze and seizes control of my focus. I snap my gaze up to his.

He smirks. I growl.

I'll race you, he says, taking off toward the trees. *First one back knots her first.*

Fuck that, I curse, chasing him. *You already knotted her in the shower. It's my turn.*

Only if you beat me to the den, he taunts, a good ten yards ahead of me.

My wolf snarls at him.

And the fucker laughs.

So I start thinking about all the ways I can kill him with a blade.

It doesn't deter him in the slightest. He's running full speed, driven by his wolf.

As much as I hate to admit it, he's faster.

Which means he beats me to the den. But rather than fulfill his part of the deal, he pauses on the doorstep to watch Caius and Clove play.

They're a sensual ripple on the bed, fucking with abandon, and utterly lost to the bliss of the moment. That sight alone is worth waiting a few minutes.

So I quietly back away to work on gathering items Clove is going to need—like food and water.

Tieran accompanies me, helping me carry everything into the room to sit beside her nesting material.

Caius is a panting mess on top of her, both of them lost to a climax that appears to be unending, until finally he rolls off of her on a sigh of relief. "Your turn," he says, settling in for the show.

Tieran grins, then glances at me before nodding at the bed. "Take her."

He won the race.

But he's giving me the prize.

Yet another reason why he's a better wolf than I am.

I shuck off my boots and jeans and crawl over a writhing Clove. She's a little sex monster, snarling with need. The minute she sees me, she bites my pec.

I groan, loving that she's claiming me all over again like it's the first time.

When she's done, I repay the favor by kissing a path down her body to bite her thigh again. She cries out in confusion, wanting my knot, not my teeth. But Tieran quiets her by capturing her mouth in a bruising kiss. I'd tell him to silence her by sliding his dick down her throat, but he's going to need to knot her next.

The whirlwind of sex is just beginning.

And Clove is *hungry* for seed.

I lave her wound as it closes, then nuzzle her weeping sex. She smells divine. "So fucking sweet," I groan, licking her deep. Then I skim her clit with my tongue on my way back up.

Tieran releases her to me, letting me take over as I slide home between her thighs.

She immediately arches into me, demanding more with an adorable little whimper that I catch with my tongue.

Her inner muscles clench around me, making me groan.

"I taught her a new trick," Caius says lazily, grinning at whatever expression he sees on my face. "You're both very welcome."

I almost say something snarky, but Clove squeezes me again and I'm utterly lost to the vixen beneath me.

Yeah, that's a talent I'm not going to fault him for teaching her.

Because *fuck*.

I thrust into her hard, making her scream.

Then I take her in my way, with brutal strength softened by tender kisses.

Her nails bite into my skin, her thighs hugging me as I take us both to another state of existence—to a place I never want to leave.

My knot claims her.

My tongue calms her.

And my soul marries her.

She kisses me as though I'm her lifeline, her body embracing mine with so much heat and warmth that I feel my heart exploding in my chest.

Clove and this clan are my everything.

My family.

My *home*.

That's the gift she's given me more than anything else —the sensation of fullness in my life.

Our clan is finally complete.

And together, we'll conquer life itself.

I roll to my back, taking Clove with me and cuddling her against my chest as my knot continues to pulse inside her. "You're officially ours now, sweetling," I tell her softly. "Ours to fuck. Ours to cherish. Ours to protect." I tuck a stray strand of hair behind her ear. "If someone so much as looks at you wrong, I'll end him without question. Because that's who I am here. I'm the guardian. I'm *your* guardian."

"We all are," Tieran murmurs, brushing his own fingers through her hair as he lounges alongside me.

"We're the savage beasts who will prove all the rumors true if anyone ever touches her again."

"The cruel, wicked tyrants who pillage and plunder our way across the packs," Caius adds from my opposite side, humor evident in his tone as he strokes his hand down her back. "We'll paint the world in blood for you, Clove."

"Kill anyone you desire," I offer, meaning it.

"Forgive anyone you tell us to forgive," Tieran says, his fingers stilling by her nape.

"Be whoever you need us to be," Caius finishes.

I just want you, I hear her whisper into our minds. *I just want all of you.*

Tieran chuckles, leaning forward to kiss her temple. "You have us, Clove."

"Always," I say.

"And forever," Caius adds.

She hums something unintelligible, nearly asleep.

Then her body spasms again, tightening around my shaft as my knot begins to subside. "Looks like you're up," I tell Tieran as I guide myself out of her slick heaven.

While I could easily take her again.

And again.

It's his turn.

And I don't mind sharing.

Not with Caius and Tieran.

Besides, I'll enjoy watching.

Maybe we'll teach her something together.

Or maybe I'll make her suck me off while he fucks her.

Hmm, no. Not yet.

We have a few days to experiment and play. For now, we'll worship her. Tomorrow, we'll start testing her limits.

Perhaps I'll even be allowed to play with my knives…

CLOVE

B lood.
		Sweat.
Sex.

I'm swimming in a sea of peppermint, ash, copper, and pine.

I never want to surface.

Swimming. Drowning. Swimming again.

But there's something not quite right. The bed is too lumpy. It's… imperfect.

And I really dislike that sensation.

I stir from my cloud of dizzy desire and hit the lump on the bed. It's soft and plushy and in the wrong place.

Growling, I move it to the corner. But then I find another misshapen clump and have to move it, too.

Which unearths a third one.

And then a fourth.

By the tenth, I'm a snarling mess, ripping apart the bed and everything on it.

Clearly, I need to make the bed again.

Once I'm satisfied with the mattress and the lack of bumps, I start over. *Carefully.*

347

I pick up sheets and shirts and jeans and towels and everything I can find, crafting the perfect bed to rest within.

My males are here.

I feel them watching me.

One of them even hands items to me, trying to help. I purr when I like the offering and snarl when I dislike it.

He's a good male.

He doesn't force me to take anything I don't want, instead giving me the correct items more often than not.

I'll invite him into our new safe haven first.

It's a little strange in appearance, not necessarily flat, but all the edges are *perfect*.

I prowl around it, proud of my creation.

My males seem to like it, too. They're purring. Mmm, I love that sound. I want to roll around on them while they rumble.

"That's a beautiful nest, gorgeous," the helpful one says.

I preen with pleasure and reach for him, wanting to show him how to properly enter our new home.

He doesn't rush me. He lets me lead. And I very much appreciate that.

Then he does exactly what I show him, careful not to dislodge any of my perfectly placed fluff.

"I'm suddenly reminded of when her wolf took herself on a tour of the house," the gruffer one says. My scary giant. He likes knives. But he only bleeds me for pleasure. So I like him. "Except she's in human form this time."

I prowl out of my safe haven, coming for him next, and catch him by the hand.

He's not as careful as the other one, his bulky form almost knocking one of my blankets loose. But he listens to me when I growl, waiting for me to move it out of his way so he can finish climbing into our new bed.

I point to the place I want him.

He goes there willingly, lying down naked on his back.

The other one is still sitting, making me consider where I want him.

Hmm, I hum, leaving him there for a moment as I go to find the leader.

He's waiting patiently for me outside, naked, just like my other two males.

I'm pleased.

I like them naked.

I wrap my hand around his, tugging him forward. Then he crawls inside with ease, not altering my design at all.

My lips curl. *Very good.*

He settles next to the helpful one.

I'm not sure if that's where I want them but decide to try it.

Slipping inside, I settle next to the scary one, then shake my head. I can't touch all three right here, and I *need* to feel them all.

I start shuffling them around, playing a game of moving mates until I finally find the ideal position.

Scary one at my back.

Helpful one at my front.

Leader between my legs.

Yes, I think. *Perfect.*

And fall back to sleep.

TIERAN

Clove is very particular about her nest.

That started around day two of her heat.

We're now on day nine, and all of us are exhausted.

"I'm not fucking you until you eat that sandwich," Volt says sternly, making my lips curl. "*Now*, Clove."

She growls at him.

He growls back.

We're not in the nest right now, but on the floor beside it.

Because we learned on day three that food in the nest creates a furious little Omega.

And we've not made that mistake since.

But she's still not a fan of eating. She just wants our *seed*.

However, we've found that withholding sex will eventually make her cooperate. Which Volt is doing now while I check in on island operations.

The power and telephone functions were finally fully restored three days ago.

Alpha Lance, Alpha Edwin, and Alpha Ion all worked as a team to help clean up the mess Alpha Kin had made.

Alpha Ebony and Alpha Pan also returned after the burial to assist.

And Alpha Dirk oversaw the restoration of telecommunications on his own.

I've reviewed it all from the den, giving assistance where I can without leaving Clove's side.

She's showing signs today that her estrus is coming to an end. It's been subtle, but there have been a few moments of clarity where I've overheard her mentally ask herself what she's doing.

Of course, then she's on all fours again in the next minute, begging to be fucked.

It's an adorable cycle, one I very much look forward to repeating in the future.

Except it's going to be at least a year until that happens.

Because our little Clove is pregnant.

A fact that makes my heart skip a beat.

We don't know who the father is yet, as it happened the first night—it's what caused her to go into a nest creation fit.

All three of us stood in wonderment, watching the Omega work, *knowing* what it meant. Her scent confirmed it, too.

We're thrilled.

And also in hyper-protective mode.

I've already started making arrangements for our future den with the Black Mountain Pack. It's a property my father secured for our clan several years ago.

But I need it properly prepared for our Omega and future child.

So I've been sending off messages the last few days, listing requirements.

Which is probably why my phone is ringing now with my father's name on the screen.

Or maybe it's just because he wants an update on our situation.

I quietly excuse myself from the growling contest going on between Clove and Volt and answer the call in the hallway.

"Hey," I say, my voice low. "I know I've sent a lot of requests. Sorry."

"Requests?" my father repeats.

"Yeah, for the house."

"Oh, right. Well, that's expected with your return to the pack. Which is actually why I'm calling. The Elders just reached out. You've been cleared of all charges."

"Really?" I feign surprise. "That's shocking."

He huffs a laugh. "I think *they* were pretty shocked. It was smart of Alpha Duncan to export the surveillance to an external server."

"Yeah," I agree.

I didn't even think about the footage being jeopardized by Alpha Kin's antics. But Alpha Pan did. While en route to Black Mountain Pack territory last week, he checked the archives and found where Alpha Duncan had stored all the surveillance footage.

Then he handed the video files to my father to give to the Elders.

I could have sent the details to them myself, but my father is the current Pack Alpha, thus giving him far more authority than a Reject Island wolf—otherwise known as me.

My father also included a letter that pretty much said, *I would appreciate it if you released my heir from your custody, you dumb old fucks.*

But more politely worded.

"He was a good man," I add, referring to Alpha Duncan.

"Yes, he was. And an even better wolf."

We both fall silent for a moment, respecting the shifter's memory.

Then Clove starts to moan in the other room, causing my groin to tighten. I'm not wearing clothes because she keeps ripping them off me. So I'm pretty much saluting the hallway now.

Thankfully, this isn't a video call.

Because that's really fucking inappropriate.

"So, *when* are you coming home?" my father asks.

I clear my throat. "Soon. Maybe next week. Clove's still—"

Her moan turns into a scream, the sound definitely loud enough for him to hear.

So I don't bother finishing my statement.

He chuckles. "I see. How about two weeks from now?"

"Two weeks may be safer," I say.

"Good. I'll make the necessary preparations for your arrival."

"Thank you, Dad. The pack is looking forward to coming home."

"I know they are. But who are you leaving behind?"

"No one," I tell him.

He's silent for a moment. "We can't just abandon the island."

"I don't intend to," I reply. "But I'm not leaving anyone behind because Alpha Ebony and Alpha Pan have already volunteered to stay. They like it here, and a lot of the rogues respect them. Alpha Dirk has also offered, but I haven't accepted it yet."

"Is he still looking into who helped Gafton get to the island?"

"Yeah. But he texted me earlier, saying he thinks he found something. I haven't had a chance to reply yet." Because Clove promptly pulled me into the nest after he messaged and I didn't prioritize replying after we finished.

"It wasn't Alpha Nick," my dad confirms. "But he's definitely Clove's father."

I'm silent at that pronouncement. Not because I'm shocked. I'm just… *angry*. I really hoped to learn that it wasn't one of our wolves who raped her mother. But after everything with Alpha Kin, it doesn't surprise me.

"Sorry, I should have softened that."

"No, it's fine. I'm just deciding what to do with the information," I admit, palming the back of my neck.

"It's technically my responsibility to assign punishment since it happened under my rule. However, I'm willing to hold back my judgment if you would prefer to be the one to handle it," he offers. "They are unique circumstances."

"I would prefer to handle it." I need the clan to decide how they want to respond.

I vote for death.

Volt will vote for disembowelment.

Caius will vote for death.

But Clove's vote will trump all of ours.

"Consider it done," my father replies.

"Thank you."

A short silence falls between us, ending with my dad saying, "I'm proud of you, son. Your mother and I are looking forward to having you home. Well, the whole clan is. The pack, too."

I smile. "We're looking forward to it."

There's some murmuring in the background, causing my father to muffle the phone a little. He chuckles and comes back on the line. "Your mother wants to know if she can help decorate the nursery."

I blow out a breath.

Of course they saw that housing request come through. All I asked for were a few minor items to make Clove comfortable during the pregnancy process.

But nothing escapes my mother.

"I'll have to ask Clove when she's more capable of coherent sentences," I reply.

Which causes them both to chuckle.

"Stop talking to us and go see to your mate," my mother chastises, but it's a playful chastisement.

"Speaking of seeing to mates," my father says, his voice low. "How about we—"

"Right. Good talk. See you soon," I interject, ending the call. Because I have no desire to hear the rest of that statement from my father.

His clan is notoriously affectionate.

Much to my chagrin.

Yet they somehow kept the pregnancies to a minimum.

It's a magic I'm going to have to ask about, because otherwise, Clove is going to end up pregnant every year.

An irony that's not lost on me, considering how concerned we were about her ability to go into a proper heat.

I should have taken my own advice and listened to my wolf that first knotting.

Oh well.

We're where we need to be now.

A complete clan.

Preparing for the future.

And ascending to our rightful place in the pack.

We're free, I tell them all via the mental link. *The Elders lifted my sentence. We can finally go home.*

We are home, Volt replies, his voice low and content.

355

I walk into the room to see him happily knotted inside a dozing Clove.

He's right.

Clove is our home.

Our heart.

The center of our clan.

Our love.

It isn't until much later that I finally reply to Alpha Dirk.

He sends me a series of surveillance photos from Wolfe Island with the date of the attack.

They all show Gafton talking to a pair of guards, one of whom is that dick Jack who tried to drown Clove.

The photos are clearly from a video camera, but Alpha Dirk cleaned up the imagery to make them clearer.

I show Volt and Caius, who both snort.

"Leave this with me," Volt says. "I'll have a nice chat with Jack and let you know what I learn."

It's on the tip of my tongue to deny him.

But he missed his last assassination assignment—something that infuriated our client. Fortunately, Caius knew exactly what would shut him up—so Volt is due another kill.

"All right," I agree. "But don't bring his balls back for Clove. I don't think she would appreciate the present."

"No balls," she murmurs, half-asleep between us. "Or heads."

Volt frowns. "What sort of trophies should I bring home, then?"

"Your knot," she hums, yawning. "Only trophy you need, V."

He grins. "Is that my sweetling talking or my sex monster?"

"Both," she says, her long lashes fluttering to reveal her beautiful brown eyes. "I don't want balls or heads. But I wouldn't mind coming with you for that chat. My wolf has unfinished business with that one guard's throat."

Volt groans. "And now I'm hard."

Clove squirms back into me as though to escape Volt's words. "I think she may be sore," I say softly.

"Very," she replies on a groan. "I feel like I've taken your knots every way possible for a month straight."

Her ass clenches against my groin, and I press my lips to her ear. "You have, but only for nine days. Would you like to continue for another twenty or so to make it a month?"

She moans, but it's not a sound of pleasure so much as exhaustion mingling with pain.

I kiss her pulse. "How about a bath instead, darling?"

That makes her relax. "Yes. That sounds better than knots."

I grin. Her heat has definitely broken. But that doesn't mean we can't worship her a little with our tongues in the bath.

Caius slips out of the nest first, going to prepare the bath.

Volt leaves next, his bulky form careful as he navigates the exit.

Clove frowns after him. "Why are we in a pillow fort?"

"It's the nest you built during estrus," I tell her.

She blinks. Then her cheeks redden prettily. "Oh. I vaguely remember that. My wolf felt very particular about the organization of the sheets." It's a statement that makes her frown as her gaze catches on something in the corner.

She crawls over to it and fluffs the fabric, then tucks it back in a particular way.

After a moment, she nods.

Then she starts toward the exit, only to freeze. "Wait…"

I grin, amused by the startled look on her face.

"No, I made the nest. *We* made it. My wolf and I." Her lips part as she faces me again, her palm settling on her flat belly. "I'm pregnant."

"You're pregnant," I return, confirming her statement.

Her eyes widen, and for a second, I worry that she's about to freak out.

Except a giant smile blooms in the next instant, and she tackles me in the nest. "I'm pregnant!" She's elated now, her eyes sparkling with a delight that echoes in her mind.

She grew up wanting to have children, maybe because her pack ingrained the need into her mind—a fact I hear her ponder for a brief second. But her heart is so warm and happy that she knows this is what *she* wants.

It's what we *all* want—something she realizes as she taps into all our minds.

"We're connected," she whispers, freezing on top of me.

I grab her hips and roll her to her back. "We're connected," I echo back at her. "We're a complete clan now, Clove. And you're our heart."

I kiss her, letting her feel all my emotions and gratitude at having found her.

She returns the favor in kind, letting me experience her joy and wonder at our union.

It's a tender moment made even more special by the life blossoming inside her.

"Let us take care of you now, Clove," I whisper. "A bath. Some orgasms. And maybe some fruit."

She grins. "You're spoiling me."

"We're loving you," I correct her. "Because you're ours."

"Forever," Caius says from outside the nest.

"And always," Volt finishes.

CLOVE

E nergy hums through the air, causing the hairs along my arms to stand on end.

But it's for an entirely different reason today than two months ago.

I'm in the same field.

Standing in the same place I once kneeled.

Only now I'm standing. I'm clothed. And I'm staring directly at the male who once rejected me.

Seeing Canton now, I can't remember why I ever found him attractive. He has nothing on my three mates.

He's a fucking pansy ass, Volt says to us all. *Look at him. He's ready to wet himself just like last time.*

That pansy ass managed to keep a hold on Clove's wolf for almost a week, Tieran reminds him. *Looks can be deceiving.*

He's right.

I remember feeling Canton's power.

He's certainly not weak.

He took advantage of an untrained shifter, Volt argues. *Hardly makes him strong.*

Also a fair point. I didn't know how to control my inner

animal, and she was pissed at me for denying her all these years. It made her easy to manipulate.

Alpha Crane clears his throat. "Well. We're here," he says, gesturing to his pack. "What do you want, Tieran?"

"*Alpha* Tieran," Caius corrects him. He's standing to my left.

Volt whistles from right behind me. His hands are on my hips, where they've been since we arrived. "Yeah, not a good start, *Alpha* Crane. Insulting your superior?" He makes a clicking noise with his tongue. "Not recommended."

Tieran says nothing on my other side, but I feel his displeasure at Alpha Crane for the clear insult to his title.

"Please excuse me," Alpha Crane says, not sounding apologetic at all. "What do you want, *Alpha* Tieran?"

Several of the Carnage Wolves behind us growl. They all showed up in wolf form rather than human form, something Tieran requested of our pack. He wanted to prove that they don't need weapons in a fight. Their teeth and claws will do just fine.

Of course, Volt, Caius, and Tieran are all armed, just in case Alpha Crane decides to commit suicide today.

We have a few surprise guests, too.

"Well, I have a problem," Tieran starts, his tone lethally serious. "You see, the Elders are under the misconception that my mate is feral. They think she killed her mother. And that's not what happened at all, is it?"

Alpha Crane shrugs. "I have several witnesses you could ask about it if you would like clarification regarding what happened that day."

"Before you call any of them forward, I just want to caution you that Alpha Tieran doesn't react well to lying," Caius says conversationally.

"He's right," Tieran confirms. "I would suggest you ask

Bryson about it. But he's a bit indisposed at the moment."

Alpha Crane studies Tieran for a long moment. "What do you really want, Alpha Tieran?" This time he speaks with a breath of respect that surprises me.

"I want the wolves who raped and killed my mate's mother to step forward so that I can see that justice is served," Tieran tells him honestly.

Silence falls as Alpha Crane considers the request. "What do I get in return?" he asks.

"Your life," Tieran replies without hesitation. "And that's twice that you've insulted me now. I don't recommend going for a third."

Our pack growls behind us, agreeing with their Alpha.

Alpha Crane's sharp gaze goes to me before he looks at Canton. "You're the one who chose the punishment, *son*. What would you like to do?" The irritation in his tone almost makes me smile.

But the memory of what was done that day keeps me from being able to grin.

Because while it's true that Alpha Crane told Canton it was his punishment to give, he ran the show. Alpha Crane was the one who said crude things about Black Mountain Pack, saying the wolves didn't understand hierarchy and were feral beasts, using me as an example.

Canton actually tried to stand up for my mother at first, confirming that the Carnage Wolves were known for their brutality.

Perhaps not an accurate statement, but it is what the Santeetlah Pack and Nantahala Pack believe.

Which makes Canton almost as much of a victim as me.

Because he's been entirely brainwashed by his father.

"I don't remember Canton giving my mother to your men," I say. "But I remember you nodding approval to two of your wolves to step forward and take her." My words are for Alpha Crane.

And oh, he is *pissed*.

His eyes are narrowed into slits, his jaw clenching.

But I'm not done.

"Canton's crime is rejecting me for being *feral* and not allowing me to shift back into human form." My statement makes Canton's brow furrow.

"I didn't trap you in wolf form," he says, causing his father to growl beside him. "But yes, I called you feral. Because you were."

"I wasn't," I correct him. "It was my first time shifting, and I couldn't change back to use my mouth. So I growled instead." And yeah, my wolf also wanted to rip his throat out after she realized what a bad mate he would be. But that doesn't qualify me as being *feral*.

Alpha Crane looks ready to explode.

But Canton appears thoughtful. He nods. "She's right. What happened to her mother wasn't my decision." He looks at his father. "However, since you're stating it was my decision, I'll correct it." He looks at his wolves. "David and Brown, step forward."

Clever, Caius says to us mentally. *He's upstaging his father to gain favor with the pack.*

By handing over two of the wolves, Volt replies. *Not sure that's the wisest way to gain favor.*

It is if the pack dislikes their behavior, Caius points out.

"Langston and Hicks," Canton adds. "You should step forward as well since I know you participated in the *punishment.*" He turns to point out all four wolves he's named, just in case they decide to disobey.

"I should have known better than to give you this task," his father says, furious. "You're proving yet again that you can't handle being an Alpha."

"Actually, I think he's doing a fine job," Tieran says. "He's taking ownership for a mistake that wasn't his, and for that, I may just let him live when this is done." He locks gazes with Canton. "You did, after all, insult my mate by calling her feral."

"And knocking her out," Volt adds.

They made me tell them everything about the ceremony a few weeks ago, wanting to be prepared for today.

I'm somewhat regretting that now.

But also not.

"He also tried to add you to a harem, right?" Caius asks me.

"Yes," I confirm.

Tieran nods. "Well. To say I'm dissatisfied with Clove's initial treatment would be an understatement." He tilts his head. "But keep being honest and perhaps my wolf won't want to rip out your throat." With that lingering threat, he pulls out his phone. "Just one moment. As I said, I want to ensure justice is served." He dials a number and waits. "We're ready."

He hangs up, his focus on the four wolves Canton called forward.

They look terrified.

And maybe a little furious.

Because there's absolutely nothing that can save them now.

The sound of an approaching car has Alpha Crane surrounding himself with his enforcers. When he gestures for Canton to join him, he doesn't. "An Alpha should be able to defend himself," he tells his father. "It's something I'm realizing you failed to teach me."

A few of the Santeetlah Wolves exchange glances,

making me wonder if Caius is right about Canton trying to upstage his father. If he is, he's doing a good job of it.

Alpha Crane appears ready to commit murder.

Something Volt is paying close attention to.

His mental humor has died, and now he's focused on any and all potential threats. It's a fascinating transition how he goes from easygoing to assassin in the blink of an eye. His thoughts shift accordingly, going from dark sarcasm to lethal intent.

My wolf likes this side of him.

As do I.

Caius is reading the crowd as well, his mind cataloging everyone's movements and reading their intentions from their expressions.

He's an expert at cues.

Tieran is listening to all of it, registering the details and thinking through potential scenarios at rapid speed.

It's no wonder these three males created their own clan. They all complement each other in their own unique ways.

I'm the heart, as Tieran likes to say.

I make them *feel*.

Something the three of them are doing a lot of now, as they can hear some of my memories of this field within my thoughts.

And none of those are good memories.

The four-by-four vehicle comes to a stop, and Alpha Dirk exits the driver's side. He opens the back door to allow two very familiar faces to appear.

Jack, also known as Mister Muzzle, from my initial trip to the island.

And his buddy, Bischel.

They take one look at me and shudder.

Or maybe it's the male behind me.

Perhaps both.

We recently had a chat with Jack and Bischel, one where Volt allowed my wolf to play a little. We expressed our concern over the bribe they'd taken from Gafton, told them what havoc he'd caused, and asked if they wanted to die or make it up to us.

They chose the latter.

And now they're here like good little guards.

But the woman in the passenger seat is an unexpected attendee.

My lips part as I realize it's my former social worker. *What's she doing here?* I ask my mates, stunned.

A friend of ours named Reese did some digging into your case for us, Caius says casually. *Tieran and Volt paid the lady a visit afterward, and wouldn't you know? She offered to help us today. Such a kindhearted individual, hmm?*

Volt doesn't reply, his focus still on the Santeetlah Pack.

But Tieran's lips curl just a little as he says, "Beverly, thank you so much for volunteering to join us today." He speaks to her like she's an old friend, but the discomfort in her hazel gaze says she disagrees.

She moves to stand beside Jack and Bischel, all three of whom are wearing similar expressions.

I would be amused if I didn't hate them all.

"Alpha Crane, Canton, I want you to meet Beverly," Tieran continues. "She's the social worker that Bryson bribed to expedite Clove's case. So I guess you could say we're old friends since her assessment is what led to Clove being sent to Carnage Island."

I'm absolutely stunned that they not only tracked her down but also brought her here.

It's clearly a gift.

One I'm very happy to accept.

Because it means they want to ensure *everyone* who

wronged me is avenged. And that just makes me melt all over again for them.

Shh, Volt says, his palm sliding from my hip to my stomach to pull me back against him. *You don't want to provoke me to fuck you in this field, Clove. Because I will. And I'll make that former intended mate of yours watch, too.*

"Beverly, Canton and Alpha Crane have introduced the four men who actually killed my mate's mother." Tieran points to the males in question, making them all visibly cringe.

The redhead on the left is thinking about running, Caius warns us.

I'm not sure how he can read that from the man's bored expression, but Volt agrees with a grunt via our mental connection.

Tieran continues speaking as though Caius didn't just issue the warning.

"They're here to testify so that you can report back to the judge regarding Clove's case and see that she's not only acquitted but also released from the Reject Island assignment program. Because, as I told you, she was never rejected. As a Carnage Wolf Omega, her only true match can be with an Alpha clan. More specifically, *my* clan."

Beverly clears her throat. "Yes, of course. I understand. Would you like the inquisition done here or back on Wolfe Island?"

"Here," Tieran says without hesitation. "Alpha Dirk will be videotaping it to make sure everything is transcribed correctly."

The Alpha male in question is already setting up the camera equipment.

Three, two—

The redhead bolts before Caius reaches *one*, and Volt takes him down with a quick shot to his kneecaps. Several wolves snarl, and two of the Santeetlah Wolves pull their weapons. Which causes Caius to pull his and take aim as Volt shifts focus to them as well.

Beverly is on the ground.

Jack and Bischel are trembling.

And Alpha Crane is vibrating with anger. "You can't just shoot my wolves!"

"I can if they run," Volt tells him. "You agreed to justice. He tried to flee. Surely you don't want that kind of coward in your pack, yeah?"

"Correct," Canton says. "My punishment, my decision, right, Father?"

Alpha Crane growls.

Canton growls back.

Tieran tops them both with a howl that makes me weak in the knees. He exudes Alpha energy, his dominance a palpable wave in the air that brings several wolves to the ground beneath the force of his command.

When Caius and Volt join him, even more wolves collapse beneath their authority.

The only reason I don't is because of Volt holding me to him.

He won't let me kneel.

Unless it's in the bedroom.

When Alpha Crane starts to tremble, my mates stop howling.

"The next reminder won't be verbal," Tieran tells him, his tone edged with superiority and underlined in acute command. "Beverly, begin your questioning. *Now*."

The four wolves in question are all on the ground with the redhead just a few feet away from them, curled into the fetal position.

It's not the kindest trial, but it beats being locked up in a cage in wolf form.

At least these assholes can talk.

And every time they even think about lying, Tieran growls.

In the end, they tell the truth and admit to raping and murdering my mom—under Alpha Crane's authority.

That last bit surprises me because I expected them to blame Canton.

But Tieran's lingering threat appears to force them to be fully honest.

Do you think Alpha Crane wanted the blame to fall on Canton? I wonder, asking my clan. *Maybe that's why he wanted him to choose what to do? To be able to pin some of the fault on him?*

I think Canton and Alpha Crane have been playing a dangerous leadership game these last few years, Caius replies. *And the student has just become the master.*

Yes, we will need to watch him carefully. But he has made some wise decisions today, Tieran says. Then he clears his throat and thanks Beverly for her service. "Jack, Bischel, if you could please escort these four wolves to Wolfe Island, it would be greatly appreciated," he says at the end.

Jack and Bischel immediately move forward to do exactly what he requested, causing my lips to twitch a little.

Mmm, I told you Clove would enjoy watching me work, Volt muses at us all. *She's a natural wingwoman, too.*

You're not taking her on assignments, Tieran replies immediately. *I only okayed this one because it wasn't dangerous.*

Volt snorts. *She's not a damsel, T.*

No, she's pregnant, Tieran reminds him flatly. *With* your *child.*

Or that's the guess, anyway.

They're going based on scents, and mine has been a bit more coppery lately.

"Are we done?" Alpha Crane demands, drawing our focus back to him.

"You're not going with your wolves?" Tieran asks. "You don't want to defend them or your own actions?"

Alpha Crane narrows his gaze. "I'll attend the trial once a date is set."

"Do that," Tieran tells him, ensuring he hears the demand in his tone. "Oh, and, Beverly?" he calls as she's about to enter the passenger seat once more. "I expect you to provide daily updates to Alpha Dirk on Carnage Island. He'll let me know if he doesn't hear from you."

Alpha Dirk nods, his stoic expression making him that much more intimidating.

Beverly visibly swallows. I'm not sure what kind of wolf shifter she is, but she resembles a deer in the headlights right now. "Yes, Alpha Tieran," she manages to say, her voice a bit raspier than before.

"That'll be all," he says, dismissing her before looking at Alpha Crane once more. "We're taking the Nantahala territory. If that's a problem for you, speak now. Otherwise, I'll take your silence as acceptance of our intentions."

Alpha Crane's jaw clenches. "You will not enter my lands."

"I'm not talking about Santeetlah territory. I'm talking about Nantahala territory," Tieran replies. "I have no need for your pack or your lands, and it'll remain that way until you give me reason to feel otherwise."

"What will happen with the Nantahala Wolves?" Alpha Crane asks, a hint of hesitation in his tone.

"That's not your concern," Tieran replies flatly. "However, as a token of good faith, I'll respond. The majority of the women and children have chosen to seek shelter with our pack. Several of the men have as well. Those who shared Bryson's pack philosophies have been given thirty days to relocate. Anyone who chooses to remain past that deadline will be dealt with accordingly."

It's a stern summary, but a fair one.

Almost ninety percent of the survivors have sought refuge with the Black Mountain Pack.

It's an arrangement I didn't expect Tieran to make with the Nantahala Wolves. But it's one I respect and appreciate since several of them were friends at one point.

And those who weren't are either dead or have fled.

For the first time today, a glimmer of respect graces Alpha Crane's expression.

He's realizing that if we ever take his land, we'll likely offer refuge to his wolves, Caius says. *That relief right there demonstrates that he does care for his pack; he just goes about it in a backward manner.*

It's the only reason he and his son are going to be allowed to live another day, Tieran replies. "We're done here," he says out loud. "Next time we meet, I expect you to bring your whole pack. That includes the women. They're wolves, not slaves."

Several of the female Carnage Wolves howl in approval of their Alpha's words, and I join them, pleased that he chose to add that final jibe.

He doesn't wait for Alpha Crane to reply; he steps in front of me, presents the other Alpha his back, and kisses me with a fierceness that knocks me off my literal feet.

Fortunately, Volt catches me. But then he spins me and kisses me just as intensely.

I've forgotten how to breathe by the time Caius takes my mouth.

My stomach clenches with a desire that permeates the air.

Volt presses his nose to my neck, inhaling deeply as he rumbles in approval. "Please tell me I can fuck her in this field."

"That would require removing her clothes," Tieran says, his nose in my hair.

"No," Caius says against my mouth. "We'll devour her in the den."

My lips curl at the mention of our den.

It's a new one in Black Mountain Pack territory surrounded by fir trees with a little creek that runs alongside it and a lot of land for running.

My mates surprised me with the beautiful home just last week. And it's absolutely perfect.

Apparently, Tieran's father gifted it to the clan several years ago, the intention to be a gift for whenever they returned. Tieran requested several renovations, one of which kept us from being able to move back as soon as he originally wanted.

But that allowed us to say goodbye to Carnage Island properly.

I miss it. Yet I also don't.

My home is where my mates are, something I hum into all their minds.

If Volt wants to take me in this field right now, I'll love every minute of it. Because it's him. Because Caius and Tieran are here, too.

However, their possessive energy tells me that's not going to happen.

Because Canton is watching us.

Which I realize is why they all decided to devour me within an inch of my life.

I don't even look at him. He no longer matters.

I only have eyes for three men.

Tieran. Caius. And Volt.

My Carnage Wolves.

My Alphas.

My *mates*.

EPILOGUE

TIERAN

One Year Later

I stand beneath a tree, watching Clove as she spins around the yard with our daughter in her arms. Technically, the baby has Volt's genetics, not mine, but all three of us consider that little girl ours, just like Clove.

She's as beautiful as her mother.

The tenderness of the moment keeps me from interrupting, as I don't have the best news to deliver. I don't want to spoil their fun.

Clove giggles as the baby babbles at her.

Then Volt swoops in to steal the little bundle of love away. He does it with a huge grin that makes Clove laugh harder, but his dark eyes catch mine and I know he's done this for me.

He can sense that I need to talk to her.

I've kept it from the mental connection, not wanting to risk Clove overhearing it in my thoughts.

But he reads me almost as well as Caius does.

"I'm going to go see if I can't coax our little beauty into taking a nap," Volt says, a purr already igniting in his chest. "Then maybe Mommy will reward me by engaging in some adult playtime afterward."

He coos the words, making Clove blush and hush him at the same time. "Shh. You can't say things like that in front of Serena."

"Why not?" he asks innocently. "She doesn't understand me yet."

I smirk. Even if she could, it wouldn't stop him.

I have a whole new appreciation for my father's relationships now and why he didn't bother hiding his affections.

It's impossible.

I'll never try it with Clove. She'll forever know how I feel. Caius and Volt are the same.

She sighs as Volt disappears with our daughter, then she wanders over to me with a knowing look. "You want to talk about something," she says.

I smile, but it doesn't feel as genuine as it should. "What gave me away? Me or Volt?"

"Both," she said. "But mostly you. It's in your eyes." She cups my jaw and traces my cheekbone with her thumb. "What's going on?"

I clear my throat. "It's about your father," I say, not wanting to beat around the bush.

Her brow furrows. "Alpha Nick?"

I nod.

"What about him?"

I'm not sure how to politely state this, so I just voice it. "He's dead."

Her eyebrows shoot upward. "What? How?"

"He ingested silver nitrate." I clear my throat. "I'm still

not sure how it happened, whether someone gave it to him or if someone poisoned his food. But he's gone."

Clove blinks at me. "Oh." Her brow pulls down. "I… I'm not sure how I feel about that."

Yeah, I wasn't sure how she would feel about it either.

That's why I didn't want to deliver the news. She asked for him to be imprisoned while she debated what to do with him. Then life sort of escaped us with her pregnancy, taking over the pack, and everything else. Time works differently for our kind since it's typically more on the infinite scale.

A year doesn't feel like that long to wait on a decision.

But apparently, it was too long for Alpha Nick.

"I think I'm relieved," she says after a beat. "He wasn't a good shifter."

"No, he definitely wasn't." Something my dad is still beating himself up about because he should have noticed the signs yet didn't.

It's an oversight I've taken into consideration with my monitoring of the pack. Caius is helping me find ways to better look for signs of such activity. It's not infallible, but it's a start.

Clove presses her nose to my chest, and I purr for her in response, my arms automatically wrapping around her in a hug.

We stay like that for several minutes, her body melting into mine.

I kiss the top of her head, happy to just exist for a few minutes.

Maybe it's a moment of silence for the father she never really knew.

Or maybe it's a moment for the mother she misses.

Regardless of the point, I'm here for her. Holding her. Giving her my strength, just like an Alpha should.

She sighs, her nose coming up to nuzzle my throat. "I love you, Tieran," she says softly.

"I love you, too, Clove," I reply, smiling.

We don't often exchange the words.

But it doesn't make them any less true.

Our clan's love pours into Clove every day.

Because she's our beating heart.

The center of our lives.

The core of our existence.

Tieran's mother just stole Serena from me, Volt informs us, making Clove smile.

My mother is obsessed with the newborn. So I'm not really surprised by the news.

Clove turns her smile up my way, her chin resting on my chest. "Well, if she's offering to babysit…" Her gaze twinkles. "Do you want to go for a run?"

I arch a brow. "A run or a chase?"

She bats her long lashes at me. "Catch me and find out." She spins out of my arms and rips her dress off over her head, revealing nothing underneath.

I'm too hypnotized by the view to focus on my jeans.

It's not until she's in wolf form that I start undressing.

I hope you're both in the mood for a little game of hide-and-seek, I tell Caius and Volt as I shift into my wolf. *Because it seems our mate wants to play.*

Mmm, Volt hums in reply. *She hides.*

We seek, Caius adds.

I grin. *And then… we bite.*

Thank you for reading *Carnage Island!*

USA Today Bestselling Author Lexi C. Foss loves to play in dark worlds, especially the ones that bite. She lives in Chapel Hill, North Carolina with her husband and their furry children. When not writing, she's busy crossing items off her travel bucket list, or chasing eclipses around the globe. She's quirky, consumes way too much coffee, and loves to swim.

Want access to the most up-to-date information for all of Lexi's books? Sign-up for her newsletter here.

Lexi also likes to hang out with readers on Facebook in her exclusive readers group - Join Here.

Where To Find Lexi:
www.LexiCFoss.com

ALSO BY LEXI C. FOSS

Blood Alliance Series - Dystopian Paranormal

Chastely Bitten

Royally Bitten

Regally Bitten

Rebel Bitten

Kingly Bitten

Cruelly Bitten

Dark Provenance Series - Paranormal Romance

Heiress of Bael (FREE!)

Daughter of Death

Son of Chaos

Paramour of Sin

Princess of Bael

Elemental Fae Academy - Reverse Harem

Book One

Book Two

Book Three

Elemental Fae Queen

Winter Fae Queen

Hell Fae - Reverse Harem

Hell Fae Captive

Immortal Curse Series - Paranormal Romance

Book One: Blood Laws

Book Two: Forbidden Bonds

Book Three: Blood Heart

Book Four: Blood Bonds

Book Five: Angel Bonds

Book Six: Blood Seeker

Book Seven: Wicked Bonds

Book Eight: Blood King

Immortal Curse World - Short Stories & Bonus Fun

Elder Bonds

Blood Burden

Assassin Bonds

Mershano Empire Series - Contemporary Romance

Book One: The Prince's Game

Book Two: The Charmer's Gambit

Book Three: The Rebel's Redemption

Midnight Fae Academy - Reverse Harem

Ella's Masquerade

Book One

Book Two

Book Three

Book Four

Noir Reformatory - Ménage Paranormal Romance

The Beginning

First Offense

Second Offense

Underworld Royals Series - Dark Paranormal Romance

Happily Ever Crowned

Happily Ever Bitten

X-Clan Series - Dystopian Paranormal

Andorra Sector

X-Clan: The Experiment

Winter's Arrow

Bariloche Sector

Hunted

V-Clan Series - Dystopian Paranormal

Blood Sector

Vampire Dynasty - Dark Paranormal

Violet Slays

Crossed Fates

Other Books

Scarlet Mark - Standalone Romantic Suspense

Rotanev - Standalone Poseidon Tale

Carnage Island - Standalone Reverse Harem Romance

Printed in Great Britain
by Amazon